CRAVE ME

SPECIAL EDITION

JENN PLUMMER

WildLupine BOOKS

Crave Me

Aspen Ridge, Book Two

Published by Wild Lupine Books LLC

Editing by Katie Ducharme - Between The Covers Editorial

Cover Art by Qamber Designs

contents

join jenn plummer's readers' group

Stay up to date with Jenn Plummer by joining her Facebook readers' group, Jenn's Harlots. Ask questions, get first looks at new books/series, and have fun with other book lovers!

https://www.facebook.com/groups/jennsharlots/

a note from the author

Dear readers,

Welcome to Aspen Ridge. Crave Me is book two in a five book, interconnected standalone series. You do not have to read them in order but for the best experience, I recommend that you do.

In some cases, BDSM/kink, can work to heal from past sexual trauma in a safe, and trusted environment with the right partner. This is in no way a how-to manual, nor is it remotely evidence-based, factual information to be used in real life. Dallas and Blaire's story is a work of fiction. If you or someone you know is looking for support for sexual abuse/trauma or how kink can be used to heal from it, there are resources available to you.

Themes in Crave Me include explicit language and sexual situations, on-page memories of prior abuse (teenager), discussion of abuse/sexual abuse (not from the love interest), discussion of fertility/infertility, and BDSM.

Please read responsibly. If you have any questions about this list please don't hesitate to reach out to me directly.

Sending all of you love.

playlist

I Knew You Were Trouble - Taylor Swift
Most Girls – Hailee Steinfield
You Proof - Morgan Wallen
Bad Habit - Steve Lacy
...Ready For It? - Taylor Swift
Slow Hands - Niall Horan
Better - Khalid
Don't Blame Me - Taylor Swift
A Bar Song (Tipsy) – Shaboozey
Greedy – Tate McRae
Let Me Love You – Mario
Sure Thing - Miguel
Willow – Taylor Swift
Too Sweet - Hozier
Fine Again - Seether
Starving - Hailee Steinfeld & Grey
Worst Way – Riley Green
Treasure - Bruno Mars

To all the queens who silently fight their demons away alone, you are my heroes. I see you.

To all the kings who have chased the demons away from your women.

To my king, thank you for chasing away mine, for saving me from everything that came before you. I love you.

blaire

"FOR THE LOVE OF GOD, WHAT IS YOUR PROBLEM?" My boss looks up at me from behind the rim of his coffee mug as he sits smugly in his stupid, fancy office chair. "There's a room full of our coworkers and their families downstairs, and you're up here pouting. This event is important to the distillery."

"It's really not important though, Blaire. It's a nuisance and I want no part of it. I've been saying that since the beginning. Let them eat and drink, play pin the tail on the damn donkey or whatever trivial shit you have planned, but I'll be up here, actually working."

My hip cocks to the side as my hand rests on it, and I don't miss the slow perusal of my body that he unashamedly makes with those sky-blue eyes. I snap my fingers loudly with my free hand.

"Eyes up here, Dallas." His eyes work their way up my body slowly until they meet mine. I have to work hard to keep my breathing steady, but I've become a professional at keeping my features and emotions in check. "It's been three months. When are you going to get over this? I don't know why you hate working together so much, but I'm not going anywhere. Sawyer hired me for a reason, and you need to learn to deal with it."

Dallas stands now, walking around to the front of his desk. Each step with purpose and composure, each step leading him closer to me. I hold my ground, not wavering or cowering, even if on the inside my body is lighting up like a live wire. He stops a solid foot away from me, towering over me at what has to be six feet to my five feet, five inches. His piercing blue eyes are cold, irritation etched into his strong features. His disdain for me is obvious in the way he looks at me.

"I don't like repeating myself, Blaire, so this will be the last time I say it. You work *for* me. Not with me. I don't care if my shithead brother says otherwise. And if I don't agree with something, I'm most certainly not going to support it. So, head back downstairs to your little party, schmooze with everyone, do whatever you've got to do to make yourself feel like you're important here, and leave me out of it."

My eyes squint into slits as I stare up at my asshole boss. From the first moment I met him during my interview, he had decided he hated me. A preconceived notion he concocted that has nothing to do with me and everything to do with him not getting his way.

I tip my head to the side slightly, giving him a wide, fake smile.

"Of course, Mr. Hayes. But I will remind you, *again*, that according to the terms of my employment, we work *together*, not the other way around. Enjoy your afternoon." I spin on my heel and pull open his office door. Looking over my shoulder I say, "Do us all a favor, though, and drown in your coffee. We'll all be enjoying ourselves downstairs while you're up here struggling to breathe. Fingers crossed it's a slow, torturous death."

My nails dig into my palms as I walk out the door, keeping my chin held high, his patronizing laugh echoing behind me. I leave his office and walk down the long second-floor hallway to the stairs that lead to the open room below. Taking a deep breath, I pull my shoulders back and join the rest of the people here to celebrate this new venture for Aspen Ridge Distillery.

The rest of the day goes by in a blur of introductions, small talk, and tours of the distillery grounds. I'm on cloud nine, but slightly anxious for the real deal tomorrow when tourists and community members arrive.

I pull my jacket tighter as I walk into the chilly Washington evening. It's much colder than I expected, and I hustle to my car, parked at the back of the distillery staff lot. My first function as the event coordinator for Aspen Ridge Distillery went smoothly and without any hiccups, minus my asshole boss storming out of the room like someone had kicked his puppy. After twenty-seven years of being on my own, you'd think I'd have tougher skin, but when it comes to Dallas Hayes, he easily slides right under, grating and digging until I snap. I've never had anyone affect me the way he does, and I wish he didn't breach my armor every day.

I quickly start my car and crank up the heat, rubbing my hands together in an effort to warm my frozen fingers. Pulling out of the parking lot, I can't help but marvel at my surroundings. Aspen Ridge is an enchanted forest, practically plucked straight out of a Disney movie. It's a small town, tucked away west of the Olympic National Forest, backing up to the Pacific Ocean. On clear days, we have a gorgeous view of the misty mountains and tall Sitka spruce trees. The cloud cover is fairly constant, but I don't mind it. The fresh air is like a healing balm for my soul, and I could never imagine living anywhere else now that I'm here.

I pull my car around to the back of an old brick building on Main Street and climb the stairs that lead to my place. Once inside, I kick off my boots and walk into my little studio apartment, if you can even call it that. I'm renting a room above Rogue, the tattoo shop in downtown Aspen Ridge. I got extremely lucky when I arrived here three months ago. Desperate for a caffeine boost after my drive across the state, I walked into Bean Haven, ordered a black coffee and chocolate croissant, and sat in the only free booth when a giant of a man walked in. Every inch of his exposed skin was covered in tattoos, but I didn't get "bad boy" vibes. He ordered a coffee and looked around for a place to sit, and considering I was by myself in a booth and the others were filled, he asked if he could join me. My intention of keeping to myself was thrown to the wayside after five minutes of conversation. Something about this heavily tattooed Hulk, who was the most soft-spoken man I've ever met, made it easy to open up. Small talk turned into me confessing that I was new to town and interviewing for a position at Aspen Ridge Distillery later in the week, but that I had no family, no lodging figured out, and I didn't know a soul. He sympathized and offered to rent me a room above the tattoo shop he owns. The fact that he didn't offer me a handout, somehow knowing I wouldn't be comfortable with one, that I needed to pay something and was determined to make my own way, was exactly why I said yes. He never once looked at me like damaged goods, instead saying, "Everyone needs some help every once in a while." So, I accepted.

The studio is cozy. Exposed brick walls give it a charming, vintage vibe, while the large window that filters in the daylight casts a warm glow across every inch of the space. A futon that I use as a couch/bed sits in the center of the room, and I actually like the options it gives me—not that I'm hosting anyone for brunch or anything. The space is completed with a little kitchenette that serves my basic needs, and a small bathroom. It's honestly perfect. Some people may scoff at it, but it's mine, and it will do until I get further on my feet and can afford something bigger. It sure beats any of the homes I lived in during my childhood, or the dorms at college, or the women's shelters I've stayed in. My salary at the distillery is way more than I expected, giving me the ability to save for the first time in my life, and I almost have enough saved for first and last months' rent. If only my student loans weren't eating me alive financially, I'd be sitting pretty already.

Moving to the mini fridge, I pull out a premade meal from my little freezer and toss it in the microwave to heat up before stripping out of my work clothes. I tug on a pair of night shorts and a large band tee and pull my crazy hair into a messy bun at the nape of my neck. No matter what I try to do, my waves are uncontrollable. I couldn't get curly hair, or straight hair, no—I inherited a wild mix of both, which results in a new look every day.

It's nights like these I wish I had a family to share my day with. While I'm content being alone, it would feel so good to tell someone how amazing today went. I love my job as the event coordinator for Aspen Ridge Distillery. These last few months, I've worked tirelessly to create an addition to their business that the Hayes family can be proud of. The CEO, Sawyer, gave me no strong parameters, so this project has been my baby. They wanted to open up the distillery to the public by offering scheduled tours of the grounds, tastings, and host events. While my heart hopes to be able to focus on weddings someday, this is an incredible opportunity to lead my own team and develop something from the ground up.

Today was the pre-grand opening, just for the employees and their family members. Tomorrow, we're open to the public for tours and tastings, and I can hardly wait.

For the first time, I feel a real sense of accomplishment, and that lonely little girl inside me who still desires praise wishes I had someone to share it with. It's too bad I don't really drink. Tonight would be a great night to celebrate myself and simultaneously take the edge off.

Pulling my meal from the microwave, I grab my laptop and get comfortable in my spot on the futon. It's not long before I'm completely lost to season two of *Bridgerton*. Anthony's season is the best one, and anyone who says otherwise is lying. There's something so deliciously addictive about an enemies-to-lovers story. The toxic bickering that's fueled by passion, the stolen glances, and when the characters finally give in to each other? Chef's kiss.

Closing my laptop, I clean up the small mess from my quick dinner and lay back on the futon, pulling my blankets and pillows out of the basket I keep them folded in. I go about my nightly routine, washing my face, moisturizing my skin, and brushing my teeth before quickly climbing into bed and pulling my comforter and fleece blanket over me. Reid told me he is already heating the place by heating his studio, and I am not about to crank the temperature up and add to the bill. I relax on my side, snuggle into myself, and prop my Kindle up on some of the bunched-up blankets so I can read until I fall asleep.

"What the hell are you doing home so early?" His voice never fails to make my heart drop into the pit of my stomach. I swallow hard, doing my best to keep calm and steady, not sure which version of him I will get today.

"We get released early on Wednesdays. I can go find something to do if you'd like me to leave. I don't mind." Please say yes. Please. I will gladly go anywhere but here so I don't have to be alone with you. I grip my backpack strap for dear life, hovering in the space between the entryway and the living room of my foster parents' trailer. I look down and kick my dirty shoes together over the stained, worn carpet. The house reeks of cat urine—even though I've never seen a cat since living here—the carpet is pulled up in places, and scratches and stains climb up the old walls.

"No, stay. Why don't you come sit and watch a movie with me? Sherry said we should bond, let's get to know each other better." His voice slinks over me like a filthy snake. The blood in my veins curdles, bile turning over in my stomach. Ever since I moved in with my new foster parents, Andrew and Sherry Cain, I've felt like I've been on borrowed time. I've been here for three months, and I've considered running away a hundred times. I'm sixteen, almost seventeen, and I know how he looks at me. I know what he insinuates when he says things like that. I'm also acutely aware that I don't look my age. Unfortunately for me, puberty hit early and it hit hard. I have large, full breasts that men's eyes are drawn to, no matter how hard I try to tape them down. My trim waist, and hips that flare out, also gain unwanted attention and not-so-innocent touches as I walk by, or when they hold open a door for me. It's hard to love my body when it brings so much unwanted attention.

"I really should go study, Mr. Cain. I have a chemistry test in the morning."

"What did I tell you to call me, Blaire?" he says as his footsteps clomp in my direction.

I squeeze my eyes shut, wishing I could just disappear. My heart races in my chest. Can teenagers have heart attacks? It feels like we can. My hands shake as I grip tighter onto my backpack. I keep my eyes closed as his steps stop directly in front of me and the brush of his wiry, hairy hand drags down the length of my bare arm. A tear slips free, but I know that won't stop him.

"Go ahead, Blaire. No one's here but us. You can say it." His hand moves to cup my breast and I wince, terrified to move.

"Sorry, Daddy."

I wake with a jerk, my heart knocking hard against my ribs, my body covered in sweat. I jump up and race to the bathroom, barely getting the toilet lid up in time for me to purge the contents of my stomach. Tears stream down my face and my body convulses. "Fuck!" I lay down on the bathroom floor, the cold tile welcome on my burning cheek, and cry. Wishing I had the comfort of someone who loved me enough to hold me through these nightmares. And maybe love me enough that they're chased away altogether.

dallas

"Careful, Dallas, you keep looking at her like that and people will get the wrong impression."

"That I'm hoping she'll erupt into flames?"

"That you're two seconds away from ripping her clothes off."

I scoff at my idiot brother. "That is not how I'm looking at her."

"Sure, sure. Whatever you say."

I cross my arms defensively over my chest. "This is a pointless shit show. I'll be in my office."

I start to walk away when my twin brother, Sawyer, grabs my arm.

"You need to stay. This is a big deal, dickhead. Show your support. You bailed yesterday, and she's worked hard to make all this happen."

"I don't support it though, do I? Hosting events here, all these stupid-ass tours and tastings, what's the point of all this? Dad and Granddad did just fine without letting everyone and their mother waltz through the doors to gallivant around our operation. Why are we?"

"I'm not getting into this with you again. You've seen the numbers; you know this is a good move. Blaire's worked her ass off to set us up to host events and tastings here in time for Christmas. Whether you agree with it or not, you're the chief operating officer and need to show face."

"Like hell I do." To prove my point, I walk away with my middle finger in the air and head up the stairs to our offices, slamming the door behind me. I relax into my new Herman Miller office chair, a gift from the same shithead brother downstairs currently pissing me off. He bought it for me after I helped save his fiancé from being abducted by her psycho ex-boyfriend.

My phone vibrates in my pocket, and I pull it out to see who the text is from. My four siblings and I have a group text thread, and it keeps our phones going off constantly, but this time, it's only from Sawyer.

Sawyer: You're a dickhead, you know that?

Me: You think I care?

Sawyer: You can't just hide in your office and ignore your responsibilities

Me: No? Then fire Blaire and cancel this shit show. As long as people are stomping through our business then you can find me in my office

Sawyer: Pouting like a goddamn baby who didn't get his way. Grow the fuck up, Dallas

Is that really what he thinks? That I'm pissed off because I didn't get my way? Frustrated, I turn my phone on silent and toss it onto my desk with a huff. This is the problem with being in business with family; the lines get blurred, and boundaries are inevitably crossed. My three brothers and I run Aspen Ridge Distillery. It's been in our family for four generations, supplying whiskey and bourbon to the Pacific Northwest, and it only keeps growing.

Since Sawyer and I are twins, our dad and grandfather weren't sure which of us would take over the CEO position from our dad, but I happily bowed out of the running, content to be his number two. Last summer, one of our younger brothers, Carter, who handles all of our PR, came up with a plan to generate more income by hosting tastings, events, and tours of the distillery. Unfortunately, Carter had done all of his homework, and everyone was on board with his proposal. Except for me. I thrive in the laid-back environment we've had going here; the only people on the property are the staff, and it's easygoing. Now I'll have to suffer through the hustle and bustle of events and gaggles of people swarming around while we work. I think we're opening ourselves up for disaster. The pressure to always be "on" because we represent the company and people are paying to be on our grounds, isn't something I'm thrilled about either. Go to a goddamn winery or brewery. This is a distillery. I live for the tranquility that this place has had my entire life. Now, with all the changes, my sanctuary has gone out the goddamn window.

To add the cherry on top, Sawyer went ahead and hired an event coordinator after I refused to fill the position like he had tasked me to. And he didn't hire just anyone. Blaire Hollis is the bane of my existence. She's the physical representation of everything that irritates me and has ruined everything we had going at the distillery. What's worse? I am so goddamn attracted to her that it pisses me off. She's easily the sexiest woman I've ever laid eyes on.

Wild, fiery red hair that is always worn down, cascading past her shoulder blades, a set of thick thighs that I've imagined tossed over my shoulders more times than I can count, a plump ass, and curves that were made for my hands to grab onto. She's a damn smoke show. A succubus sent by the devil himself to torture me, and I've nearly beat my cock to death in the bathroom after every interaction I have with her.

I can't stand her.

My dick doesn't agree.

Yesterday was Blaire's launch party. Everyone who works for the distillery was invited and encouraged to bring their families to celebrate. I lasted about five minutes before I bailed. Today is open fucking season and worse than I could have imagined. Seems like everyone within a fifty-mile radius came out to catch a glimpse behind-the-scenes of the mysterious Aspen Ridge Distillery. Knowing I need a way to release this energy, I relent and pull up my sibling group chat.

Me: Hey fuckers. Dom's tonight?

I bounce my knee, waiting for one of them to confirm they're free to meet up. My brothers, Sawyer, Liam, Carter, and I have been boxing together at Knockout since Sawyer and I were teenagers. As soon as our dad realized that our first response to a fight was to react physically, he threw us into lessons. It's been an outlet for stress ever since, and tonight I'm feeling worked up enough that I know I'll combust soon if I don't get it out.

Sawyer: Would love to beat your ass today but Ivy isn't feeling well so pass

Liam: Can't today.

Me: Fuck you both. Carter you in?

Carter: Nah man. Ask Reid or I can meet you at The Night Owl around 9

Reid is Sawyer's best friend, whom he met in college, and the two of them are as close as brothers. I'm not surprised that Sawyer won't meet up, he's had his head stuffed right up his girl's ass since shit went down with her. In September, I got a tip from Wes, the PI Sawyer hired to keep tabs on Ivy's ex who was harassing and stalking her. Shit went down hard. The whole thing was enough to make Sawyer act all caveman, protective of her, barely letting her out of his sight. As if he wasn't nearing that point before she had a stalker.

I'd be the same way, so as much as I want to pummel his face in for the shit he's causing at work, I get it and respect it. But maybe what Carter has in mind is a better idea. Drinks and pussy. Both foolproof stress relievers that are just as good as using my fists in the boxing ring.

Me: See you at 9

I park my Audi in the back parking lot of The Night Owl, the only bar in Aspen Ridge, ready for a drink. My brother, Carter, is already at the bar chatting up a pretty little blonde I've never seen before. I take a seat on the empty stool next to him and flag down Ruby, the owner and bartender.

"Been a while, Dallas, what can I get for ya?"

"Just a beer to start with."

I nudge my brother with my elbow, getting his attention. "Hey, lover boy, you invited me and you're already bailing? Some wingman you are."

"Can't help that the ladies flock to me. Why don't you worry about getting yourself laid and less about me?"

"Fucker," I mumble. I pick up my cold beer and take a look around. Aspen Ridge is small. I usually head into the city for what

I'm looking for and to keep it under wraps. My sexual appetite is on the darker side, and that news would spread like wildfire if I slept my way through AR like my brother.

The beer is refreshing and cool as it goes down, a much-needed drink after a long day. Setting my beer back on the bar top, my eyes scan the room and lead me to the door like a moth to a flame. In walks Blaire with Cole-motherfucking-Barnes right behind her. Her eyes connect with mine, instantly going wide, just as shocked to see me here. Cole removes his jacket and helps Blaire shrug out of her winter coat. My eyes roam her perfect body, and my dick stiffens in my jeans. She's wearing her work clothes—a tight pencil skirt that hugs her shapely hips and thighs, stopping just above her knees, and a blouse in a light blue that makes her hair look even more red. She's in fuck-me heels that aren't practical for the weather, and has gold link necklaces around her gorgeous neck. She's so fucking sexy.

Her attention darts away as Cole leads her to a booth, his hand planted on her lower back. Cole and I have a history, and it isn't a positive one. Growing up, he was always trying to one-up me, but never quite had the edge I did. He's a top-tier douche canoe, and it's no secret that we don't get along. The coupling actually makes sense, and an obnoxious snort leaves me as I come to that realization. She looks up at him and gives a genuine smile, her face lighting up at something he said, as I use my palm to adjust my aching cock that's always standing at attention when she's nearby.

Fuck this. You know what, a quick fuck wouldn't hurt. I reach over, grab Carter's glass of liquor, and toss it back before washing it down with half my beer. I let my eyes scan the room without looking too eager.

Bingo.

Sitting at the end of the bar, is Ava Jones. Cute, petite, not my usual type—I like 'em a little less breakable—but hot enough and giving me fuck-me eyes that can't be misinterpreted. A little too young for me, but she's legal and seems down for a night of no-strings-attached orgasms. I lift my beer in her direction and give her a nod. Cheers. Ava smirks before picking up her drink, a margarita by the looks of it, and sashays over to me, sinking down on the barstool on my other side. I lean into my brother and whisper under my breath, "If you've already been in this one, for the love of God tell me now. We're brothers by blood, don't need to be fuckin' boner bros on top of it."

He laughs and glances over at Ava.

"Nope. You're good."

With the all clear, I turn my body to face her, fully aware of Blaire's presence the entire time. I can feel each time she looks my way, her eyes grating over my skin like a sharp razor. Little terror can't even let me enjoy a drink with my brother.

"So how ya been, Ava?"

"I've been good. Yourself?"

"Better now." I give her a wink. She smiles seductively at me, pushing the hair out of her face and behind her ear, showcasing a decent enough rack that's pushed up and out of the top of her shirt. Oh yeah, she's down for letting me hit it. I sneak a glance over at Blaire, finding her already looking my way. She jerks her head away, focusing back on her douchebag date. More patrons file into the bar, lining up to order drinks, shuffling around me, Carter, and the girls.

"Here, let's make more room," I suggest as I move Ava from her barstool onto my lap. She loops her arm around my neck and shimmies her ass directly over my cock. My hand stays on her thigh, one on my beer, disappointed that I'm not feeling any excitement or eagerness about this prospect. My dick shriveled up the moment my eyes left Blaire. Fuck, this is bullshit.

"Definitely more comfortable than the stool." She rubs her ass against my lap again, but it's not doing a goddamn thing for me. I feel absolutely nothing. Fuck. My dick and I need to get on the same page, the bastard. I look back over at Blaire as she's standing and walking toward the restroom. I pat Ava on the thigh, signaling her to get off my lap. She turns to face me and pouts, but I'm completely unaffected. I follow Blaire to the bathroom, walking right into the ladies' room behind her, bending down to check that it's clear of anyone but us before flicking the lock.

"What the fuck are you doing in here, Dallas?" she snaps in the vicious tone I've come to expect from her, the same one that turns me on.

"What the fuck are you doing here with *him*?" My feet are on autopilot as I prowl her back against the bathroom wall. Her eyes widen in shock, but not alarm.

"What I do in my free time has nothing to do with you! Are you serious right now? Leave!"

I don't know what comes over me, whether it's the way she sucks her bottom lip between her teeth and drags it free, her hooded, hate-filled eyes, or her deep breathing, but fuck I know she feels it too. Maybe it's the alcohol, maybe it's this toxic, heated energy between us, but all I want to do right now is fuck the attitude out of her. I reach my hand up to cup her cheek, and she lifts her chin in defiance.

"Fuck, princess. You make me fuckin' crazy. You know that?" I say through clenched teeth.

"Fuck you, Dallas."

My hand moves down to her throat, and she fucking whimpers.

Whimpers.

Not in fear. Goddamn it, she likes it.

I squeeze lightly around her pretty neck, watching the motion as she swallows, and I imagine what it would look like covered in a pearl necklace of my own making. How my cum would glisten around her collarbone. That damn plump lip is being held hostage between her teeth again, her chest rising and falling rapidly, brushing those voluptuous tits up against my arm and chest. My mouth waters as I imagine what it would be like to rip her blouse open, the buttons scattering across the floor so I could free them and feast on them. They'd spill over my hand, much bigger than a handful, and I'd suck on her pert nipples until she was begging me to let her come.

Fuck.

Why do I want her this badly? I meet her glossy, heavy eyes, and there's no mistaking the arousal I see in them. For the first time since meeting each other, we're quiet, suspended in this intense moment, both of us frozen. I move my hand back up to her face, swiping my thumb over her lip, pulling it free. I have the biggest urge to kiss her right now. Something I never do.

"He's not right for you," I growl.

"Yeah? Then who is?" she challenges. Her voice is almost a whisper, clouded with lust and desire. It shouldn't shock me, because she meets me head-on at every single opportunity, but given the close proximity, I find myself surprised at what she could be insinuating. Like I've been soaked by a bucket of cold water, I release her face and shake my head.

What the fuck am I doing? I can't stand this woman, and I'm just pissed that she's seeing that asshole, dickweed, Cole. Nothing more. I can't act on any of my physical desires for this woman. As my employee, she's seriously off-limits.

"I don't give a shit, just anyone but him." Her head bops back slightly, and her expression looks jarred. She quickly schools her features, but I swear I saw something that looked a whole hell of a lot like disappointment. Fuck.

"Oh. Well, if you're not careful, Dallas, it may seem like you actually care."

"I don't. If you want to fuck him, go ahead and enjoy that needle dick. I'd be surprised if he figures out where it goes."

"Real mature as always, Dallas. Go fuck yourself!"

I run my hands through my hair and take one last look at her. Her face is still a little flushed, but she's otherwise composed and still looking hot as fuck. I unlock the bathroom door and bolt out of there, leaving her to herself. I don't stop until I'm in front of my car, ready to head home for the night, not willing to sit back and watch her leave with Cole.

blaire

THE MORNING LIGHT STREAMS IN THROUGH MY window, and as much as I could stay tucked under the warmth of my blankets and sleep the rest of the morning away, I want to make the most of my Saturday. Last night was so unexpected that I tossed and turned and barely got any sleep. Dallas cornering me in the women's restroom rattled me. I felt his jealous rage just as fiercely as his lust. He wanted me, and for a moment, I thought he was going to kiss me.

His behavior came out of nowhere. It's no secret how much he dislikes me, but he's also not as sly as he thinks he is when he's checking me out. The distillery has an insanely lax atmosphere, so I'm not worried about the fact that I told him to fuck off, but his behavior would probably get him in trouble if I wanted to report him.

I was supposed to be on my first date with Cole. We met at the end of summer bonfire at Grace Beach my first week in town, and he asked me out during a tasting yesterday. While I'm not overly interested in him, it sure beats spending another lonely night at home. Dallas being there was just the icing on the cake, and I'd be lying to myself if I didn't admit how much his dominance turned me on. Something I need to dissect later, because that is usually a hard line for me.

I couldn't imagine a sexual relationship that is built on having a trust so deep that one person can hand over their desires and needs to another with no reservations. I'm no virgin, but I can't imagine being willing to let someone control me in the bedroom; I need to play an active part in controlling the situation. I'm sure that can be blamed on one person. For a kid who grew up the way I did, I consider myself lucky. My need to not take any shit from anyone and be in constant control are all coping mechanisms. Even if Dallas' unexpected dominant side definitely turned me on.

I slowly rise and pull on some athletic clothes—a pair of black fleece-lined leggings, a long sleeve top, and a baggy sweatshirt. Tucking my wild hair under a beanie, I slip on my sneakers and head out. Aspen Ridge is breathtaking, especially in the morning. Fog kisses the ground, and it smells like snow is on the horizon.

The walk down Main Street is like a trip inside a Hallmark Christmas movie. Complete with brick sidewalks, light posts decorated in twinkly lights that give off a warm, festive glow, and wreaths hanging on doors. I can't help but stop at each window display and marvel at the holiday cheer. I open the door to Bean Haven, welcoming the warmth of the shop.

"Morning, Blaire!" Hannah chirps from the other side of the counter. "I just pulled chocolate croissants out, would you like one with your coffee?"

Hannah Haven runs the town's only coffee shop. To say she's gorgeous would be a drastic understatement. She has beautiful violet-colored hair, styled in loose waves, and a full sleeve of intricate, fine line floral tattoos up one arm. She's also the most genuine, sweet person I've met here so far, and I always look forward to talking with her.

"That sounds like heaven actually, please! Good morning, Ms. Nettie," I say to greet Hannah's grandmother, who is sitting at a small table in front of the shop window, her small dog lying peacefully in her lap.

"Mornin'," the older woman replies without giving so much as a look in my direction. When I first moved to Aspen Ridge, she would sit outside just like that, watching everyone as they went about their lives around her. Now that winter has moved in, she sits right in the front window.

While I wait for Hannah to make my coffee, the bell chimes, signaling more customers, and Ms. Nettie's dog loses her mind, jumping out of her lap and yelping loudly. I look over to find Ivy and Sawyer walking in holding hands. They're the epitome of what two people who were made for each other look like, and from what little I've heard from people chatting, especially Ms. Nettie, they were together all through school and then were separated for ten years but made their way back to each other. It's pretty romantic actually. Apparently, Sawyer waited for her—never even dated—and was convinced he'd get her back someday. Can you even imagine? That kind of stuff doesn't happen in real life and is totally romance book material.

Ivy glows, happiness exuding from her. Her long black hair is worn down and makes all of her facial features pop. I absentmindedly run my fingers through my wild, untamed, red hair.

"Ms. Nettie, why? Why? Minnie, get off!" Sawyer drawls in an obviously irritated tone.

"It's Winnie!" Ms. Nettie and Ivy yell at him. I laugh to myself while watching Ivy scoop the little dog up, her teeth planted firmly at the bottom of Sawyer's pants. She wrangles her free and sets her back with Ms. Nettie before they turn in my direction.

"Hey, Blaire! Good to see you!"

"Hi, Ivy. Hey, Sawyer. What are you guys up to?"

"Ivy's craving apple cinnamon muffins and these are the best."

Ivy smacks Sawyer in the chest and gives him a pointed glare. I'm not sure what the issue is, it's no secret how mouthwatering Bean Haven's apple cinnamon muffins are.

"What about you? Any plans for the weekend?" Ivy asks me.

"Nope. Just kinda hanging around." Alone. Cause that's

what you do when you have no family and haven't made any real friends in your new town yet.

"Morning, you two!" Hannah sets my coffee and croissant on the counter and rings me up. "Usual?" she asks the pair.

Sawyer nods and confirms, "Yep."

"Really? When are you going to stop this madness? Get something you actually enjoy," Ivy says to him.

I watch as Sawyer leans down and whispers something into her ear. Her face flames in a vibrant blush and I can't hold back a smile. They're so in love.

"You and Charlie coming tomorrow, Han?" Sawyer asks. I grab my coffee and paper bag and turn to leave.

"Wouldn't miss it!" she replies.

"Hey, Blaire, if you don't have plans tomorrow, why don't you join us? Sawyer's parents host a mandatory Sunday dinner at their house. It's super informal, usually pretty chaotic actually, but it's good food and it isn't just family. Hannah and Charlie usually come, and Reid is always invited but never shows. But it's fun, sometimes others bring a friend or two. You should join us."

I give her a genuine smile, but the idea of going over to my employer's parents' house for Sunday dinner doesn't sound like the best idea. Dinner opens up getting-to-know-you questions, and questions are never good when you basically made up an entire story about your past to make yourself sound better and not so pathetic and damaged. They think I'm a military child who grew up around the world, returning to Washington to live with my grandparents—who don't exist. The last thing I wanted out of moving here was a pity hire.

"Thank you for the invite, honestly, but—"

"Don't be ridiculous, you need to come. Plus, the look on Dallas' face will be worth it. You enjoy pissing him off, right?" Sawyer chimes in, slinging his arm around Ivy's shoulders. I know my face brightens at the mention of my other boss. While Dallas is indeed a huge prick, he's so sexy that it's actually painful to look at him. Memories of last night flash through my mind—how his eyes were filled with a blazing inferno, how he looked at me like he wanted to devour me. But then the way he left me hot and bothered, confused, and shocked, yeah, I'd love to spend my Sunday pissing him off in retaliation.

"Actually, that sounds great. You convinced me."

Sawyer laughs. "Atta girl. Ivy will text you the details."

"Sounds great. See you all tomorrow."

We all go our separate ways and head back out into the winter chill. I'm lost in looking at the holiday displays and don't notice when I run into a hard wall of a human leaving Book Bound, the indie bookstore. I bounce backward, lucky not to spill any of my coffee.

"I'm so sorry about that!"

"For fuck's sake. Can't you watch where you're going?"

Dallas. Because of course it would be Dallas.

"What part of sorry did you not hear?"

"You wouldn't need to say sorry if you were watching where you were going."

"You would think that wouldn't you? Because you never make mistakes. Speaking of, I'm sure the innocent girl you were going to corrupt last night is thankful you weren't another notch on her bedpost."

"Cheeky as always, princess."

He leans down into my space, his head next to mine as he whispers in my ear, making my pulse race and sending chills down my spine.

"Trust me, nothing about what I would have done to her would have been considered a mistake. She'd be left more than satisfied and come back begging for more."

My eyes flutter closed for a brief moment as thoughts of all the things Dallas could do behind closed doors flash before them, then I shake clear of the spell he has over me.

"You tell yourself that all you want, buddy. Whatever helps you sleep at night."

Refusing to let Dallas get under my skin today, knowing that he'll get a rude awakening at dinner tomorrow, I walk away, deciding to head into Rogue to check on Reid before going upstairs to my apartment. Especially because I don't need Dallas seeing where I live. Lucky for me, he's not currently tattooing any clients.

"Hey, you," I greet him. He looks up from his workstation, his iPad displaying a gorgeous design he's working on. The artist in me wants to look at the details, but I don't ask. He takes off his glasses, which are such an enigma because the man is the size of an extra-angry Hulk, covered in tattoos from the neck down, and has shoulder-length hair. His occupation checks out.

"Hey there. What, no coffee for me?"

I pale, realizing the rudeness of my behavior.

"Oh my gosh, I'm so sorry! Last minute decision to swing in to say hi," I say sheepishly. He reaches down by his feet, picking up a Bean Haven to-go mug that matches my own, and smirks at me as he takes a long pull from it.

"Dick," I tease while taking a seat across from him. "So, guess where I was just invited."

"Hayes Sunday dinner."

"What the hell? How'd you know?"

"'Cause you just came from Bean Haven. Which means Liam was probably there, and since Ivy can't get enough of those damn apple cinnamon muffins, there's a good chance she was there with Sawyer. Plus, they're always trying to extend that invitation."

"Smarty pants. They said you have a standing invitation but you don't ever go. What's up? Is there something I'm missing? There's not some weird cult thing happening over there, is there? My roommate in college got sucked into one of those."

He laughs at that.

"Nah, they're good people. The best, actually. I just can't bring myself to go. Got something else going on Sundays and don't do family stuff like that."

There's something in his tone that brings me pause, taking a moment to decide whether I should press or not.

"I can see your brain working overtime, B. Just spill it."

"Why can't you go? From what I've seen and heard, you and Sawyer are best friends, you seem close with all of them, actually."

He sighs before leaning back on his stool, resting his large, tattooed arms across his station behind him.

"It's complicated. It's just the family dynamic. It has everything to do with me and nothing to do with them, and going there just reminds me of everything that I've lost. Plus, I have a standing appointment that day."

Now that, I can relate to. I don't want to ask further questions on the topic, I understand more than anyone the need to keep our secrets close.

"So, I guess I'm going solo then. I'll let you know how it goes. I'm positive it's going to ruin Dallas' day, so that will be my highlight."

He laughs and takes another sip of his coffee, then sits up straight and looks at me with huge eyes.

"Wait, you actually know someone who got pulled into a cult?"

"How are you just now hearing that? I swear men's brains are bizarrely wired. I'm so not making it up. My roommate in college got involved with one. Took over her entire life, like consumed her. Couldn't talk about anything else. Kept trying to get me to join. Hard pass, by the way. But we lost her to it. The CrossFit gods claimed her."

The look on his face is priceless, as shock morphs into a deep laugh that triggers my own. It feels so good to have a friend. AR is finally starting to feel like home.

I decide to head back to my apartment upstairs to get some work done, choosing to spend the rest of the day with my Post Malone playlist on shuffle, working on my laptop, and going over plans for Sawyer and Ivy's upcoming wedding. They wanted to have it on the distillery property, something intimate and beautiful, and being asked to plan it has been such an honor. While I'd worked on weddings at my previous job, I've never taken the lead until now.

Planning weddings has always been my dream, and this is as close to reaching it as I'm going to get right now. Creating someone's happiest moments and giving them something spectacular to look back on, would be goals for me.

Before I know it, four hours have passed, and I'm forced to set my laptop down next to me on the couch and rub my strained eyes. I stretch my legs out and pick up my phone to scroll aimlessly through social media, when I find a missed text.

Cole: I had a great time with you last night. I'm glad you agreed to go out with me.

A soft smile comes to my face. Despite Dallas flustering me in the bathroom, I had a good time with Cole. The conversation flowed easily, and he was present and attentive, sweet even. But he didn't light me up. There weren't any initial sparks. But maybe that takes time. Perhaps if Dallas hadn't messed with my head, I'd feel differently. I want so badly to make it work here in Aspen Ridge, and dating is a part of that. I don't want to be alone forever.

Me: Thank you for taking me out. I had a good time as well.

Cole: I was hoping that was the case.

Unsure of what to say in response, my fingers hover over my keypad. Feeling slightly awkward about how to keep the conversation going, I toss my phone to the side and pick up my sketchpad and pencil, adding some finishing touches to a new wedding gown design I've had floating around in my head. Designing wedding dresses was my first passion, but going to art school was too much of a gamble. I needed to make sure that I could settle down with a stable job, and let's face it, unless I wanted to teach, getting my degree in art was going to make finding a career more challenging. With no one to fall back on but myself, going to school for hospitality management and then studying my ass off to get my project plus certification was the closest I could get to creating dream weddings. I may not be designing brides' dream gowns, but the event process is just as fulfilling.

Looking around the sparse room that is my apartment, I can't help but wonder what tomorrow will be like at Dallas' parents' house. I've seen the relationship dynamic between the Hayes brothers, and their closeness must be partially due to their parents and their upbringing. As much as I'm eager to see the shocked look on Dallas' face, I'm nervous to be asked questions about my own family, because I'm seriously lacking in that department. I'll have to get creative to keep my secrets locked up close.

But I've been playing this game my entire life.

CHAPTER 4

dallas

SUNDAY AFTERNOONS ARE ALWAYS SPENT AT MY parents' house, and my mom expects your presence unless you're on your deathbed. I walk into the house I grew up in, raucous noise echoing off the walls. I'm stunned still when I leave the entryway and bump into none other than Blaire fucking Hollis, princess of my nightmares. She's wearing a cream-colored sweater that hangs slightly off one shoulder, exposing the expanse of her collarbone, and the memory of my hand wrapped around her throat on Friday night makes me flex my hands into fists at my sides.

"The hell are you doing here?"

Blaire's face pales, which surprises me. It's only a moment before she schools her expression and snaps back at me, "I was invited, dickhead. I don't make it a habit of just showing up at people's homes on a Sunday to crash their dinner."

"That nickname is reserved for family," I say, pointing my finger in her face, "and who the hell invited you?"

"I did," Ivy chirps, coming up next to Blaire. "Problem? I ran into her yesterday at Bean Haven and Hannah and I were talking about dinner. Sawyer was thrilled I invited her and encouraged her to come. Don't be rude."

Blaire gives me one of her signature smug smiles and waltzes away with Ivy, arms linked together like they're best pals. I'm fuming. This is my space, the last thing I need is her in it. She's already taken over the distillery. I go on a hunt for my twin brother, ready to rip him a new one.

"Hi, my wild child. Hope you're hungry," my mom says as I lean in and kiss her cheek.

"Always hungry for your cooking, Mom. Where's Sawyer?"

She stops stirring the pasta on the stove and looks at me, her eyes squinting in speculation.

"Don't cause any mayhem. He's in the living room. No roughhousing, Dal."

I feign shock, pulling back like she slapped me and placing my hand over my heart.

"Me? I would never."

"Mhm. Go. Just don't be destructive."

I drop a kiss to the top of her head and walk through the house and into the living room. Lucky for me, he's sitting nice and relaxed on our parents' couch with his back to me. I slink up behind him and hook my arm around his throat, squeezing tightly and restricting his airflow. His hands immediately rise up, one grabbing my forearm, the other reaching behind my head to grasp the back of my neck. I lean down to his ear and whisper through my teeth, "Why the fuck is Blaire here, shithead?" I pull back, forcing him to arch on the couch as he grunts. He plants his heels on the cushion and kicks off hard, sending us both flying over the back of it and onto the ground. The force of the fall and his weight on top of me knocks the wind out of my lungs. I'm quick to recover and don't lose my hold around his neck right away, but the moment he loosens my arm, he flips us. I take a punch to the stomach before I clock him in the ribs twice, my free arm blocking a punch to my cheek. We grapple on the ground, rolling around and bouncing into the wall.

"Holy shit, is this normal for them?" I hear Blaire ask from not too far away while I work to overtake my asshole twin.

"Yep. They've been going at it like this since they shared a womb. Their poor mother is a saint," Ivy tells her.

I grab a fistful of Sawyer's hair and yank him back, throwing a fist to his stomach.

"Grow the fuck up, Dallas!" Sawyer yells.

"You first, fucker!"

We roll once more, tossing punches wildly at each other before Liam and Carter pull us apart.

"You two are animals. Mom wants us to throw you outside. Pull yourselves together!" Liam shouts at us. I shove out of Carter's hold and shake out my arms, adjusting my clothes and running my hands through my hair.

Sawyer reaches for Ivy, wrapping his arm around her waist and pulling her flush against him. He drops a kiss to her temple and takes a deep breath. It's clear she settles him. I find myself strangely jealous watching the interaction. Not of him and Ivy specifically, but the connection between them. He makes eye contact with me and points with his finger. "You're a dickhead, Dallas."

I throw my arms out to the sides. "Yeah. You've all said it. I get it. I'm a dick." I shoot a glance at Blaire and narrow my eyes at her before walking into the lounge where my parents keep their bar. I pour a heavy-handed whiskey neat, not wanting to dilute the burn as it goes down. Gripping the counter, I toss it back and pour another. If I'm going to be forced to endure Sunday dinner with Blaire in attendance, I need to get a good buzz going.

"Dallas?"

"What, Blaire?" I snap, not bothering to look her way.

She walks up next to me, her voice low, almost insecure.

"Look, I'm sorry if I crossed a line by being here. Sawyer and Ivy invited me. I declined at first but . . ." Her voice trails off and I'm forced to look at her. For the third time since we met, her composure has slipped. She's unsure, hesitant, and wary. All traces of the headstrong, difficult, stubborn asshole are gone. I don't understand it, but I don't like what's standing in front of me right now. I slide my glass of whiskey down the smooth grain of the bar, and she looks at it like she's never seen one before.

"Just drink it, Blaire."

She looks up at me with those big blue doe eyes, and I'm immediately lost in them. The dark blue of her irises is so stormy and uniquely her, it would be impossible to recreate the color. My anger dissipates, leaving nothing but frustration behind. She picks up the glass and takes a hesitant sip. I watch as she swallows and then immediately starts coughing.

"Holy shit. Fire," she gasps. "How do you drink that?"

I shrug. "You get used to it."

A beat of silence passes between us as Blaire shifts on her feet.

"I can leave if you want me to."

I turn to face her and instantly regret it. She's so fucking pretty.

"Don't go soft on me now, princess. Let my family see what a feral creature you are."

She nods, but at least she's smiling again. She places my drink in front of me and walks back into the other room, leaving me alone for a few precious moments before dinner is served and I'm forced to embrace the chaos. I don't know what it is about this girl that drives me fucking wild. Her sad eyes awaken a protective side that I have no control over. No matter how frustrated I am with her, I can't fight these feelings she brings out of me.

"Dinner, heathens!" my mom's voice bellows through the house. I grab the glass, studying the mark Blaire's luscious lips left behind. I swipe my tongue over the spot before tossing the remainder back. After pouring another, I walk into the dining room and take a seat at the table as everyone else does the same.

"Here, Blaire, make yourself comfortable," Sawyer says, taking a play out of my book, being the little shit-stirrer as he pulls out a chair for her directly across from me. I wait for her to look down before giving him the finger.

We all take turns passing around the chicken, eggplant, pasta, and red sauce. It's hard to keep my focus off Blaire as she interacts with my family.

"You know I'm gonna ask, so tell me how work is," our dad says with a bit of a slur. Last year he suffered a few strokes that left him with some physical and cognitive challenges. He never complains and he doesn't let anything hold him down. Because of it though, he did step away from his position as CEO of the distillery way before he was ready to. The four of us know he likes to be kept in the loop, so we do our best to fill him in and let him be a part of as much as possible. He's enjoying early retirement at home with my mom, where they're happiest.

"Actually, I've got news," Liam says while trying to wrangle Charlotte into the seat between him and Hannah.

"Let's hear it, son."

"I'm workin' on something new. It's gonna be long-term and may take a bit to get it right since the rules are stupid specific, but hopefully, in two years we'll be tasting our first straight bourbon whiskey."

"Are we really?" my mom asks.

"I mean, we gotta make sure we do it right, which I'm confident we can. The fermented corn has to be distilled to no more than 160 proof and aged in new charred oak barrels, which we can do. There's more to it, but I'm damn excited about it."

"Seriously, it's all I've heard about for weeks now. He hasn't stopped researching and talking about it, even though I don't understand half of what he just said," Hannah chimes in.

Hannah and Liam have been best friends since they could walk. One is never far from the other, and we all thought they'd end up together someday. Little Charlotte came unexpectedly, courtesy of Hannah's piece of shit boyfriend, Levi. He's in and out of both of their lives, but Liam stays put. Whether any of them admit it or not, Liam's been a surrogate father to Charlie since the day she was born. She may have been a surprise, but that little girl is an honorary Hayes, and we all love her so much.

"It sounds great, Liam. Blaire, we have loved seeing what

you've done in such a short amount of time. The event went so well, and all the changes are such a beautiful addition."

Blaire replies to my mom with a smile on her face, "Thank you. That means so much to me, coming from you. It's been such a pleasure." Her voice takes on a happy, enthusiastic tone reminiscent of Tinkerbell rather than the vile Maleficent she reserves just for me.

I choke on a bite of pasta, coughing into a quick laugh. "Sorry, sorry. Please, Blaire, continue," I say while taking a swig of my whiskey.

"How do you like working at the distillery?" my mom asks her.

"Honestly, it's been incredible. I'm thankful for the opportunity to create this additional business for you all. I love the event aspect, and Sawyer, Carter, and I have a meeting after the new year to discuss hosting larger events like weddings. Sawyer and Ivy's will be the first, and while it's very small and intimate, it's going to give me a great—"

"You're not serious, right?"

"Dallas," my mom admonishes.

"Mom, you guys can't be on board with this. Weddings? Why not just call in a damn circus. Hell, a petting zoo would bring in more business, too, if we're just fuckin' off with any idea. Let's do that. Liam! We know anyone who's got livestock for sale?" I yell down the table.

My sister, Kinsey, slaps me on the back of my head. "Dallas, stop being such a dickhead! Can you seriously not be nice?"

Kinsey is the youngest of us five, and with four older brothers, she's a perfect mix of feminine and take-no-shit. While she doesn't ever box with us and is half our size at least, I'd bet good money she could kick our asses.

I rub the back of my head when Blaire speaks up, my eyes shooting to hers.

"Kinsey, it's okay, really. Dallas didn't get his way, and like most toddlers, is struggling with having big feelings right now.

Aren't you, little man?" she says in a condescending, mocking tone that is all her.

The room goes silent for a split second before they all erupt into raucous laughter. I've never seen Blaire smile so big and bright that it lights up her entire face. I clap my hands slowly.

"Well done, princess. I knew you could show them," I say directly to her with a wink before finishing off my drink.

"Alright, alright," Sawyer says, getting everyone's attention. "So, Ivy and I wanted to talk to you all ahead of the wedding next weekend." I look over at my mom, whose eyes are already glassy, as she covers her mouth with her hands. Everyone here knows what he's about to share. The two of them have been talking about it since we were teenagers, and we've all been waiting for the announcement since Ivy returned. "Ivy's pregnant. We're having a baby!" he yells before leaning down and kissing her head.

The table erupts into cheers as everyone clambers out of their seats to get to Sawyer and Ivy. I lean back in my chair and look at my twin brother. We all knew that as long as Carter didn't accidentally knock someone up, and Ivy found her way back to Sawyer, he'd be the first to be a dad. He's wanted to put a baby in her from the moment she got back into town, and based on the timeline, he did just that.

"My niece or nephew is in there?" Kinsey asks, her palm on Ivy's tiny stomach.

"Yes! I want to say that it doesn't feel real, but the constant morning sickness would make me a liar."

I wait for everyone to give their congratulations before I get up and move toward my twin. I pull him into a big hug, slapping his back. I've never seen him so happy, and after everything he went through losing Ivy and then getting her back, he deserves every bit of the happiness.

"Didn't waste any time, huh?"

"Fuck no. We lost ten years, I'm not waiting another second. I'm going to breed her until she can't take it anymore."

I laugh as Ivy slaps him on the chest, which causes me to

laugh some more. Making room for my mom to hug him again, I step back, ready to return to my seat, when I catch Blaire's heated stare in my direction. I don't know what she sees, but there's no mistaking the look in her eyes. My dick wakes up just from the look on her face. Fuck, why am I so attracted to her? She scoots back out of her chair and excuses herself quietly. I watch her head for the bathroom, and since everyone else is occupied with the love birds, their baby news, and their upcoming wedding, I follow her. I blame the alcohol flowing through my veins because just as she starts to close the door, I stick my foot in, stopping her.

"What the—"

Pushing open the door, she steps back just as I'm stepping in.

"Somethin' on your mind, princess?"

"What are you rambling about now, Dallas?"

"You think I didn't notice the way you were looking at me back there?"

She sucks her bottom lip into her mouth, and I have to use my palm to press down on my thickening cock to readjust it behind my zipper. Her eyes track my movements, widening in shock before meeting mine in a challenge. Fuck does she get under my skin. I take a step forward, closing the distance between us. Her chest rises and falls, and I can't take my eyes away, so jealous of the creamy ivory sweater that gets to rest over her full breasts. My resolve is slowly chipping away, the alcohol muddling the restraint I know I need. She's just so goddamn tempting. She places her hands on her hips, and I let my eyes roam over her perfect hourglass figure.

She's so sexy.

So seductive.

So tempting.

I want to tie her up, wrists and ankles bound so I can bury my face between those gorgeous legs, spread that pussy open wide, and fuck her mercilessly with my tongue until she squirts all over me. I want to fucking drown in her. Death by Blaire's sweet cunt is a fate I'd accept.

"Dallas."

Her voice brings me out of my fantasy, forcing me to look into her eyes, pupils blown wide over the stormy blue. She has the same dirty thoughts as me.

Shit.

What the fuck am I doing? I run my hand over the scruff on my jaw and walk out of the bathroom. Once again leaving a stunned, confused, Blaire behind.

I stumble into Carter on my way to the lounge for another drink when an idea strikes me.

"Hey, lover boy, want to bail? My style?"

"You're speaking my language, brother. I'll drive since you've been pregaming."

Carter and I kiss our mom and say bye to our dad before putting on our jackets to head out.

"Where are you two heading? Celebrate with us here!" Ivy coos.

"We love you, Iv, but the night calls! Congratulations, you two. We'll celebrate next weekend at the wedding."

***

An hour in the car later, Carter and I are walking into Temptations, an invitation-only, high-end sex club. Our other brothers are aware I'm a member and frequent it from time to time. I vouched for Carter last year and got him an invitation, but this is the first time we've come here together. Not that either of us are shy about what we like, we just try to stay clear of having public sex while the other is in the room.

I pull out my membership card and scan it on the second set of doors before they open. The music is blaring, base thumping, and the smell of sex is heavy in the air. Fuck yes. This is the outlet I need to get Blaire out of my mind. Carter and I walk through the main floor and head to the bar to order drinks. Taking a seat on the leather stool, I take a good look around, my eyes roaming across the open expanse of the main floor. Across from me, a beautiful woman lays back on a couch with her legs spread wide, a man massaging her breasts, sucking and pulling on her pert nipples, while another woman's face is buried in her pussy. Her back arches as the man pulls her legs up, spreading her wider for the woman to eat her out. I'm too possessive to share, but fuck if my mind doesn't conjure Blaire splayed out like that so I could direct someone else to lick her pussy and make her come apart at the seams. She'd writhe and squirm and I'd prolong it until she was begging to come. Fuck. Why can't I get her out of my fucking head? Only now does my dick decide to come alive.

I turn back to the bar and accept the shot the bartender placed in front of me, clinking it with Carter's. "To women and never being locked down by one!" he cheers as we toss back the liquid.

"Heading to the floor. Where you gonna be?" Carter asks.

Knowing exactly where I'm called to, I stand and smooth out my shirt.

"Red Room."

He nods before heading into the crowd to find someone to play with for the evening. I walk through the floor, heading into a long corridor that lines the front of the voyeur room. The light is on, meaning there's a show in progress. A few couples watch from the hallway, eagerly touching and groping each other, getting off to watching someone else so openly and intimately. I make my way to the end and relax into the shadows before a pretty, petite woman slinks up next to me, her hand lying flat on my chest, rubbing upward to my shoulder and back down again.

"You here alone?" she whispers. Her hand moves down, on a path to grab my junk. I clasp her wrist loosely and remove it from my body.

"Sorry, not interested."

She nods and walks away with her head held high. Gotta give her props for shooting her shot, but she's not my type nor what my dick seems to fucking want. I finally take in the scene in front of me. A female sits on her knees, her ass resting on her feet, legs slightly spread with her palms facing up on her thighs. She's the perfect sub, waiting for instruction. Her Dom prowls her, circling around her slowly, dragging the top of a riding crop up and down her arms, the length of her spine, and over her breasts, before walking away and sitting relaxed in a large, tufted chair. He slings his arm around the back of it before tugging on his hard cock with his free hand.

"Crawl to me." His voice plays over the speakers so the audience can hear everything. His sub doesn't hesitate, she leans forward on all fours and slowly, seductively crawls to him until she's right between his spread legs. Sitting back on her heels, she waits, never breaking eye contact with him. Fuck, what I would give to see Blaire crawl to me. Her gorgeous blue eyes trained on me, her large breasts swaying with each step. Goddamnit, she makes me crazy. My dick thickens in my pants, pushing painfully against the zipper.

I focus ahead, her head bobbing on his lap, his cock shoved down her throat while he pets her hair lovingly, his words of praise echoing through the hallway. I wonder how Blaire would respond. I know she loved my hand around her neck, so I'm going to bet she likes it rough. Fuck if I don't want to see how she'd respond to me being dominant with her, if she'd like it. I'd love to break her. She's so goddamn strong. Fuck if I don't want to see her on her knees, putty in my hands for me to fucking mold. I'd make her feel so fucking good she'd crave me after, needing to come back for more because no one could satisfy her like I can. My cock throbs painfully and I rub my palm against it, hoping to alleviate some of the pressure. Normally, I'd have someone sucking me off already. I look around the hallway and find a woman pressed up against the wall, her thigh hiked up around a man's waist while he finger fucks her and sucks on her neck.

"We can help you with that big problem you've got there. Want to join us?"

Running my hand through my hair, I give her a slight smile.

"You two enjoy yourselves."

Turned on, I leave the dimly lit hallway and walk through the throngs of half-naked bodies, the sound of pleasure and music mingling, the smell of sex heady. I make my way to the bathroom, walking into one of the stalls and locking the door behind me. Unbuckling my pants, I groan as my stiff cock is freed, grabbing it tightly and running up the length, my piercings pulling and giving the sting of pain I live for. I close my eyes and Blaire appears, her wild red hair splayed out across my bed, her wrists tied above her head, her sweet pussy on display for me. That curvy, sexy-as-fuck body ready for me to ravish. I'd edge her until she was compliant, until she learned to listen and could hand over her pleasure to me. And boy would I come through for her. I'd turn her into a screaming, writhing mess under me, making her pussy weep, soaking the sheets under her. My orgasm hits me out of nowhere, my balls drawing up, my cock hardening further.

I come harder than I ever have in my life. And she was only in my head.

I'm fucked.

blaire

It was impossible not to fall in love with the Hayes family. They're everything I used to wish for when I was a little girl. Open, loving, close, and so many of them. It was hard not to feel jealous of everything they have, while also feeling happy for them all. Dallas' parents have clearly worked hard at building a beautiful life with adult children who have strong relationships with their parents and each other. If only.

When I was growing up I got moved around so much I started to shut myself off from developing those relationships, knowing they'd end eventually. I'd be lying if I said I didn't wish I had a sister or brother of my own. Even if the banter is wild and heated, it's so clear as an outsider that the love between those Hayes siblings runs deeper than anything else. Except for maybe Sawyer's love for Ivy. In my twenty-seven years, I've never seen a man love like he does. I can't even fathom what that would feel like. To be the absolute center of someone else's world, to feel safe and comforted, happy with another person who knows you so deeply and intimately. It's the dream, honestly. A dream that would require me to be transparent about who I am and where I truly come from.

Like every day, I get ready for work with my music playing to drown out the quiet, doing my best to tame my wild hair, putting on a thin layer of makeup, and dressing in a navy blue sweater dress with tights and boots. Today I have two tours, a meeting with Ivy to finalize the plans for her wedding on Saturday, and anything else that comes up. Grabbing my coat and purse, I close up my apartment, ready to take on the day.

I love my morning drive to work. The hushed stillness of the early morning hours magnifies the beauty of our town, creating a sense of enchantment that's impossible to ignore. I drive along the narrow, winding road through town, flanked by the towering Sitka spruce and evergreen trees. Twinkling Christmas lights glow from every lamppost and give a whimsical addition to the already charming vibe. Wisps of smoke curl from the chimneys of the older, rustic homes and cottages. Fog still coats everything, a frigid winter chill in the air, everything quiet and hibernating. As the sun begins to rise over our sleepy small town, I pull onto the long gravel road that leads to the gorgeous property. The distillery sits in the most scenic part of town, and the view of the snow-capped peaks of the Olympic Mountains is breathtaking. I love winter, and Aspen Ridge is the epitome of a winter wonderland. I know deep in my bones that I want to settle in here and make this paradise my forever home.

I climb out of my car, grab my bag, and beeline it to the office doors on the other side of the building with five minutes to spare. When I round the corner, Cole is standing at the entrance in what looks like a heated discussion with Dallas. There goes my peaceful start to the day.

"Morning, boys," I greet them as I approach.

Cole takes a step toward me, coming into my space and leaning forward to place a chaste kiss on my cheek. My face flames from the unexpectedness of it, slight embarrassment washing over me.

"Good morning. You look beautiful today. I brought you a pick-me-up."

Dallas, who is still standing off to the side, scoffs loudly, and I look over at him just as his eyes are rolling. His muscular arms are crossed over his broad chest, the sleeves of his button-up shirt rolled up to right below his elbows, showcasing the half-sleeve of tattoos on his right arm. A chill works its way down my spine, scattering goosebumps across my flesh. I know it's not from the winter chill. I shake my head and return to Cole.

"Thank you. That was really sweet."

Dallas makes a choking sound and I shoot him a glare.

"Pumpkin spice. I know all the women are obsessed with this."

I do my best not to let my shoulders deflate. I take a small sip and hold back my gag. Pumpkin Spice lattes are the worst drink on the planet, and my tastebuds salivate, doing their job to try and wash away the vile taste currently working its way down my throat.

"Mmm. Thank you, Cole. That was really thoughtful."

Presumptuous. But thoughtful.

"Don't you have a job to do today, Ms. Hollis?" Dallas interrupts.

"Surely she can be a few minutes late. Give us a moment to chat. I'm sure the big boss can be lenient for the pretty lady. What do ya say?"

My eyes open wide, slightly shocked by Cole's tone, but these two clearly have a history and this is a pissing contest that I have no desire to be a part of.

Dallas cocks his head to the side and studies me, but before he can open his mouth, I speak up.

"It's okay, really. Dallas, I'll be right in. Cole, thank you for the latte. It was thoughtful."

"I have to admit, it wasn't completely selfless. I was hoping to take you out again."

"Oh."

"Blaire!" Dallas' voice is thick with irritation and something else I can't quite place.

"I'll text you, okay? Thank you again."

Dallas holds the door open for me and I slink inside the entryway, the warmth from the heat instantly flushing my face. Dallas walks away from me and I scurry to catch up to him just as his foot hits the first step that leads to our offices on the second floor.

"Dallas."

He continues to walk up the stairs, not acknowledging me. This man is so infuriating. Attractive or not.

"Dallas!" This time I grab his forearm, electricity shooting through me. I pull my hand back like he burned me. He stops walking and looks down at the place my hand was before meeting my eyes. God, he is so good-looking. His facial hair is cut close to his skin, coarse stubble that I imagine leaves burn marks if trailed across fragile flesh. His eyes are a mesmerizing sky blue and so much depth and emotion swirl within the light shade. My eyes trace over his features as the heat starts to rise in my body.

"What, Blaire?" he snaps. But his expression tells me he is completely aware of the thoughts I was having. Shit. How long was I just staring at him?

"You can't snap at me like that, especially not in front of my friend."

"Is that what he is Blaire? Your *friend*?"

Is he serious right now? Does he think just because he keeps cornering me in bathrooms and telling me his feelings about Cole that I will just listen?

"That's none of your damn business."

He takes a step down the stairs and closer to me. My breath hitches.

"I told you he wasn't right for you." His eyes shamelessly look down at my lips before meeting my eyes again and holding me hostage. He thinks he has the upper hand in this game, but I'll drown a slow death before I give in. This time, I take a step into his space, making his eyes widen. I run my free hand down the length of his tie, smoothing it against his firm, muscular chest. The growl that leaves him comes from somewhere deep and forbidden. I glance at his lips, my pussy throbbing and wet. His hand reaches out slowly toward my waist just as I speak.

"Like I said, that is *none* of your business, Mr. Hayes. Now excuse me, I have a job to do."

I walk up the stairs, leaving Dallas behind me, not feeling an ounce of shame for the way I let my hips sway side to side with each step that takes me farther away from my infuriating, sexy boss. He doesn't follow me, and for that, I'm thankful.

Once I'm safely in my office, I hang up my coat, drop the coffee cup into the trash can, and take a seat in my chair at my desk. It's hard to believe I have my own office, and most mornings I can't help but take a peaceful moment and look around at the space. I come from less than nothing. I worked hard in school despite the trauma that was going on outside of it. I knew that my education would be my ticket to freedom, and that the only thing separating me from the streets would be busting my butt to get into college and taking out student loans.

I worked tirelessly, keeping to myself and staying focused so I could someday sit in a place like this. To be here now? The event coordinator for a huge distillery, building a piece of their company that they're proud of, creating memories for tourists and the people of our community? I'm filled with pride.

I pull out my laptop from my bag and open it up to check my schedule, email, and plans for the day, feeling more clearheaded than when I got here.

Nothing will rattle me today.

dallas

"You're fucking kidding me."

"Nope. Enjoy shadowing Blaire for the day, dickhead. You want to moan and complain that she shouldn't be here? You want to bail on your commitments? You get to follow her around for the entire day and see what a positive influence she's having on this place. People love her."

I scoff and run my hand across the rough hair on my jaw. Well, this should be an interesting day after the morning we've had.

"I find that hard to believe. She's a menace."

"And that's why you're going to shadow her. So, get the hell out of my office and get to work."

"You're a shithead, Sawyer. This is a real low blow and you know it."

His face returns to his laptop, ignoring me. The asshole. I stand up and exit his office, walking to the end of the long second-story hallway to Blaire's office. I give the door two raps with my knuckles and walk right in. Her back is to me, body bent over, adjusting a pair of boots that come to her ankles. The fabric of her dress stretches taut over her perky ass and my dick instantly comes to life. I grind my palm against it, shifting it in my pants to a more comfortable position since the fucker likes to stay rock hard in this terror's presence. I stand frozen in my spot, leaning against her doorway, watching her, and it's only a moment before she stands, adjusting her dress.

"Come i- Ohmygod!" Her hand flies to her chest and she stumbles backward. I take a step forward, my hand extended as if to grab her and prevent her from falling. I quickly drop it back at my side, unsure why the fuck I care if I scared her or not.

"Dallas. What the hell?"

"I knocked."

"But just walking into my office, without permission, negates the knock. Did anyone teach you etiquette?"

"You clearly haven't met me if you need an answer to that question."

I walk around her desk and take a seat in her office chair, rocking in it slightly. Yep. Mine is definitely better.

"What are you doing, Dallas?"

"Seems that you're stuck with me for the day, princess. Sawyer just informed me I'm to shadow you. See all the wondrous and glorious things you do for the distillery," I tell her as I wave my hands around with a flourish. "He seems to think you're spreading pixie dust and rainbows around and I plan to inform him that it's more of a virus, killing us slowly from the inside out."

Her face pales and she shifts on her feet. My heart rate accelerates as I anticipate her retort but I'm shocked when it doesn't come.

"Have I . . ." She pauses to clear her throat, emotion clogging her voice. "Have I done something wrong? Could I lose my job?"

I straighten in the chair, my hands gripping the armrests. The girl standing in front of my parents' bar is back, her confidence faltering, and right now she seems extremely insecure and worried. I shrug my shoulders.

"Depends on who you ask." I let a beat of silence pass between us and watch Blaire's unease before continuing. "He wants me to shadow you so I can see what an asset you are."

The color comes back to her face and her shoulders relax.

"Ahh. Well, that makes more sense. Because you see me and my position as unnecessary and causing more harm than good."

There she is. Her hands rest on her hips. Fuck if I don't want to grip them, leave finger bruises on them from how hard I hold her still while I fuck the brat out of her.

"Correct. So, if you don't mind, let's get on with proving me right."

"Happily. Right now, we're going to meet a small group for a tour, followed by a flight tasting. Try not to scare anyone away with that ogre persona of yours."

I watch her walk to the door, wide hips swaying, her fiery red hair wavy and draped to her mid-back. My dick throbs, reminding me that it wants attention and only wants it from the spitfire in front of me. I stand, following her to the door before pausing to spit out my gum in the trash can. Her latte is tossed inside, the contents spilling out into the plastic bag. Hmm. So she doesn't like pumpkin spice. I picked up on her slight wince when she took a sip of it outside, and sick satisfaction fills me, seeing that she threw out Cole's morning gift. The idiot.

"Are you coming or are you going to ask it out on a date?" Her voice snaps me out of my thoughts.

"Cheeky. Lead the way, princess."

She gives me a dramatic eye roll before walking ahead of me, leading us to meet her first group of the day. We reach the large bay windows that line the entirety of the front of our office building before she pulls open one of the doors.

Fuck my life, because waiting for us is a group of six people, all in matching obnoxious Christmas sweaters, looking as out of place as a fuckin' snowman on the beach. Goddamn tourists. Who vacations to Washington State in the middle of December? Besides going to Leavenworth for a Bavarian Christmas, there's no damn point—unless freezing to death is your personal brand of torture.

"Good morning! Welcome to Aspen Ridge Distillery. My

name is Blaire, and lucky for all of you today, I have a special guest accompanying us. This is Dallas Hayes, heir to this incredible company."

A bunch of oohs and aahs escape our festive guests and I give them a head nod, trying to embrace my inner Sawyer and be somewhat professional.

"Let's start with your names, who would like to go first?"

A shorter woman in the front raises her hand wildly and Blaire nods to her, motioning for her to go ahead.

"Well, I'm Sharon, this is my husband Aaron, my sister Erin, and her wife Karen. These two here are our friends Robby and Bobby. It's a delight to be here!"

Of fucking course that's their goddamn names. What in the hillbilly kind of shit did I just walk into? Blaire simply smiles brightly at them like it's just another day in the twilight zone and this is the most normal shit ever.

"It's nice to meet you all, we're happy to have you here with us this morning. If you'll all follow me, we'll head to the rickyard first."

The crowd walks ahead and I lean into Blaire's ear to whisper, "What the fuck? Who marries someone who has a rhyming name? And there's three sets of 'em!"

She elbows me in the stomach and shoots me a glare. "Shh. Be nice!"

Once we survive the freezing walk to the rickyard, Blaire begins to talk about my family's business. She's surprisingly knowledgeable about the history of the distillery and the whiskey-making process and seems to have planned her tour around the steps we take to create our product. Everyone smiles and eats up every single word. I have to admit that she's infectious.

"The distillery was founded in 1925 by Dallas' great-grandfather, William Colby Hayes. We're the largest supplier of spirits to Washington and Oregon but have recently expanded to Idaho and the rest of the Pacific Northwest."

I can't help but watch and listen to her speak with rapt attention along with the rest of them. Everyone is drawn to her, and I can understand why. There's this undeniable aura about her, a magnetism that leaves you feeling tethered, hanging on every word she says. It's not just how breathtakingly beautiful she is, it's how she holds herself, how she looks at each person like they matter, like she truly cares about the job she's doing. She's captivating and makes it look so effortless. The world fades to the background as I lose myself to watching her work.

Which shocks the shit out of me.

"You need to be on your best behavior for what's next. I mean it, Dallas, don't fuck with me in this meeting."

"Oh, princess. What you're asking is near impossible. Who are we meeting with anyway?"

Like I summoned them, there's a knock on the office door. Blaire stands from the chair and wipes her palms down the front of her dress before combing her fingers through her hair.

"Quit fidgeting with yourself. You look . . ." I struggle to find words that are workplace appropriate. Fuckable, sexy, and stunning come to mind, but won't work. "Presentable."

She arches a brow at me. I study her for a moment before standing and taking two steps to the door and opening it.

"Oh! My boy! What a nice surprise! I was going to stop in and see you before we left," my mother coos.

"Mom? Always happy to see you but I wasn't expecting you."

"Oh, that's because we're meeting with Blaire. Ivy made a pit stop to see Sawyer. She'll be right in."

"Ahh. Wedding stuff?"

"Of course. My first baby is getting married! I always hoped they would find their way back to each other. Now here we are. Planning their wedding, and a baby on the way. It's so good to see him happy again, isn't it?"

Ivy was forced to run away by her very controlling mother

after we graduated high school. She hid herself away for ten years before finally returning. My twin was never the same after she left, and since she's returned? He's been so wrapped up in her that I don't see much of him outside of work. Which, if I'm being honest, hasn't been the easiest adjustment for me. While we've always gotten under each other's skin, he's my best friend, my twin, and having him occupied with Ivy means that I haven't had him around. The alternative isn't something I'd trade though. I don't know if I believe in the soulmate bullshit, but those two were born for each other.

"Yeah, Mom, it's great. Don't tell me it lit a fire under you to start nagging at the rest of us to follow suit . . ."

"Oh heavens no. You five will do whatever you want to do when you want to do it and that's all your father and I need. No pressure coming from me."

I believe her. My parents worked hard to provide a good life for the five of us, only having basic rules and requirements—go to college or learn a trade, be smart with your money, and be happy —they've never put pressure on us to do anything but what makes us happy. We hit the parent jackpot.

Blaire comes up next to me, putting her hand out to shake my mom's, but she's pulled in for a tight hug. Blaire stiffens momentarily before relaxing and returning the embrace.

"It's so good to see you, sweetie."

I have to stifle the groan. Blaire is the farthest thing from sweet, no matter how intoxicating she is.

"You just saw her at dinner yesterday, Mom."

Blaire shoots a glare my way before returning to my mom.

"It's good to see you, Mrs. Hayes. Please come in, we can chat while we wait for Ivy."

"She'll probably be a bit. Sawyer wouldn't know a quickie if it bit him in the ass," I joke.

Blaire chokes on her water, coughing and gasping for air. I smile wickedly at her while I watch her struggle to clear her lungs and breathe. Fuck, if only it was from my cock down her throat.

"Dallas Wyatt Hayes! Don't be so crass! Blaire, honey, are you alright? He's feral. I apologize. I can't imagine what it must be like to work with him. I love my boy, but he is a textbook middle child."

"I'm your firstborn, Mom. Sawyer and I are twins," I deadpan.

"You still came out second, son. And you're my wild child. You know it. I know it. Hell, the whole town knows it."

"You have met Carter, right? Your actual middle child?"

She rolls her eyes at me. Carter is the baby, even though he's second to last, and Kinsey is the youngest. She'll make excuses for him until her last breath. He can do no wrong.

"At least he's quiet and doesn't give me a hard time about anything. You, my love, have always been hardheaded, stubborn, and destructive."

I keep my eyes focused on Blaire while my mother lists all of my negative qualities. She's composed herself and is nodding along with everything my mom says. Fuck. They're going to bond over how difficult I am.

"But you're also the most loyal, passionate, and protective of my five."

I turn to give my mom a halfhearted smile before returning my attention back to the stunner sitting across from me, her red hair falling into her pretty face. I have the strongest urge to reach out and tuck it behind her ear.

"Well, I haven't seen any of the latter qualities but boy do those first ones sound familiar," Blaire says.

The two women laugh lightly at my expense and something inside me softens. Ivy arrives, so I give up my chair to her, moving to the back of the room and taking up residence on the chaise lounge. I pull out my phone for a distraction, allowing them the privacy to talk wedding shit.

Me: Grandpa caught me drinking his whiskey again

Liam: Location?

Sawyer: Ignore this idiot. You can't abuse the code phrase dickhead.

Me: I'm not abusing it. I need out asap

Liam: What's going on?

Sawyer: I made him shadow Blaire all day and he's being a whiny little bitch

Liam: Dude c'mon

Carter: You did what? *Laughing emoji*

Sawyer: Yep. Got sick of him bitching about her job being pointless so now he can spend his day learning otherwise

Liam: Reigning with an iron fist

Me: Yep. Napoleon Complex at its finest

Sawyer: Do I look small to you?

Me: I mean . . .

Liam: You're playing with fire brother

Carter: Let him. They're animals remember?

Kinsey: I'm trying to enjoy my winter vacation, can you all behave?

Liam: Seems like Dom's is needed. Tonight?

Me: I'll be there

Sawyer: Yep. But I'm bringing Ivy

Kinsey: You four are ridiculous

. . .

I snort and the three women look over at me.

"Sorry, something on my phone. Ignore me. Please, continue."

Me: Of course you are

Me: Sooo is anyone gonna come bail me out?

Sawyer: *Middle finger emoji*

Liam: No

Carter: No

Kinsey: No

Rolling my eyes, I pocket my phone and recline further into the seat, crossing my legs and resting my ankle on my knee. I'm not sure how much time goes by but just as I start to doze off, I'm jolted awake by someone shoving my foot off my leg. I open one eye to see all three of them hovering over me like a flock of mother hens.

"Which one of you did that?"

"Why do you need to know?" Ivy asks.

"Retaliation."

"You don't need to know then. Wake up. I'm sure you have better things to do than nap in Blaire's office. Why are you here anyway?"

"Why don't you ask your man, lil' sis."

Ivy laughs while my mother rolls her eyes and says something under her breath that I didn't catch.

"We're heading out. Don't fire her. She's amazing and I like her," Ivy says as she points to Blaire.

"No promises. I'll see you tonight."

"Wait, why? what's tonight?"

"Dom's."

Ivy's eyes go wide before she's driving her pointer finger into my chest. "I swear, Dallas, if you leave a mark on him days before our wedding I will ruin you."

"Settle down, pipsqueak. It'll be fine," I reassure her, lightly smacking her finger out of my space.

"What's Dom's?" Blaire speaks up and asks.

Ivy turns to face her, and I swear my heart freezes. I need to stop this train in its tracks before shit gets out of hand.

"Alright, time for you to go! Move out!" I start to corral my mother and Ivy toward the door, trying my damndest to circumvent what I know Ivy is about to do.

"Knockout. The guys box there. You should come. Sawyer usually brings me to watch and I just stand there by myself. Come with me!" Ivy practically yells over her shoulder as I push them out the door. The growl that leaves me comes from somewhere deep. Fuck my life.

"Easy there, alpha. We won't get in the way of you guys burning off your ridiculously inflated male energy."

Blaire's reply comes quickly, I'm positive she caught onto my discomfort. "Sure! I'm not doing anything and that sounds interesting."

And just like that, Blaire is digging deeper into every aspect of my life, leeching into every area.

A virus is right.

blaire

I'M NOT SURE WHAT I EXPECTED WHEN I PULLED INTO the lot of Knockout, but now that I'm inside, standing with Ivy, I feel ridiculously out of place. Dallas, Sawyer, Liam, Carter, and Reid are already shirtless, with their hands fitted into boxing gloves. I slide up next to Ivy just as Sawyer climbs into the ring.

"Hey, girl. You ready for this?"

"I honestly don't know what to expect. Do they just beat the crap out of each other?"

"Sometimes. But they've been training since they were teenagers. They're all pretty good. Especially Sawyer. If he wasn't in love with the distillery, he'd want to do this for a living." She gives me a long-dejected look. "I'm glad he's CEO. Watching him with his brothers is hard enough." She hip-bumps me and focuses back on the ring.

"Hey, pretty ladies." Reid walks up to us and leans against one of the large beams in the middle of the floor.

"Don't let Sawyer hear you say that, Drogo. He'll drag your ass in there instead of Dallas."

I laugh. I can't imagine anyone standing a chance fighting Reid. All of the men are larger than average, but Reid is on a different level. You'd be nuts or have a death wish to fight that man, gloves or no gloves.

"You don't fight with them?" I ask.

"Nah. I stick to the heavy bag, weights, and running. They're too smart to fight me, even if they're trained, they know I'm stronger. Wouldn't want to break their pretty faces," he says with a wink.

A laugh escapes me again and I settle in a comfortable place. I adore both of these humans, and I'm happy to be here with them. Even if I am about to watch my extremely sexy bosses pummel each other in a boxing ring.

Dallas walks past us and climbs into the ring to join his brother while Liam and Carter hang back below it. It's hard to focus on anything but Dallas. He's wearing a pair of athletic shorts that hang low on his hips and a thin gold chain around his neck, nothing else. It's clear he works out hard. His body is defined, his muscles rippling over his abs. He has a light dusting of hair over his chest that he keeps trimmed short, but it's his half-sleeve of tattoos my eyes shoot to next. They define his thick, corded forearms and I want a closer look at them. I can't help the carnal reaction watching him brings out in me.

Sawyer bounces on his feet, stretching his arms across his body while talking. "You ready, dickhead?"

Dallas cracks his neck and focuses on his brother.

"You're gonna pay for the shit you pulled."

"Yeah? Bring it. You learn anything from the day you had today?"

My heart tumbles in my chest. I turn to face Ivy and she cringes, her face transforming to sympathy.

"Wait, this is about *me*?"

"Kinda?" She winces. "Their back and forth has been going on long before you. But Sawyer forcing Dallas to work next to you all day set Dallas off."

God, he is so infuriating. So hot and cold. I can't stand it.

Why does he hate me so much? Then in the next breath, he's acting like he wants to rip my clothes off.

"Am I that bad?"

"No. God, no! It's not you. It's more like, Sawyer flexes his weight and Dallas hates it."

I suppose that makes sense. Still, I know Dallas despises my position at the distillery and all the changes that come with me being there. It's hard not to take it personally.

As I watch him in the dimly lit gym, my heart races with a mix of emotions. He frustrates me to a level only he can take it to, but my body responds to him in a primal way. There's something about him that makes me feel at ease, almost *safe*. I'm drawn to him even though he drives me insane.

The sight of him sparring with his brother ignites a blazing fire within me, one that I can't seem to shake. My breathing increases as my heart rate accelerates. The raw aggression and strength from each of his movements draws me in, and I don't notice that my feet have propelled me forward toward the ring.

Closer.

Closer.

Closer.

Dallas throws a hard punch into Sawyer's ribs, and I vaguely hear Ivy's wince behind me. My heart thunders in my chest. Dallas' body glistens with sweat. His arm pulls back, muscles tightening and flexing, his entire body hyper-focused on his opponent. I never imagined any type of violence could awaken a deep, dark, arousal within me. My core clenches, desperate to be filled, and my panties dampen. The world disappears around me as I take every movement in. Dallas pulls Sawyer in close with his arm hooked around his neck, holding him tight against the ropes. Sawyer swings wildly but the punches are futile against Dallas' hold.

"Pull them apart. Now, Liam!" Ivy pleads.

Sawyer spins out of Dallas' hold, twisting quickly. He lands two rapid punches to Dallas' face that push him back against the ropes, blood leaking from his eyebrow. Reid and Liam climb into the ring and separate them, both men panting. They take a minute to calm down, Liam holding a towel against Dallas' eye.

Sawyer steps into his twin's space. "We good?" he asks.

Dallas nods his head in agreement. They hug each other before Sawyer climbs out and picks up Ivy, her legs wrapping around his waist, and his sweaty face buried in her neck. My heart yearns for that. I look back at Dallas, who is still standing in the ring, bouncing on the soles of his feet, shaking his gloved hands at his sides, eyes glued on me. I involuntarily lick my lips, pulling my bottom one into my mouth.

He gives me a knowing smirk before turning to Liam. They do the same thing, gloves touching in the middle before taking a few steps apart and circling each other. Liam is gorgeous. Bigger than all of his brothers, with longer, lighter hair than the rest of them. He could pass for Charlie Hunnam's look-alike honestly. While I can appreciate his good looks, my body doesn't seem to have the same reaction to him that it does to Dallas.

"What do you think, B?" Reid comes up next to me, bumping me with his shoulder. I lean my head against his bicep for a moment in a friendly nudge just as Dallas is glancing at me. His momentary lapse in focus gives the perfect opening for Liam. Dallas staggers back from the force of the blows to the side of his face and his ribs. I gasp and cover my mouth.

"He's fine. Trust me. These boys have been doing this most of their lives. Although it seems Liam is fighting for something today, he's usually a bit more reserved than this," Reid reassures me.

It's only a beat before Dallas regains his control, letting loose on Liam. The power behind each punch is magnified in comparison. He's feral, his eyes laser-focused. He forces Liam back against the ropes, his hands held up, blocking each punch, his knee coming up to cover his ribs. After what feels like an eternity, Liam shoves Dallas hard, causing him to stumble back.

"The fuck is wrong with you, Dal?" Liam shouts.

"They're fine. Dallas is just being an asshole." Reid's voice reminds me that we're in public and that I'm not having a normal reaction to watching them fight. I school my features, straightening my spine and putting my composure firmly back in place.

"Of course. They've got this. It's just wild to watch. I don't know what I was expecting but it surely wasn't this."

The brothers share some words that only they can hear for a few moments, hug, and both climb out of the ring, covered in sweat and blood. Reid walks away from me to talk to Liam as Dallas steps into my space.

"Enjoy the show, princess?"

"Ehh. Your brothers sure know how to fight."

His eyes narrow, his head tilting to the side as he studies me with a cocky, shit-eating grin. He's reading me like a book.

"You seem a little flustered. Feeling okay?" I want to smack that knowing smirk off his smug face but as his eyes trail over my body, heat flames my face again.

"Nothing I can't take care of by myself at home." His eyes widen, his face transforming to unadulterated hunger. I smile sweetly before turning and walking away. I don't stop until I'm safely in my car and can finally catch my breath.

What is he doing to me?

Once I'm back alone in my apartment I'm still sexually charged. I go about my nighttime routine, washing my face, tying my wild wavy hair up in a silk scrunchie at the top of my head, and pulling my futon down flat. I climb into bed and pull the blankets over me, thoughts of Dallas' sweaty body working hard while in the ring repeating in my mind.

My fingers trail aimlessly up and down my stomach, circling my soft belly, and between my breasts. Warmth pools between my legs, my core clenching, a deep ache in my lower abdomen. It's been so long since I've been with anyone. It's hard for me to let all my walls down in order to enjoy sex, so it isn't something that happens often. Or at all.

My fingers drift down, over my panties, and run along the

length of my seam. My hips nearly jolt off the bed. I'm so sensitive, so swollen and needy. Knowing that I need to release this primal pressure within me, I shimmy out of my panties, tossing them to the foot of the bed. My hands cup my large breasts, massaging, pinching, and twisting my nipples, sending shock waves down to my clit. I know that with enough time I could come from this alone.

My eyes close and I let myself go to fantasyland. I'm not surprised when Dallas appears. His sexy, muscular body, sweaty and glistening from his fight. Adrenaline coursing through him with nowhere to go. I slip my fingers easily through my slick center, dipping a finger into my core and pumping a few times before dragging them back up to circle my clit. I imagine it's Dallas' tongue instead of my fingers, his mouth feasting on me like I'm his favorite meal and he'll never get enough. My fingers move back down, slipping two inside, wetness coating them, and my palm rubs firmly on my clit while I fuck myself with my fingers. I imagine Dallas between my legs, licking me into oblivion, my hips grinding on his face, his facial hair rubbing my sensitive skin raw. It's euphoric. I chase my orgasm, my hips moving in sync with my hand.

"Yes. Yes. Fuuuuck. Dallas!"

I come completely undone, coming to thoughts of my asshole boss' tongue between my legs.

***

The rest of the week passes in a blur, and I spend most of my time avoiding Dallas. The tension between us climbed too high at the gym, and after masturbating to the fantasy of him eating me out, I didn't want to face him, even if I did feel him everywhere I went, and he fucked with me in various ways.

Every day something annoying happened and I know it was him. On Monday, all of the glasses that are usually in the bar for my tastings went missing. On Tuesday, I was double-booked for a tasting and a tour, and on Wednesday during a meeting, Dallas congratulated me on hosting an all-day event scheduled for Thursday for the retirement center's weekly day trip. Not surprisingly, that event hadn't been on my schedule until I checked after he brought it up. The worst part was that although every single thing irritated me, the fact that he was spending time trying to get under my skin just made me think of him more.

By the time Friday rolled around, I was exhausted. Walking into my office, I do a double take around the room. Everything has been rearranged. The desk, which was perfectly positioned in front of the large window, is now at the back of the room facing an empty wall with the back of my chair to the door. My shelf has been moved to the front of the window, blocking all of the natural light and the view of the mountains. My plants are missing completely, and instead of the photos I had hung of various famous wedding dresses in magazines, my walls are lined with empty frames.

I'm going to kill him.

Throwing my coat and purse onto my desk, I march down the hallway to his office, pushing right into it without knocking, not giving a damn what could be going on behind the door. Unfortunately, it's empty. My eyes roam the room as I contemplate how to cut him where it hurts when they land on his precious office chair.

I move quickly, wheeling the chair out of his office and down to the storage closet. Pushing it to the far back behind the shelves, I pull as many boxes down as I can to stack on top of it and keep it covered before closing the door and returning to my office.

"WHERE IS SHE?"

Dallas' voice echoes through the expanse of our office suite. I laugh lightly under my breath. She. Of course he'd give a female pronoun to an inanimate object whose only purpose is to serve him and keep him comfortable. Asshole. He barges into my office, smoke practically steaming from his ears.

"What did you do with her?"

"I don't know who you're referring to. Be more specific, Mr. Hayes."

"My chair. Gloria. Tell me where she is, Blaire."

"Do you like my new office layout? I gotta say, not having natural light really makes me appreciate the fluorescents. And having my back to the door? Brilliant, right?"

"Blaire . . ."

"Yes, yes, I know. You don't like to repeat yourself. But I don't know where your precious chair is. Go ask one of your brothers." The lie tastes so sweet on my lips.

He glares wickedly at me, and for a moment, he looks slightly unhinged and I second-guess my decision to steal his beloved chair. He shakes his head at me before storming out of my office.

By the time I get back to my apartment around ten-thirty after spending the entire day and evening getting everything set up for tomorrow's wedding, I pop a bag of popcorn and collapse onto the futon. Turning on my guilty pleasure movie, *Pride and Prejudice*, I relax until my phone chimes with an incoming text.

Cole: Hey pretty lady, how's it going?

Can't say I'm fond of that nickname. Cole is nice enough and I know he means well; I just wish my body responded to him the way it does to Dallas. Cole seems like Dallas' opposite in almost every way. He's clean-cut, soft-spoken, confident and sure, but also respectful—all qualities I thought I would melt for and be lucky to find in a partner. Dallas is rough around the edges, brash, domineering, stubborn, and has no filter. That shouldn't turn me on like it does. Especially with the trauma I come packed with.

Me: Hey

Cole: How was the rest of your week?

Me: Entirely too busy trying to make sure Sawyer and Ivy's wedding is the fairytale they deserve.

Me: How was yours?

Cole: Outside of only seeing you once? It went well. Work kept me busy.

Cole: I'd love to see you again . . .

Maybe this is what I need. To focus on someone else. Cole is sweet and he'd make a good boyfriend, and I honestly should see where this goes. Maybe one more date will give me clarity on whether to see him again or just stay friends.

Cole: Ouch. Way to leave a guy on read.

Me: I'm so sorry! It's not that.

I bite my lip, nervous and unsure if this is a good idea or not.

Me: Are you free tomorrow? I know it's short notice . . .

Cole: Absolutely. Won't you be at the wedding though?

Cole: Unless you're asking what I think you are

Me: Yes. That's the thing though. I will technically be working, but you can be my plus-one? Are you comfortable hanging by yourself there while I work?

Cole: I'd love nothing more than to be your plus-one. I'm sure your boss won't have an issue with it.

Kind of a weird thing to add in. It doesn't give me the warm fuzzies, but I try to shake it off.

Me: I'll send you the details right now. See you tomorrow, Cole.

Cole: Tomorrow. Night pretty lady.

I send him the itinerary before turning my phone on silent for the night and go through my nighttime routine. Once I've got my futon laid out and I'm curled up, I work through my mental checklist of everything that needs to get done in the morning in preparation for the wedding. I want this to showcase my work and give Sawyer a reason to be glad that he hired me and trusted me with his own wedding. But most of all, I want to give them memories that will last a lifetime.

I try to stay focused on making sure I'm not forgetting anything, but thoughts of Dallas keep sneaking in. I wish I knew what it was about him that caused my body to react the way it does, and I hope inviting Cole as my plus-one doesn't cause any issues tomorrow.

Avoiding him this week only made me think of him more. I can't fight the fact that I crave those piercing blue eyes when he shamelessly checks me out. The way he slowly peruses my body from head to toe when I walk into a room is addictive. No one has ever made me feel good from that kind of attention, and I want more of it. Maybe if I give Cole a chance, those feelings will arise. But something deep within me is whispering that it's Dallas. Only Dallas.

Sleep comes before I'm ready, and I drift off, hoping like hell the nightmares stay away.

CHAPTER 8

Sawyer

IVY FLOATS DOWN THE AISLE TOWARD ME AND I CAN'T hold back my emotions. The tears in my eyes spill over and I wipe them away.

Blaire and her team overhauled the distillery's old, empty barn, and they outdid themselves. I know Ivy would have married me in a dirty alley if it meant becoming my wife, but giving her a dream wedding fills me with pride. Wooden benches line both sides of the aisle, our family and friends—the people closest and most important to us—fill the rows. Fairy lights are strung from the rafters, and the walls are stacked with empty whiskey barrels. I stand under a simple white arch covered in greenery and more tiny lights.

My beautiful girl takes confident steps in my direction, on the arm of Reid. Since both of her parents have passed, she wanted my father to give her away, but his mobility issues would have made that challenging. Reid was happy to step up. He and Ivy have a special relationship, and while I wasn't happy about it at first, it's one I am thankful for now. Her dress fits like a glove. The sleeves are made of skin-tone mesh, sprinkled with delicate vines of lace that curve and wrap around her arms and down to her dainty wrists. The bodice matches, and lace dips low between her

69

small breasts, connecting to a tight satin skirt that flares out slightly to the floor. The back is the same flesh-tone mesh, with beaded pearls down her spine and small train. The gorgeous raven-black hair that I'm obsessed with is worn down to her waist, just how I'd hoped she'd wear it. She looks like a fucking dream.

Reid walks her directly to the altar before hugging her and placing her little hand in mine. Her beautiful emerald eyes are glassy, but her smile is huge. God, she's the most beautiful woman I've ever seen, and she's all mine. It took ten long years of emptiness, but my baby found her way back to me, just like I knew she would.

"Hi, butterfly."

She laughs lightly, just for me to hear.

"Hi."

The ceremony goes by in a whirlwind, my eyes never leaving my girl. When the officiant tells me I can kiss my bride, I don't hesitate. Grabbing Ivy around the waist, I pull her tight, her little body flush against mine. I comb my fingers through her hair and grasp the back of her head with one of my hands, cupping her cheek with the other, and dip her slightly. I kiss her deeply, putting every bit of emotion behind it. I kiss her like she's the only girl in the world I've ever loved, like she's the center of my fucking world. Because she always has been. I pull back slightly, straightening her and resting my forehead against hers, sharing air.

"Hi, wife."

"Hi, husband."

"It is my great honor and privilege to introduce to you, Mr. and Mrs. Sawyer Hayes!"

The crowd erupts in cheers and applause, but it's all silence around me as I stare at the only woman I've ever known and loved all of.

My Ivy.

My wife.

dallas

"ANOTHER," I TELL THE BARTENDER. THE BEST THING about my brother's wedding, besides him marrying his childhood sweetheart, is the open bar. The bartender, I think he said his name is Chuck, sets another Aspen Ridge whiskey in front of me —because what else are you going to serve at your reception when you're the CEO of a distillery—and I turn to face the dance floor again. The music is loud; some of Ivy and Sawyer's throwback favorites boom through the speakers. Scanning the crowd, my eyes stop on the sexy-as-fuck redhead talking animatedly on the opposite side of the dance floor. She's wearing a little black dress that hugs her body perfectly. Her head is thrown back in a laugh, her hair cascading down her back. My dick responds like a teenager who's never fucked before.

Rock hard.

If it wasn't for that fuckface, Cole Barnes, standing in front of her, I'd be content to sit here and watch. Instead, my hand squeezes the tumbler, and I toss back the amber liquid like a shot, the liquor burning slightly as it slides down my throat. I welcome it. Cole reaches out, grabs her forearm, and leads her onto the dance floor.

"Hey, man, it's our brother's wedding, maybe you should lose the scowl," Liam says to me, pulling my attention away from Blaire and Cole. "What's got you looking like such a sourpuss?"

"I don't look like a sourpuss, idiot."

"You definitely do. Now why are you shooting daggers at Blaire and Cole?"

"What does she see in him?"

"Counter question, why do you care?"

"She's our employee, newish to town, and c'mon man, it's fucking Cole Barnes. That guy is a total assclown. I fuckin' hate him."

"Again, why do you care, Dallas? It's good that she's seeing someone, if that's what they're doing. This isn't a company event either, so she can do whatever she wants. Let it go or do something about it. But don't sit here and be a judgmental dick."

Liam walks off and leaves me to ponder his words. I set my tumbler back on the bar top and signal the bartender for another one. Drink in hand, my eyes go back to Blaire, only to find her eyes already on me. The mood shifts at the same moment the song does.

She's not dancing as if no one's watching her, instead, as if only I am. Her eyes don't leave mine as her hips sway in a slow, sultry rhythm, her hands gathering and pulling her hair up off her neck before dropping the waves back down, her arms above her head as she sways side to side.

Little temptress.

The tension in the air is palpable, she's so fucking sexy, and right now, she knows it. She knows exactly what she's doing to me, and I can't have that. What a little minx. She sucks her bottom lip between her teeth before resting her head back on Cole's shoulder. Just like that, I'm doused with a bucket of ice water. I move easily through the crowd, my eyes firmly set on Blaire. Her chin lifts in a defiant challenge that I am all too eager to meet. At the last second, I shift my body, shoulder-checking Cole and spilling my drink down the front of his shirt. Blaire jumps out of his hold and spins on me, anger written all over her pretty features.

"Oh, sorry man! My bad!" I tell Cole.

"Sure you are, Dallas."

I'll give it to him, Cole keeps his composure, wiping his hands over the cold liquid soaking his shirt, sloshing it onto the floor.

"Napkins are over there, man." I point in the direction of the food tables.

Cole excuses himself from Blaire, who is still looking at me like I'm Satan himself. I shrug my shoulders, feigning indifference before walking away, needing to get the hell out of here and get my head on straight. She has me flipped the fuck around and I don't know which way is up anymore.

The fiery redheaded princess stomps her feet after me, following me away from the party and into the distillery's office building.

"Dallas!" she whisper-shouts behind me. I keep walking ahead of her, up the stairs, and into my office. She slams the door behind us. "Why are you such a dickhead, Dallas? Your siblings are spot-on with their nickname, by the way. It suits you." Her voice becomes shrill when she gets worked up, and it feels like I'm taking an icepick to the skull. I lean back against my desk and cross my arms, content to just let the brat go off on me some more, doing my best to tune her out.

"You totally did that on purpose! What did he ever do to you, anyway? You know what? I can't live like this anymore, Dallas. Every chance you get, you bulldoze or sabotage me. I have been working my ass off here, and I'm good at what I do! I thought you saw that this past week! You won't even give me a chance."

She paces back and forth in front of me, her hips swaying side to side, her full breasts slightly bouncing in the top of her dress. She's got the sexiest hourglass shape I've ever seen, wearing a tight-as-fuck little black dress that hugs her curvy body like a second skin, not leaving much to the imagination. The top dips low, exposing her neck and the tops of her perky tits. It's hard to hear what she's saying when my focus is on the curve of her ass and the dip above her hips. Fuck, I'd love to hold on to them while she bounces on my cock. Or bury my face in those perfectly round, voluptuous tits. I can't fight this desire anymore. I'm crazed for her, her attitude and irritating presence in my life be damned.

"What is it about me that you don't like, Dallas? I can't change who I am. You need to find a way to work with me and deal with your problems because I can't live like this anymore. I'm so over it!"

Fuck it.

I take a few measured steps in her direction, backing her up against the door. Her cheeks heat to a bright crimson that spreads down her neck and to the top of her chest. Her mouth falls open, and her breasts rub against my chest on each intake of breath. She's surprised but turned on. My eyes move to her plush lips, the urge strong to lean down and kiss her, to taste her. I don't ever kiss. *But I want to kiss her.* So, I do something I never do.

My lips crash down on hers.

Her lips are soft like rose petals, delicate, and such a contrast to every other part of her. I kiss her hard and demandingly, licking along the seam of her lips, begging her to open for me so I can taste her. When she refuses, I pull back enough to look at her face. She's stunned, her face flushed and her lips a shade darker than before. Fuck, I want to bite them and see what other shades I can make them.

"What the hell was that? You can't freaking do that, Dallas! What is wrong with you? I'm telling you what a dick you are, and you decide to kiss me? What the fuck?"

"You know, I bet if my cock was down your throat you'd finally shut the fuck up."

Her eyes widen in equal parts shock and horror.

Yup. I'd say that did it. Pretty princess doesn't have anything to say to that.

"Wh-what did you just say to me?"

"I don't like repeating myself, princess."

"You can't talk to me like that, Dallas. What is wrong with you?"

"Don't act like the thought of my thick cock in your mouth doesn't turn you on. You can't hide from me; I see right through you. Does *he* talk to you like this?"

"Fuck yo—"

"Get on your knees, Blaire."

She lets loose a quick gasp as her mouth falls open and her eyes narrow into slits.

"Don't make me say it again."

I wait for her to call my bluff. I want the upper hand on this one. There's no way she'll kneel for me, and any moment now she's going to run right out my office door in outrage and right into Cole's pathetic arms. But he'd never give her what she truly needs. She needs someone to put her ass in its place while taking control and taking care of her.

I cock my head to the side as her deep blue eyes dart back and forth between my own, searching for something she won't find. I've never noticed just how pretty they are, such a unique dark blue that they could almost be purple. Her cheeks are dusted with freckles, and as my eyes trace over them, her tongue peeks out between her luscious lips and swipes slowly across to wet them. My cock thickens further in my jeans to the point of pain.

She meets my eyes just as her hand comes up and rests flat on my chest. I expect her to shove me away before spinning and storming out, but she pushes gently and I take a single step back, allowing just a foot of space between us. She's finally not running her mouth and I should be basking in the silence, but instead, I'm anticipating her next move, my heartbeat ringing in my ears.

She's just as calculated as I am and I wish I could prepare myself, but she's so damn unpredictable that I can't do anything but challenge her and wait. I'm not running from her this time. If she doesn't want this, then the door is right there.

"Run along, Blaire, or get on your knees and suck my cock like a good girl."

Her eyes narrow as her hands move to her thighs. She holds my gaze, her eyes drugged and crazed, like she has never been spoken to like this before and had no idea that she needed it. I watch her movement, the dress tight around her body as she pinches the fabric between her fingers, inching it up, exposing her knees and the top of her thighs. I maintain my composure, not willing to let her see how she affects me. When she moves her hands to place them on my hips, my eyes dart back to hers. She's unreadable as she slowly kneels to the floor, dragging her hands down my thighs to steady herself.

Fucking she-devil thinks she's calling my bluff. She thinks I'll run out on her like all the other times. Not a damn chance. You want to play, Blaire? Let's play.

"Fuck, look how pretty you are on your knees."

She fucking *hums* in response and my dick jerks. Fuck, does this strong-as-hell woman melt for praise? She's going to be the death of me, a fate I'll happily accept if it means I get to feel her like this. If it means I can finally give in and take control of this strong, fiery woman. I run my hand across her soft cheek until my fingers rest under her chin. Tilting her head back to look at me, I can't see an ounce of hesitation on her face. There's only lust, passion, and eagerness.

"You want my cock, princess? Show me. Take it out." I rub my hands through her wild red hair, loving the soft feel of it, and nudge her closer, waiting for the moment she stands and leaves. There's no way she'll see this through. Somewhere in the recesses of my mind, I'm keenly aware that I took this too far the moment I told her to get on her knees in my office. She'd be within her rights to report me to my brother, HR, and press charges. But I know she wants this just as badly as I do. The tension between us is too taut, it was bound to break.

Her hands are steady as they move to my belt buckle, pulling the strap out before unfastening it. She flicks the button open on my dress pants before meeting my eyes again.

"This is what you want?" she asks, all confident and

composed, but below that, she seems eager, willing, excited. Fuck, what I want is to rattle the shit out of this woman. Since the first moment I met her, I've been torn between wanting to shake the shit out of her or fuck her brains out, and right now, given the steel rod pressing painfully against the zipper of my pants, I want to fuck her until she's a whimpering mess, even if I can't stand her.

"I don't want to hear your mouth, Blaire, I want to see it work around my dick."

She moans slightly as she slides my zipper down and pushes my pants down over my hips. The outline of my cock is on full display against the thin fabric of my black briefs. I'm harder than I've ever been, and she hasn't even touched me yet. I hate that my body responds to her this way.

There's a fine line between hate and desire, and fuck if my dick isn't confused. Her hands rub up my thighs, squeezing and massaging as she goes. I watch as her soft fingers dip into the elastic waist of my briefs and begin to pull them down. The tip of my cock is freed before her breathing hitches and picks up a steady, deep rhythm. She only hesitates for a split second before pushing them down to meet my pants at my ankles.

Now it's my breathing that picks up. I can't believe she let it get this far. Her face transforms—her plump pink bottom lip is pulled between her teeth, her fair skin flushed from her freckle-dusted cheeks down to the top of her busty chest, as she takes in my cock for the first time. If I thought her face was red before, it's nothing compared to her complexion right now. I fucking *love* her reaction and it shocks the hell out of me. The energy around us crackles like a live wire as she looks me over—thick, long, and veiny, pointing straight up to my navel. But I know it's not the size that has her eyes huge and her mouth slightly ajar.

"Dallas . . ." she says on a rushed breath.

"It's a Jacob's ladder, I take it you've never seen a pierced cock?"

Her eyes snap up to mine, looking at me like I'm the biggest dumbass that ever walked the earth. "Do you think I'm stupid? I know what it is, asshole."

She reaches out hesitantly and slightly clinically before grasping my thick length, her fingers not able to close completely around it, and it jerks in her hand, happy to finally be touched by the only woman it craves. She runs her hand from my base up to the tip, squeezing and twisting as she goes, her palm hitting each of the barbells. The groan that works itself loose from my chest is deep and long.

"You like that?"

"I'd like it better if it was down your throat. Be my good girl and show me what that mouth can do other than talk back."

Her eyes are set on mine as the flat of her tongue licks up my length, going over each of the six barbells before swirling slowly around my engorged head. I nearly come on the spot.

"Fuck, baby girl. That feels good." I thread my fingers through her thick, wild waves of hair before pulling her forward. "Now suck it," I growl.

She moans around my crown before opening her mouth and descending on me. Fuck. My eyes roll involuntarily to the back of my head.

Her mouth feels *so* good.

Too good.

So warm and wet, her tongue smooth like velvet, like nothing I've ever felt before. Why the fuck does it have to be her? She takes me all the way to the back of her throat before sucking me hard, her cheeks hollowing as she comes back up for air.

"Such a good girl on her knees. You should see yourself right now. I knew your filthy mouth would feel this good. You're sucking me like you can't get enough. You like my cock, baby girl?"

The sharp drag of her teeth up my length is her only response. I know she was trying to make a point, but she just learned the hard way exactly how I like it.

Rough.

My hips jerk forward, pressing me deeper into her mouth. "Fuck yes, you're taking me so well. You're making me feel so good, baby. Do it again."

She moans around me, the vibrations scattering and edging me closer to release. She drags her teeth again and this time I don't hold back the moans that come out of me. My balls draw up, my spine tingling as my orgasm rapidly approaches. She continues her rhythm, rotating between sucking me down hard like she wants to drain the cum out of me, and dragging her teeth up my length. She has a death grip on me, her fist jerking me at the base of my cock. I'm losing my goddamn mind. Nothing has ever felt this good.

"Where do you want my cum?" My voice is a deep, husky rumble. She answers by sucking me deeper, her gags music to my ears, her free hand moving between us to roll my balls firmly in her grasp. "Fucking take it then, princess. Don't spill a drop," I order as I hold her face between my hands.

Her palm tightens around my balls, squeezing them as she takes my cock down her throat. It sets me off. My orgasm barrels through me like a tidal wave, and I don't take my eyes off the scene in front of me—Blaire on her knees, tears streaming down her face, while my cock is buried to its hilt in her mouth, pulsing ribbons of cum down her throat. I'm overloaded with sensations. I've never come so hard in my life and all I can think to do is what comes naturally.

Praise her.

My hands release the death grip on her head, rubbing gently and affectionately through her silky waves of hair.

"Such a good girl for me. Fuck, that was so good, Blaire. You did so well." She hums her appreciation as she pops off me. She sits back on her heels and peers up at me, and fuck if she doesn't look like the most perfect, most natural sub I've ever seen. I bet she doesn't even know it either. I look down at my still-hard cock, a bead of cum leaking from my slit. Cocking my head to the side, I decide to test her, push her a little further while she's lust-drunk. I grab my dick in my hand and hold it out, ready to feed it to her.

"I said don't spill a drop, baby."

Her eyes look down at the bead of cum and she doesn't even hesitate, leaning forward and licking it clean.

I wasn't expecting this turn of events. This spitfire of a woman who takes me on harder than anyone else, who doesn't back down from anything, actually behaves when told what to do sexually, and fucking *preens* at my praise. Goddamn brat just needs to be told what to do. It makes dealing with her crazy all day that much hotter. This changes everything.

I don't understand it. I can't stand this woman. She makes my life difficult every day and is responsible for everything changing around here. My heart does a weird flip in my chest that I've never felt before. Seeing her so pliant, thriving under my demands and praise after fighting me for so long, does something to me.

Fuck. Suddenly she's not just the irritating, bitch of an employee that gives me a hard time, and I just so happen to want to fuck. The tension between us just snapped, and nothing will be the same now. Especially not after that mind-blowing blowjob and what I've learned about her.

Blaire stands, swiping her fingers across her puffy lips and adjusting the skirt of her dress, smoothing the fabric down flat with the palms of her hands while I tuck my dick back into my pants. She doesn't meet my eyes as she combs her fingers through her disheveled hair. I watch her composure slip back into place, like carefully worn armor. When she turns to walk away, my heart tumbles in my chest, not ready for her to leave.

That's new.

"Where the fuck do you think you're going?" My arm shoots out to grab her as she tries to leave, forcing her to turn and face me.

"I think we're done here, Dallas, you made your point." Her voice is flat and monotone, and she's not looking rattled at all, except for the nervousness in her eyes.

"The fuck we are. Get on my desk and spread your legs."

"What? No . . ."

"I didn't ask. I showed you mine, now you show me yours."

"What are you, twelve?" Yup. Ice princess is back. All submissive qualities have gone out the door, and fuck if that doesn't turn me on. I'll happily break her down again, more than happy to fuck her into submission.

"Based on how I just came down your throat, I'd say no. But fair is fair."

"You're not serious right now, Dallas."

I drag her a few steps to my desk before pushing her up against it. Crowding her space, I pick her up by the hips, loving the feel of her curves under me, and set her on the edge of my custom wood desk.

"Quit being a fucking brat and lay back. Has anyone made you come with their mouth before?"

"Like I'd give you the satisfaction of knowing either way."

That's a hard no. Good. I want to be the first.

"I'll take that as a no. I'm going to show you how good you can feel when a real man is taking care of this pussy."

"You know what, Dallas? Fine. Show me what you've got, you raging, pompous dickhead. You want to eat me out? Do it then."

"Fuck, princess, I love when you talk dirty to me."

I push her to lay flat on my desk before shoving her dress up around her waist, and rubbing my hands slowly up her thick, gorgeous legs, loving the feel of her smooth skin under my palms. I stop at her thighs, grabbing a handful of flesh and squeezing, losing my fucking mind at how perfect her body looks and feels. She winces from the pressure, but I quickly release my hold, rubbing gently back over the area. I continue upward to my final destination, hooking my fingers into the thin fabric of her panties and pulling down her lacy thong before bunching it in my fist. I bring it to my nose, taking a deep inhale of her sweet, musky scent.

My dick hardens again behind my pants as if I didn't just

come. She smells fucking divine. Like the sweetest nectar. Moving each of her heels to rest on the edge of my desk, I spread her knees wide and get my first look at the pussy between her legs. She's bare of any trace of hair, freshly waxed, plump, pink, and already glistening for me.

"Fuck, that's a pretty pussy." My mouth waters, eager to taste her and make her come on my tongue.

Not wanting to waste any more time, I devour her. There's no teasing, no finesse, I eat her pussy like I'm starved, telling myself that it's to prove a point and not because I'm craving it. Craving *her*.

"Ohhhh," she moans, and it fuels me further. I grasp her thighs tightly, pushing them up to her chest and spreading her wide open for me, my fingers bruising into her soft, supple flesh as my mouth feasts on her, her taste exploding on my tongue, loving every inch of her. Hitching her thighs over my shoulders, I run my hands under her ass, dragging her closer to the edge and lifting slightly for better access. My tongue spears into her wet center as her thighs start to tighten around my head.

"Aah! Dallas, oh, god," she yells, body trembling in my hands.

"Fuck, this pussy tastes so damn good," I tell her, loving the taste of her on my tongue, the sound of her moans in my ears, and the feel of her curvy, sexy-as-hell body in my hands.

I lick eagerly back up to her swollen little clit, swirling my tongue around and around, enjoying the feel of her throbbing nub against me. I've never minded eating pussy, it's easy and I'm good at it. But love it? Never until this one. This is a meal I want every day.

I move my hand between us, sucking three of my fingers into my mouth before pushing two of them into her warm center, my pinky rimming her asshole. She jerks against me, and I can't help but wonder how far she'll let me take this.

"Shhh, baby girl. Let me take care of you now. You'll love it."

I breach her tight little hole, pushing in to the first knuckle and fucking both holes in tandem while I swirl my tongue around her swollen clit.

"Ohmygod, ohmygod!" she moans. Fuck if I don't like seeing her like this. Her wound-up-tight self in a puddle on my desk, completely at my mercy. She hands over her pleasure to me on a gold platter and I am fucking here for it. She's better than I imagined. I seal my lips around her pussy, sucking her clit into my mouth. She comes completely undone for me and fuck if it isn't the prettiest damn sight I've ever seen. Sick satisfaction fills me, knowing that I'm the reason for it. I'm the one who melted her icy exterior.

"That's it, baby. Give it to me."

"Ohh fffuuck, I'm coming!" Her hips gyrate against my mouth, her tight pussy squeezing the life out of my fingers, legs shaking on my shoulders, and I don't pull back until she's ridden every last wave of her orgasm, loving the flood of arousal I'm gifted in return. I give her one last languid lick along her seam before standing, using my palm to adjust my hard-on, not bothering to wipe her arousal from my face.

"You're much more tolerable like this."

"Fuck you," she seethes.

"So sweet." I give her a wicked smirk. "Your pussy is at least."

blaire

"Shut up and fuck me."

"Say please," Dallas says smoothly while he pushes his hand through my hair, angling my head to look up at him. His crystal blue eyes are such a contrast to the mirth and dark promises dancing in them, his mouth still glistening from going down on me.

The fucking arrogance of this man will be the death of me. Even if right now it's not entirely misplaced, and he knows it. I've never let anyone even attempt to give me oral before. In fact, I've never even orgasmed with a partner, but that was one that will go down in the history books. Now all I want is for him to fill me, but I'll be damned if I beg anyone for anything.

"Fuck you," I spit with as much venom as I can muster.

His head cocks to the side as his eyes squint into slits. I move to sit up on his desk and pull my dress back down, feeling extremely exposed now that he isn't touching me. He steps further between my legs, pressing a large hand to the center of my chest, forcing me to stay on my back. I heave in a deep breath.

"I said to ask nicely, princess. Now ask me to fuck you. And don't forget the please this time."

"Fuck. You. Dallas." I enunciate every goddamn word to drive it home. Before I can register his movements, he's on top of me, both of my wrists pinned above my head, and I find myself face-to-face with a snarling beast of a man.

"Do I have your attention now, Blaire? I won't repeat it again. When we're together, I'm in control. You're going to behave, or I'll spank the brat out of you. The moment you dropped so eagerly to your knees sealed that fate. Do you understand me?"

I look up at him, his T-shirt wrinkled, eyes wild and feral with desire. For me. This gorgeous, sexy man wants me. Why does he have to be my boss? The man who makes my life here so difficult? Why do my brain and body go to complete mush when he bosses me around like this?

"I understand, but I'm not sure if I'm going to listen." He releases a deep rumbling sound from his chest that can only be described as a growl. I don't know why I continue to poke the bear, there's just something about riling him up that feels so good. His hand moves to my center, pushing two fingers into my wet pussy, hard, the other one pressing down firmly on my lower abdomen. My back bows off the desk, arching into it.

"Beg."

"Fuck off!" I yell between clenched teeth.

He drives in again, rubbing a sensitive spot deep inside me that makes my legs shake. My breaths come in pants, the pressure building inside me.

"Don't make me say it again, Blaire."

I turn my head to the side, refusing to look at him as he touches my body like he's known it forever. My vision blurs as tears leak from the corners of my eyes from the pleasure. His thumb moves to my clit and my orgasm climbs. I do everything I can to hold back my moan. Just as I'm about to peak and fall off that glorious cliff, he pulls his hand away. I whip my head back in his direction, a whine leaving my lips.

"I told you I don't like repeating myself. Only good girls get orgasms. Brats get punished. Are you going to be my good girl, princess?"

I don't know what I expected Dallas would be like during sex, but it sure as hell wasn't this. His dirty talk is expert level and he knows it, he can see the proof of his effect on me as arousal leaks from my center down to my ass. I've never been so hot and turned on in my life. There's something he's unlocked in me that I didn't know existed. I *want* to please him. I *want* to do what he says. This morning, I wouldn't have let him jump-start my car out of fear of him rigging it to explode on my drive home. But here, now? I can't help the trust I hand over effortlessly.

"Fuck me, Dallas. Please. I want to come. Please make me come. I'll behave." I move my hips, scooting down further to the end of the desk, wanting him, hoping he'll take me and deliver what I know he can give me.

"That's a good girl. Has anyone else made you feel this good?"

"Never."

"Good, because I'm about to erase every memory you have of every man that came before me. After I've had you, princess, you won't even remember their names."

He wastes no more time talking. He kisses me, it's bruising and raw, his tongue demanding entrance, and this time I open eagerly for him, the evidence of my orgasm exploding on my tongue as our mouths clash together. The rest of my fight drains out of me quickly and I melt for him. His hands roam up my thighs, spreading them further to make room for his waist to settle between my legs. He steps back, pulls me to a seated position, and releases my mouth.

"I want to see all of you while my cock is inside you." His voice is husky, deep, and resolute. Strong hands grab the hem of my dress that's around my waist and pull up in one swift motion, leaving me completely naked on his desk.

My hands automatically go to my soft tummy, instinctually wanting to cover up, and feeling extremely exposed, while he is still partially dressed. I've always loved my body, I'm curvy and voluptuous. My curves are what have always boosted my confidence. But lying here in front of this Greek Adonis, insecurities start to creep in. Dallas bats my hands away just as quickly.

"Don't you dare hide from me. Fuck, Blaire. Your body makes me lose my mind. Look at you, baby girl. So fucking sexy." Any insecurity that was edging itself in, flies out the window as Dallas fuels what I've always seen in myself. His hands push his pants that were left undone down his waist, revealing that huge, pierced cock.

"Tell me you want it just as bad as I do." His confession stuns me. While I'm fully aware of the tension that's always been between us, and I've caught him checking me out on more than a few occasions, I didn't expect him to want me like this. He hates me. For some reason that I don't dissect right now, I can't find it in myself to care.

"I want you. Now fuck me or I'll go fi—"

His hand comes up around my throat, cutting off my sentence, his fingers squeezing just enough to get my attention. What's shocking is that this situation should scare the living shit out of me, but he just lit the match to an inferno that set my entire body on fire.

My pussy throbs, needing to be filled by him. He notches his cock at my entrance before slamming home in one powerful thrust that jerks my body further onto the desk. I've never felt so full, and I can't control the scream that leaves me as my body rapidly tries to adjust to the intrusion. His piercings add an entirely new sensation, and I feel myself getting wetter around him. He releases my throat and grabs my hips in a bruising grasp, pulling me back to the edge of the desk. He hooks my legs over his forearms, holding me tight as he pulls out halfway and slams back home.

"Aah! Yes!" My moans and whimpers come out unabashedly.

"You're taking me so well. Look at this greedy pussy swallowing me. You're gripping me, Blaire. So. Fucking. Good." He slams into me over and over, hitting a spot deep inside me that makes my toes curl and my eyes drift closed.

"Don't stop! Please, just don't stop," I beg. He pulls my legs to wrap around him and I lock my ankles together at the base of his spine, holding him in place. Dallas leans forward over me, his big hands grabbing each of my breasts, squeezing them together around his face. He licks up the center before descending on one, sucking my nipple harshly into his mouth. My spine arches and my hands surround his head, holding him to me. My hips gyrate on their own, chasing my orgasm.

"I can't get enough of you. Goddamn it, Blaire. You're fucking perfect. Why do you have to be so fucking perfect?" His words go straight to my throbbing clit as I moan out my appreciation. He alternates between each of my nipples, sucking and lapping at me while his hips keep their brutal pace, thrusting that thick, long cock deep inside me. Moving to stand again, his hand goes between us, thumb pressing firmly down on my clit.

"Come for me, princess. Come. Right. Fucking. Now." My body greedily listens, like it was waiting for his command. My orgasm thunders through me, my back arching, my legs squeezing tight around his waist, my inner walls clenching and spasming around him. It's like nothing I've ever felt before.

"Goddamnit, baby. Your pussy is fucking milking me, I'm gonna come, Blaire." He grabs my hands and moves them between us. "Spread yourself wide for me, baby." I move my fingers to either side of my lips, spreading myself open for him as he abruptly pulls out, his hand grabbing his dick roughly and jerking it hard, using my wetness coating him as lubrication. His fist pumps from root to tip, his grasp brutal and tight, while I watch with rapt attention, my breaths coming in heavy pants. He comes on a loud, masculine groan, ropes of pearly white cum pulsing from his engorged head, coating my pussy. It's the hottest thing I've ever seen. I move my hand between my legs, rubbing my fingers through his cum over my overly sensitive clit, his face watching in rapt attention.

A growl works its way up his chest.

"Good. Fucking. Girl."

I melt.

After putting myself back together in Dallas' en suite bathroom, where he insisted he clean me up and was surprisingly caring and attentive, I returned to the wedding reception on wobbly legs, as if my life wasn't just flipped upside down. Lucky for me, the party was in full swing, and I was officially off duty. Everyone just needed to enjoy themselves, and we had people hired to clean up over the weekend. The snow had started to come down heavily outside, and the winter chill helped settle my nerves. Walking straight to the bar, I order the strongest liquor they've got stocked, and with shaky hands, toss it back before ordering another through my cough.

"There you are." Cole's hand rests on my lower back and I jump out of his touch. "Whoa. Everything okay?"

"Yep. It's good. Everything is great. So sorry about your shirt."

Holy shit, I'm a terrible person.

"Don't worry about it. Dallas and I go way back. He's a prick. I should have seen it coming."

Yep. I'm officially the worst person on the planet. Guilt consumes me. I left my plus-one after my boss spilled a drink on him and instead of coming right back to Cole, I fucked Dallas in his office. What is wrong with me?

"Still. It sucks and I am so sorry."

"Don't apologize for him, I've got what he doesn't and that makes everything worth it."

I cringe at his statement. He doesn't have me. No one does. We've been on two dates, and this hardly counts as one of them. Is he only pursuing me because he thinks Dallas wants me?

"Do you want to get out of here?" His hand returns to my back, sliding upward and grasping around the back of my neck. My skin prickles in warning, and my heart starts to race in fear. This is the complete opposite of what I felt in Dallas' office when he took control. This right here is my normal reaction to men touching me, which is why I haven't been able to let myself go to a place where I could orgasm with one.

Until Dallas.

I shrug out of his hold and luckily, he lets me go, completely unfazed by the reaction he just set off in me.

"I actually have to stay late. You head out though, it'll be a long night and I won't be much fun because I'll be working," I lie.

His face deflates but he relents.

"Okay. Call me and we'll plan something?"

"Sure thing. Thanks for coming," I say as sweetly as possible.

I spend the next two hours floating between guests and the bar, tossing back drinks. I don't see Dallas again, even though I find myself looking for him. Sawyer and Ivy spent the entire evening on the dance floor, and it was so beautiful how the world completely melted away around them. They truly only have eyes for each other.

As the night calms down, everyone gathers and talks around the bar. Sawyer has Ivy wrapped tightly in his arms, and I look from them to Dallas, seeing him for the first time since earlier in his office. His eyes are already on me, his face a mask of indifference, but also something else that I can't quite place. I look away from him quickly, shame and worry starting to creep in. I can't explain what came over me, and looking back on it, it feels like a fever dream.

"Sawyer, Ivy, thank you for letting me be a part of your special day. I hope it was everything you imagined."

Ivy looks up at Sawyer and smiles brightly before looking back at me.

"It was perfect, Blaire. We can't thank you enough. You're truly talented. The transformation of the barn was stunning. We're glad you're here, and not just for the gorgeous wedding. As a friend."

As if my heart needed to hear those words, my eyes tear up. Ivy smothers me in a huge hug and we say our goodbyes. The newlyweds are the first to head out, leaving the rest of us to make sure the crew hired to clean up knows the plan. Since Liam lives the closest to the distillery, he offers to stay to make sure everything is secure for the night.

"You've been drinking, I'll drive you home, B. I drove my truck," Reid offers.

"I can take her," Dallas says firmly, irritation clear.

"Yeah, that's not going to happen. I'm ready when you are, Reid."

"I'll go get the truck and pull around since it's so cold, I'll be right back."

"Same, I'm out of here. Night, losers!" Carter yells as he throws up a peace sign behind him, leaving me alone with Dallas. Which is not a good thing. My body wants his even if my head is screaming that I can't let this happen.

"The fuck do you think you're doing, Blaire?"

"Going home. You should do the same."

"I mean leaving with fucking Reid. Is there something going on there?"

I roll my eyes at him and look away.

"You're unbelievable. He's my friend, jackass. I'm going home to my grandparents'. And I don't answer to you."

"I didn't say you did, princess. But I can still taste your cum on my tongue, excuse me for not wanting to watch you leave with another man."

"That's a you problem, Dallas. We both know this was a mistake. I'd really love to keep my job, so if we could please be adults and pretend like it never happened, I'd appreciate it."

"You think I'd do that to you?"

I laugh maniacally.

"I don't know, Dallas. You've done a ton of other shitty things since I started working here. You tell me."

"I'm not evil, princess. I wouldn't do that. And don't ever say that what we just did was a mistake because you know damn well you don't regret a thing."

"Whatever, Dallas. It's not happening ever again."

Reid pulls up and jumps out of his beloved all-black Ford F-150 Raptor, and takes a few long strides to open the passenger door.

"Have a good night, Mr. Hayes."

I walk away before he can reply and haul myself into Reid's truck, my brain a jumbled mess for me to sort through.

Did I just ruin everything I've worked so hard for?

dallas

THE FOLLOWING MONDAY, I'M EAGER TO SEE BLAIRE. I spent the rest of the weekend replaying everything that happened in my office, feeling like shit that she could think I would use having sex with me as leverage to make her quit, fire her, or get her to comply. I'm fully aware of the line I crossed, but fuck if I could take one more minute without touching her. And the way she melted for me? Fucking hell. Vixen.

Sunday afternoon, I went into the distillery to put her office back together. Messing with her last week and making her life difficult gave me a sick kind of pleasure. Riling her up feels good, but now that I've found other ways to get those cheeks to brighten to a pretty shade of pink, I want to do that more. I can still hate her and want to fuck her again.

Pulling into the distillery parking lot, my eyes scan for her busted-up silver Ford Focus. Surprised that I'm here before her, I head into my office to see what's on my agenda today, annoyed as fuck that I still haven't found Gloria. I know it was Blaire who took her, just like she knows it's me who keeps fucking with her schedule. I don't want her to get too comfortable here, so I planned to drive her insane. Now I just want to fuck her senseless like my own personal sex assistant.

An hour into my day, I get a team meeting reminder on my laptop, grab my tablet, and head to the conference room. Blaire is already there, wearing what can only be described as a black bodysuit, which forms to her curves, and tucks into high-waisted, wide-leg denim jeans. She's usually not dressed this casually at work but I'm not going to complain. Her back is to me, talking to our intern, Marcus, and I let myself appreciate the way the jeans hug her perfect, heart-shaped ass.

"Alright, everyone take your seats. Let's get this going," Sawyer says as he enters the room. We all take a seat at the long conference table, and I purposefully sit directly across from Blaire. Her eyes squint at me before looking away and listening to my brother ramble on. After a presentation from our CFO, Lorelei, Carter starts his.

"Alright, let's get into the biggest news first. We've won, for the third straight year, Washington State Whiskey/Bourbon Distillery of the Year!"

Everyone erupts into applause, and I watch Blaire smile brightly.

"Next, we've been invited to attend a masquerade ball in the spring, where our whiskey will be the only brand served, more details to come, but, Hayes boys, pull out those tuxes." Carter drones on about how we've grown to distribute our product, as of today, to sixteen states and British Columbia, as well as some other public relations and marketing plans, but I tune him out, my eyes focused on Blaire and how attentive she is to each item on the agenda. She takes notes and it really seems like she's trying to learn everything she can about the company.

Liam goes next, and as our head blender, he discusses sourcing rye and barley from Walla Walla, plans for creating a straight bourbon whiskey, and current imports of wood.

"Our whiskey is different from that in Tennessee. It's smoother. We've got the temperature for it—the Olympic mountains to our east and the ocean to our west—we're in a prime spot to continue to deliver a product that is different from anywhere else in the world . . ."

The meeting goes on for another hour, and when it's done, I speak up, "Excuse me, Blaire. Meet me in my office."

I don't bother waiting for a reply, and leave the conference room to head to the comfort of my office with Blaire hot on my heels. She follows me in, and I wait for her before I close the door behind us. She moves out of my reach, but her sweet jasmine smell lingers in the air and my cock stirs to life.

"Yes, Mr. Hayes?"

"Don't start with that shit, princess. You don't call Sawyer 'Mr. Hayes.'"

"Sawyer doesn't throw his weight around and act like a maniacal overlord."

"That is literally the definition of Sawyer," I deadpan.

"Whatever. What do you want? I need to get to the tasting room and make sure all of my glasses are where they should be so I don't look like an idiot again."

Instead of answering, I approach her, making her eyes widen, and she takes a step back for every one of mine until her back is flush against the wall. My hand moves to the side of her face, threading my fingers through her hair. It's so soft between my fingers and smells just like her.

Delicious.

"I haven't been able to think about anything other than this. What did you do to me?"

"Maybe you should see a doctor. You're a masochist if you enjoy this toxicity between us."

"Then I'm a masochist. It doesn't change how addictive you are."

Her face flushes, crimson spreading over her cheeks, neck, and the top of her chest. I lean in to kiss her, something I've been craving since Saturday night, when she jerks her head to the side.

"Dallas, this isn't happening. It was a one-time thing. A lapse in both of our judgment that can't be repeated."

"That doesn't work for me, princess. Now that I've tasted your cunt, now that I've experienced what it feels like to fill you, there's no world in which I don't want a repeat of what happened the last time we were in this room together."

Her eyes flash momentarily to my desk, and I know she's imagining what it was like to be spread out on top of it while I licked her pussy and fucked her so good she drenched my cock and balls when she came.

"I'm serious, Dallas. It was a one-time thing to get it out of our systems."

"It doesn't have to be," I whisper as I reach out and put my hand on her hip.

"Dallas. This could ruin my job. So kindly, piss off."

"Oh, baby girl," I say as I grab her hand and rub the palm of it over my pants so she can feel my hard cock, "when you talk back to me it just turns me on more."

She pulls her hand away and pushes against my chest for space. I go willingly, taking a large step away from her.

"Then lucky for you, you have two working hands that can take care of your problem. That won't happen again." Her voice lacks conviction, laced with lust and fighting against her desire, her body betraying her words.

She walks out of my office and fuck if I don't love how she fights me. The buzzing of my phone in my pocket steals my attention from watching Blaire walk away.

Carter: Party Friday for Kinsey's birthday

Liam: You think we need a reminder for our only sister's birthday party?

Carter: Yup. You're dumbasses lint licker

Liam: That nickname is outdated

Me: It stays

Sawyer: Agreed

Kins: You guys are idiots. I'm on this thread

Me: You literally planned it Kins, it's not a surprise

Kins: But still! It's my birthday! Make it special!

Carter: We will. By getting you drunk

Kins: Like I haven't gotten drunk before

Sawyer: You haven't

Me: We don't wanna hear otherwise

Liam: She would never

Kins: Morons. Make it special

Me: No pressure or anything

Knowing that Carter took over plans from Kinsey a while ago, I don't bother checking in. Since she's a December baby, born the week of Christmas, my parents always went all out for her. They wanted to make sure there was a separation between her birthday and Christmas celebrations and that she never got passed over. Now that she's an adult, she still expects to be treated like a queen on her birthday. We're happy to oblige, but whatever man she marries someday will have huge shoes to fill.

Friday night rolls around after being given the cold shoulder by Blaire all week, and I'm annoyed as fuck by it. I let her have her space, but I caught her eyes wandering over me multiple times throughout meetings and in passing. On Wednesday, my brothers and I met up at Dom's to box and release some energy and it barely took the edge off.

Getting ready for Kinsey's birthday party, I dress in a pair of denim jeans, brown boots, and a plain white tee with a navy plaid shirt over it.

Walking back into work, the party is already in full swing. The tasting room area was transformed with black and gold decorations. We blocked off the area for a closed party, but it seems Kinsey invited everyone she knows anyway, so it was probably pointless. Her best friend, Livvy, and friends Lily, Harlow, and Emma surround her, the five of them slamming shots together at the bar. I walk up to them, grabbing my sister in a huge hug.

"Happy birthday, Kins. Can't believe you're already twenty-three."

"Thanks, big brother."

"Ladies, good to see you. Enjoying your holiday break?"

Harlow looks at me with a devious smirk and unashamedly eye fucks the shit out of me. She's a pretty girl, way too young for me and not my type, but man if she isn't making her interest obvious. A strong hand pats my shoulder blade in greeting, and I turn to face Wes. He's an Aspen Ridge resident and one hell of a private investigator.

"Hey, man, how's everything?"

I watch him move directly behind Lily and wrap his arms firmly around her tiny waist, hauling her back flush against him. She looks up at him and smiles brightly.

"Things are finally right in the world. You?"

Shocked as shit, I have to pick up my chin from the floor. Lily is twenty-one. Wes has to be pushing forty here soon, even if he looks like a solid thirty. That's one hell of an age gap, and I'm pretty sure Lily was dating his son over the summer.

"Happy for you two. When did this happen?"

"Around Halloween. Just kinda hunted her down and made her mine."

"Well, good for you guys. It's good to see you all. Kins, I'm gonna go find our brothers. Behave."

"That is not what tonight is for! Tonight is for getting hammered and living it up! So be gone! Let me live for a change!" Kinsey singsongs.

Finding my brothers standing in the back with Reid, Ivy, Hannah, and Blaire, I join the group to find them in a heated discussion about tattoos. Reid, who's covered from his neck down to his toes, and a highly successful tattoo artist, is speaking in support of them while Carter is speaking against them. Which is not surprising.

"Do you tattoo your friends?" Blaire asks after the conversation settles down. I look at her and cock my head. Like fucking hell is Reid going to touch her body to put a tattoo on it.

"Yeah, from time to time. I did Dallas' half-sleeve. It was a good time. I don't mind tattooing friends, just as long as they're sure about what they want so they don't come at me pissed later."

"How'd you decide on the trees on your arm, Dal?" Ivy asks.

"Aspen Ridge. It's my peace. Wanted it with me no matter where I went."

I meet Blaire's eyes and she seems a bit taken aback by my answer. Like it surprised her. I'm not always a dickhead, princess. I give her a wink and she rolls her eyes before walking away from the group. The conversation is good, my brothers and I give each other shit, and Sawyer hangs all over Ivy.

My eyes linger around the room, not believing the turnout to celebrate my sister, when they settle on Blaire talking to some dink at the bar. Jealousy courses through me as I watch him order her a drink.

"Dude. Are you even listening? Who the hell are you looking at, dickhead?" Liam asks, pulling me away from watching Blaire get hit on.

"Looking for a hookup. What's it to you?"

"Looks like you're trying to shoot daggers from your eyes like

Superman. Those weren't hookup eyes, those were I'm-gonna-fuck-you-up eyes."

"Shut the hell up. You don't know what you're talking about."

"Whatever you say."

"Why don't you worry about yourself, lint licker?"

Liam smacks me in the chest before walking away, and I focus my attention back on Blaire. She smiles brightly before walking away and heading toward the bathrooms. My feet are on autopilot before I realize that I'm following her. I pull the door open right as it closes behind her and quickly check the stalls to make sure we're alone.

She spins on me, her attitude on full display, head cocked to the side and arms waving around as she raises her voice.

"What is with you and women's restrooms? Could you not follow me in here, just once? Get out!"

"Shut up, Blaire, don't pretend you don't like it."

Her face flames and she nervously pushes her wild, wavy hair behind her ear.

"I don't," she says, surprisingly convincing, but I know better.

"Such a little liar. What did I tell you about what happens to brats?"

She swallows and I track the movement, mesmerized by how her throat bobs. It reminds me how it felt to have her swallow my cock down and I'd give a whole hell of a lot to feel that again.

"Are you telling me that your pussy isn't wet right now?" I grab both of her wrists in my hand and hold them above her head, putting my free one around her neck. She lifts her chin and glares at me, making my cock throb behind my jeans. "You're not thinking about how good it felt to have my tongue inside you? How your legs trembled when I made you come? If you don't want me, princess, then say it, otherwise I'm going off everything else, and your body is screaming that it's mine."

I move my hand from her throat and drag it over her chest, between her breasts, and downward until I'm sliding under her dress, my fingers grabbing onto the thin strap of her panties and pulling hard, ripping them from her body. I bring them to my nose, inhaling her sweet, musky scent, and her mouth drops open as she watches me in a lust-filled haze. Her wet panties get stuffed into my pocket before my hand returns between her legs, cupping her bare pussy roughly. She mewls and it's the sexiest fucking sound. She's so slick already, and I fucking love how responsive she is to me. I grind the heel of my palm against her clit, and her hips immediately respond.

"I want to watch you come, it's so fucking pretty when you do."

"Dallas—"

I press harder as I capture her mouth with my own, opening and finding her tongue. She responds by meeting me halfway, moaning into my mouth.

"Goddamnit, Blaire. Why do you have to feel so good?"

I continue to hold her in place, devouring her mouth while I rub over her pussy with my hand, her juices soaking me. Her hips gyrate just as the handle clicks against the lock of the door, followed by a knock.

Blaire pushes me off her, straightening and combing her fingers through her hair.

"I'm so sorry! I'll be right out, spilled my drink and needed to dry my dress! Give me five, please!"

"No prob," comes a voice from the other side of the door. I look at Blaire and take a step back in her direction.

"Five minutes is plenty—"

"Nope. I said this can't happen again. You're the worst, Dallas! I'll check that the coast is clear."

Instead of lunging for her like I want to, I bring my hand to my mouth, licking it clean like an animal, feral for her taste. Her eyes are heavily lidded, her breaths coming out in pants. She's such a dirty little liar. Taking one step in her direction, she puts up her hands to stop me.

"Stop. You need to go."

Before I can argue, she unlocks and opens the door, peeping outside and checking that we won't be caught before opening it completely and shoving me through it. She doesn't immediately follow, and the disappointment that consumes me is unwarranted and unwanted.

But I can't fight how badly I want her. At least my hand will smell like her the rest of the night.

CHAPTER 12

blaire

KINSEY'S BIRTHDAY WAS ONE SHE SHOULD REMEMBER . . . or maybe not considering the amount of liquor she consumed. Everyone showed up for her, and even though she's Dallas' sister, I love being able to celebrate her because she's the sweetest. I tried not to let Dallas cornering me in the bathroom again get to me by drowning myself in shots. I don't drink often, so it didn't take much before I was feeling the effects plus some, and now I am swaying on my feet. Reid left a few hours ago, claiming he had something important to get to, and then over the last hour the crowd started to dwindle.

"Hey, we're heading out, the storm is picking up quickly outside and I don't want to get stuck in it," Sawyer tells the group, which consists of his brothers, Kinsey, and Ivy. I lay my head down on the cold bar top, the coolness feeling so good against my flushed cheek.

"I'll bring this she-devil home in a bit, she's clearly had more than she should," Dallas tells Sawyer as he walks away with his arm slung over Ivy's shoulders. The rest of his family follows, leaving me alone in Dallas' domineering presence.

I pop up from my position on the bar, sitting up on my barstool, trying my best to keep from swaying off of it, and making a quick decision to choose violence, 'cause I've had enough of the audacity of this infuriating man, even if he is hot as hell and knows exactly how to fuck me.

"The hell you will, Dallas, you arrogant dickhead! I'm not going anywhere with you!" I yell at him.

"You'll do whatever I tell you to do, Blaire, now let's go."

"No way. Fuck you!"

"Watch your mouth, princess," he says through gritted teeth.

"Or what?"

He leans in close, grabbing me firmly around the back of my neck and yanking me so my face is only a breath away.

"Or I'll fuck it. Remember how much you enjoyed gagging on my cock?"

All the blood drains from my face.

"What? Suddenly at a loss for vicious words to spew my way? Walk out of here with me so I can get you home safely, or so help me, Blaire, I'll fucking carry you. But either way, you're leaving with me."

"You are such an arrogant dick. I'll leave here with whoever I want. I'll find—" His fingers tighten around my neck, pulling my face directly to his. The space between us is nonexistent, our noses practically touching now, his breath hot on my lips.

"Finish that sentence, I dare you."

His eyes dance down to my mouth, and I can't fight the feeling his touch and filthy words ignite in me. I feel how slick I'm starting to get as my core aches. I should worry about how his dominance turns me on, but I don't. I know deep down I want a repeat of what happened in his office. I've never come so hard in my life. I never imagined my mind and body reacting the way they did to Dallas' commands, and I've been avoiding dissecting that. His little show in the bathroom only made me want him more. Time passes between us without a response from me, and he takes it as obedience.

"Good girl," he praises. I know he sees the moment my features soften and my body relaxes. I don't understand why I react to him this way. It's not me. He brings out something in me that has long lain dormant, and I can't explain the primal urge I feel to please him, to relax in his presence, especially when he's the one in my life I am usually playing defense with.

He releases his hold on me and grabs my hand. I look down at where they're joined, and my heart stutters in my chest. No one's ever held my hand before, no one's ever cared enough to. I follow him out of the distillery and into the night, the freezing Washington winter air sobering me.

We hustle to his fancy car, which looks entirely too nice for driving in the snow, but he seems to handle it just fine. He lets go of my hand and takes all the warmth with it. Opening my door for me, he motions for me to get in. I climb in quickly, rubbing my hands together, seeking the warmth he took from them. I study him the entire ride home, his chiseled jaw is covered with prickly facial hair, and the urge to run my hands over the coarse stubble is strong. I watch the way he focuses on the road as the snow rains down on the windshield in a thick blanket, the movement of his legs as he releases the gas and pushes in the clutch, his muscled arm shifting gears. He's so hot it's painful.

I'm so lost in the image in front of me that I don't realize we've pulled up in front of a large, northwest contemporary home, the garage door sliding open in front of us.

"This isn't my place, Dallas."

"You're so observant. It's mine. I asked you three times where you lived but you haven't answered me. I'm tired and not going back out in the storm, so I have a guest room you can crash in."

Panic sets in. Shit.

"Dallas, I can't stay at your house. I must have zoned out, I rarely drink. But I definitely cannot stay the night here."

"Don't be a pain in the ass. I'm not going back out in this. Look outside, Blaire, it's a fucking freak blizzard. We're here, so get out and let's get inside to get some water and ibuprofen in you."

His voice softens at the end, and I don't like what it does to me. His concern over my well-being is foreign and does weird things to my heart. It needs to stop.

"Fine. But I'm not your problem to worry about. Just show me where I'm sleeping, and I'll be gone first thing in the morning."

"Blaire, it's not a big deal. Calm down."

I scoff and roll my eyes at him.

"Tell me a time in history when a man has told a woman to 'calm down' and she actually did it. Fuck off, Dallas."

He looks at me blankly for a moment before opening his car door and climbing out, slamming it shut behind him. I follow him into his house and am immediately engulfed in his scent. Woodsy and clean and so him. His house is surprisingly modern for this area, with sleek, clean furnishings, hardwood floors, and minimal decor. We walk in silence into his kitchen, where Dallas hands me a water bottle and two pills. My hand goes to my hip, and I look up at him with the attitude I know he loves so much.

"Do you always have to be such a goddamn brat? Take the fuckin' pills and follow me."

Placing my hand out flat in front of him, Dallas drops the ibuprofen into my palm before snapping open the water bottle and handing it to me. I toss them back with an exaggerated eye roll.

"Atta girl. Now let's go," he says before putting his hands on my lower back, steering me around the corner and down a hall-way. There are three doors, and he opens the only one on the left.

"My room is right across the hall if you need anything. There's an en suite in here and I'll go grab you some clothes. Be right back."

He leaves me alone to take in the space. It's a pretty traditional guest room—a queen size bed in the center, a dresser, and a settee in front of a large window. There are no curtains and the moon lights up the room in a shadowy, silver ambiance. I drift over to it, looking out into the night. The snow is still coming down heavily outside.

"Hey, here's a shirt and a pair of sweatpants. That'll hold you over till tomorrow."

I give him an appreciative smile. "Thanks."

The tension ratchets up as we stare at each other. I move toward him, all inhibitions going right out the window, wanting nothing more than a repeat of what happened in his office now that I'm in his home, no matter how stupid it is, when he takes a step back.

"G'night, Blaire."

As if the storm had blown the winter chill through the window, that blazing heat is doused, leaving me feeling stupid and insecure. That was a one-time hookup. A misstep. There's no way he'd want that again, he was probably just fucking with me earlier in the bathroom because he likes to rattle me. Feeling like an idiot, I close the door behind him and strip out of my clothes, pulling Dallas' shirt over my head. It goes to the top of my thighs, and it feels so good to be swimming in a man's shirt. I'm not a petite girl by any means, but there's something so comforting and feel-good about wearing his shirt and having it hang off my body.

Pulling back the blankets of the bed, I slip into the sheets that feel so soft on my skin, and do my best to fall asleep. While I'm no stranger to sleeping in new places, it is so weird to try to fall asleep without a movie playing or a book to read. Both keep my brain from being idle and relax me, even if the content riles me up in other areas.

I can't believe the events of the day have led me to spending the night at Dallas' house. After I let my asshole boss defile me in his office in a dominating way, and freaking loved it, I knew I had to stay away from him. Never would I have imagined any of this happening. When he's ordering me around the office, it comes so easily to snap back and fight him on everything. But the moment he told me to get on my knees, all the fight left my body. The moment he caught me earlier in the bathroom, I caved. My nervous system recognizes something in Dallas, something I'm not sure I want to investigate.

Without anything to keep me busy, I look out the window and watch the snow fall gracefully from the sky. I've always loved winter, and the massive window next to me, plus the skylights above, give me the feeling of being inside a snow globe. The white flakes float from the sky, each one unique and inherently their own. It's hard not to marvel at the magic of it.

Wide awake, I decide that a hot shower and washing off the night will help relax me further. The bathroom is gorgeous, and almost the size of my entire studio. I look around for a towel and come up empty-handed. Really wanting a shower, I leave the safety of the bedroom and step across the hall to Dallas' room.

Door already slightly ajar, I push it open and take a hesitant step into the room. "Dallas?" The noise of a shower coming through the opened bathroom door stops me in my tracks. Shit, he had the same idea. I just need a towel. I bite my lip between my teeth. He's naked, just thirty feet away from me. It seems criminally unfair that I've given this man a blowjob and let him have all of me, but I haven't seen him fully naked. Curiosity wins as I tiptoe to the entryway of the bathroom, slowly peeking inside.

I send a silent thank you up to the powers that be for having my back because his shower is exactly like the one in my bathroom, and glass doors give me a full view of Dallas' naked body. From my angle, I have a perfect side view of him. One of his arms is braced against the tile, his back to the spray, and the plains of his body are defined, the water rippling over each of his sexy, chiseled muscles. He's hunched forward, and holy fucking shit. I suck in a gasp and quickly cover my mouth with my hand. His arm pumps in front of him as he strokes his very hard cock.

I know I should walk away and that this is crossing a major line. I just moved into stalker territory. His moans and breathing pick up and his head slowly moves to the side, his eyes connecting with mine. He doesn't look surprised to see me, as if he felt me the moment I stepped into his room. Turning to face me, he continues a slow but bruising assault on that thick cock. His forearm muscles rippling, his abs taut and flexed. I lick my lips before pulling my bottom lip between my teeth.

"Don't just stand there, princess. If you're going to watch, at least give me something to get off to."

My heart stumbles in my chest, my breath hitching. I don't move.

"Such a little voyeur you are. Get in here, Blaire. Now."

I close my eyes for a moment before stepping into the bathroom and leaning the top of my ass on the edge of the bathroom sink.

"Pull up the shirt, Blaire, I know you're bare under there, I have your panties. Let me see that gorgeous body you're hiding."

I bite down hard on my bottom lip as I grasp the hem of the shirt and pull it up to just under my large breasts. His eyes drop to my bare torso and his eyes widen with hunger.

"Take it off. Don't make me say it again."

I pull the shirt over my head, tossing it to the side. Slowly, I drag my fingers down the center of my chest, over the soft flesh of my tummy, and then trace the area around my pelvis. I watch as his eyes eat me up, lust-filled and focused. His free hand bats the shower head so that the water hits the wall and then he opens the glass door that was fogging up and distorting our view of each other.

"Such a pretty pussy. Spread your legs and touch yourself. I want to see how wet you got while watching me fuck my hand."

I do as he says, propping myself up on the counter, spreading my legs and exposing myself to him. I drag my fingers through my center, finding myself already slick with arousal, my eyes glued to that big dick, the barbells of his piercings glimmering in the light as his fist works himself over.

Up and down, up and down.

I moan out loud, and the erotic, dirty scene playing out has me hovering on the edge already. I swirl my fingers around my clit before moving them lower, pressing them inside, and dragging my palm across my clit with each stroke.

"That's it. Fuck yourself. You want to be a little voyeur? Now you're going to make yourself come while I watch."

It's all too much. My knees shake as I hang right on the cusp, and just as the orgasm starts to hit me, Dallas steps out of the shower, the water sloshing off his naked body and soaking the floor. He drops to his knees in front of me, grabbing one of my legs and holding it out further with his hand, spreading me impossibly wide. His mouth descends on my throbbing, swollen pussy and I shatter. His talented tongue swipes through my pussy, piercing into me before sucking my clit in quick pulses like he knows exactly what I need. My body shakes as I convulse from the power of the orgasm. His hand is still between his legs, working himself over, and as one orgasm fades, it rolls right into a second.

"Oh god, Dallas! Yes! Fuck, yes! Don't stop!" I grab the back of his head, holding him close to me as my hips grind wantonly on his face. I fall rapidly, the waves washing through me with force. As I start to come down, he releases me and stands, putting his hand on my shoulder and pressing me down.

"On your knees. You know the rules. Don't spill a drop."

I collapse down in front of him, my knees weak and trembling, and open my mouth wide, sticking my tongue out just in time to accept the warm, thick ropes of cum into my mouth. I lean forward and eagerly suck his engorged head between my lips, sucking and pulling every bit of cum I can from him, wanting to milk him dry. I grab his length with my hand and pull off with a loud pop. I lap at his still-firm cock, cleaning him up and making sure I don't leave anything behind. When I'm finished, I look up at him as he's dropping down to his knees in front of me, grabbing my head with both of his hands. He kisses me, sucking my tongue into his mouth, the lingering taste of both of our releases mixing together. He pulls back and looks me in the eyes for a moment before speaking.

"Fuck, you're addictive." He leans in again and presses his lips to mine before standing and pulling me to my feet. "Get back to bed. I'll see you in the morning."

Sobering, I quickly throw his shirt back on over my head and walk back to the guest room, thoughts of getting a towel or taking a shower long gone. I collapse onto the bed, pulling the blankets over me, and watch the snow fall rapidly from the sky until I drift off to sleep, asking myself how the hell I let this happen again, even if I was craving it.

I wake up later than normal, the sky a dark gray and the snow still coming down in large white flakes. I walk to the window and I'm shocked that the ground as far as I can see is blanketed in a deep layer of fresh snow, with more coming down on top of it. I pull on the sweatpants Dallas gave me last night, realizing that I'm still without a pair of panties. I open the door with a low creak and pad across the cold hardwood floor in my bare feet in search of Dallas.

As I walk through his house, a steady beat of bass gets louder and louder. I follow it to a closed door at the back of the house. Pulling the door open, the music is much louder, coupled with the hard-to-miss sounds of grunting and a rhythmic hammering. Deciding to scope it out, I walk blindly down the steps to Dallas' basement to find his back to me.

He's wearing a pair of gray sweatpants that hang low on his hips. His back and shoulder muscles tighten and flex as he punches unforgivingly on a large, hanging punching bag. He lands punch after punch with his gloved fists, moving to the beat of Nine Inch Nails. His body turns to the side as the bag sways with each of his heavy hits. He straightens his spine and grabs the bag between his gloves.

"Such a little creeper."

"I wasn't creeping on you. I was looking for you and found you, I was being polite. I didn't want to interrupt your workout."

"Is that so? I have reason to believe you're a closet voyeur. Sorry to disappoint you with the sweatpants. I'm happy to take them off now if you'd like." He faces me completely now, sweat making his body glisten. I bite my lip to stifle an appreciative moan. I need to change the subject before he distracts me further.

"The snow seems like a problem. Any word on how the roads are so I can get home?" I say with a bit more of an attitude than is necessary.

He moves to pull his gloves off, grabbing a towel, and wiping the sweat off his face and neck.

"All the roads are closed. Supposed to turn to freezing rain tonight. Everything is shut down. Looks like you're stuck here."

My mouth slackens, dropping open in shock. This can't be real life.

"Dallas. No."

"Here we fucking go." He moves swiftly, grabbing my wrist in his large hand and pulling me behind him. Up the stairs we go into his living room, where he flicks the news on. The reporter's voice fills the room, confirming what Dallas had told me.

". . . winter storm warning. Closing roads, highways, as the state shuts down . . . emergency . . . prepare for power outages."

"Dallas, what the fuck am I going to do? I can't stay here."

"Did you not hear her, Blaire? You're staying. Now stop being so goddamn difficult for once in your life and deal with it. You think this is ideal for me? You're everywhere! You've invaded the distillery, Dom's, Sunday fucking dinners at my parents' house, and now you're in my house. I can't escape you, Blaire, and it drives me fucking crazy. *You* drive me fucking crazy."

I stumble back a step as if he slapped me.

"Wow. The fucking arrogance on you . . ." At a loss for words, I close my mouth and stare at him as he runs his hands through his hair. He's still wearing nothing but those damn gray sweatpants, and my face flushes. They hang so low on his hips, exposing that mouthwatering V. I shake my head and look away from him. His body turns my brain to absolute mush. He walks up to me, running his hand across my cheek and combing his fingers into my hair.

"I see how I affect you. Even when I'm yelling and pissed off with you, just being close to me turns you on, doesn't it?" His voice is softer now, seductive, but still laced with that arrogance he couldn't shake if he tried. I straighten my spine and look at him.

"No. It doesn't."

His eyes rise in a challenge as his hand curls around my hair, pulling my body into his space. His free hand dips under my shirt before slipping in the loose band of the sweatpants I'm wearing. His fingers trace down my slit, easily slipping through my folds and dipping into my center. He pumps twice before removing his hand and holds his fingers out between us, the evidence of my arousal proving him right. He slips them into his mouth, licking and sucking my moisture from them before leaning down to meet my eyes straight on.

"Liar."

CHAPTER 13

dallas

"Here's how this is going to go. We're stuck here and I don't know when the roads will open up, sure as shit ain't gonna be today. Our bodies clearly want each other. So, we can either be at each other's throats the entire time, or we can fuck like animals. If I had my way, we'd do both."

She looks at me a little stunned, and I brace for the fight that I know is coming. Hell, I welcome it. Crave it. I surprised myself a bit, but if I'm going to be stuck in my own house with this sexy terror, I'm at least going to make the best of it.

"You're out of your fucking mind."

Called it.

"Yep. Out of my mind for you, princess. For some fucked-up reason that I don't understand. Trust me, I've tried."

"Wow, Dallas. Way to make a girl want to jump into bed with you. You woo me, my king!" She dramatically puts the back of her hand to her forehead and feigns swooning.

I grab her hips roughly, jerking her into me so she can feel how hard she makes me.

"Say it again."

Her palms flatten on my chest, but she doesn't push me away.

If she did, I would stop right now. But I know she wants this; she just doesn't like to admit it.

"You know exactly what I want to hear. I don't like repeating myself."

Her pretty eyelashes flutter closed briefly and when she looks up at me again, she's that sexy submissive that I want so badly. Fuck, I love bringing this strong woman to her knees. She's such a challenge, so feisty and hardheaded, but when I break down those walls and she gives in? It's fucking *magic*.

"My king."

A deep, uncontrolled moan releases from me before I rip the shirt off her and devour her lips. Her hands come up and curl around my neck, pulling me closer. The kiss is bruising, demanding, and hurried. My hands roam her body and I shift to pick her up, her thick thighs wrapping around my hips. I nip at her neck, licking and biting in a line down to her shoulder. I move us to the couch where I lay her on her back, dropping to my knees between her spread legs, and pull the sweatpants off, leaving her naked in front of me.

"Shoulda asked you this in my office but, birth control or condom?"

"IUD. Fuck me."

Fuck. Heaven help me, I'm going to lose myself in this woman. I line up my cock with her wet center before slamming into her without warning. Her body jerks back and I grab her hips, dragging her to the edge of the couch as I pull out to my tip and drive back in. My piercings make each thrust more sensitive and I know it makes me feel ribbed inside of her. Based on her eyes rolling to the back of her skull, I'd say she fucking loves it.

"Fuck, this pussy is so good, princess. You're soaking me, gripping me so tightly. So. Fucking. Good."

Her moans echo off the wall as I drive into her over and over with forceful thrusts. I fucking love this position. Her naked body is on full display for me, and her breasts bounce every time I slam into her. Leaning forward, I grab one roughly, it's huge and heavy in my large hand and I'm finding myself quickly becoming obsessed with them. Sucking her nipple into my mouth before biting it, I drag my teeth across her sensitive flesh, loving making her squirm. Her screams and moans are a symphony that I'm creating with her body, and I love the melody it creates.

"Goddamn it, Blaire. I can't wait to fuck these. So sexy. So fucking perfect."

"Yes, Dallas, yes. Take it!"

I quickly pull myself free from her body, grabbing her hips and flipping her onto her stomach. My palm connects with her ass cheek in three rapid slaps as she screams out.

"What did you call me?" I rub softly over her reddened skin.

"Dallas! Fuck!" She squirms against me, wanting me back inside her.

"Such a greedy pussy. Say it, Blaire. Who's fucking you right now? Who are you begging for?"

My hand comes down hard on the other cheek twice.

"My king! My king!"

"Mmm. That's right. Such a good girl." I praise as I spread her cheeks and slide my cock back into her wet, waiting center. Her channel is so tight, but even more so bent over like this. I fuck her hard and deep, gripping the flesh of her ass in my hands, loving how she feels. I lean over her and tap her lips with my thumb.

"Suck."

She greedily pulls it into her mouth, her tongue swirling around, getting it nice and wet. I pull it free and spread her cheeks once more. Looking down at her pretty, tight little hole, I spit right onto it before rubbing my wet finger over the puckered area. Her moans get louder as her hips start to push back on me. She's going to fucking kill me. I don't even have to try that hard, she's like fucking putty in my hands to mold and do what I want with. Good thing I know how to make her feel better than she ever has before.

"Fuck, you're so dirty. You want it?"

She pushes back on me and my thumb breaches that tight rim. I work it in slowly, letting her adjust.

"Harder, Dallas!"

My free hand connects with her ass cheek on impulse. Hard. I love how her fair skin blooms from the impact, love how wet she gets after each slap.

"Fuck! Harder, my king! Harder! Please!"

She's bucking wildly now and I'm feral for her like this. Wanton and careless, chasing the high of an orgasm only I can give her. I fuck her ruthlessly in both holes until I feel her pussy fluttering around my cock. I'm edging myself at this point, I want her to come with me, need her to come with me. She feels like nothing I've ever experienced before. My balls draw up and tingles shoot down my spine.

"Come, princess. Right fucking now."

She clenches tightly around me, her walls gripping me and holding me in, I pound into her one last time before emptying inside her.

"Jesus fucking Christ. That's it, baby, milk me. That greedy cunt can take it all. You like it when I fill you up?"

"God, yes!!!"

She screams through her orgasm and it's the prettiest damn thing I've ever heard. She's so goddamn addictive when she's like this. My cock jerks inside her until I'm completely spent. I pull myself from her body and move to sit next to her while we both work to control our breathing.

"So, you in?"

She turns her head to look at me, a smile on her face. She really is just so damn beautiful. Especially like this. Freshly fucked, coming down from an orgasm, her wild hair dancing around her face, and my cum leaking out of her. How she hasn't been wifed up yet is crazy to me.

"Yeah. I'm in. But there needs to be rules."

"Let's hear 'em."

"This ends when I leave here. No strings attached."

"Okay. What else?"

"We keep it to ourselves. Despite what you may think, I really do love my job, and I can't lose it because I'm sleeping with my boss. I also don't want to be looked at like a hussy, don't forget I'm new here."

"I can do that. Anything else? Should I open my notes app?"

That earns me a slap on my bare chest. I can't help but grab her wrist, bringing her palm to my mouth and biting the skin under the inside of her thumb.

"No. What about you? Anything to add?" she asks.

"Just one question." She looks at me thoughtfully, waiting. "Any limits?"

Her smile fills her face.

"Apparently none with you."

* * *

"Can I ask something without you being an asshole?" Blaire asks as she looks at me from across the bar, where she's seated in a clean Aspen Ridge Distillery T-shirt of mine.

"Not a very nice way to start a conversation, Blaire, but try me."

"I'm used to needing control. I shy away from men, no offense, like you. But with you . . ."

"With me you like it. More than like it."

She looks up at me with those vulnerable eyes and my heart flips in my chest again. I rub my knuckles into it to ease this awful feeling. I kind of figured she's never been with someone with my tastes before and knows nothing about this type of sexual lifestyle.

"I just expected to not like anything remotely close to what we've done, I'm trying to understand why."

"Here's a question for you, why does it matter why you enjoy it? Does it feel good?"

"Just forget I asked."

I walk around the bar from where I'm making our breakfast

and pull her around to face me. Her legs open and I step between them, grabbing her chin and forcing her to look at me.

"Answer me. Don't make me repeat it or I'll bend you over my lap right now and punish you."

Her eyes flutter closed as her breath hitches. So responsive.

"Yes. It feels good. I was just trying to understand why. What we've done, what I've let you do, those were hard lines before."

I boop her nose with my finger.

"That's just it. What *you* let me do. You think that because I'm the one being dominant means that I have all the control? That's all you, baby. At any point you could tell me to stop, pause, go, and I would."

"So, what do you get out of it?"

"It's the exchange that does it for me. Whether you're going to like this next part or not, it's the truth. Your mind and your body trust me enough to hand it all over to me. You're able to completely let go and know that I'll keep you safe and make you feel better than you ever have before. It's the exchange of trust. Having someone give themselves up wholly to me? Fuck, Blaire. Yeah, that does it for me." My cock starts to thicken behind my sweats just thinking about it.

She pulls her bottom lip between her teeth, quiet and contemplating everything I just told her. I return to the kitchen to assemble our breakfast sandwiches and pour coffee, giving her time to digest my small explanation.

"How do you like your coffee?"

"Black."

"That explains why you didn't like the pumpkin spice latte."

"Please don't remind me."

"That bad, huh?"

She laughs and it's the prettiest sound. I don't know if I've ever actually heard it before and now I know I want to hear it again.

"I don't really have a sweet tooth. Or at least I'm really picky about it. I do love Hannah's chocolate croissants. But coffee should be smooth and rich and not need all the cream, sugar, and added flavoring." She makes a disgusted face, and I can't control the chuckle that comes out of me at the sight.

"So black coffee good, flavored coffee bad. But chocolate croissants are fine."

"But only Hannah's."

"Got it."

"What about you?" she asks after a moment.

"Same on the coffee, black. After I graduated from high school some things went down with Sawyer and Ivy. Long story short, they were together from the very first moment they met in the sixth grade, and about a month into the summer after graduation, Ivy just disappeared. Her mom forced her to run off, get out of AR, and live the life she never got to, even if it wasn't what Ivy wanted. But it almost killed Sawyer. Anyway, he fell into a deep depression. Our dad was working long hours at the distillery and my mom was worried sick about Sawyer while trying to be there for Liam, Carter, and Kinsey. Kins was still pretty little. I stepped up to take care of my mom and all the extra shit. Didn't know the first thing about drinking coffee, so I just started pouring it black. It stuck."

I clear my throat, not quite sure how I ended up opening up to her, and focus on my breakfast sandwich in front of me, not wanting to face her reaction.

"Wow. I had no idea they went through all of that. I mean, I put it together that a bunch of stuff happened in the fall, but I had no idea about the rest. Your mom is lucky to have you. Is that why you two are so close?"

I meet her eyes then, full of something I can't quite decipher. It almost looks like jealousy or envy, and I realize that I haven't tried to get to know anything about her on a deeper level. Deciding to make the best of the time we have snowed in together, I make a mental note to get to know her. All of her.

"Yeah, I think that was the start of it. Sawyer was never the same after Ivy left. Even though we're twins, he definitely took on the firstborn role and I was able to fuck around. It wasn't until he checked out that I had to step up and I just never stepped back." I laugh at that sentiment. "Must be why we go round and round so much. He wants control back and I'm not giving it up. I like taking care of my family. I'd do damn near anything for any of them."

I look up from my meal just as Blaire swats a tear from her face. I cock my head to the side and study her. She's so much more than I initially thought. Sure, I've been madly obsessed with her feisty personality and sexy-as-hell body, but she's managed to surprise me.

"That's really sweet, Dallas. They're lucky to have you. Honestly, you're all lucky to have each other."

"Yeah. And we're only getting bigger with the way Sawyer plans to breed Ivy."

She chokes on her coffee, and I throw my head back in a laugh.

"You're joking."

"I wish I was. He's pretty open about it. Surprised you haven't heard the fucker. They want a hockey team. I'll bet you right now that she's pregnant again before the first baby turns one."

"Oh my god, Dallas!"

We both laugh and finish our breakfast and coffee with easy, comfortable conversation. It's the longest we've spoken without ripping each other's throats out and I don't hate it. In fact, I want more of it, even if I know I shouldn't.

blaire

AFTER A LONG-NEEDED SHOWER, I WRAP A TOWEL around me and pad across the hardwood floors into Dallas' room, stealing a clean shirt from him and tossing it over my head, letting the towel drop to my feet. Bending over to grab it, I flip my hair forward and use the towel to wrap it up when hands glide over my bare ass. I yelp and jump forward, only to be held in place by those firm hands around my hips.

"Dallas!"

"Walking into my room to find you already in here, bent over, bare-assed in nothing but one of my T-shirts is a fucking wet dream."

I relax into his big arms as they pull me closer, his hard length pressing into my back.

"I just got clean; can you wait a bit before messing me up again?" I beg, even though my pussy is already throbbing, wanting him.

"Maybe I don't like you clean. Maybe I prefer you dirty, with my scent all over you and my cum leaking out of every hole."

His words trigger a moan as one of his hands wraps around my waist and the other slips between us, heading south, my body on fire. He rubs between my legs, fingering my center, and my arousal is quick to respond. He dips in, pushing deep before pulling out and slipping upward, pressing and swirling around my asshole.

"Have you ever been fucked here?"

I shake my head.

"Only what you've done with your fingers."

"Good. Now get on the bed."

I do as he says, my body on autopilot, letting him lead me into the abyss. He strips out of his clothes before walking over to his end table and pulling out a bottle of lube. He tosses it next to me and kneels on the bed between my legs. Running his hands up my thighs, he spreads them further so his big shoulders can fit between them. He settles in, his face right at my center, but he doesn't do anything but stare.

"Such a good pussy, princess. You're already weeping for me."

He leans in, smelling me for a moment before he spits. I'm so shocked all I can do is whimper, torn between the shock of the action and how degradingly hot it is. He spits again, letting it fall from his lips and drip onto my center before finally leaning in and licking me. He drags his tongue from ass to clit, over, and over, and over again until I'm a dripping, moaning mess under him.

"Please, Dallas. Make me come. I can't take anymore."

"That's it, baby, beg for it."

His fingers meet my center, pressing into my pussy, the noises embarrassingly loud. I can hear just how wet I am, feel it dripping down to my ass where I know he wants it. He fucks me with his fingers until I'm a squirming mess under him. When I'm right on the edge, he pulls them out, moving them lower to my asshole, rimming it, pulling my wetness to it before he presses in with one finger. I know I can handle this, he's done it before, but I still clench slightly from the intrusion.

"Gonna need you to relax, you know how this works, you've taken this much before."

He licks my clit in flicks, driving me wild while his finger works into my ass, pumping in a few times. My body starts to press into him, my hand moving to grasp around the back of his head, holding him to me, wanting him to make me come.

"Please, please. Please. I need to come."

He sucks my clit into his mouth and the orgasm finally crests, causing my toes to curl and forcing tears from my eyes as I shake under him. Just as I'm falling, I feel the pressure in my ass increase, realizing he's added another finger. He scissors them, stretching me and preparing me to take his huge, pierced dick. His words of praise echo around me as I melt into the bed.

Once he pulls his fingers free, sitting up between my legs and uncapping the lube, I watch in a trance as he covers his cock with the liquid, pumping it in his fist and then adding more. He pours some on two of his fingers, rubbing along my hole and pressing them in. He watches his actions, his face transfixed and hungry. His hips gyrate slowly, fucking the air while his fingers move in and out.

"Fuck, you should see what you look like right now, baby girl. So open for me. So fucking pretty."

I moan, his words doing just as much for me as his fingers are. Finally, he pulls free, leaning over me and lining up his fat cock with my entrance.

He cups my face with his clean hand and looks into my eyes.

"You're going to breathe for me and let me take care of you, just as I have been. You understand?"

"Yes."

"That's a good girl."

He kisses me as he presses in the thick, mushroom head of his dick. I gasp into his mouth, his fingers rubbing against the side of my face, calming me.

"Shh. It's going to feel so good. But you've got to breathe and let me in. Relax," he whispers against my lips.

I take a deep breath, allowing myself to relax, knowing how good this will feel if I allow it. He presses in a bit more and I feel the first of the six barbells that climb his length.

"Such a good girl, that's one. Five to go, baby."

He kisses me, fucking my mouth with his tongue, holding the side of my face tightly in his hand. I moan against him as I feel him press in again, deeper this time.

"Halfway there, beautiful. You were made to take this. Fuck, you're so perfect, Blaire."

"Oh god, Dallas, I feel so full."

"Almost, baby."

He presses in again, two more piercings grazing my rim as he fills me. The feeling of each of them drives me insane. He finally, *finally*, presses all the way in, filling me completely, and stops, giving me time to adjust and relax.

"You took all of me, Blaire, you did so well. You like it? You like having your ass filled with my cock?"

"God, yes, Dallas."

I wiggle against him, loving the sensation it gives me. He moans, deep and masculine, and then he starts to pull out. Each piercing is evident as he withdraws slowly and presses back in, impossibly deep.

"Shit, you feel so good. So. Fucking. Tight."

I relax further, loving the feeling, and start to meet him thrust for thrust. The pace is torturously slow, and I want more, I want it harder. I trust him not to hurt me. I press my hands against his chest, pushing him away from me. He gets the hint and moves to his knees between my legs, pulling out completely and grabbing my hips. His strong arms roll me, flipping me onto my stomach and pulling my hips back up to him. His hand goes to my head, pressing it down into the mattress so that my ass is in the air. I hear the squirt of lube and then he's notching that head back at my entrance and pressing in. It's much easier this time since I'm stretched and ready to accept his girth.

"Oh, fuck, such a dirty little princess. Your ass is swallowing me, Blaire, taking me so fucking well."

"Aah. Dallas! Holy shit."

His thrusts are stronger now, deeper, his moans becoming louder and mixing with his dirty words.

"Touch yourself, baby. Make yourself come while I fuck this pretty ass." His palms grip into the meat of my ass, grabbing a handful and squeezing, massaging. "Fuck, this ass. I could fuck you like this every day, dirty girl."

I move my hand between my legs, easily slipping through my wet center and finding my clit. I press down firmly, swirling my fingers in small circles, pleasure racing up my spine.

"Dallas, I'm going to come. It all feels too good."

His palm comes down and slaps my ass, my cheek shaking from the force of it. I moan loudly at the sting.

"Wait for me," he growls.

I whine, slowing down my movements and trying to hold out, but it's too hard. The pleasure is too much.

"I can't, please," I beg desperately.

He thrusts into my asshole once more before groaning loudly, "Come, baby, fucking come for me!" I press down firmly and that's all it takes. I'm washed away in euphoria as the pleasure takes over. My legs shake, collapsing down onto the bed, and Dallas follows me, lying on my back. I scream out his name as I'm lost to it all.

"You're incredible. You just blew my mind."

"You're lying," I pant, unsure why I'm looking for confirmation that he isn't feeding me a line of bullshit, but there's a huge part of me that lives for his praise. Something I've never wanted or needed before, but with him, I crave it.

"I don't bother with lies. There's no point in them. I've never been like that-no one has ever-fuck. I'm at a loss for words, princess. But that was mind-blowing, and I've never come so hard in my life. Thank you for giving me that part of you."

His words fill me with satisfaction, and I smile into the mattress. After we've caught our breath, he climbs off me, pulling me with him. He starts the shower, gets out two towels, and hangs them on the hooks next to the walk-in shower. We both step in, Dallas pulling me into the spray. I let him, and the warm water feels so good on my body. When he grabs the shampoo and moves to wash my hair, I grab his wrist, stopping him.

"Please. Let me clean you up."

"Washing my hair isn't cleaning me up after sex, that's something else entirely. Thank you, though. I can do it."

He concedes, knowing that I'm right. We finish our shower and dress in comfy clothes, because why would we get dressed? Not that I have anything here anyway.

The rest of the day goes by slowly, but somehow we avoid deeper conversation about me. He tells me about growing up at the distillery. How he and his brothers used to play hide and seek in the barrel stock house, and then once they got older, used to sneak girls into it to fool around. He talks about his parents and their love for each other, how his dad has worshiped his mom for as far back as he can remember. His stories fill my heart with happiness for him and his family, but also make me yearn to have one of my own someday. It's not even that I am desperate to have children, because I'm not, but I hope whoever I end up spending the rest of my life with has a family like the Hayes. It's incredibly rare to be so close and love each other so fiercely. At least, it is in my world.

CHAPTER 15

dallas

AFTER LYING AROUND ALL DAY, I'M EAGER FOR SOME fresh air. Grabbing everything I need—a bottle of Aspen Ridge whiskey, and two towels—I open up the back door and step onto my covered back porch. Lucky for me, my house backs up to the woods for ultimate privacy. Not that I've had a woman over here before. I set everything down on the patio table before lifting the lid to my hot tub. Turning it on to heat up, I flick the string lights on and the overhead light off and head back inside to find Blaire, excitement flaring to life inside me.

Rapping my knuckles on the guest bedroom door is the only warning she gets before I open it and walk into the room. She's lying on the bed, sprawled out with a movie playing on the flat screen in front of her. Her eyes light up slightly when she sees me enter, and I don't fight the smile it brings me.

"Didn't want to invite me to movie night?" I tease as I drop down next to her on the bed, my big body brushing against hers.

"Like you'd really want to watch *Pride and Prejudice*."

"Only if it's Keira Knightly and Matthew Macfadyen."

Her head spins so fast I'm positive she has whiplash. She bounces up on the bed, her knees tucked under her, facing me. I arch my neck back to look up at her.

"How did you know that? This is my favorite movie of all time. My favorite book."

She's so damn cute like this, in nothing but one of my T-shirts, barefaced, excited, and relaxed at the same time. I like this version of her. A lot.

"My mom. It's also her favorite."

Her face falls slightly and it confuses me. I thought that would make her happy. She seemed to really get along with my mother.

"It's classic. My guilty pleasure movie. I watch it more often than I dare admit, honestly."

"Your secret is safe with me. Care to take a break from it?"

"What do you have in mind?"

"C'mon and I'll show you."

I grab her hand in mine and drag her from the room. She follows me in silence, which is surprising, she's usually always got some smart remarks to make. I lead her to the back door when she starts to pull on my hand.

"Dallas, I'm in just a shirt. I'll freeze to death!"

"You'll warm up quickly, trust me."

I slide open the door and step onto the large wooden deck, watching her face as she takes in the surroundings. The twinkling lights illuminate her beautiful features as she smiles brightly. Once she sees the hot tub, bubbling and steaming, her body relaxes, and she sighs. She's so fucking beautiful. So easy to make happy. I want to do more of it.

"Dallas, it's so beautiful out here. So quiet and peaceful."

"Compared to where you live?"

"Wouldn't you like to know?"

"How else am I supposed to sneak in and fuck you while you sleep?"

Her body stiffens, her face turning ashen, and I have no idea why that would upset her. Her reaction was quick, but I caught it right before she masked it.

She smacks my chest playfully and I move just as quickly to

wrap my fingers around her wrist, hauling her to me. She laughs but stutters once she feels my hand sliding up the top of her thigh, slipping under the T-shirt, and pulling the fabric up with it.

"No clothes. Hot tub rules."

She smirks at me but moves to the elastic of my joggers.

"Same goes for you then, Mr. Hayes."

We strip and climb into the warmth of the hot tub, the steam rising from the heat and the cold winter air. She relaxes deep into the water as I hand her the open bottle of whiskey. I watch as she takes her first swig of whiskey straight from the bottle. Her mouth forming an 'o' around the opening, and I immediately think of those luscious lips wrapped around my cock. She's so eager. Easily gives the best head I've ever had. I don't even remember anyone before her. She swallows the alcohol, her face scrunching up as a shiver runs through her body. She visibly shakes, and I try not to laugh at her. Instead, I want to play a game.

"Truth or dare?"

She eyes me skeptically for a moment before answering.

"Dare."

Not surprising at all, my little spitfire.

"I dare you to tell me something honest."

Her face pales momentarily before she relaxes further into the bubbling water, the tops of her double D's bobbing at the surface, tempting me.

"Hmm. That's not how this game is supposed to work. But, fine. You may already know, but, I have a tiny tattoo behind my ear of a dove."

My eyebrows shoot to my forehead and she laughs at me. I'm moving before she has a chance to stop me, threading my fingers through her hair and pushing it out of the way, turning her head in both directions until I find it. On her left side, sits a tiny tattoo of an expertly done single dove. I thought I had my mouth on every inch of this woman's body, but I'm proven wrong. She bats my hands, pushing me in the chest.

"Why a dove?" I ask as I move back to my seat across from her.

"Nuh-uh. That's not how the game works, punk. My turn."

I shoot her a grin before waving my hand between us, urging her to go on.

"Dallas, truth or dare?"

"Truth."

Let's see if I can get her to do the same next. I want to get to know her better.

"Did you always want to work at the distillery?"

"Easy, baby girl. Yes. I grew up running around that place. Each of us loves it for different reasons but I've always had this chaos within me, this live energy that I never knew what to do with. The only place I ever felt calm was at the distillery. So, yes. I've always wanted to work there. I never considered doing anything else."

"That's why you are so against the tours and opening the place up for visitors. Dallas . . ."

"Don't. I don't want to ruin this. Just let it go."

Her eyes are full of sympathy and guilt, and I don't like it one bit. I move across the hot tub to her, cradling her face in my hands before kissing her, shutting her up. My tongue swipes across her plush, silky lips before she opens for me. Her tongue is warm and wet, and I can't help but suck it into my mouth, muffling her moans. I pull away, returning to my seat, leaving her eyes heavy-lidded, and a smile on her face. "Truth or dare, princess?"

"Dare."

Brat.

"I dare you to come put those tits in my face."

She doesn't hesitate, moving into my space and standing between my legs. I keep my arms splayed out across the edge of the tub, giving her full control. Straddling me, she lifts those full, sexy breasts with her hands, lifting them and swiping each nipple across my lips. I stick out my tongue, feeling her smooth skin glide across, before she feeds one into my mouth. I greedily suck her nipple, pulling it taut, my tongue lashing across the stiff peak. I open wider, pulling her entire areola into my mouth, sucking hard. Her body jerks forward at my onslaught, her hands gripping my shoulders to hold herself up.

"Dallas, holy shit." One of her hands slides through my hair, grasping the back of my head and holding my face to her. Her hips start to gyrate, and I wonder if I can get her to come just from this. I suck harder, rotating between suckling and biting. My free hand finds her other breast, twisting and pinching at her nipple while she continues to moan, her hands threaded through my hair, her body trembling, and fuck if I don't love this.

"Dallas, you're going to make me come if you don't stop," she says, her voice breathy and thick with lust.

I pull back and look up at her. "Now, why would I stop?"

Alternating between her breasts, I focus on each one, lavishing them, sucking, biting, and twisting. Within minutes she's a shaking mess in my arms. One more hard suck, and my tongue swirls around before an orgasm hits, her body shaking slightly in my arms.

"Aah! Oh! God!"

I look up at her, breasts still in my face, and swipe my tongue across my lips.

"Delicious."

"God you're going to kill me."

"Back to your spot."

She steps back from me reluctantly, breathing heavily, post-orgasm haze written all over her face.

"Truth or dare, Dallas?"

"Dare."

"I dare you to go jump in the snow. Buck ass naked. Don't forget to roll around in it."

I gape at her for a moment, slightly shocked, but it's not like it's something I haven't done before, growing up with three idiot brothers. But I bet it's something she hasn't. That's going to change right now.

I stand up, shake the hot water off, and step out of the hot tub, taking a moment to decide the best way to grab her without making us both crash to the ground first.

"Don't I get a good luck kiss first? I'm about to turn my balls into ice cubes. It's the least you can do."

Like a good girl, she stands, turns to face me, and leans over the edge of the tub, ready for me to kiss her. Looking at her plush, sweet lips for a moment, I lean in and press mine to hers. I typically stay away from kissing partners, but kissing Blaire comes as naturally as breathing. I moan into her mouth the moment our tongues touch, losing myself in her for just a moment before grabbing her around the waist and yanking her out of the hot tub. Her arms grasp around my shoulders, a scream piercing my ears.

"Don't you fucking dare, Dallas!"

Holding her close to me while her arms push against my chest and her feet struggle for purchase, I lift her up, bridal style, and run across the deck, diving off of it into the feet of snow covering my backyard. The cold assaults me like a thousand tiny knives and pulls the breath from my lungs. Blaire's scream stops and she frantically tries to climb back out.

"Oh, no. You said not to forget to roll around, baby girl."

Grabbing her around the waist, I drop onto my back and roll us back and forth. Her scream turns into a deep laugh that fuels my own. The sound is so fucking pretty, and I want more of it.

"You're the worst, Dallas Hayes!" she says through her giggles. Standing, I grab her hand and pull her through the snow, up the deck steps, and back to the hot tub, where we both sink into the water to heat up, her teeth chattering together. The smile on her face reaches her eyes and I know I made the right decision.

"Maybe. But now you can say that you've rolled around naked in the snow."

"If I don't die of hypothermia!"

"Don't be a baby, you're fine!"

"Whatever. Your turn."

"Truth or dare, baby girl?"

She hesitates for a moment, biting the inside of her cheek while she contemplates. Come on, give me a truth. Just one truth.

"Dare."

Goddamn brat. I should spank it out of her.

"I dare you to take a long pull from that whiskey bottle without wincing."

"You dick!" she says as she grabs the bottle and brings it to her lips, pulling the warm, amber liquid into her mouth. Her face immediately sours, and she lets out a small cough that she tries to cover with her hand. Laughing at her, I take the bottle and take a long pull, my face casual and composed.

"You're the worst."

"You like it. Your turn. I'll make it easy on you. Dare."

The smirk that she gives me is so fucking devilish, and if my cock wasn't already hard from being in here naked with her, it would be from that look alone.

"Bring it, baby. What are you waiting for?"

"I dare you to get me off in under a minute."

Fuck. Yes. That I can do.

"Done. But you're going to count. If you stop counting, time stops."

"That's not fair."

"Then don't stop counting."

I lift her then, placing her ass on the edge of the hot tub and spreading her legs so I can easily fit between them. Goosebumps erupt across her wet skin and her nipples stiffen to tight, firm peaks as the winter chill hits her. I'm not worried, I know this won't take long, and her body will be molten on the inside.

"Count."

"1, 2, 3 . . ."

I swipe my tongue up her slit, finding that swollen sweet spot and swirling around it, plunging two fingers inside her wet heat. I curl them up toward her stomach, keeping them in deep and rubbing that place inside her that will make her cry tears of pleasure. I lick her thoroughly, alternating between swirling and flicking, her hips bucking into my face.

"19, 20, 21 . . ."

She moans out every number, her voice starting to stutter, while her legs begin to shake on either side of me. She stops counting and I pull back, delivering a quick, hard slap right between her legs. Her yelp echoes into the quiet, still night. My fingers are instantly flooded with her arousal. Thank fuck, I was hoping she'd respond like that.

"Count."

"29, 30 . . ."

I return to licking her, inhaling her sweet scent, and devouring her delicious taste. I add more pressure with my tongue, licking and suckling at her engorged clit.

"45, 46, 47, 48 . . ."

Done messing around, I push in deeper with two fingers and press down on her lower abdomen with my free hand, sucking her clit into my mouth at the same time. She shatters. She throws her head back as her orgasm hits, her body shaking. She stops counting, but I decide not to torture her. I lick her through it, the flat of my tongue soaking up all of her, letting her sweet release coat my mouth and chin. A hand combs through my hair, grabbing a fistful and pulling me off. I look up at her from between her legs and smile, knowing I have every reason to be smug right now.

"Enough, please. Too sensitive. That was insane. It literally causes me pain to admit how damn good you are at that."

The laugh that comes out of me is unfiltered and raw. She looks at me, stunned for a moment, before joining in. She sinks back into the hot tub, rubbing her arms with her hands to warm up.

"Wh-whose turn is it?" she stutters before dipping her shoulders below the surface.

"That would be yours. Truth or dare?"

"Truth," she surprises me by saying.

Finally. Caught off guard, I think for a moment, having

waited for this, knowing I want to make it count but unsure what to ask now that I've been given the opportunity. But I also want to ensure she keeps playing this little game with me, not ready to spook her and have it end.

"Tell me something you dream of."

Her answer comes quickly, as if it was already on the tip of her tongue. Something she thinks about often and desires.

"A family."

My heart squeezes and I want to press for more, but I know that's the wrong move. Instead, I pocket that piece of her, and I'll hold on to it for a later date.

"Truth or dare, Dallas?"

"Truth."

"I'm going to preface this, you said you like the power exchange, that you like to be in control. But are you a Dom? What are you into?"

Her eyes get heavier the more she speaks, the tops of her breasts rising and falling in the water as her breathing increases, as if just the idea of it is turning her on. I knew she'd be curious, but I didn't expect to want to show her as much as I do. I'd love to demonstrate how it works, fuck, I'd love to take her to the club. I can picture the blush that would bloom across her fair skin.

"Yes. I'll show you."

<hr>

"You want to know what I'm into, Blaire, what my kink is? There are different Dom-sub relationship dynamics. Some are purely sexual in nature, and some are in it twenty-four-seven. Some are monogamous, and some are poly. I'm too possessive to share, and I only want the sexual relationship. Although, I love the cat and mouse game and the bratty behavior during everyday moments, because it feels so good to break a woman down in the bedroom." I pull the towel that's wrapped around her body loose, letting it drop to the floor so she's standing in my bedroom completely naked. Her eyes don't leave mine, not an ounce of unease reflected in them.

"The relationship can be whatever the two, or more, want it to be. But communication is key. I love the power exchange. There was nothing hotter than seeing you give up control to me, trusting me to keep you safe and take care of you, both before, during, and after sex. That's why I've insisted I clean you up. You gave up that control to me, and I hope it made you feel powerful, but I want to show you that after sex or a scene, I'm still present. I want to check in with you and know you're okay." I run my fingers up and down her chest between her breasts while I continue to talk.

"What's even better than you giving up control though, is that you enjoyed it. It has to be mutually beneficial or it doesn't work. I don't want you on your knees for me, bending to my will, unless it's what you want. In my opinion, like I've said before, you hold all the power."

She nods, and her face says she understands, but I want confirmation.

"Does that make sense?"

"Yes. So far."

"There are various things that people in the BDSM community can explore, but since I've already asked if you have limits, and I'm not into impact play, blood play, or anything dark—and for the sake of only having right now together—we don't really need to go over those. Any questions?"

"I want you to show me, now. Please."

I love how eager she is. How genuinely she seems to want this. So much has changed in the last forty-eight hours, and while we're stuck together in our snowed-in bubble, I can't wait to explore it all. I lean down and kiss her lips, running my tongue along the seam of them before pulling away.

"Red means stop, yellow means slow down. No questions asked, baby."

"Okay."

"Good. Show me how well you listen, my little menace."

She moans as I rub my hand down the center of her chest before dipping my hand between her legs, grabbing her pussy roughly, and jerking her closer to me.

"I'm going to get a drink and you're going to sit here like a good girl and wait for directions. Can you do that for me?"

She nods.

"Good. Remember, good girls get rewarded and brats get punished."

The noise she releases is strangled and I smirk at her.

"Kneel. On your knees. Spread them slightly, palms up."

She obeys, and fuck if she isn't so pretty. I can't help but drag my hand over her head lovingly. I walk to my bar and dump a few ice cubes into my glass before pouring two fingers of whiskey. Returning to the bedroom, I take a seat in the center of the chaise lounge and look at her, taking a small sip of the alcohol. That damn lip is tucked between her teeth, her hips moving slightly back and forth.

"So needy. Crawl to me. Slowly."

She hesitates for a moment, and I arch a brow at her. I'm more than happy to break down my little brat, but I want her to want to obey me. I want her to give up her pleasure to me wholly, trust me enough to take care of her and give her exactly what she needs, without her having to think about anything. That's the real power play that gets me off. I watch as she swallows her pride and leans forward slowly onto all fours, those large breasts hanging low and swaying slightly as she prowls toward me. My cock hardens where it rests heavy against my abdomen.

"Fuck. Look at you, baby girl. So hot. So sexy. All fucking *mine*."

Her eyes shoot up to meet mine, but she doesn't stop. She sits on the floor between my legs and waits.

"Good girl."

I run my fingers through her hair before pulling it back to arch her neck.

"Open your mouth for me."

I take a long pull of my cold whiskey and lean forward, hovering above her face, my eyes connecting with her deep blue ones. I slowly release the liquid, letting it steadily drip into her mouth. Leaning forward so we're nose to nose, I whisper, "Swallow."

She obeys, swallowing the liquid without a cough, and holds back her wince from the burn I know she's feeling.

"Mmm. You like it better straight from my mouth?"

"Yes."

Lifting my glass, I repeat the process, except this time I kiss down her neck, stopping at the top of her chest and releasing the liquid. I sit back and watch as it cascades between her breasts when an idea hits me. Something I've wanted to do since the first day I met her.

"Get on the bed, on your back."

She takes a deep breath before standing and doing exactly as I asked, her sexy body waiting for me in the center of the bed. I stand, walking naked to the front of the bed, while her eyes rake over every inch of me. My cock is rock hard, aching for the release only she can bring. I climb on top of her, whiskey in hand, straddling across her waist.

"Do you have any idea what you do to me? How beautiful you are?"

I couldn't have held back the confession if I wanted to. This woman has buried herself deep within me and there's no fucking getting her out. I lean down, squeezing one of her huge tits in my hand, her flesh spilling over my large palm. Fuck I love their size. I suck her nipple into my mouth, pulling hard until it's a stiff peak before repeating on the other side. Her moans fill the air as her hips gyrate below me.

"Squeeze them together for me, baby girl." She uses both of her hands and lifts her breasts, bringing them tightly together in the center of her chest. I slowly drip the rest of the whiskey down the crease before setting the glass on my end table. She lets out a gasp as the cool liquid moves through the crevice created with her tits. Grabbing my cock tightly in my fist, I stroke it twice before leaning forward over her.

"Let me in."

She lets them fall apart so I can slide my dick between her perfect breasts before she pushes them around me again. The cold whiskey around my dick, and the smooth silk of her skin, has my eyes nearly rolling to the back of my skull.

I fuck her perfect tits, sliding my cock back and forth between them, the cold whiskey keeping her slick. She keeps them pushed up tight around my cock and it's fucking heaven.

"Just like that. Fuck, you feel so good. I'm going to fuck you everywhere, Blaire. There won't be an inch of you left that my cock hasn't touched. You ready for my cum, princess?"

"God, yes, Dallas. Give it to me. Come for me."

That's my undoing. My cock jerks between her breasts as I spray cum across her chest, covering her neck and the tops of her breasts. "Shiiiit. Blaire, oh, fuck!" My head drops back on my shoulders as my orgasm rolls through me, my cock pulsing out ribbons of cum.

"God, you're a dream. So good, baby."

She releases her breasts and I sit back, slightly admiring the mess I made of her flawless skin. I knew it would look this good, she wears my pearl necklace so well. Swiping my fingers through the cum and whiskey, I gather it up between two fingers and feed it to her. Her mouth opens, sucking my fingers in and swirling her tongue around the digits. It's one of the hottest things I've ever seen, her eager lips suctioning around my fingers, devouring my cum.

"Mmm."

God, she's so damn perfect for me. How is this possible?

I collect the rest of my cum and whiskey off her chest and let her lick my fingers clean before pulling them out. Our eyes meet, both of our chests rising and falling rapidly. Bracing myself on my forearms resting on either side of her head, I kiss her. The taste of my release and alcohol are still on her tongue, and I lose myself to kissing this woman. My hands move to slide into her hair—the fiery red locks that frame her beautiful face. My cock starts to harden again, never getting enough of her. Fuck, what's happening to me? She's so damn intoxicating. I can't get enough. It's never enough.

I break the kiss and slide next to her, flipping us so that I'm on my back and she's straddling me, and fuck if seeing Blaire on top of me isn't a sight that'll be burned into my memory forever. Her red hair is wild and rumpled, a mix of waves and curls that cascade over one shoulder. Her breasts are full, the skin red and angry from being squeezed and fucked. Her waist dips in before her hips flare out, leading to thick thighs that I want wrapped around my head. She lifts herself slightly, bracing her hands on my chest, and before she can get the chance to sink down on me, I drag her forward.

"Grab the headboard, baby."

"Dallas, no. I can't, please."

"You can and you will. You're going to sit on my face, right fucking now."

"Dallas, you can't be serious."

I pull her thighs up so that she's straddling my face, locking my arms around them and holding her in place.

"Sit, Blaire. You're doing so well behaving, don't make me punish you for disobeying."

Her eyes roam mine, panicked. I lift my head slightly, dragging my nose through her folds, inhaling her scent into my lungs.

"God, you're divine."

"Dallas . . ."

I lift my hand and connect with her ass, hard, the slap echoing through the room. She yelps before moaning as I run my hand over the spot to soothe it.

"I won't repeat myself, princess."

She hesitates, so I smack the same cheek again, this time slightly harder.

"Fuck! Dallas!"

Gripping her hips, I pull her down on me, her pussy settling perfectly against my mouth to devour. I spear my tongue into her drenched slit, fucking her with it, her taste exploding on my tongue. She's so damn sweet. I lick through her lips, finding her clit and sucking. My hand slaps her ass again, forcing her to jerk forward on me.

"Oh god, Dallas, that feels so good."

Another smack, the palm of my hand connecting hard with her ass cheek, the flesh burning. Wetness floods my mouth. Fuck yes, she loves it. I grip her hips, showing her just how I want her to move on me, rocking her back and forth on my face. Her body takes over, rotating and gyrating on me while I lick and suck her thoroughly.

"That's it, baby. Fuck my face. So fucking good. Drench me."

"Aah. Dallas. Oh god!"

Her legs start to shake around my head, her movements jerky and uncoordinated, her little nub swelling. I slap her ass in three rapid-fire movements while sucking her clit into my mouth, pulsing my sucks. She collapses forward, resting her forehead on the headboard as her orgasm tears through her, and I pulse around her, working her through her pleasure until she's come down.

I release my hold on her clit and lick her languidly, her sweetness coating my tongue, and I hum in approval. Her body responds so perfectly to me. Helping her lift off of me, I lay her down, back to my front, pulling her flush against me. Positioning her leg over my thigh, spreading her open for me, I line up my cock with her heat and sink in smoothly, her walls clenching around my length. She's so damn tight, but it's a perfect fit. Her body arches into me as she reaches back to grasp my neck, pulling me into her.

"You feel so good inside me," she whispers like a confession. My heart beats erratically in my chest, flipping over itself and falling. I grip her chin with my hand, pulling her head back toward mine so I can kiss her. Our tongues caress slowly, in no rush to reach the finish line. I pull back enough to talk, my lips ghosting over hers while I speak.

"Yeah, baby, like nothing I've ever experienced before."

I fuck her slow and deep, never pulling all the way out, staying buried as far as I can get, until both of us are coming, losing ourselves again to the pleasure of each other.

Tonight was supposed to be about showing Blaire how I like it, and it turned into something else entirely.

Something I like more.

blaire

I WAKE UP ALONE IN DALLAS' ROOM AFTER OUR NIGHT together. I hadn't intended on sleeping in his bed, but after the last round of sex, he cleaned me up with a warm washcloth, wrapped me in his arms, and I fell asleep quickly. It was the best sleep of my entire life. I didn't hover in the in-between space of awake and the dream world, fearful of drifting too deep where my nightmares could reach me.

My heart flips in my chest as I struggle to come to terms with why. There's something about Dallas that my subconscious recognizes. Something that calms my nervous system. I don't want to get too attached to that thought because this ends the moment the roads are clear. It'll be nothing more than a blip in my memories of a time that I got to live out an extremely pleasurable, wildly intense sexual experience. An experience that will make our working relationship slightly uncomfortable, but we're both adults.

Having laid here long enough, the smell of Dallas surrounding me, I get out of bed—pulling the sheet with me to cover up—grab a shirt from Dallas' dresser, and pad across the hallway to the guest bedroom I'm staying in. Once in the bathroom, I crank the shower as hot as it will go and wait for the steam to fill the room and fog the mirror before stepping in.

The bathroom door opens and shuts loudly, causing me to jump, my hand covering my heart.

"Holy shit! You scared me! Don't you know how to make yourself known before you barge in on people?"

"Apparently not, now let me in. I'm sweaty from my workout."

"What are you doing, Dallas? Your shower is in your room."

"What's it look like I'm doing, princess? Showering with you."

I move farther into the water as he steps into the shower and closes the door behind him. He wastes no time crowding my space to get under the spray.

"FUCK, Blaire! It's hot as shit! How are you not burning?" he yells as he shuffles out of the spray of the hot water. I double over laughing at his reaction, but he seems genuinely concerned and pained, which makes me laugh harder.

"I like it this hot. It's relaxing."

"Of course it is. It's not burning *you* because it's hell water, you demon. Turn it down some so I can shower without melting the skin off my bones."

My laughter is uncontrollable at this big, strong, muscular man as he whines and shies away from some hot water. I reach up on my toes and turn the faucet in his direction, causing him to move farther away, against the tile wall, his leg bending up in defense.

"Blaire!" he yells, his eyes going wide.

"Okay, okay, okay!" I say through laughter as I move the faucet back and adjust the gauge to a more tolerable temperature. He moves into my space in one large step, grabbing my hips and jerking me to him, pushing my back against the tile wall.

"Glad to see you're mortal after all," I tell him.

"You're a menace."

"You love it," I chuckle as he brushes the wet hair from my face.

I don't know why that comes out of my mouth, and based on his reaction, he's feeling the same way. He doesn't move though, he just continues to look at me like I struck a chord, suspending us in a tense moment that neither of us moves to break. His eyes are so crystal blue they're almost transparent, and being the center of his focus makes my heart beat rapidly in my chest.

"Yeah, princess. I do," he says before he kisses me. His kiss is the same as it always is, passionate and demanding, and my heart tumbles around frantically, making me feel things that I shouldn't. His fingers slide into my hair, holding my head in his big palm, angling me exactly where he wants me. Our tongues caress in the center and I lift my leg, attempting to hook it around his waist. The height difference makes it hard, but he grabs my thigh with his hand and squats down, lining his thick length up with my core and working his way in with a few powerful thrusts, each piercing making him feel so much thicker.

After a moment, he's sliding home, and the feeling is indescribable. Those damn barbells rub the inside of me, making me see stars. He pounds into me, still holding my head and never breaking our kiss. He keeps his cock buried deep, grinding it into me, rubbing my clit on his pelvis. The hair on his body is trimmed short and the rough stubble adds a painful sensation to the pleasure, something I'm realizing I love. But deep down, I know it's so specific to him.

I moan into his mouth as he kisses me, his fist in my hair tightening brutally, his other hand digging into the flesh of my thighs. He fucks me hard and I love every minute of it.

"This isn't going to take long, princess. You feel too good. Always so good."

"I don't care, just don't stop."

I run my hands over his back, the muscles straining and strong, the water cascading down over us. He sucks my tongue into his mouth before pulling away and resting his forehead against mine, his hand never leaving my cheek, our breaths mingling.

"Fuck, fuck, fuck," he huffs, his mouth slightly parted, eyes hard on my own. He feels insanely good, hitting every part of me and lighting me up from the inside. My orgasm doesn't build, it slams through me like a freight train. My moans are smothered as he captures my mouth with his, pressing our lips hard together as he pumps into my body two more times before releasing. Our bodies tremble against each other as we ride this wave of bliss.

When we come up for air, the water has run cold, and I start to shiver. We take turns rinsing off quickly before Dallas opens the door and grabs a huge fluffy towel, wrapping it around me as I step out. He steps out behind me, grabbing one for himself and drying off. It's bizarrely comfortable and domestic.

"Hungry?" he asks.

"God, yes."

We dry off and throw on comfy clothes, Dallas in a pair of black, low-hanging joggers, and me in one of his T-shirts. Spending the last few days without panties has been a bit strange, but with how often Dallas wants to be inside me, it's been beneficial. Speaking from experience, he's the kind of man that will rip them off you if they stand in his way. We move to the kitchen and work together to make pancakes when his phone alert starts to go off in rapid succession, vibrating on the bar in front of us. Then it starts to ring.

"I should answer this to make sure everything's okay."

"Of course, I'll finish these."

He grabs his phone but only walks to the other side of the bar, answering the call.

"Hey, Momma."

My heart squeezes. I've never been able to say those words and I have to swallow down the envy. I try not to eavesdrop, but he isn't doing anything to make his conversation private. I focus on my task, flipping the pancakes and watching them cook on the flat top.

"Merry Christmas to you and Dad, Mom."

My eyes go wide, and I look at him, his equally as large. It's Christmas? I quickly do the math in my head. Kinsey's birthday was on the twenty-third. I've spent two nights here so far. Holy shit, it's Christmas Day. I woke up Christmas morning in my boss' bed and then was fucked by him in his shower. We've been so preoccupied living in this little bubble it seems we both forgot the date. His house isn't decorated at all for the holiday, so it wasn't even on my radar. Christmas is usually a sad reminder of how alone I am. I have a few traditions of my own that I hope to share with my family one day, but I don't go all out and celebrate. Dallas finishes up his phone call, talking to his mom, dad, and sister, Kinsey. I plate our pancakes just as he's returning to the kitchen.

"Looks like we've been a little preoccupied and forgot about Christmas."

"Yeah, I guess so," I say with a bit of a fake laugh, slightly uncomfortable with the situation.

"Do you need to call your parents and grandparents?"

I stiffen, my body tense, my hand hovering with the spatula extended to place it in the sink.

"I, uh, my phone died sometime yesterday. I'll reach out to them later."

He doesn't ask any follow-up questions but moves in front of me, putting his hands on my hips, his touch light and comforting. I relax into him, releasing a deep breath. He leans down and kisses my cheek, sweetly.

"Merry Christmas, Blaire."

"Merry Christmas, Dallas."

We spend the rest of the day on the couch, taking turns picking Christmas movies and eating an obscene amount of popcorn. I wanted to string it together to make a garland, but Dallas lacks the string and needles. Being with him is the complete opposite of what I thought it would be. He's so much more complex than the brash, arrogant dickhead I see at work. He has a huge heart, loves his family more than anything in the world, and is one of the most genuinely caring people I've ever met.

After being locked up with him for days, I've learned that the brute side of him comes out of pure protection over what and who he loves most. The distillery is one of those things, and regardless of his own twin brother hiring me and his younger brothers and parents supporting it, I am the sole representation of the disruption to what he loves. I shouldn't feel guilty because I love my job more than anything, but I do.

"Favorite candy?" he asks.

"Twizzlers Pull 'n' Peel, on the rare occasion I eat candy. You?"

"Twix bars. Favorite music genre?"

"Post Malone."

"That's not a genre."

"I will fight you on this. He can do any and all genres, so he is a whole genre himself. Don't knock him because my claws will come out."

"Touchy! Okay, favorite song?"

"'Chemical' by Post Malone. You?"

"Wow. I listen to everything, but right now it's, 'Feel Like That' by Sublime and Stick Figure. Dogs or cats?"

"Neither. Especially not cats. Never cats. You?"

"Dogs. Can't stand cats. They're temperamental and I swear to fuck they hold grudges."

"Alright, it's your turn, we've already watched *A Christmas Story*, *Jingle All the Way*, *Home Alone*, and *Die Hard*, which isn't a Christmas movie, by the way."

"Agree to disagree."

"Fine, with that logic, I'm picking *A Nightmare Before Christmas*."

"That's a Halloween movie."

"Like hell it is, Dallas! You made me sit through *DIE HARD*. And Halloween should be celebrated year-round because it's the best."

"You're one of those adults who dress up still, aren't you?" he asks.

"Oh, I absolutely am. And I splurge on all the candy and love giving it out to all the kids."

"That's cute. What do you dress up as? I want to picture it, paint it for me."

"You're an idiot. This year I dressed up as a witch, the year before that, Wanda Maximoff, before that, a zombie Princess Ariel, which only went over well with the older kids . . ."

"That's actually pretty awesome. Maybe next year you can dress up as a schoolgirl for me."

I swallow hard at his words and look away. There won't be a next year with him and I need to remember that. I pick up the remote and find *A Nightmare Before Christmas* and turn it on, relaxing into the songs and story of one of my favorite movies. After the movie is over, we work together to make grilled cheese sandwiches and tomato soup for dinner. We eat together in silence, but the tension is thick and strained, my walls slowly being put back in place. It was so easy to get caught up in how effortless it was being alone with him. But this doesn't change anything. I need to focus on creating a life here in Aspen Ridge, and that banks on keeping my job. You don't get that by sleeping with your boss, who has no idea who you actually are.

"I'm exhausted, I think I'm going to bed," I say after we clean up from dinner.

"I'll meet you there, want a bath first?"

While that sounds incredible, I know it's not a good idea. Baths are sweet, romantic even. That's not what this is.

"Raincheck? I think spending the entire day being a couch potato actually made me more tired." Which is a lie. After the sleep I got last night in Dallas' bed, I'll be lucky if I can sleep tonight. Clearly reading me like he always does, he nods but doesn't push. Which is appreciated.

"Yeah, maybe tomorrow. I'll let you get some sleep."

"I had a good day, Dallas. Merry Christmas."

"I had the best day, princess. Merry Christmas."

I head to bed, working through my sad attempt at a nighttime routine, using water to wash my face, and brushing my teeth with the spare toothbrush. Snuggling up under the blankets of the guest bedroom isn't the same as sleeping in Dallas' bed with his strong arms wrapped around me. Even if it was for only one night, it was the peace he somehow brought me that carried me through a night of sleep like I've never had before.

I lay on the soft sheets with the blankets wrapped tightly around me and stare out the big window again. The moon isn't as bright tonight, blocked by Aspen Ridge's near-constant cloud cover, but it looks like the snow has finally stopped. I lay here and think about the last few days and how quickly everything changed. I do everything I can to convince myself that falling for my boss is a terrible, awful idea, until sleep claims me.

I'm wide awake, never able to fully rest since moving in with the Cains. The turn of my doorknob sets alarm bells off in my head and I quickly roll to my side, squeezing my eyes shut, hoping that he'll just go away. The door opens for a moment before closing again and I hold my breath tightly. Maybe it was just Sherry checking that I didn't sneak out. I wait in silence for a moment before the soft patter of his steps comes closer and closer to my bed. My body begins to shake, fear racking my limbs. Flight or fight aren't the only two options. Sometimes fear has such a strong grip that you're frozen.

"I know you're awake, Blaire. I know you're waiting for me. I can smell your arousal calling to me."

I don't move. I don't breathe. I hate my life. I hate that my parents were coked-up drug addicts who would rather shoot up than take care of their child. I hate the foster care system. I hate that I don't have any power or control. I hate my body and the attention it brings.

His rough hands drag the blanket off of me, exposing my body to him. I purposefully wear as much clothing as possible in hopes of deterring him. I never want to give the wrong impression and am so aware of what men see and want. His hand dips under my sweatshirt and I lock my arm down to prevent him from going any higher.

"Don't play hard to get. I know you want this. Let Daddy take care of you." My stomach turns while my head swims with what to do. His hand starts to dip south, and I no longer have control over my body, I jerk upright and throw up all over my blankets, my body emptying itself from the fear and adrenaline coursing through my bloodstream.

"You disgusting bitch!" His hand comes down hard and fast across my cheek, bouncing my head off the wall next to me. "Clean this fucking mess up. I'll be back, Blaire. This is happening. You owe me for all the shit we do for you."

"Baby, it's okay. Blaire, wake up, it's just a nightmare, you're safe. Baby, come back to me."

I'm pulled from my nightmare by Dallas' voice, and his body surrounding mine. I'm tangled in the bedsheets, my body drenched in sweat, and my chest heaving as I gasp for air. My eyes fly open to find him in only his briefs, one big arm wrapped around me, the other brushing the hair out of my face and cupping my cheek.

"There she is. Breathe. You're at my house in my guest room, you're safe. Just breathe for me, yeah?"

The nausea settles as I gain control over my breathing. His smell envelopes me in a warm caress, and I allow myself to lean into it. I've never been able to calm down after one of these nightmares so quickly. But right now, I feel so comforted, so safe—a first for me.

"That was some nightmare, princess. Are you okay?"

"No . . . I'm really not." My voice is hoarse, barely audible. I must have been screaming. I wait for embarrassment to wash over me, but it doesn't come.

"C'mere." Dallas untangles me from the sheets and crawls under them with me, pulling my body flush against his. His body is warm and envelopes me completely, his arms wrapping around me, his hand running up and down my spine. I take a deep inhale of his scent and my heartbeat slows. Wrapped in a bubble of comfort that I've never experienced before, I rest my head on his large chest and listen to his steady breathing, his calm heartbeat. Sinking into him, I allow myself this rare moment of safety.

"Sleep. I've got you. I'll chase all your demons away."

Tears escape my eyes, because for the first time in my life, I don't feel alone.

dallas

WAKING UP TO BLAIRE'S SCREAMS FROM MY GUEST bedroom had me hauling ass across the hall to get to her. I wasn't prepared to find her fighting something in her sleep, tossing and turning, while her voice turned hoarse from her cries. Comforting her was the only thing I could do; I can't fight something that isn't in front of us. Her warm body is tucked into me, and I let my hand roam her soft skin to soothe her. She fits so perfectly in my arms, and I want nothing more than to hold her and give her peace.

I've never wanted this before; to comfort someone so affectionately and intimately. Fuck, even kissing. That's always been a hard line for me. Kissing leads to feelings and I haven't found anyone that I've ever wanted to chance it with. But kissing Blaire is a need. I struggle the rest of the night between what could be terrorizing her sleep and the aftermath of the last few days together. Can I really just go back to normal after this? Can I walk away from this woman and not have her again?

I hold Blaire until the morning when she starts to wake. She's still on her side, her thigh thrown over my hip, her head nuzzled into my chest. I never knew it could feel so good to have someone wake up in my arms like this. Her sleepy eyes flutter open, giving me my first glimpse of the stormy blue hue.

"Good morning."

"Hi. What time is it?" she asks, her voice groggy from sleep.

"Doesn't really matter when we're snowed in, does it?"

"Your nickname really is perfect, you do know that right?"

I swat at her ass and she giggles, moving away from me. She stands from the bed, and I'm surprised at the feeling of disappointment that washes over me. I want to pull her back in here with me, keep her wrapped up in my arms the rest of the day.

"Meet you in the kitchen?" she says sheepishly. Her posture is all wrong and it immediately makes me nervous. Her arms are folded across her chest, her shoulders slumped forward. I'm hoping that it's just that she wants me out so she can do her business in private, which is stupid since I've been inside her in every way imaginable. I get up and kiss her forehead.

"I'll make some coffee. Take your time."

I leave her to do her thing, stopping by my room to pull on sweats and grab my phone from its charger. While coffee brews, I pull up my texts and get caught up on the missed messages. I scroll through two days' worth of texts in my sibling group chat and pause to read the last few.

Liam: I'm over this shit

Carter: You're over it? I'm stuck here with you. I'm over it.

Liam: You're such a whine ass

Kins: It's not terrible. But I'm at Mom and Dad's. It's been a good break.

Carter: Whatever Kins. Singing the ABC song got you that tired?

Kins: Hey! I can only handle one dickhead brother and that spot has been claimed! Cut the shit!

Sawyer: Will you all shut the fuck up? It's a snowstorm, it'll pass. We've been through it before

Kins: Yeah, but it's over Christmas! We didn't get to be together!

Carter: Says the CEO who's holed up in his big house with his wife

Liam: Kinda a low blow man. We're stuck here keeping everything running and making sure pipes don't freeze and we don't lose power.

Sawyer: There was no fuckin way I was leaving Ivy home alone while pregnant, kiss my ass

Same shit different day, apparently. I shoot off a quick text so they don't send out search and rescue because of my silence.

Me: Jumping in here to give proof of life. Otherwise, I'm checking out. Talk to all you fuckers later.

Next, I check the ones from my mom. She's the sweetest woman and has a heart of gold. You'd have to, to successfully raise five humans. Out of all the relationships, she and I are the closest. I leaned on her a lot growing up, and when I was nineteen, things went to total shit when Sawyer's long-term girlfriend, who happens to be Ivy, took off without saying goodbye. He slipped into depression, rarely getting out of bed. Our dad still worked long hours at the distillery and our brothers were still a bit young. I stepped up and took care of things to make life easier on her.

Mom: You doing okay over there by yourself my boy?

Me: Hey momma, sorry for the late reply.

I hesitate for a moment, thinking it through, my fingers hovering over the keyboard.

Me: I'm actually here with someone

She responds right away.

Mom: Blaire?

Me: How'd you know?

Mom: Beautiful girl. I had my suspicions that something was going on.

Me: I could never fool you. I'm really into her but she's got these walls up, she'll only let me in so far

I laugh at that. Blaire's got no qualms with letting me in deep in every other way, but emotionally? She's only giving me so much.

Mom: Just takes time. You really like her?

Me: Yeah. I think I do.

Mom: Well be sure and then just take it at her pace

Me: Thanks Mom. You two doing okay? Kins driving you all nuts yet?

Mom: We're good, no complaints. You know we love winter.

Mom: I'll check in soon. Love you

Closing out of the chat, I bring up the local news and my heart stops.

The roads are clear.

Our little bubble is about to burst. I contemplate keeping it from her, playing stupid just to prolong our time together. I turn my phone on silent and toss it down on the bar top just as Blaire walks into the room. Her hair is wet and falls around her face in a wavy mess. I hate that I didn't have anything to make her more comfortable here, even if she hasn't complained.

Coffees poured, I hand a mug to Blaire and settle in on the leather couch next to her, in front of the fireplace. I take my first sip, relishing the slow, smooth taste as the caffeine goes down, needing the boost to help me through this conversation. The storm has trapped us here together for a while, but that's not to say she won't spook and lock herself in the guest bedroom or bolt the moment she learns the roads are cleared and she can go home.

I focus my attention on Blaire sitting next to me, looking nothing like she did when we were at Kinsey's birthday party a few days ago. She's wearing nothing but one of my large T-shirts, and I know she's completely naked underneath. Her hair is unbrushed, and her face has been bare of makeup since our first night here. It's such a stark contrast to when we arrived here together. I hated having her in my space, and now the thought of her leaving creates a sick feeling in the pit of my stomach.

The sight of her tear-stricken face, blotchy cheeks, red-rimmed, puffy eyes, and the sound of her screams has me wanting nothing more than to pull her hard into my chest to wrap her in comfort.

I set my mug down on the coaster and pull her legs into my lap, holding one of her feet in my hands, massaging it. She watches me intently, her mouth slightly agape as she relaxes into the couch, humming softly as my thumb rubs little circles up the center of her foot. I can't help but let the fixer in me lead this, it feels too good to love on this woman when she lets me.

"Are you okay?" I break the silence and ask her.

She stiffens. "I'm fine."

"Let me help you. Whatever it is." Either she's going to tell me on her own, or I'm going to contact our old friend, Wes, the PI, breaching all of her trust. But fuck if I'm going to sit back and let whatever play out when there's a chance I can get ahead of it. Not after what happened to Ivy. Not after we were almost too late. Nightmares happen, but not like that. She's battling something dark. She pulls her feet from my lap and curls into herself. Fuck, I'm losing her.

"Baby girl, that wasn't just any old nightmare. That was something much darker. Talk to me."

"I'm not your baby girl, Dallas. I said I was fine. Drop it," she snaps.

Fuck this shit. She's gotta make everything so damn difficult.

"No, I'm not going to drop it. I wake up to you screaming, tossing around in bed, and crying and you tell me you're fine?

Fuck that. That is *not* fine. Why won't you talk to me? Let me help you," I bite out louder than I meant to.

"No! You don't get to have access to all of me. Absolutely not. You don't get to order me around like you do when we fuck. I let you do that. That's all this is, fucking! I don't have to tell you shit and you don't get to demand it from me. Fuck you!"

She gets up and stomps to the guest bedroom, slamming the door behind her. How did this go so badly? She's hiding something and I'm going to figure out what it is.

I follow her to the bedroom and gently rap my knuckles on the door before opening it.

"Thought you should know the roads are clear. I'm in no rush for you to leave, but when you're ready to—"

"I'm ready."

She gets up and pulls on the dress she was wearing when we got here, minus the panties, which are hidden away in my end table drawer. Not willing to fight with her over this, I let her win this one, as much as it's hurting me to not fix it for her. Or to at least help her fix it.

"Okay. Let me pull some clothes on and I'll take you home."

By the time I'm ready to go, she's bundled in her winter coat and waiting at the door.

"It ends here, remember."

I look at her and can't hide my disappointment. I grab her face between my hands and kiss her like I've never kissed her before. It's firm but slow, my mouth gently coaxing hers to open, my tongue languidly meeting hers in the middle. She melts in my arms, and I moan into her mouth. I kiss her passionately, putting everything into it, doing my best to show her that I don't want this to be just sex. But because she's a goddamn stubborn brat, as I break away from her, I pull her bottom lip back between my teeth, dragging it out until she pops free from me, reminding her that I can be everything she needs.

She blinks rapidly before composing herself, not saying a word, but I know she's lust-drunk and confused. We walk into the garage, and I open the door, revealing a freshly plowed driveway. I'm thankful to Liam for being out at the ass crack of dawn and handling it all for us.

The drive is slow, and the roads are still pretty bad, but drivable. She's quiet, wrapped around herself and looking out the window.

"Where am I headed?"

"Hmm?"

"You still haven't told me where you live."

"Oh. Uhm. You can drop me off at Bean Haven."

"Like fuck I will. Where do you live, Blaire?"

She huffs and drags her hands down her face. What the fuck is she keeping locked up so tight?

"Actually, shit, I need to get my car. Just take me to the distillery."

"Do you hear me right now? No. I'm taking care of getting your car back to you. Now tell me where you live."

"Why are you so fucking pushy, Dallas? Boundaries. Learn to respect them. I told you to stop ordering me around. You're not my Dom. We're done fucking, so that ship has sailed. Drop me off at the distillery so I can pick up my car or I'll get out here and walk."

Her words sting and I don't bother hiding my wince and disappointment.

"Fine, princess. You win. Again. But I'm only going to follow you home so I know you got there okay. The roads are still shit."

Her eyes go wide for a split second, and if I hadn't glanced at her in that moment, I would have missed it.

What the fuck is she hiding?

blaire

Dallas drops me off at the distillery to pick up my car, only to find it buried under an exorbitant amount of snow. He forces me to sit in his warm car while he works to clean mine off and get it warmed up for me. When it's clear of all snow, he opens the passenger side door and helps me climb out of it.

"I'm good to go?"

"I'm following you, but yeah, it's running and warm now."

"You didn't have to do that, but thank you."

"I wanted to, Blaire. Now get in the car where it's warm, and drive slow."

I get settled in my car, feeling a mix of emotions, but thankful for all of his hard work, and pull out of the lot. I take it slow, Dallas behind me in his souped-up Audi. The snow is piled high on the side of the road from being plowed recently. Gray clouds cover the sky from the sun, blocking any view of the mountains, and the tall Sitka spruce trees are heavily blanketed with a thick layer of fluffy white snow, making everything look like a true winter wonderland. I'm thankful for the salt on the roads as I navigate back into town, but I still drive at a crawling pace.

Dallas is such an enigma. This brute of a man can be so compassionate and caring. A natural caretaker. My face flames at the reminder of him cleaning me up after sex, no matter how many times I told him I could do it myself. When he explained it was part of the dynamic, and that it makes him feel good to take care of me after and it gives him the opportunity to check in with me, it was hard not to swoon. He's so much easier to deal with when he's being a dick. I know what I'm getting and can handle myself. But when he's almost . . . loving? I'm at a loss. Letting him comfort me after my nightmare last night was a weak moment that I won't let myself repeat. I can't let him find out that I lied to him and Sawyer. And even if I could get over that part, it would change everything.

Dallas would regret everything we've done, he'd look at me differently, and worst of all? He'd handle me with kid gloves. It took me years, and lots of therapy through college, to learn and accept that what happened to me was just that. Something tragic and awful that happened *to* me, through no fault of my own. Someone who was supposed to be my caretaker, my safe space, exploited me and took advantage of their position of power over me in the worst way possible. I wasn't in control of what happened to me, but I am now, and I'll be damned if I let that evil bastard claim any more power over me and my future. I don't have a place for anyone who doesn't support that. It's bad enough that he still haunts my nightmares.

I know Dallas would look at me with pity, and he definitely wouldn't go all Dom on me. Not that I'm planning to repeat anything that's happened between us. But I'm positive he would recoil from me quickly, and I can't possibly survive that. Not after how he made me feel over the last few days. Which I still don't understand.

I take the turn for Main Street and I'm sure Dallas assumes I live on the other side of town. I drive past Rogue, refusing to let him know that I live in a rented studio above a tattoo shop, and instead pull into the only empty spot in front of Bean Haven. I turn off my car and climb out to see Dallas parked behind me, his arm resting on his rolled-down window.

"What do you think you're doing, Blaire?"

"What's it look like? Getting coffee. In case you don't remember, I didn't get to drink mine at your place."

I swear to all things holy the man growls at me. Actually growls.

"Wait here for me. I'm going to park around back."

"No! No. Absolutely not. I'm not going to walk into Bean Haven with you. Especially not in the morning. Please just go, Dallas. I'm good. I'm a big girl. I don't need a knight in shining armor. I'll see you at work."

He drops his head in defeat and my heart stutters in my chest uncontrollably. When he meets my eyes again, he looks almost hurt. But this is Dallas we're talking about here. That's impossible. Right?

"Alright. Be safe. I'll see you at work."

I nod to him before he drives off. I pull my coat tighter around me, concealing the fact that I'm wearing the clothes I had on at the party, and walk into the warmth of Bean Haven. Hannah is working behind the counter with her little girl on her hip. The coffee shop has the cutest bohemian vibe, and it feels so welcoming. The walls are a creamy off-white, while one was left with the traditional brick that the building is made of. "Bean Haven" is painted in a gorgeous loopy font above the counter in the prettiest green. Live plants hang from the ceiling in some of the corners, while others are in huge wicker planter baskets that she's draped Christmas lights over. There are four booths that line the wall across from the display case and register and one small table for two, where Ms. Nettie sits when it's too cold for her to sit outside. I walk up to the display case, which is surprisingly already filled with Hannah's mouthwatering creations.

"Morning, Hannah. Hi, little one." Hannah's three-year-old daughter, Charlotte jerks away from me, flipping her head the other way. Hannah bounces her on her hip and rubs her back.

"Don't mind her, she is so grumpy today. I had no one to

watch her this morning so she's been up since four with me so I could bake."

"Oh, Hannah, that's so hard. That's an early morning. Hopefully she'll nap for you?"

"I can only hope. How are things with you? Survived the snowstorm I see. You look good."

I know my cheeks pinken when I realize that I must have that "freshly fucked" look going on, and I'm suddenly very conscious of the fact that I'm not wearing any panties. I don't know if I'll ever be able to replicate the kind of sexual chemistry I found with Dallas. It has to be that once-in-a-lifetime kind of thing.

"I did. I love winter, and the break from life was pretty perfect. You guys do okay?"

"Oh yeah, we're good over here. I agree, the break was nice. You settling in and finding your groove here?" she asks. She's so damn sweet and genuinely seems interested in getting to know me.

"I am. I really love it here. Who wouldn't fall in love with this area? It's perfect."

"Aaaand what about a certain Cole Barnes?" she says with a wink, and I bristle, unsure how to answer. I don't want anyone to think something is there that isn't, but at the same time, there is no part of me that wants the town to know I just spent the last three days locked up fucking my boss at his home. Lucky for me, the door opens and the bell above it rings. Hannah and I both turn toward the door to see Liam stomping his feet clean of the snow caked to his boots.

He walks in, eyes focused on Hannah and Charlie.

"Hey, beauty. I'm sorry I wasn't here. I had to get everyone plowed out. She make it hard on you?"

"You know her better than to ask."

"Hi, peanut. Have you been good for Mama?" I watch as Charlotte reaches her hands out to Liam and he scoops her into his large arms. She snuggles into him, wrapping her arms around his neck, happy and content.

"I'll take her upstairs and get her back to sleep. See you at work tomorrow, Blaire?"

"Absolutely."

Liam takes Charlotte into the back, and I can't help but give Hannah that look.

"What?" she asks innocently.

"Tell me to shut up if I'm overstepping, but you two aren't . . ." I wave my hand around in front of me hoping she puts together what I'm asking.

"Me and Liam? No, never."

"Really? You guys are so comfortable together. Did he call you 'beauty?'"

"That comes from being best friends since we were Charlie's age. Literally. Yes, he did," she says with a laugh. "I was obsessed with *Beauty and the Beast* growing up and have been a lover of books for as long as I can remember. He's been calling me that for just as long. He's so good with Charlie, and I definitely need the help since I've only got my grandma. My sisters are always busy doing their own thing when they're home. I swear they only show up around the holidays lately. Liam's parents help a lot, too, but with his dad's medical issues, I try not to lean on them too much."

"I get that. Are your parents not in the picture?"

"Oh, they are. They're great. But they're snowbirds. They live in San Diego from early October through April. They hate winter. Seasonal depression is real for my mom, so my dad whisks her away to the sun."

"God, could you imagine? What a life."

"What about yours? How do they feel about you living away?"

I try to keep my features casual and inwardly cringe. I was so lost in the easy flow of conversation that I inadvertently opened myself up to get-to-know-you questions. Idiot.

"You know, they really don't mind at all. I'm so happy to be here, so that's really all that matters," I say with the confident smile I've perfected.

"Good for you, Blaire. Live your life, baby! Now, what can I get you?"

I take my warm chocolate croissant and coffee to go and head back into the winter chill. Deciding it's just easier to walk, I leave my car parked in front of Bean Haven and walk the two blocks down the street to Rogue. The silence and emptiness of my studio is a stark contrast to being at Dallas' the last three days.

After I devour the warm, perfectly flakey croissant, licking the chocolate from my fingers, I connect my dead phone to its charger and decide a long shower is needed to help get my head straight. Then, with nothing to do the rest of the day, I'm left with my thoughts and sketchpad.

The last three days spiraled out of control so quickly. It was the most fun and easy three days of my entire life, so naturally, it would end in a shitshow. I mentally admonish myself.

Sex has always been a difficult experience for me because of my history of sexual abuse. The few encounters I had before Dallas were short-lived. I need to be in control. We have to be in my environment, and I have firm limits. What man wants a woman who flinches when you're more dominant than she is? But with Dallas? My body handed everything over to him like it was the easiest thing in the world.

I lean my head back into the spray and let the hot water cascade over my body. The heat triggers goosebumps and Dallas' phantom touch. Grabbing my soap, I run my hand over my body, noticing every hickey, bite mark, and finger bruise Dallas left on me. My hands trace over my skin, realizing that there isn't anywhere that Dallas hasn't touched with his hands, mouth, or dick. My heart starts to quicken in my chest, my breathing increasing. I close my eyes and lean further into the water, letting it wash away the reminders of him and everything we did. I have to let this go.

I'd be okay if it weren't for him seeing one of my nightmares. It had to end there anyway, so it shouldn't matter if he saw me in such a vulnerable state. But it was the way my heart soared in fulfillment when he enveloped me in his arms, the way he comforted and protected me while I slept. That can't happen. I let him get too close, and if he's too close he'll know the truth. What would that mean for me? My job? My new life in Aspen Ridge? No. I can't let that happen, no matter how incredibly life-changing the last few days were with him. It's over. It has to be. I want it to be.

dallas

IT'S BEEN THREE DAYS SINCE I LEFT BLAIRE STANDING IN front of Bean Haven. Three days spent going fucking crazy and taking it out on everyone around me. My house is empty without her in it, her absence so noticeable that I've been filling my time, trying to be anywhere but there. Her smell has almost left altogether, and it pisses me the fuck off. My brothers have had enough of my shit and they won't even box with me anymore, so tonight I have plans to meet up with Reid. Man is six foot four and over two hundred pounds of pure muscle. Ivy nicknamed him Drogo, and she's actually spot-on. He's even got the long hair and tattoo thing going on. My brothers and I aren't small guys, but none of us have been stupid enough to take Reid on in the ring. Sawyer jokes that it'd be two hits, one from Reid and one as we hit the ground. But I'm feeling just worked up and crazy enough to take the fucker on.

It took me an hour after I dropped her off in front of Bean Haven to send a text to Wes, the private investigator, asking him to look into Blaire and her background. Not too long ago, Sawyer asked me what I would do if my girl was in trouble and whether or not I'd breach her trust to get ahead of the problem. I didn't hesitate. There's nothing I wouldn't do to protect and care for what's mine. But is Blaire mine?

My brother drones on in front of me from behind his desk while my thoughts are lost to Blaire. I've given her space but I'm not happy about it. She spooked, and I don't know how to make it better without her getting even more cagey. As if I summoned her from my thoughts, her voice pulls me back to the present.

"Excuse me, Sawyer?" Blaire peeks into the office after knocking lightly, nerves written all over her pretty face. She avoids meeting my eyes and it makes me angry as fuck. Like I didn't have my tongue in her pussy a few days ago. Like she doesn't know what it feels like to have my cock buried inside her.

"Come on in, Blaire, what's up?"

"Could we have a moment to speak privately?" Sawyer looks at me cautiously, unsure how to navigate the situation. I haven't come right out and told him what happened between us, or how I'm feeling, but he's my twin, and he knows something is up. I don't take any chances and speak up for him.

"I'm not leaving if that's what you're insinuating, Blaire. Feel free to talk with me here." I gesture to the seat next to me and she shifts on her feet before pushing her wild red hair behind her ears. Fuck, she's so damn beautiful.

"Okay. Well, I'd like to request some time off from work. I know this isn't ideal with everything going on here, but I have a family emergency that I need to take care of as soon as possible." I sit up straight, cock my head to the side, and study her. She still won't fucking look at me. What the fuck is going on?

"Is everything alright?"

"Yes and no. I just need to handle some things, my grandparents need me to visit as soon as I can get leave from work. The sooner the better."

She lives with her goddamn grandparents. I recline further into my seat and do my best to appear relaxed, even though this news just put me on edge. It takes all the control I have not to call her out in front of Sawyer, but I know by now that cornering her will only ensure her claws come out.

"Of course. Send Dallas and Carter over everything that you have on your plate this week and we'll take care of it. Let me know when you plan to leave and when to expect you back."

"Thank you, Sawyer. I appreciate it. I know this isn't ideal. I'd like to try to leave tomorrow morning. I'll get to work right now on wrapping things up to send them and hope to be back shortly after the new year."

"I don't want to pry, so just let us know if you need anything, yeah?"

"I will. Thank you."

I watch as Blaire hurries from Sawyer's office, leaving the door open behind her. Body on autopilot, I stand and follow her, not giving an ounce of shit what impression my shithead brother gets from it. I catch up to her in front of a utility closet, and without thinking, I grab her arm and yank her in behind me, kicking the door shut. She spins on me, her eyes shooting daggers in my direction, her mouth parting to lash me with whatever vicious words she has on reserve. I don't plan on giving her the chance though, and my mouth collides with hers, my hands threading through that wild fucking hair I can't get enough of. My kiss is just as brutal as always, bruising, devouring her mouth like I need it to live. Maybe I do.

She meets me in the middle, her tongue pushing through and clashing with my own. Fuck, I missed this. The way she feels in my arms, the taste of her kiss. And it's only been a few days. I yank her closer to me, her breasts pushed against my chest, my already hard cock pressed against her lower abdomen. Her hands roam my back as her body melts into mine. I tighten my hold on her hair and slow our kiss, nibbling on her bottom lip, pulling her head backward to arch her neck, forcing her to look up at me.

"Now that you're nice and compliant, wanna tell me what the fuck that was back there?"

Her eyes go wide, the submissive and dominant sides warring

with each other in her pretty little head. "Talk, Blaire." Her body slackens in my arms, her eyes closing in defeat. I wait, giving her the patience she deserves, but knowing full well I'm not letting her leave this closet until I've got the answers I need to help her. Unable to stop myself, I gently trace her hairline with my fingers, tucking a strand of hair behind her ear. Her eyes flutter open and the look on her face stuns me. It isn't lust, or that vile little attitude she likes to give me. It's a look I don't ever want to see on her face again.

Fear.

"Hey. Talk to me. What's got you so worked up?" I rub my hands up and down her arms as a tear slips free from her eye. That's all it takes. One tear. My body softens toward hers, wanting to do everything in my power to make sure I never see another tear that isn't from happiness or pleasure ever again.

Wiping her tear away with my thumb, I lean down to kiss her again. I take her tenderly and kiss her like I've never kissed anyone but her. Cautious to take my time, worshiping her mouth in a slow, passionate kiss that makes my heart beat erratically in my chest. Those plush lips like satin pillows against my own drive me crazy. Whatever she's about to tell me, I'm certain that no matter what it is, I've got her. I pull back and open my eyes, finding hers glassy and vulnerable. I've never seen her like this before and it rattles me. I'd do anything to help her, she's just got to talk to me.

"I just can't, Dallas."

"Princess, *please*." Her eyes dart around the room, looking everywhere but at mine. I can't let her pull back from me now. "You said you live with your grandparents. Why do they need you to come visit if you live with them?"

Her eyes snap back to mine, her mouth parting slightly. That got her attention, and she realizes her misstep because it's written all over her face.

"You ready to tell the truth now? You know I don't like repeating myself, but you need to start talking or we can go back into my brother's office and you can explain it to both of us." She rears back like I smacked her, her reaction catching me off guard. Fuck, I knew the moment the words left my mouth it was the wrong thing to say. She takes several steps back, her armor firmly back in place, and I know I've lost her.

"They're visiting family. It's none of your business. It's a family emergency. Not a workplace one. I requested emergency leave, and I am taking it because I have no other choice. Butt out." Her shoulder bumps purposefully into me as she yanks open the closet door and storms out. I drop my head back in a huff.

"FUCK!" Why does she have to be so goddamn difficult? I want to shake the shit out of her. Taking a moment to try to settle down, I spot a black object in the corner of the room with boxes stacked around it.

Fucking Gloria.

Defeated and pissed, I push my favorite chair to my office, finishing up my tasks to get this miserable day over with and head to Dom's to expel some of this shit brewing inside me before I explode.

Reid's stepping out of his truck as I'm pulling into Knockout, energy coursing through me at a volatile rate.

"Hey, man. How's life?" he asks.

"Shit. Ready to beat the shit outta something."

"Happy to help, you sure as shit can try."

Reid's not a trained fighter. Sure, he'll knock around a heavy bag like it's an inflatable, but he doesn't fight unless he has to. He's more of a weightlifter and runner. I know I got his ass in both speed and experience, even if one of his punches is enough to send me to sleep for a month.

After wrapping up and stretching, we climb into one of the boxing rings. Tapping gloves in the center, I don't hold back. My first punch lands on his ribs, and even through the gloves, it's like connecting with a concrete wall, the reverberations spreading through my fist and up my entire arm. I bounce on my feet and shake my hands to my sides. He keeps his hands up to block his face but otherwise lets me slam my fists into him.

"Fucking fight back, Reid!"

He shoves me off of him.

"Why don't you tell me what's up your ass, huh?"

I send a right hook to his face that he narrowly dodges.

"Dallas! You know this is fucking stupid, man. I'm not going to hit you back. Just get it out of your system."

I ignore him, and instead, land two quick jabs to his ribs, pain ricocheting again through my arms. This time he does hit back, one solid punch, right to my face. I stumble back onto the ropes, tossing my arm over it to hold myself up as blood pours from under my eye.

"What's got you so riled up that you wanted to get in here with me? No one is crazy enough for that."

I snap. The pressure of the last week bubbling over to an all-time high that I can no longer contain.

"Blaire! That's what's gotten into me. Fucking Blaire! She's under my skin like a fucking disease that I wouldn't shake even if I could. I'm obsessed with her, every piece of her. I don't even know how it happened. We hooked up once and then got stuck at my house during the snowstorm and everything changed. But she's hiding something big, man, and she won't fucking let me in. She won't even tell me where she lives! Fuck!" I pace around the mat, trying to calm myself down. "When she got here she said she lived with her grandparents, and I didn't even think to ask who they were. Today she asked for leave from work for an emergency and I caught her in a straight-up lie. She bolted and I don't even know how to fucking find her. So instead of spending my night going fuckin' door to door all over Aspen Ridge looking for her, I'm here to fucking hurt somethin'."

Reid's quiet as he climbs out of the ring and degloves, pulling the elastic out of his hair and retying it so it's out of his face. He gathers himself before facing me, throwing a towel in my direction.

"Look, brother, I can help you, but this shit sucks. I'm only telling you this because you said she's got an emergency and that doesn't sit right with me knowing what I know."

"How the fuck do you know anything? Do these girls just flock to you and open up?"

He laughs at that, but the humor is lost on me.

"Ivy and Blaire were both right place, right time. I ran into Blaire when she first got here, before she even interviewed with Sawyer. She needed some help, and I was in a position to give her what she needed at the time."

So help me, if he's fucked her I'll fucking kill him.

"Get that dumbass look off your face, I've never touched her you stupid fuck. What is with you and your brother? You're Neanderthals. I gave her a place to stay."

"She's at your fucking house?" Rage boils to the point of overflowing, especially after he rolls his eyes at me.

"No. I let her rent the room above Rogue. It's a studio and has everything she needs while she gets on her feet."

"Because her grandparents don't fucking live here. She's above Rogue?"

"As far as I know. I'm not telling you more. You gotta ask her.
"

"Thanks, man. I owe you."

I'm out the door and hauling ass into my car to get to the bottom of this. Whatever she's going through, I'll be damned if she goes through it alone. Within ten minutes, I'm pulling up and parking on the side of the street in front of Rogue Tattoo. I walk around back, find the stairs that lead to the second floor, and take them two at a time, pounding my fist on the door. Blaire opens the door meekly, and her tear-stricken face nearly takes me to my knees.

"Baby." My voice softens as I push open the door and reach for her, bending and picking her up, and carrying her into the room, kicking the door shut behind me. In the center of the room is a futon, and I sit us down on it. Her hands come up to cup my face, angling me from side to side while she looks me over.

"Dallas, your face. What happened? Are you okay? We need to clean this up."

In my hurry to get to her, I completely forgot about my busted face and realize I probably look alarming.

"I'm fine. I was boxing. Are you?"

She closes her eyes and tears break free, I watch for a moment as they trickle over her perfect freckles and cascade down her beautiful face, debating on the best way to get through to her.

"Princess, I'm addicted to you in ways I can't explain. When I'm not with you, I crave you. And it pisses me the fuck off."

She looks up at me then, eyes curious, darting back and forth between my own.

"But I wouldn't change a fucking thing. I'm in this. Whatever is going on, I want you to know that I have your back. I'm not going anywhere."

She takes a deep breath, shock morphing into worry.

"This is going to change everything, Dallas." I already guessed as much. What she hasn't figured out yet is that I'm so damn gone for her that she could tell me she dismembers bodies in her basement and paints murals with their blood in her spare time and I would probably ask if I could join her just to spend more time together. These few days away from her have been miserable after knowing what it's like to have her.

"Try me. I don't scare easily."

She takes an audible gulp of air into her lungs before talking.

"My parents weren't in the military. I wasn't raised around the world. I've never even left Washington. My parents are Curtis and Natasha Hollis, two drug addicts who lost custody of me when I was five when they were arrested on drug distribution and child neglect charges." She pauses and takes a deep breath. My head is reeling with this new information. My poor girl.

"I was put into foster care and bounced around quite a bit.

No one wants a five-year-old kid with drug addicts for biological parents. Turns out they didn't want me at any age, because I was never adopted after my parents' rights were relinquished." Blaire wipes away a few rogue tears while I spin out of control and process what she's saying. I knew she was hiding something, but this, this I don't even know what to do with. I thought she came from a happy home and moved all over the world. Anger courses through my veins at what she's been through, it wars with sympathy and my need to fix her pain, forcing me to work hard to keep my breathing steady so she doesn't spook again. Even though my mind is reeling, I rub my hands over the soft skin of her arms.

"Tell me more, baby. I want to hear the whole story," I plead with her, hearing the tremble in my voice. She takes a deep breath before speaking again, her voice barely above a whisper, her hands trembling. I grab them, holding them between mine, hoping that I'm providing the comfort and safety I know I can bring her.

"While I lived in a total of seven homes, only one was a nightmare and scarred me for life. The last home I was in was for almost a year and a half. From sixteen through right before I turned eighteen. It was pretty bad. The nightmare I had at your house, they come and go still. I don't know what my triggers are, but they sneak in sometimes and unfortunately very vividly portray the type of abuse I received."

"Fuck, Blaire. Whatever happened, I promise it wasn't your fault."

"I know that now . . . He harassed me. And beat me. And raped me. I lived in hell."

"Goddamn it," I whisper, squeezing my eyes closed tightly and trying to breathe through my nose, processing what she's been through.

"I'm sorry . . ."

I run my hands through my hair, doing my best to digest this. Moving directly in front of her, I hold her face in my palms, forcing her to look at me. "Why are *you* sorry? You have nothing to be sorry for and I don't want to hear you apologize for that again. That shit happened to you at no fault of your own. You did nothing to deserve that. Fuck, baby, don't ever apologize for that." Nausea rolls through me at the thought of this precious girl being harmed by some low-life piece of shit. She nods her head, chewing on the inside of her cheek.

"It went on for a while before one of my teachers saw some signs and pulled me aside. As a mandatory reporter, an investigation was opened and I was removed from the home, along with four of my foster siblings. He was charged with child neglect and endangerment, child abuse, sexual assault of a minor, rape, among other things, and got twelve years in prison."

"I can't believe what you've endured and survived. I'm so sorry. I'm at a loss for words."

I release her face and drop my back against the couch as the realization of what I've done hits me like a semitruck. I immediately panic.

"Jesus Christ, Blaire, I am so sorry. I had no idea. I never would have-I never would have been so demanding with you. Holy shit." I take a deep breath, feeling like the selfish dickhead that I am. It's hard to catch my breath as it sinks in, my chest aching in a way I've never felt before.

I fucking forced her.

I know her body was giving me all the signs, but I was still pushing her. "Please forgive me. I never would have been so dominant and forceful with you if I had known," I beg, dropping to my knees in front of her and grabbing her hands, bringing her palm to my mouth and kissing it.

"Stop. Dallas, please just stop. First, don't look at me like I'm damaged, I'm not. It took me years to understand that I did nothing wrong. That I didn't ask for what happened to me. It took me years to love my body again. Second, for the first time in my life, I wanted to give up my obsession with needing to be in control. It wasn't even really a choice, it just happened. The moment you were that way with me, something snapped into place, Dallas. I wanted to do whatever you asked or demanded or whatever you want to call it. It came naturally to me to submit to you for whatever reason. I'm still trying to wrap my head around it. I even did research this week to help understand it myself. There are tons of articles on how kink can help treat post-traumatic stress in sexual assault survivors. But the point is, I *wanted* it. I *still* want it, even though I shouldn't." Her eyelashes flutter closed for a brief moment as she whispers, "That's new for me."

I'm fucked. Because I know I should be reeling in anger toward myself right now for my role in our sexual encounters, but after hearing her confession, how can I be? Now I want to do the same research and find out how I can continue to help her heal from her past. I could kill the bastard who hurt her. I'm pissed at the system for making it possible for shit like this to happen every day. But I'll be damned if I make her feel bad. Handing over that control to me takes so much strength on her part, without the trauma. But with it? Fuck. I'm so damn proud of her. It also means she feels completely safe with me. But overall, this confirmed one solid thing for me.

She's mine.

And there's no way I'm walking away from her now. I'll walk through the belly of hell for this woman. No one will hurt her again.

Mine.

I pick her up by her ass, her thighs wrapping tight around my waist, and lay her back on the futon. I'm eager for her to take her power back and experience exactly what she wants. She's the one who reigns here.

My fucking queen.

blaire

"WHY DO YOU CALL ME PRINCESS?"

"Because you're a goddamn brat." He looks at me, his face darkening, lust filling his eyes even though we've been at it all night. "And calling you my queen in front of anyone else wouldn't have been appropriate."

My smile must reach my eyes because he leans in and kisses under each of them.

"Fuck, I love your freckles. It's like someone painted them on, just a dusting under each of your eyes. You're so beautiful."

"As much as I love Dickhead Dallas, I'm really enjoying this sweet side of you, too. Who knew it was in there?"

"So, what happened today? Who do you need to go visit if you've got no grandparents?"

"Yeah, well. I panicked because a man walked into the distillery that looked exactly like my abuser and I spiraled. Exactly like him. So much so that I had convinced myself it *was* him, Dallas. The court has to notify me when he's released, but I've changed my address so many times that I assumed I didn't get the letter. I just had to get out of there. With New Year in a couple days, I thought it best that I just hide out for a bit."

"Baby, I won't let anything happen to you. No one will ever hurt you again."

His words go straight to my heart, and I know that I'm falling rapidly for this man. I couldn't stop it if I tried.

"Have you done an inmate search? I can look for you if you give me his name."

"Not yet. I will. Thank you, but I'll handle it."

"You don't have to handle things on your own anymore. I'm not going anywhere."

"I've just never had that before. It's not going to be easy for me to just lean on someone and accept help. I don't know how to do that because I've only ever had myself to rely on. Everyone else has let me down or hurt me. You're going to have to be patient with me. If you're up for that."

Ever so softly, he cups my cheeks with his large hands, cradling my head between them, his thumbs gliding softly across my cheekbones.

"I'm not going anywhere. I don't care how long it takes, but you'll believe me one day. I'll show you."

My eyes flutter closed at his sweet words just as his lips connect with my own. The kiss is soft, almost loving, and as I moan into his mouth, the restraint I know he was using snaps. His hand moves to the back of my head where he tightens his grip around my hair, pulling my head back to arch my neck. He rubs the coarse scruff of his face across my jaw and nuzzles into my neck before biting and sucking at the soft skin of my shoulder.

"I just, I'm not ready for everyone to know about us. Until we figure out what exactly this is."

He moves his face in front of mine, looking at me dead-on, his eyes full of concern.

"Then we keep it to ourselves. Your secrets are safe with me. But I want to know them all." He licks up the length of my neck, scattering goosebumps in his wake, pulling the lobe of my ear between his teeth before whispering, "I want all of you, Blaire." He licks again, back down to my shoulder, and nibbles, descending further to the tops of my breasts. "Every raw and bare piece." He continues working his way down my body, kissing, biting, sucking. I arch into him, his hands holding my hips flush with the mattress. "Every lie. Every truth." He pushes open my legs before settling between them, his face in front of my pelvis. He licks a line from hip to hip, biting at the soft skin there, lapping at me and sending waves of emotion and pleasure through my body, causing my heart to flip over itself into the abyss. I know without a shadow of a doubt that I'm starting to fall for this man. "I want it all, princess."

My breathing staggers as he looks up at me, there's no misunderstanding the conviction and truth written all over his face.

"Then take it all, my king."

He growls before dropping his face into my pussy, his wet tongue swiping through my center in that perfect way that he does. He's not gentle or slow, he's ruthless and demanding, and I love every minute of it. He swirls around my clit as two fingers are pushed into me, making that "come hither" movement deep inside me that has my eyes rolling into the back of my head. My climax hits hard and fast, and just as I start to crest, about to fall off that glorious euphoric cliff, he pulls away from me and sits up, grabbing my hips and pulling me onto that thick cock. I scream as my body ignites, clenching and throbbing around his length.

"You're so pretty when you come on my cock. Fuck, I love the way you squeeze me. You're so tight, Blaire."

He fucks me through it, and just as it starts to ebb, he licks his fingers and presses them down onto my clit. I spiral right back into that bliss that only he gives me.

"That's my good girl. Give it all to me. I'll take care of you."

"Dallas! Oh. My. God!" I scream, moaning unintelligible words that are muffled to my ears. My legs shake around his hips, my body spasming as I dig my nails into the sheets under me. I've never felt such pleasure before, and he holds it all. I trust him. That is the key.

I relax into the mattress, and he slows his speed. He pulls one of my legs over, shifting me to my side while his length is still firmly inside me, tucking my legs up high into the fetal position.

"Yeah, just like that, baby girl. Let me have my way with you."

His words are so filthy and go straight to my already drenched center. I know he feels me throbbing wildly around him. He grips my hip with one hand while the other digs into the flesh of my ass cheek. He's rough, bound to leave bruises on me, but I couldn't care less. All I want is for him to feel as good as he makes me.

"Fuck me, Dallas. Please. Hard."

He slaps my ass once, twice, three times before driving into me over and over. He sets a ruthless pace, pulling almost all the way out and slamming back in until his base is flush with my skin. I feel him everywhere. It's all-consuming. Heat rises through my body from my toes to my face—I'm engulfed by him.

Another orgasm builds, surprising me, and I arch into him as his body collapses on top of mine. I grab his face, kissing him hard, stealing the breath from his lungs. He pushes into me once more, staying deep as his cock jerks inside me, the warmth of his cum painting my insides. He releases my mouth and rests his forehead against mine before sliding to the side and pulling my body flush against his, tucking me into him. I work on catching my breath, grabbing his hand in mine and pulling him closer, holding it at my chest. He kisses my head before relaxing his body with mine.

"You're incredible. Let me stay the night with you. Please."

I stiffen in his arms.

"Dallas, we can't. I live above Reid's studio. It's bad enough you're here now. Wait, how did you find where I live anyway?"

"Reid."

"That fucking traitor."

"He kinda has that track record. He means well. But I don't want to talk about another man while I've got you naked in my arms," he practically growls.

I giggle and roll out of his hold.

"We need to take this slow. We've jumped straight to sex and sleepovers, and we need to back up some."

"I already agreed to it. I'll go at your pace. I don't fucking like it, but I'll do it."

Anxiety starting to dissipate, I shuffle out of his arms to stand on my feet and move to pick up his clothes, holding them out to him. He grabs my wrist instead and pulls me to straddle his lap. His hands go to my hips, squeezing the flesh in his palms.

"Mmm," he moans, nuzzling his face into my chest between my heavy breasts.

I pull back, bracing my hands on his shoulders and trying to put space between us.

"Dallas! No more, you need to go. It's late."

"Oh, you mean now?"

"Uh, yes! People can't see you here. I live downtown."

I start to panic again, looking around the room for my phone to check the time. Dallas grabs me, demanding my attention. His hands are on my face now, cradling me between his palms.

"Hey, listen to me. Everything is going to be okay. No one is going to find out your secret, no one is going to find out about us until you're ready."

He kisses my forehead before stepping away from me and pulling on his clothes. I pull out a shirt from my drawer and slip it over my head before walking him to the door, with my heart in my throat.

"Tomorrow, we'll act like everything is normal. I have no doubt you'll find some asinine way to piss me off and no one will know any better," he says while stroking his hand over my hair and tucking it behind my ears.

"And I'm sure you'll be just as grumpy and pig-headed as you always are."

He laughs and I smile up at him.

"I'll see you at work, princess."

I shut the door behind him, body racked with a multitude of feelings, and get ready for bed. Laying down on my bed for the night, I snuggle into my thick blankets, cocooning them around me tightly.

I lay in bed wide awake, like every night this week, waiting, anticipating when he'll come back for me. I know it's only a matter of time before he finds his moment and takes what he wants. Like I summoned the devil, my doorknob creaks as it's turned. Wishing it was clicking against the lock I'm not allowed to have, I hold my breath while the door to my bedroom is slowly opened. My heart pounds loudly in my ears, a steady drum that gets louder and louder.

I keep the blankets cocooned around me like a protective barrier, as if they could stop the monster entering my room. I know there isn't a God. This wouldn't happen if God was real. But that doesn't stop me from praying. To God, to anyone who will listen, end my suffering. I beg of you.

The blankets are peeled back, but I don't open my eyes. I go to the place I know that will keep my will to survive.

"You can pretend to sleep all you want. I know you enjoy this. This pussy doesn't lie when it gets wet for me."

My bottoms are pulled from my body, pain ricochets throughout, and my mind floats away as it dissociates. Someday I'll be away from this hell, someday I'll be married, I'll have a man who loves me, who protects me, who will make me feel safe and secure. We'll have a house in the woods, just the two of us, madly in love. I'll be successful, happy, and loved for once in my life, and none of this will matter anymore...

I wake heaving in breaths, looking frantically around my room as tears pool in my eyes, wishing like hell I could escape these nightmares. I lay back down into my blanket cocoon, steadying my breathing and trying to relax. I can't help but crave the warmth, safety, and comfort Dallas brings me.

Maybe I should have let him stay after all.

CHAPTER 21

dallas

WHEN I WAKE UP THE NEXT MORNING, I HAVE A PLAN IN place to show Blaire that I'm not going anywhere. I shower and get ready for work, dressing in a pair of denim jeans and a button-up shirt, and pull on my boots as I slip out the door. The drive into town this early in the morning is always beautiful, and I know that I take it for granted. Being born and raised in Aspen Ridge, with the mountains surrounding our town, I got used to them hovering over our existence.

Today the sun is peeking over the mountain range, casting a bright reflective glare off the snow in front of me. We're typically under constant cloud cover, which I thrive in, but the sun is welcome. I wonder what Blaire prefers. I pull onto Main Street and into a parking spot before pulling out my phone to text Sawyer.

> Me: Walking into Bean Haven. You want anything?

> Sawyer: Nah. Was already there this morning.

193

· · ·

How fucking early does he go in to work? I grab what I need from Hannah and head to the distillery, slightly nervous about surprising Blaire but knowing that I need to do this. I want this woman to realize that she isn't alone anymore, that I want to take care of her—that I enjoy it. The drive to work goes by in a blur, the roads still heavily caked with dirt and salt.

I stop by my desk, grab a Sharpie, and write on the side of her cup.

Not pumpkin spice

Picking up her chocolate croissant, I head to her office in hopes of beating her there. I knock softly on the door, and when I don't hear anything, I hesitantly open it. Free of her beautiful face, I slip into her office and leave her black coffee and pastry on the center of her desk before slinking back out and shutting the door softly behind me. Once back in my office, I settle into my chair and open my laptop to get to work when my phone chimes with an incoming text. My heart flips in my chest as I anticipate a text from Blaire about the surprise I left her, but it isn't her. My face falls in disappointment.

Ivy was added to the chat

Me: What is this blasphemy?

Sawyer: Be fucking nice, dickhead

Kins: Aww, sis! Why didn't I think to add you to this?

Carter: Cause you're too busy with a bunch of
snot nosed kids all day

Kins: Har-har. And why didn't you add her,
lover boy? Too busy getting your rocks off?

Carter: *Wink emoji*

Kins: *Vomit emoji*

Ivy: I wanted to invite you all to Barrel House
for New Year's Eve. I officially have the go-
ahead from the owners to create my own
menu and I thought you all would be good
guinea pigs.

Ivy: You can bring a guest obviously, but I'd
love to have you

Sawyer: They'll be there, baby, don't worry

My excitement is short-lived when I realize I can't bring Blaire as
my date since she wants to keep us a secret. I'll have to figure out a
way for her to get an invite from one of them. Ivy seems to really
like her, so it's not far-fetched that she would extend an invitation.

Me: Who's all going to be there?

Ivy: Outside of Sawyer and I? You all, the
Haven sisters and maybe Levi and Blaire who
might bring Cole but I haven't asked her yet.

One problem averted only to stumble into a new one. Like fuck
she'll be bringing Cole. She isn't seeing that dumb fucker again
and she had better make that damn clear to him and everyone else.
My blood pressure starts to rise at the thought of my beautiful girl

bringing Cole with her. I'll break his hands, finger by finger if he ever tries to touch her again. Blaire may not understand the relationship, or lack thereof, between Cole and me, but even without that knowledge, she dodged a bullet. He's a goddamn twat.

My phone chimes again, but this time Blaire's name pops up, and just like that, my mood is settled. Her text comes right after a photo of her coffee and pastry sitting on top of the white pastry bag.

Blaire: Was this you?

Me: And if it was?

Blaire: I'd say thank you.

Me: No need, princess. I hope you have a good day.

The next text is a photo of her smiling while holding the coffee cup. I bite my lip hard to stifle the groan that wants to release. This woman. She has no idea what she does to me. My cock hardens behind my zipper, pressing painfully against the fabric. I'm half tempted to fuck her senseless bent over her desk, but I control my urges and continue to check my emails. One in particular stands out to me.

Wes Draven Info you requested

A little late, asshole. I open his email to a link to download the file he put together on Blaire. Downloading the info, I save the file to my desktop. I don't have plans to open it, there's no need to breach her trust and privacy, right now at least. But if there's a rainy day and I need to in order to protect her, I won't hesitate, and I'll deal with the repercussions later. There isn't anything I won't do to keep what's mine safe. And she is.

Mine.

Barrel House is located in the cellar of an old brick building on Main Street. It's the only fine dining restaurant in Aspen Ridge and is open for lunch and dinner service. Ivy was hired there shortly after she returned to AR and is the head chef. Gotta give props where props are due, the girl can cook and create in the kitchen. The entrance is on the side of the building, down a set of stone steps that lead to a heavy steel door. Its speakeasy vibe is elegant while also being edgy. With exposed brick walls, hanging lighting, and emerald-green tufted booths, it fits with the Pacific Northwest vibe. The bar and tabletops are dark cedar wood with a matching green epoxy river through the center, similar to the one Blaire had installed in the distillery. By the time I walk in, everyone is already here. My eyes immediately spot Blaire, dressed in a pair of tight denim jeans that fit her curvy body like a glove, black boots that come to her ankles, and a leather jacket. My mouth salivates as I take her in. Her fiery red hair is down, framing wildly around her face. She's standing at the bar, her head thrown back in a laugh. Ivy touches her arm, laughing just as hard. My heart warms, satisfied and happy that she's finding her home here.

Kinsey and the Haven sisters are sitting on stools next to them —Hannah, Harlow, and Hailey. I wish I was joking. Their parents really did a number on those girls. The women all seem to be getting along, so I walk up to them to find out where my brothers are hiding. Blaire's eyes light up momentarily as she sees me approaching and it makes me feel damn good.

I lean in and give my sister a quick half-hug.

"Hey ladies, how are you tonight?" I don't miss the way that Hannah's sister, Harlow, checks me out, and apparently Blaire doesn't either. Her face morphs into one of jealousy and annoyance.

"Hey, Dallas. Haven't seen you since before Christmas. How are you?" Harlow asks.

I chance a look at Blaire, her face paling slightly before she turns to face Hannah, asking her something I didn't catch.

"I'm doing pretty great lately, Harlow. You doing good? When are you heading back to school?"

"I'm free until mid-January," she nearly purrs. Right in front of everyone, shamelessly. She's in her last year of college and it must be doing good things for her confidence.

"Well, enjoy your break," I say, my tone kind but clipped. I turn to face my sister-in-law. "Where are my brothers? Or did I just crash a girls-only New Year's Eve?"

"They're in the kitchen pulling out drinks and food. Sawyer was being his overprotective self and wouldn't let me carry the beer out."

"Good. I agree, gotta keep my niece or nephew safe in there. I'll be back. Ladies, good seeing you. I'm going to go find my brothers."

I excuse myself and walk through the large dining room and back to the kitchen where all of my brothers are, plus Reid. Lucky for everyone here, especially Blaire, Cole-fuckface-Barnes is nowhere in sight. Hopefully he's spending his New Year's Eve rutting into the hollowed center of a fucking tree stump.

"Hey, boys! How's everyone doing tonight?"

"Hey, man. 'Bout time you made it. Girls still keeping it together out there?"

"Got held up taking care of a few things. Yeah, they're doing good."

"Good, now help us carry all this out."

"Jesus, she made a damn feast of appetizers," I joke. But

honestly, there's tray after tray of food. She must think she's feeding an army, cause there's no way all of this will get eaten.

Sawyer points at each of us before speaking. "Yeah, she's been working hard on it, so you assholes better fucking eat it all."

We each grab what we can and carry it out to lay on the bar top. She's made cranberry brie bites, bacon wrapped dates, various dips, crab stuffed mushrooms, breads, tarts, crème brûlée, and so much more. Everyone praises Ivy before digging in.

"Okay, Blaire, why didn't you bring Cole?" Ivy asks, and I can't help but listen over my shoulder even though I'm a ways away from them and straining to hear.

"He's not my type. We went on one real date, and he was just a little pushy after, and I can't stand men who are so forward," Blaire says, and I snort.

"So, the date wasn't good? You brought him to my wedding, I kinda assumed . . ."

"He brought me to The Night Owl for our first date. Which is fine, I guess. But not my ideal first date."

"Okay, now I want to know, what is Blaire's dream date?"

"Oh gosh, that's actually pretty easy. He'd take me somewhere new, someplace that shows me who he is, somewhere I could experience what he likes through his eyes."

"Well, Blaire Hollis! I was not expecting that. I like it!"

And just like that, I know I'm taking Blaire on our first date and exactly where I'm taking her.

"What about you, Kinsey?" Ivy asks my sister.

"I'm so lame and such a homebody. Probably something intimate and quiet? I don't really date."

"What?" all of the women snap in unison at my sister. Her face pales and I stiffen, not liking her being put on the spot. My brothers all seem to feel the same as their body language changes as well.

"Well . . ." Kinsey sweeps her hand out to all of the men standing around with their arms crossed, visibly agitated. "I'm a Hayes, first of all, and second, I've got those four brutes for older brothers. No one has had the balls to touch me. And the ones who have? Well, why don't you ask Sawyer."

Ivy's head whips to her husband. But it's Harlow's big mouth that keeps Sawyer from being able to defend how he broke Alex Ford's hand when he caught him grabbing Kinsey's ass after a football game she cheered at in high school.

"Wait, you're not a virgin, are you? There's no way!" Harlow practically yells.

"Whoa! Whoa! Whoa!"

"What the fuck?"

"Nope! Do not answer that, Kinsey!"

"Shut your mouth, Lo!"

Our voices fight over each other as we all shut it down. Even Reid bristles, standing up straighter and clenching his fists.

"Lo, I love you, you're my friend, but definitely not a conversation to have in front of these four."

"Okay, so point made," Ivy declares, and at least everyone can laugh.

"How are things with Levi, Hannah?" Blaire asks innocently, probably not realizing it's another hot topic in the family. I look over at Liam as he tosses back a shot and pours another. He's been best friends with Hannah since we were all kids. While Levi has been out fucking around and skipping out on his parental duties to Charlie, Liam's been there. He's never admitted to having any feelings for Hannah, but I know he's just as protective of her as Sawyer and I are about our women.

Our women.

"Oh, it's rough. Per usual," Hannah declares.

"I'm sorry, I didn't know," Blaire says sweetly. It's such a contrast to the tone she reserves for me.

"Oh, god, it's fine. Why would you? No harm done. Levi is a selfish asshole. I was forced to grow up when Charlie came, and he chose not to. He's just never around. He's a smooth-talking deadbeat and most days I feel like I'm trying to force a square peg into a round hole."

I watch as Liam downs another shot.

The conversation flows the rest of the night, and I fall harder for Blaire. Watching her let loose and hang out with my family and friends, seeing that she fits so easily, fills me with pride. The only thing that's killing me is that I can't touch her. Can't pull her into my lap. Can't kiss her neck, or breathe in her sweet, sweet, jasmine smell. It's crazy that this wild woman ever drove me mad to the point that I didn't want her around. Even if the only reason I fought her presence was because I craved her, and it took everything in me to fight that desire.

Blaire excuses herself to the restroom and I wait for the break to sneak in behind her. Everyone seems occupied with conversation, so I slip off my stool and go after my girl.

I step into the women's bathroom, locking the door behind me while she's at the sink drying her hands.

"Dallas! Oh my god, no. Someone will catch us," she hisses, and she tries to shove me back out the door.

"Baby, no one is coming."

I stalk her until she's up against a wall, my hands going straight to her tits, massaging and lifting them. I love their heavy weight in my palms.

"Do you know how good it feels to be here with you this time and be able to touch you, knowing you won't push me away? All those other times I cornered you, fuck, it was so hard to hold back."

Her eyes flutter closed at my words, and when she opens them, she leans forward, wrapping her arms around my neck and hauling me closer. Her lips descend on mine, licking into my mouth and sucking my tongue into hers. I moan, deep and long, while pressing my hard-on into her abdomen. I push her backward, severing the connection of our mouths. Leaning into her space, I nuzzle into her neck, loving the evidence of me that she's been hiding all night with her hair. My love bites are peppered all over her, I know this isn't the only spot.

"You're coming home with me tonight."

"It can't happen, they'll know something is up."

"Did you honestly think I was going to let you go home by yourself? Or that I'd let you leave here with another man?" I growl into her ear while running my hand over her denim-clad ass, squeezing a palmful.

"I wouldn't leave with anyone else except for Reid. He's just a good friend."

"Not gonna happen, baby. The only man you're leaving with is me."

"How's that going to work when no one can know we're sleeping together?"

"Just trust me. I've got plans for how you're going to ring in your New Year, baby, and all of them involve you tied up on my bed."

"Fuck, Dallas, when you talk like that," she moans, pushing her chest into me, lifting her leg and trying to pull me in.

"Be a good girl and wait. It'll be worth it."

I give her ass one last squeeze before turning and walking out of the bathroom. I adjust my stiff cock behind my jeans before joining my family and friends back at the bar, ready to get the night over with so I can celebrate alone with my girl at my house where she belongs.

blaire

THE WEEK AFTER NEW YEAR, DALLAS SPOILED ME EVERY day. My Bean Haven favorites were waiting on my desk each morning when I came into work, always with a different message scrolled onto the side of the cup. Each day was a different question, and I would text him my answer with a smile on my face.

Favorite flower?

Me: Peony

If you could do anything, what would it be?

Me: Design wedding dresses

Favorite food?

Me: Mediterranean

What does your tattoo mean?

Me: Peace.

Night in or night out?

Me: A mix of both.

Favorite pizza topping?

Me: Pepperoni and pineapple with garlic dipping sauce

Summer or winter?

Me: Winter

Hobbies?

Me: Sketching

By the time the second week rolled around, I started to look forward to what he would write next. When we weren't at work, I was sneaking over to his house to have the most mind-blowing sex of my life and staying up way too late talking. Neither of us could be satiated. He does his best to convince me to sleep over, and it's getting harder and harder to say no. When I sleep next to him, my night is quiet and undisturbed by the demons of my past.

It's Friday morning, and as I pull into the staff parking lot of the distillery, butterflies take flight in the pit of my stomach, anticipating seeing my morning message on my coffee cup and going about my day. Grabbing my purse and pulling my coat tight around my body, I hustle into the front entrance of our building.

Sawyer and Dallas are in a heated discussion in front of the tour check-in desk. Deciding the coffee can wait, I walk up to them, my heart in my throat at the sight of Dallas. He trimmed his facial hair down to a coarse stubble that I want to run my hand across. He's wearing denim jeans with a navy blue button-up shirt, the sleeves rolled to his elbows, and the mountain and tree tattoos on his right forearm make my mouth water. I take a deep breath and school my features. I've got to keep this locked down. Sawyer can't know.

"Good morning, boys. You two seem like you're starting your day with violence, per usual."

"Morning, Blaire," Sawyer greets while Dallas just nods his head. My heart tumbles in my chest.

"Anything I can help with so you two don't end up bruised and bloody?"

Dallas huffs and Sawyer crosses his arms like he needs to keep them from reaching out and decking his twin.

"Go ahead, dickhead. You can tell her the good news."

"It's not fucking good news, you shithead."

"Blaire, Carter got us a feature in a large Pacific Northwest travel magazine."

"Oh my god! Seriously? Congratulations! That's amazing!" I nearly squeal in excitement. I look at Dallas, who is glaring at me. Of course he wouldn't be happy about this. A feature in a magazine will put the distillery on the map, which will pull in tourists, essentially ruining his peace. But I can't let on that I know that in front of Sawyer. Or anyone else for that matter.

"Dickhead here is pissed. Because why wouldn't he be mad about the potential of more money?"

"That's not what the fucking problem is, brother, and I'm about sick and fucking tired of you thinking otherwise."

"Get your head out of your ass, Dallas. This is good for all of us. Blaire, this will potentially increase your workload, so I'd like to talk about a raise if that happens. Be ready for people booking tours and tastings."

"Just what we fucking need. More goddamn people here. Fuck you all."

I try not to bristle at his words as he stomps away and up the stairs to our offices. I sigh and Sawyer catches it.

"He'll get over it. I'm sure you're used to his grumpy ass by now. Believe it or not, he means well."

"It's fine. This is really great news; I'm really excited for the future here."

"We're happy to have you along for the ride, Blaire."

I nod and head up the stairs to my office, hanging up my coat and bag before beelining straight for the breakfast that's waiting on my desk. I take a seat and pick up the white to-go cup with the Bean Haven loopy scrolled logo on it and turn it around in my hand until I find Dallas' handwriting.

Tonight. 7 p.m.

My face flames and I pick up my phone to see I already have a missed text from him.

Dallas: Wear a nice dress. No panties.

With a smile I couldn't contain plastered to my face the entire day, I managed to get my morning work done, one tour, emails, and a meeting with Carter on his thoughts about the feature and what he'd ultimately like to make sure they highlight. By the time noon rolls around, I'm ready for a break. Just as I relax into my chair, the office phone rings. I'm tempted to ignore it, but I know that isn't professional.

"Hello, this is Blaire."

"Come to my office." Dallas' deep voice travels through the phone and leaves no room for argument. He doesn't wait for a reply before hanging up.

I stand and leave my office, heading toward Dallas, my legs walking with a slight nervous tremble, unsure what I'm walking into after our interaction this morning. I knock twice on his door and wait to be invited in. Instead of his voice ringing out through the wall like I expected, the door opens. Looking as gorgeous as always, he opens the door wide, and motions with his free hand for me to enter. I take a few hesitant steps into his office when the door closes behind me, the click of the lock being latched into place. I turn to face him, and I know I'm in trouble.

"On your knees."

I hesitate. We're at work. If someone comes looking for either of us, how will we explain why the door is locked?

"Blai—"

I sink to my knees before he can finish saying my name. The position reminds me of our first time together, weeks ago, and how turned on I became when I first heard him order me to get on my knees. We haven't fooled around at work since then, keeping everything confined to just his house, but he's been teaching me at home.

"Good girl," he praises, my body already softening for him, trusting that he's going to keep me safe. He walks away from me, goes to his desk, and sits down. I stay in a seated position on my knees, my ass on my heels, with my palms resting on my thighs, and wait. I know he's testing me, and I don't want to fail. I watch him from the corner of my eye as he finishes typing something on his laptop and then closes it. He slowly reclines back, pushing a foot away from his desk and rocking slightly.

"I love this chair. It was a gift from Sawyer since I kept stealing his. It's quite expensive. A few thousand I believe. Funny that I found it in the storage closet, I wonder what menace put it there?" He pauses, and I try not to vomit over the obscene cost of a freaking office chair. "You're going to come suck my cock in it."

My breath hitches as I wait for him to call me forward. He doesn't make me wait long, and my mouth is suddenly salivating, wanting him.

"Crawl to me, princess."

And I do. Crawling across the hardwood floors of my boss' office, I'm eager to get between his legs. He moves out a little further, spinning to the side and opening his legs for me to sit in the center of them. He reaches down and strokes my head sweetly.

"Such a good girl. Go ahead, take out my cock."

I do as I'm told, pulling his belt through the loops and unbuckling his pants. He lifts off the chair so I can pull his pants down his legs. His big cock springs free, his piercings on full display. I meet his eyes, waiting for permission to finally put him in my mouth. He moves his hands to the side of my throat, pulling me into his crotch. I stick out my tongue, dragging it over his balls and sucking one of them into my mouth. He moans as he releases my neck, moving to thread his hands through my hair, pulling it out of my face.

I grip him, his cock heavy in my hand as I rub my thumb back and forth over the lowest barbell. The room is quiet except for Dallas' heavy breathing. I lick up over each of his piercings, running my tongue along the cool metal until I reach the tip. My tongue swirls around the head, flicking at it before sucking him into my mouth. I drop my head down, pulling as much of him into my mouth as I can. He's so big, filling me quickly. I pull back up, dragging my teeth up his length in a way that I know will make him go feral for me.

"That's it, fucking suck it, Blaire, give me those teeth." I double down on my effort, going down as far as I can, tears springing to my eyes, and suck hard back up to the tip, dragging my teeth. His hand moves to the back of my head, pressing me down farther than I've gone before, my gags audible as I struggle to breathe.

"Breathe through your nose, baby girl."

I do, small breaths in and out as he holds me down on him, his dick down my throat. I gag once more as he pulls me back up. I heave in a breath right before he does it again, sliding me down and holding me there, forcing me to swallow around him. His phone rings and I startle, trying to pull back. He lets me, a devilish smirk on his face.

Oh, fuck.

"Better be quiet, princess, I have an important call to take."

My eyes must be huge because he just chuckles before answering his office phone and pressing a button on the pad.

"This is Dallas."

"Hey, man, it's me," Sawyer's voice rings out over the speaker.

Dallas' hand moves to the back of my head again, pushing me to continue to suck him off. I look up at him, pleading and he mouths "suck it now."

I tighten my hand around him like a vise grip and his hips jerk forward. He fucking likes it, the asshole. I drop my head back down, sucking hard, tears leaking from my eyes, and pull back, returning to the tip and desperately suckling on it.

"You wanted to talk? What's the issue now, Dal? If this is about the article . . ."

"I get that it's good for the distillery, what I don't want is to increase the number of goddamn visitors we see on our property every day. Have you run any projections for what that could possibly look like for us? Are we even in a position to handle a mass uptick? The supply isn't going to meet the demand if we climb too quickly."

His hips buck into my face as he continues to talk to Sawyer, his hand grabbing a fistful of my hair.

"Jesus, fuck, Dallas. Of course I've run the numbers. After Carter did. And our CFO. And our product manager. And every other fucking person involved. The question is, have you looked at them? Have you run your own?"

I swirl my tongue around and move my hand between us, cupping his balls tightly in my hand. He doesn't answer Sawyer right away, his head falling back against the chair, his grip on my hair squeezing.

"Dallas? You there?"

"Gonna need to call you back."

Dallas slams his hand down on some buttons until the line disconnects. He returns both hands to my head, holding me still and lifting his hips, fucking my mouth. I open wide and flatten my tongue, relaxing my throat the best that I can.

"Oh, fuck yeah, baby girl. That's it. Fuck."

He continues to fuck my face, his hips bucking wildly. It's so erotic and has me leaking through my panties. Sucking him off like this makes me feel so good. Powerful.

"Oh, I'm gonna come. Fucking suck it."

His movements become choppy as his dick thickens, his balls rising up in my palm.

"Fucking take it all. Don't spill a drop," he growls as he comes. The moan that comes out of him is louder than it should be, but right now, I'm so lost in my Dallas bubble that I couldn't care less.

"That's it, baby, oh fuck, yes."

My mouth overflows with his cum, his taste exploding on my tongue as I do my best to swallow it down. When he pulls free of my mouth, I take a deep inhale of air and sit back on my heels. I know my mouth is wet from saliva, my lips bright red and swollen, but he's looking at me like I hung the freaking moon.

"That was supposed to be punishment for the shit earlier, my little menace, but dammit you're too good at that. I guess you need a new punishment."

My eyes widen as he pulls me to stand between his legs. He adjusts my dress pants and sweater, pressing the wrinkles from them before slapping my ass.

"Go back to work, Blaire."

"Wh-what?" He's just going to leave me like this?

"You heard me. Don't make me repeat it."

I turn to walk away but he grabs my wrist, hauling me back into his lap. He grabs my face and pulls my mouth into his, my body immediately relaxing and meeting him in the middle. He kisses the hell out of me, sucking on my tongue. I know he can taste himself, and that it turns him on, which spirals me further into this crazed lustful feeling.

"You were so good, baby girl. Thank you," he whispers against my lips.

He taps my thigh and I stand, leaving his office and walking back to my own. It should be a walk of shame as I pass several people, but I can't bring myself to give a damn, so consumed with this man and everything he makes me feel.

I go back to my office when I'm hit with an idea. I'll need to do the research, but I think I'll be able to propose a plan for the distillery that would give Dallas the best of both worlds—bring in money and events, while keeping the day-to-day to a minimum. I spend the rest of the afternoon researching and crunching numbers between tours and tastings. It'll take me some time, but hopefully before the journal interview, I'll have the proposal complete and approved by everyone.

Racing up the stairs to my studio, I jump in the shower, shaving my legs and pampering myself. Butterflies fill my stomach, having no idea where he's taking me. He knows that we can't be out in public. After blow drying and taming my wild wavy hair, I put on some makeup, keeping it light and adding roll-on perfume along my collarbones and in between my breasts. The short black bodycon cocktail dress that I chose to wear slips over me like a glove, and I know that it'll drive Dallas crazy. The top is a sweetheart neckline that hugs my breasts perfectly, and the space over my chest is a thin lace that connects to long lace sleeves. It hits mid-thigh and screams *sexy*. It showcases my hourglass figure and I feel gorgeous in it.

I'm just slipping on a pair of pumps when there's a knock on my door. I walk over to it, knowing that it's Dallas, and open it wide. His expression is everything. His face lights up in awe, his mouth dropping open slightly as his eyes roam over my body.

He steps into my studio, hands going right to my waist and pulling me into him.

"Baby girl, you look gorgeous."

"Yeah? I wasn't sure how dressy to go since you didn't tell me where we're going."

"This is perfect."

I blush as I take him in. He's wearing black slacks, similar to what he wears to work, paired with a black button-up shirt, the sleeves rolled up to his elbows, the top three buttons undone, and his thin gold chain noticeably hanging around his neck. His facial hair is short, and my body nearly purrs knowing exactly what that feels like against my skin.

"You look good yourself. You clean up well."

"Are you ready?"

"I am, just need to grab my coat."

He takes my hand and leads me out the back entrance to his Audi, opening my door and letting me slip in. He leans into my space, buckling me in and kissing me on the forehead before shutting the door and walking around the front of the car to the driver's side. I turn in my seat slightly, facing him, watching as he shifts gears and holds the steering wheel. It reminds me of the first time I was in the car with him weeks ago, when everything changed between us. As much as I want to tell myself this is just sex, it's so much more than that. I'm addicted to him. To the way he makes me feel. To who I am when I'm with him. I'll never get enough.

He leaves Aspen Ridge and merges onto the interstate, heading north out of our secluded part of the forest. The drive is quiet, his hand on my thigh when he isn't shifting, and we sit in comfortable silence while I watch him.

"Are you going to tell me where you're taking me?"

"It's a surprise."

An hour later, we exit the interstate and enter a little city. I look around at the businesses as Dallas slows the car and pulls up to a nondescript building. He turns to me, grabbing my face and bringing me in for a short kiss.

"You trust me?"

"I do."

"Let's go have some fun, princess."

My heart pounds in my chest as we leave the safety of Dallas' car and enter the building. After the first door, there are two bouncers and a reception desk. The carpet is a deep ruby red, the walls black, with empty, ornate gold frames in various sizes hung about. Dallas guides me to the receptionist, his hand moving from my lower back to the back of my neck, in a claiming, dominating move that I don't hate. Quite the opposite actually. He hands her a plain black card with gold script on it. After scanning it, she nods to one of the bouncers who scans a card and opens a heavy door. The music escapes, blaring from whatever is going on inside.

Dallas urges me forward, his hand moving down to my lower back as we walk through the door and onto the floor of a club. But not just any club. Women and men alike walk around in various styles of clothing and lingerie, some are completely naked. A gorgeous woman walks hand in hand with another equally beautiful woman with a strap-on around her pelvis. My eyes dart everywhere as my pulse beats erratically and my breathing hitches. Dallas' hand strokes up and down my lower back, grounding me. His breath is hot on my ear as he leans his face into me.

"If it becomes too much, just say the word and we'll leave. But while we're here? There's only one rule."

"Okay . . ."

"No one touches what's mine."

A shiver trails down my spine at his possessiveness. I turn back to the crowd as Dallas grabs my hand, pulling me toward the bar and setting me on a stool next to him. He orders us two drinks, a whiskey on the rocks for him, and a Midori sour for me. When our drinks are set in front of us, I pick mine up eagerly, taking a large sip, letting the Midori and vodka settle my nerves.

"You brought me to a sex club."

He smiles ear to ear in a devilish way that is all him.

"I did. What do you think?"

I look around, taking it all in. The scene playing out on the couch across from the bar has my heart rate quickening. The sight of two men and two women is erotic and taboo, and I feel my core throb just from watching them. Their hands touch each other everywhere, with no care about who is who, they pleasure each other. When one man drops to his knees and sucks the other's cock into his mouth, a small moan leaves my lips. Everywhere I look there are bodies seeking pleasure, letting loose—living. Consensually, in a safe environment. I can't help but look around, my eyes lingering on certain people as they are lost in the throes of pleasure.

Dallas stands, coming into my space, yanking on my hair to force my head back to look at him.

"I knew you were a little voyeur. You like what you see, princess?"

"You know I do."

He gives me a satisfied smile.

"You come here?" I ask. He nods in confirmation, his brow furrowed.

"Does that bother you?"

I think about it for a moment before answering, unsure how he'll take it, but say it anyway.

"Not if you're only coming with me now. I don't share either."

He dips his head to my ear before whispering, "I've only been here once since I met you, and I couldn't touch anyone. You consumed my thoughts even then. My desires. My pleasure. I turned two women down before jerking off in the bathroom to thoughts of you . . . And that was way before I ever even had a taste of you."

He sucks my earlobe into his mouth before dragging it between his teeth. I sigh deeply, my heart pounding in my chest, my pussy throbbing at his confession.

"Finish your drink and I'll show you my favorite part."

"There's more?"

"Oh, my girl, this is only the main floor. There are different rooms for different things depending on your interests. There are private rooms and voyeur rooms for different scenes. You'll see."

We finish our drinks, his hand inching higher and higher on my thigh. I know he said no one else touches me, but does that mean he'd let people watch *him* touch me? The thought equally terrifies and excites me. Before we get up, a gorgeous woman saunters toward us, wearing a silk robe. It's loosely tied, one side hanging off a shoulder, exposing one of her breasts. I can't help but look at her, her nipple pierced and perky. She reaches out to touch me before Dallas growls out his words.

"She's off-limits."

The woman turns to face Dallas and arches a brow, clearly asking if that means he is too.

"We're just here to watch. Thank you for the offer though." He's much more polite to her than I would expect, and I can't help but wonder if there's a layer of unspoken respect here, or rules that the club has in place to protect its members.

She walks off unperturbed, and Dallas grabs my hand, pulling me to follow him. He keeps me close, his finger rubbing back and forth on my palm. He leads me through the main floor to a long, dark hallway. There are a few other people in it, standing against the wall across from a massive floor-to-ceiling window. It's completely dark, both in the hallway and on the other side of the window.

Dallas takes me to a spot on the wall and leans against it, pulling me in front of him, his hands going to my waist.

"What are we doing?" I ask, my eyes struggling to adjust to the pitch-black.

"Shh, baby, just wait. You'll see."

The next moment, a light at the top of a door turns green, and dim lights behind the window come on, illuminating a large room. It's set up as a bedroom, with a four-poster bed in the center, and a lounge chair in front of it. There's an armoire against a wall not far from the bed. A door on the side of the room farthest from us opens, and in walks a gorgeous man and woman. He's got the most beautiful tan skin, with long black hair, a sculpted, hairless chest, and washboard abs. He could be a GQ model and no one would question it. The woman is equally gorgeous, but she looks like . . . *me*. Her body isn't perfectly thin, her waist isn't trim. She's full and curvy, her breasts hanging heavy on her chest. I look up at Dallas, and his eyes are on me, not on the scene in front of us. He kisses me, igniting that fire inside, and I whimper against his mouth before he pulls away.

"Watch," he says as he turns my head away from him. "Watch how she trusts him to take care of her. She doesn't have to think, make a decision, or do anything at all. She simply gets to be, knowing that he'll do all of those things and make her feel better than she could have ever imagined. Watch how he delivers. How taking care of her in every way possible makes him feel like a king."

I watch as she kneels and the man praises her, his voice coming through a speaker in the hallway. He calls her forward to climb onto the bed, where he ties each of her wrists to a post on the headboard. He leaves her ankles free. I don't notice that Dallas has pulled me back further into him, that my body starts to move against him, my hips rocking ever so slightly.

The man climbs on top of the woman and kisses down her chest, stopping to lavish each of her breasts, massaging them, cupping them, and sucking on her nipples. Dallas' head moves down to my neck, kissing the tender spot below my ear, moving down and sucking at the skin above my shoulder. I push my ass further into him, his hard cock stiff against my back.

This is the last thing I'd expect to ever enjoy, or even think I would do, but here I am, practically begging my boss to fuck me in a hallway of a sex club while we watch a couple do the same.

What has he done to me?

dallas

I CAN'T TAKE MY EYES OFF BLAIRE. THE WAY HER ASS pushes back into my hard cock, the flush that's spread across her fair skin that only I can see in the dimly lit hallway, she's so turned on, and fuck if I don't want to take care of her right here. I kiss her neck, sucking that delicate flesh into my mouth, and when she reaches back and threads her hand through my hair, pulling me closer to her, a low moan slips from my lips. She keeps her eyes focused on the scene in front of us, while I keep my focus on my girl. My hand on her hip holds her flush against me while the other pulls up her dress, inch by inch. The hallway is dark, but everyone around us is already either touching themselves or a partner, if not both. If she stops me, I won't question it for a moment, everyone has limits and I'll always respect hers. But fuck do I want her right now, just like this. Right here in this club.

My fingertips glide over the silky-smooth skin of her thighs, and I moan into her ear, letting her know what she does to me. As I continue my path upward, her legs spread of their own accord, and I couldn't be fucking happier to be given the permission to keep going. When I reach the tops of her thighs, I skim over the sticky wetness already coating her. She's so turned on she's dripping down her legs.

"I'm going to take such good care of you."

My fingers brush across her puffy lips, slick with her arousal, and I hum my approval. I glide two fingers through her center and feel the tremble of her legs as she moans softly, relaxing further into me.

"That's it, baby girl, I've got you. Don't take your eyes off them, watch as he pleasures her."

My fingers continue to trail across her delicate flesh until I return to her center, pushing two fingers in deep, her pussy fluttering around me, and fuck if I don't wish it was my cock. I arch my hand, staying impossibly deep, stroking the sensitive spot inside her before pulling out and moving up to her clit. The female's moans echo into the hallway as Blaire's hips move in time with my fingers, and my other hand moves up to palm her breasts over her dress.

"You're dripping all over my hand, you like me fucking you with my fingers while you watch him eat her pussy? See how he takes care of her?"

"Yes, god, yes."

Her hips start to really move, chasing her release.

She trembles in my arms, her knees shaking

"I need . . ."

"Tell me what you need, princess. I'll give you anything. Everything."

"I need you, I need you inside me. *Please*," she practically whines.

I don't think, I just react. Pulling my fingers from her, I quickly free my length from the confines of my slacks. My hands drag up the side of her thighs, pulling the back of her dress up so that she's completely bare only to me. Sinking low, I line myself up with her wet heat from behind and drive home, filling her completely in one thrust, her dripping cunt easing my way in. I groan, loving the way her pussy clenches around me, the way my piercings pull as I drag myself out and thrust back in. I stay deep, fucking her in hard, uncontrolled thrusts.

"That what you need, baby girl? You needed to be filled by my big cock?"

"Ye-yes. God, yes."

She leans her head back against my chest, eyes locked on me as I ravish her pussy. Oblivious to any onlookers, I claim her mouth, kissing her deep and hard before releasing her, both of us gasping for air. Her walls tighten around me, sucking me in, her breathing picking up.

"That's it, come for me, take me over the edge with you. Make me come," I whisper into the shell of her ear, the scene in front of us long forgotten.

"I'm coming! Ohmygod!"

Her body stiffens before her knees give out, her entire body shaking as her orgasm takes over. I hold her up in my arms and thrust in once, twice, three more times before pushing in deep, doing exactly what she asked me to—ropes of cum pulsing out of me as my orgasm goes on and on.

"Such a good fucking girl. So good for me, baby."

***

"So, what did you think?" I ask as we lay naked together in my bed after leaving Temptations. I was nervous, wanting to give her a new experience and something completely out of the ordinary. A date like she said she would enjoy, a place that gave some insight into the person she's dating. Walking out of there with her little hand in mine, my cum leaking from her pussy, was something I'll never forget. If I could have her leaking me every day, I'd do it.

I look at her now, relaxed and satiated in my arms, looking so beautiful. She's been staying over more and more lately, leaving early in the morning and heading to work before me, refusing to go together. But sleeping next to her is everything.

"I'm sure you could tell how surprised I was, a little jealous imagining you there without me and everything you've probably experienced, but I want to go back."

"Princess, I don't remember life before you, none of that matters. My heart started beating the moment I walked into Sawyer's office and saw you sitting there."

She blushes, crimson spreading across her pretty face and making her freckles pop.

"You're a sadist," she jokes.

"You really want to go back?"

"I do."

"I've been doing research on what you told me, about BDSM and how it can work to heal past trauma. You've never been triggered with me or by anything we do?"

Her eyes fill with unshed tears, making the dark blue of her irises look like the depth of an ocean.

"Baby, don't cry. I didn't tell you that to make you sad."

"That means so much to me, that you seriously took time to look into that. No, I never have. You make me feel safe, I feel powerful in the sexual moments with you, and at night when I sleep next to you, you—"

"Chase your demons away."

"Yeah. You do."

The fucking gratification that fills my chest knowing that I can provide her relief from her past does something to me.

"Is there anything you want to try?"

"I think so. But I don't want to freak you out."

"Nothing would freak me out. I promise you. It could be anything."

She chews on the inside of her cheek nervously and I wait patiently, not feeling an ounce of worry over what her request will be. I would do anything she needed to take control back.

"My nightmares are specific because it always happened at night. He would sneak into my bedroom when I should be sleeping, and I would lay there terrified, wrapped in my blankets, waiting, wondering if that night was going to be the night he'd come in again. It was always inconsistent, so I never knew. It was torture. All of it."

The rage inside me boils, threatening to overflow hearing the details of what my baby survived. Without her continuing, I know exactly what she's asking, what she needs, and I won't make her finish.

"Give me a key to your apartment. You don't want to know when?"

She shakes her head no.

I'm not usually into dubious consent, I've played around with it once or twice, but there's nothing I won't do for her, and if this will help her heal from her past trauma in a controlled, safe environment, it's easy for me to go through with it.

"I understand, just remember your safe words and that you're in control the entire time. I would never hurt you."

"I know. That's why I'm asking you."

Her words mean more to me than she knows, and I don't know how to tell her. Being away from her for a few days is going to suck. I usually look forward to our annual boys' trip all year long. Two days at Mount Baker, just the four of us, snowboarding, drinking beer, and chilling. We live on the slopes all day and sit by a fireplace at night and catch up, leaving the distillery back in Aspen Ridge for a few days to clear our heads. But this year? This year I have somewhere else I want to be. Someone here I don't want to leave.

"I told you that I'm leaving for a few days, right?"

"I think you mentioned it and I've heard your brothers talking about it. Two days?"

"Two and a half-ish, but two nights away. We go every year the first week in February. It's a tradition I can't get out of, trust me, Sawyer tried."

"He doesn't want to leave Ivy, huh?"

"Never. Especially since she's pregnant. I think in a month or so he'll start working from home. I know he plans to take a while off after the baby is born."

"You boys really had amazing role models."

"I don't disagree with you. We were lucky and I know that. I wish you had the same. Have you ever looked your parents up?"

"No. And I don't want to. There's a big part of me that blames them for everything that happened to me. I wish I had been enough of a reason for them to get their lives together. But I guess that's addiction for you."

"I'm sorry, baby. I know it doesn't mean much, but I'd kill them all if I could. You should be so proud of yourself, you're a survivor and you're damn amazing. Look at how far you've come with no support and starting out with the shitty life cards you were handed. I'm going to keep you safe; I won't hurt you."

"I believe you."

The next morning, I wake up alone, her spot on the bed cold, and clothes long gone. Blaire tends to sneak out of my house before the sun comes up, like a little thief in the night, still terrified of anyone finding out about us. I roll over and grab my phone, sliding the alarm off and pulling up her texts.

> Me: You're a menace

> Me: When will you let me wake up to you and bring you to work?

> Blaire: Says the dickhead who steals my panties, I'm running low by the way so if you could return the ones you have

A smile spreads across my face as I lean over and open my end table drawer, pulling out a baby blue polka dot thong. I bring it to my nose, inhaling her sweet pussy, and turn my camera on to take a selfie. I snap a quick photo and send it to her.

> Me: These? Nah. How else would I be able to smell your cunt when you refuse to be here?

> Blaire: Dallas! You're a freak. That's not sanitary

> Me: Fuck if I care. I could have my face buried between your legs right now

> Blaire: You're distracting. Let me get ready for work.

> Me: Imagine all the things I could do to distract you if you were next to me

> Me: Where you should be

> Blaire: See you at work, boss

Groaning, I toss my phone to the side and walk naked to my bathroom for a shower, not thrilled with the idea of washing her off me. I hurry through my morning routine, throwing on a pair of jeans and a button-up shirt since it's Friday, knowing that I don't have time to pick up coffee for Blaire from Bean Haven, and rush out of the house.

Once I make it to work, I head straight for my office only to find our intern, Marcus, waiting at my door.

"Hey, Marcus, everything okay?"

"Yes, sir, everything is good. Liam wanted me to personally wait for you and tell you in person, and I quote, 'get your ass to the fucking fermenting vats.' Sorry, Mr. Hayes, but he was adamant and he's quite scary when he wants to be."

I laugh at Marcus and pat him on the back.

"Don't worry about it. Seeing as how I just got here and there is no explosion or fire happening, I'm going to put my stuff down, and then I'll go meet him. Go take a break, you look like you need it."

Marcus eyes me warily and I realize that he's most likely used to me being a grouchy asshole the majority of the time. I do as I said I would, dropping my stuff off at my desk and walking back through the distillery office buildings and grabbing a golf cart. I head to the vats and easily find my brother pacing, running his hands through his shaggy hair—something he does when he's worked up. I mentally give myself shit for being distracted lately. I look around to find the place empty, minus him.

"Hey man, you summoned me?"

"Yeah, I'm losing my shit and I need you to talk me off the ledge. You weren't answering your damn phone."

Shit. I must not have turned the ringer back on from last night at the club.

"What's going on? Tell me what you need."

"It's fuckin' Hannah. I'm so goddamn tired of Levi jerking her around. I'm so sick of seeing her treated like shit over and over and over again. You know where I was last night? Fuckin' holding her while she cried because she's running on fumes."

I can tell by the look on his face that the story doesn't end there. Holding Hannah through the shit Levi has put her through isn't new and it wouldn't get him that worked up.

"What'd you do, Liam?"

He looks at me, his shoulders stiff and face blank.

"I drove to Seattle to find the asshole and tell him to get his ass back in Aspen Ridge and take care of his family. And you know what I found?"

"Shit, man. Does Hannah know?"

"Know that her lying, piece of shit baby daddy that she thinks she's still involved with has a girlfriend he's living with? That she's fucking pregnant?!"

"Oh, fuck."

My heart sinks for Hannah and Charlotte.

"You didn't beat the shit out of him, did you? That's the last thing Hannah needs to deal with."

"I saw it, right in front of me at his door and I turned and left. Dal, it was the hardest fucking thing I've ever done, and the longer I stay here and keep it from her . . . fuck. I want to fucking kill him. How could he do that to them?"

"We'll all get her through it, they're going to be okay."

"You don't get it. Her parents want to cut her off, Dallas. With Ms. Nettie getting older, unless Hannah gets married and settles down because of Charlie, they're selling Bean Haven. Her mom is sick of going back and forth every winter and they want to move to San Diego permanently."

"What kind of fucked-up ultimatum is that?"

"I don't know how to tell her about Levi. I want to go put him six feet under. That's what he fuckin' deserves."

"I agree with you, brother, but that's not how this can be handled. Levi's a fucking weasel and he'll make Hannah's life hell because of it."

"What do I do?"

"Just sleep on it. You know her better than anyone else. But you get your shit straight and then talk to her. You'll know what to do."

I leave my brother, feeling like shit for him and Hannah. She's such a good girl and has been around my family for the majority of her life. Needing a pick-me-up and to clear my head, I go in search of my girl, because all I want to do right now is wrap her in a hug and know that she's having a good day.

blaire

GETTING READY FOR SUNDAY DINNER AT DALLAS' family's house comes with a mix of emotions. Hiding our relationship from everyone at work is fairly easy. But at his parents' house, in front of his entire family, that's a whole different ball game and one I'm not sure I'm up to facing. The last few weeks I've found myself craving his attention, his comfort, his touch, his dickhead quips, and the way he pushes my buttons. I know I'm falling for him in a way that I don't think I'll recover from if it ends. He's opened me up to an entirely new world—one I'm thriving in.

I finally feel at home here and I can't help but feel like I'm waiting for the other shoe to drop. Hopefully, Dallas and I can figure out what we are and a plan to move forward before this combusts.

Despite Dallas' protests, I drive to the Hayes family home by myself and park my little car out front. Nerves catch up to me as I walk across the driveway, the packed snow crunching under my feet. I take a moment, standing in front of their door and steadying my breathing, giving myself a mental pep talk that everything is fine and there's no way anyone will find out. I knock twice and only wait a moment before it's opened.

"Hi, Blaire! I'm so glad you could join us again! I love having a full house," Amy, Dallas' mom, greets me. "Come in! Everyone is downstairs in the rec room."

I slip off my snowy boots outside the door before walking through the entryway behind her, following her into the kitchen.

"Thank you for having me. I made these, I hope they're okay. I'm not nearly as talented as Ivy, but the recipe I used on the back of the Tollhouse bag seemed legit," I say with a nervous laugh as I hand her a tray filled with chocolate chip cookies.

"Tried and true! I'm sure they're delicious. Thank you, sweetie."

"I know you said everyone is downstairs, but do you need any help with anything?"

She looks at me for a moment with a big smile on her face before answering, "I would love some. Here, wash up, and then if you don't mind rolling out the pastry dough I have right here?" She points to several bowls with plastic wrap over them. Four stone pie dishes sit in front of a plastic mat with various circles etched into it.

"It smells amazing in here, what are you making?"

"One of my favorites, Liam's favorite, too. Chicken pot pie. Comfort food today."

My mouth waters.

After washing my hands, I get to work rolling out each pie crust and pressing them into the pie dishes.

"You seem to be settling in nicely in Aspen Ridge, do you plan to stay for good?" Amy asks after a few minutes of silence.

"I am, I really love everything AR has to offer. I love my job—"

Dallas barrels into the kitchen, interrupting me, yelling something unintelligible behind him, but when he rights himself, he stops in his tracks, looking at the scene in front of him. I stop rolling out the dough, both of us frozen in a moment where everything else around us disappears.

My lips turn up in a smile as I mouth the word "hi" to him.

He smiles back with an expression that looks a whole hell of a lot like satisfaction, or maybe something different, as his eyes bounce across the kitchen scene. Whatever it is, it's unfamiliar, but it wraps around my heart and squeezes.

"Hi, baby," he mouths back before turning to the fridge and opening it. "Hey, Mom, do we have any more of that Elysian Bifrost?"

"If you're not seeing it with your own two eyes then we're out, son."

"And you wonder where I got my snark," Dallas closes the fridge and says in my direction. I can't help the snort that comes from me and I quickly cover my mouth with my hand to hide the laugh that follows.

"Go ahead, laugh. But it's true whether she'll admit it or not. Everyone thinks she's the sweetest thing in the world, but she can be a snarky one, just like her son."

"I suppose you're not wrong. The only difference is I've learned when and where, and you, my son, never learned any tact."

"You talkin' about Dal?" Liam says upon entering the kitchen with Charlotte hanging by her ankle upside down in his hand. I cover my mouth and laugh at the sight. He's so incredibly good with that little girl, it's shocking to me that he's not her biological father. It's clear he loves her like she's his own. As someone who spent years wishing for that type of relationship, I know she's going to value it for the rest of her life.

Their mother gives Dallas a pointed stare that reads, *told you,* and I laugh some more.

"Something funny, princess?"

"Just glad to see that your ogre personality isn't reserved for just me."

"Did you just compare my mom's personality to an ogre? She's a goddamn angel!"

I pale, realizing quickly how what I said can be taken.

"Oh, my gosh, I am so sorry, that is not what I meant," I say to his mom.

The three of them laugh and my face changes from deathly white to a bright red tomato.

"Blaire, he's just giving you a hard time. His sense of humor matches the other traits, I'm afraid."

"You're the worst," I tell him.

He looks at his brother and mom to see they're occupied before mouthing "you love it" to me. I have to bite the inside of my cheek to keep myself from smiling as I rewash my hands and return to my task of rolling out the pie crust.

After the pot pies are assembled and set in the oven to bake, I follow the noise that leads me downstairs to a finished basement. All of the Hayes siblings are playing a game of beer pong as I walk into the large, open room. I make my way toward Hannah and Ivy, who's resting her hand on her tiny baby bump. She's just starting to pop out and she's so cute.

"Quite the sight, huh?" she asks.

"It's wild here, they're all so full of life."

"They are. It's always been like this. Rowdy, loud, crazy," Hannah says.

"I secretly love it. What's the dynamic with Kinsey, do they let her win?"

"Oh, god, no. Never. They make that girl work for it, so she's tough, but if you think you've seen protective from Sawyer with me, it's nothing compared to what Kins has had to deal with from the four of them."

"Can you imagine having four older brothers?"

"Hell no. Are you an only child, too?"

"As far as I know," it slips from my lips before I can stop it, and I try to stay calm, hoping she'll read it as a joke.

"Ha. Same. We definitely don't need any more Turner genes running around. I hope this baby is all Hayes."

I couldn't agree more about my genes. The Hollis line should surely die with me, even if I do crave a family of my own.

"He or she is going to be so loved, that's for sure."

We spend the next thirty minutes watching the five of them go back and forth playing beer pong, all of them getting louder and more heated as the rounds go on and on.

"Fuck off! You're a bunch of goddamn cheaters!" Liam yells as he walks in our direction.

"How can you cheat at fuckin' beer pong, lint licker?" Dallas yells back.

Liam keeps walking until he stands next to me and Ivy, looking irritated as all hell.

"They're cheats, huh?" Ivy asks.

"They're assholes. All of them."

"But, lint licker?" I have to ask, knowing that I'm probably going to regret it.

Ivy covers her mouth and laughs as Sawyer walks up to her. He grabs her wrist and pulls it away from her face. "What did I tell you about covering up your laugh?"

"Not to?" she asks while still laughing.

"That's Liam's nickname. You haven't heard it yet?" Sawyer asks.

"Apparently not. How did he get such an awful one? No offense to you and the other two, but," I turn to face Liam before continuing, "Liam's the most level-headed one out of all of you, so how does he end up with the worst nickname?"

"Cause they're all assholes and they don't like that I'm bigger than them."

"Size doesn't mean shit. How many times have I taken you? I'm happy to do it again right here,"

Liam steps up to Sawyer, getting right in his face. I take a step back, giving them space since these boys like to be so physical with each other. Sawyer pulls Ivy behind him, and I can't help but glance in Dallas' direction. He's standing at the far end of the ping pong table with his arms crossed, his eyes focused on me and the situation three feet away.

"What the fuck is your problem lately? You got some shit you need to work out, then you let us know, but we're not here to be treated like shit by you, so what's it goin' to fuckin' be?" Sawyer raises his voice, and Liam doesn't back down, instead, he jerks toward him, which was the wrong thing to do. Sawyer tackles him, bending down, his arms wrapping around his waist and taking him back several steps. It all happens so fast. Liam bends over Sawyer's back, throwing a punch into his side. Dallas and Carter move quickly to their brothers, while Kinsey, Hannah, and I move toward Ivy, all of us stepping back to stay clear of them while they fight.

"Get it out of your system, little brother," Sawyer huffs.

"Fuck you!" Liam spits.

"Dinner, heathens!" Amy calls from upstairs.

Everyone except Sawyer and Liam, who are currently locked around each other in some weird positions on the ground, look at each other, unsure whether or not to leave them here. Dallas walks over and ushers us up the stairs, making the decision for us.

"Liam's been looking for a fight. He's working through some shit. He'll be fine once he burns some energy. Go get started, we'll be right up."

"Dal . . ." Ivy hesitates, Sawyer and Liam banging around behind us.

"He'll be fine, Iv. Don't worry about it."

"They're fine. Annoying, but fine. Let's go eat. It smells delicious." Once we're at the halfway point on the stairs, Kinsey turns and bolts back down, yelling, "Liam! Mom made your favorite!"

Dinner gets started with everyone but the four boys who stayed downstairs to work through whatever issues are weighing on them. One of the pies is passed around, each of us taking some out before passing it on.

"It's nice of you to join us again, Blaire," Dallas' dad, Craig, tells me, and my cheeks warm. His voice has a bit of a slur from his strokes, but he is the most genuinely sweet, kind, soft-spoken man. It's hard to believe he could have an overly protective, growly side like his sons.

"Thank you, sir, it's so nice to be here again. You have such a lovely family." I finish my sentence as the four boys shove each other through the narrow entryway into the dining room like a group of wild teenagers.

"Lovely, huh? My children are feral animals, Blaire, you don't have to be so formal. We know better than anyone that it's utter chaos."

"Except for me, I never do anything wrong because they're all too busy taking center stage," Kinsey adds.

We all eat and catch up. I don't bother asking about why Reid is a no-show again, because I know he can't bring himself to come.

After dinner and cleaning up, I excuse myself to the bathroom. Not having closed the door all the way yet, Dallas pushes it open and steps in, locking it behind us and trapping me in here with him.

"What are you doing? Get out!" I panic.

"Princess, I have been cornering you in bathrooms for months." He drops to his knees in front of me and rubs his hand up my legs, stopping at my thighs. "You should expect nothing less by now. Now let me see that pretty pussy," he says as he looks up at me from his knees, already starting to hike up my dress and pull down my tights.

"Dallas, we can't, someone will find us."

"Better come quick then. You know I can get you off with my mouth in under a minute."

Without waiting for my reply, he lifts and hooks my leg over his shoulder, spreads me wide with his thumbs, and suctions his mouth around my pussy, nearly making my knee give out. I love when he does this. I lose myself to the sensation, his lips pulsing little sucks around me. I brace myself on the bathroom sink, letting him devour me the way that I know he loves. Footsteps walk past the room, and I stiffen, covering my mouth with my hand. Looking down at him on his knees, he is completely unfazed. Two fingers press inside me, curling toward my stomach, and within another moment, I'm coming. Wetness pools between my legs, soaking around his fingers. He licks me through it before pulling his fingers out and putting them in his mouth, sucking my arousal off of them, in an erotic display of obsession.

"Fucking delicious."

"You're the worst, ever," I say through panted breaths. "I need to get back out there before someone comes looking for one of us."

He pulls up my panties and tights and fixes my dress, putting me back together. I turn to look in the mirror, making sure my face doesn't scream *recent orgasm by mouth,* when Dallas stands directly behind me. His hands move to my waist, pulling me lightly flush against him.

I meet his eyes in the mirror, before looking over both of us, loving what I see reflected back at me.

CHAPTER 25

dallas

LEANING AGAINST THE WALL, I WATCH BLAIRE AS SHE speaks to a group of tourists before taking them to the tasting room. They can't help but be captivated by her effortless charm and warmth, and I feel jealous that they get her time. Despite life's relentless attack on her, her light isn't dim from the unfair hand she's been given. Her resilience and strength leave me in awe of her. She's such a goddamn light.

Knowing her schedule, I jump in my car and drive ten minutes into town to grab us both a cup of coffee. Once I'm back at the office, I scrawl out a message for her and leave it on her desk. Focusing on my work and preparing for a meeting with Liam and our operations team, I lose track of time until Blaire walks through my door.

"You wanted to see me, Dallas?"

She walks into my office, her Bean Haven coffee cup in her hand. She's wearing a sage-green sweater dress today, paired with a cream cardigan and leather knee-high boots. She's breathtaking. Her hair is pinned up high in a bun with loose curls falling free around her face. Her beauty stuns me silent for a moment.

"Yeah, I do. Lock the door."

She looks at me hesitantly before obeying, albeit reluctantly.

"On your knees."

She pulls up her dress just enough that she can bend her knees as she sinks to the ground. Spreading her legs slightly, setting the coffee mug off to the side, and placing her palms face up. Fuck, she looks so fucking good like this. She's so perfect for me. I walk up to her and run my hand over her cheek, caressing her soft skin with care and affection. My heart pumps rapidly in my chest at the sight of her.

"Such a good girl. You make me so happy."

She looks up at me with her big, pretty blue eyes, with all the satisfaction in the world. She's so damn perfect. I walk over to the chaise lounge and sit in the center, spreading my legs wide, my arm draped over the back. I palm my already hard cock with my other hand. He's known who he belongs to longer than I have, the bastard already ready to get to work.

"Crawl to me, princess."

She leans on all fours and saunters like a fucking cat in my direction, her eyes never leaving mine. Her hips sway side to side and the sight makes me go crazy. Knowing what it feels like to grasp those sexy hips and drive myself deep into her waiting heat is as heavy as a drug in its most addictive form. She comes to a stop when she's right between my legs, sitting back on her heels and waiting, not saying a word, and never breaking eye contact. Even though she should be looking down in a more submissive position, I fucking die for this. It fully encompasses both sides of her. She'll go to war with me every chance she gets, and melts to be submissive, but only so much. This is her way of reminding me. She's perfect for me. No one else will do. She's it. She's my endgame.

Fuck.

The realization hits me with force.

I'm in love with her. I don't know how it happened so fast, but I know what it is. I'm fucking done for over this woman.

I love her.

I look down at her, still waiting, and suddenly I just want to be inside her. All games and kink aside. I reach for her, hauling her up and into my lap. She adapts quickly, straddling my thighs as I hike her dress up to her waist, grabbing the thin string of her panties and pushing them to the side. Her core is already weeping for me. We're a frantic mess of hands as she reaches for my belt, unbuckling it and opening my pants, pulling my cock free, and running her palm up my piercings. Groaning, she lifts with me, lining up my cock and sinking down until she's flush with me. I grab her around the neck and pull her face to me so that her forehead rests on my own. We both moan quietly as we start to move.

Fuck, I love this woman. *I love her.*

I thrust up into her as she rocks back and forth, dragging her sensitive little clit on my pelvis, chasing her pleasure. The soft strands of her wavy hair thread through my fingers as I grab her, sealing my mouth to hers, kissing her deeply, trying my best to consume her in the same way she's done to me. She's a part of me now, and fuck if I'll stop before she feels the same.

Every year during the first week of February, my brothers and I go on a trip, just us. It started when we were younger, Liam and Carter were only little kids. Our dad would pack us up, leaving my mom and Kinsey at home to have girl time, and bring us up to Mount Baker. It's half a day's drive with stops, so we leave early to get up there and get settled. With plans to check in on Blaire and get inside her one more time before I don't see her for nearly three days, I leave my house hours before I'm due to meet everyone at the distillery and head downtown to Blaire's studio.

It's around two in the morning when I fit the spare key into Blaire's locked studio apartment door, my nerves in my fucking throat.

Before the door is even open completely, I can hear her whimpers. I rush through the open room in several long strides. She's sprawled out on her futon, tangled in a mess of blankets, her body tossing and turning, fighting the demons that can no longer physically hurt her. I know she's not fully asleep, always hovering in a state of semi-awake due to the past that haunts her. Fuck, maybe this will help her work through it. She'll know it's me. I know she asked for something like this, but she's already dreaming, and I don't want her to get the two confused. But I'm positive she'll know it's me, she has to. I speak to a part of her that even she barely understands. I'm going to give her a new memory, one to replace the nightmares. This will work. It has to.

I touch the edge of the blankets and pull them back slowly, exposing her body. She jerks slightly but doesn't make a single sound. Her smooth porcelain skin nearly glows in the moonlight, and with my cock already hardening behind my sweatpants, I drag my fingertips over her warm legs. Goosebumps scatter across her skin as my touch trails over her. I slip into bed behind her, and she startles, waking up, her little gasp and flail causing me physical pain. When she opens her heavy eyes, I see tears leaking from the corners and I nearly break.

"It's me, princess. I'll never hurt you." *I love you.*

I run my hand up her stomach, grabbing her breast and pulling her back flush against me. I'm rough with her, massaging her tit and twisting her nipple before releasing it and dragging my hand back down her body. Running my fingers along the trim of her panties, I hook my fingers into them and yank hard, pulling them until they give, ripping them from her body. She yelps but then relaxes her ass into my crotch. That's my good girl. You know you're safe with me.

"You're safe now, baby girl, I'm going to take care of you."

She moans as I push her onto her back, tucking her under me. I shove my sweatpants down to my thighs before rolling on top of her, pulling her legs up under my arms. My cock finds its home at her entrance and I prod at her, slowly working into her until her pussy becomes slick around me, easing its way in. I hold her legs up, pulling her out wide and keeping her open for me as I start to thrust in and out of her, hard, grinding my pelvis against her with every stroke. She's so tight, even with how slick she is, it's difficult to pull out and push back in. She's heaven, gripping my dick like it was built just for me.

"Shit, I love your pussy. I want to be inside this sweet thing every damn day, baby."

"Dallas, you feel so good inside me. You make me feel so good, I've never felt good before." Her voice cracks and breaks as she speaks. I stop moving, staying deep inside her, and release her legs so that I can hold her pretty face between my palms. I can feel the wet tears slowly dripping down the side of her head. Goddamn it, I love her so fucking much.

"I always want to make you feel good, I've got you. You're safe," I utter softly. With her head cradled in my hands, I kiss her slowly and passionately as I start to move inside her. For the first time in my life, I let go of my need for control. I don't fuck her, hell, I don't even have sex with her. I make love to her, completely lost in the deep connection and intense closeness between us. Her hands drag slowly down my back, pulling me into her as she wraps her legs around my waist. I hold every part of her as close to me as possible, kissing her, and feeling her skin on mine. Every moment before this one has been completely different, both in intent and intensity. *Nothing* can compare to this right now.

I swallow her breaths, her moans, both of us trying to breathe through our noses so we don't sever the connection. I want all of her, and while every part of us is touching and combined, we're still not close enough. The base of my spine starts to tingle, my balls drawing up close to my body, my orgasm on the brink of ecstasy.

"Blaire, I'm so close, I want you to come with me. Come with me, princess."

"I'm right there, baby, don't stop." And it's the baby that does me in. Unable to hold back, I thrust deep into her, my cock thickening, and right before I come, I feel her walls flutter around me, sucking me in, as her body trembles under me. My cock jerks inside her as we come in unison, our mouths crashing back together until the pleasure ebbs.

I pull back slightly, resting my forehead against hers. "Fuck, I will never stop craving you. You're an addiction I never want to shake."

She doesn't reply with words, but rather runs her fingers from my temples down my cheeks, scratching lightly over my short beard and then pulling me back down to kiss me. It ignites us both and we spend the next hour repeating something entirely new to both of us.

CHAPTER 26

dallas

"You're late, dickhead," Sawyer spits at me.

"So, blow me, shithead."

I toss my bag and gear into the back of Carter's SUV and move to help tie down our snowboards to the roof.

"Off to a fantastic start fam! Sooo excited to be stuck in a fuckin' car with you three cheerful Sally's for the next six fuckin' hours," Carter chastises.

"Are you leaving your pregnant wife behind, Casanova?" Sawyer quips back.

"Ah, so lover boy is out? I'm good with Casanova. And fuck no, I will never be a father. I'll be the cool-as-shit funcle who lets them have extra cake on their birthday and try weed for the first time when they're teenagers," Carter says, and I laugh loudly.

"Do you wanna die, asshole?" Sawyer says through his teeth. Carter's right, he's much grouchier than normal, so I simmer down a bit.

Sawyer and I step on the side bars on opposite ends of the SUV and reach over to lock everything in place on the roof.

"Hey, you doin' okay? Kinsey is staying with her, she'll be fine, you know that, right?"

"I'm just not ready to be away from her. I just got her back."

"I get it. But you made her your wife and put a baby in her, she's not runnin' this time."

"Yeah. You're right, just uneasy."

We tighten the straps down tight, making sure our precious cargo doesn't go anywhere when we're flying down the highway. Sawyer double-checks the straps before speaking, "Yep! that ain't goin' anywhere. Alright, we're good to go. Get in, idiots, we got a mountain to get to!"

Signaling the end of our conversation, the four of us climb into the car and get comfortable for a long-ass drive up north. Mount Baker, get ready for the Hayes boys.

About an hour into the drive, Carter pulls out his cooler with road sodas and cracks one open, handing it to me before doing the same for himself. I take a long pull of the beer, even though it's the ass crack of dawn still. My head is still fuzzy from everything that happened with Blaire. I've never experienced anything like that before, so fully lost to another person. She's so damn perfect. I fucking hate that I have to leave her for two days.

Liam continues to play his shitty-ass music from the passenger seat, nineties alternative rock blaring from the speakers. If he plays something by Third Eye Blind one more time I'm tempted to tie him by his ankles and drag him from the tailgate the rest of the way to Demming. I relax in my seat and try to tune out the noise, looking out my window at the cars we pass on the highway like I did when I was a kid, bored out of my damn mind.

"Hey, Casanova," I say to my youngest brother, "dare you to moon this semi comin' up."

"Hold my beer."

Carter hands me his drink, unbuckles and lifts himself so his ass is in the window, drops his pants, and does a little shake just as we're passing the semitruck. A horn blares several times and we both lose it, laughing in our seats.

"Are you two fuckin' ten? You're gonna get us killed. Haven't you seen *Joy Ride*?" Liam yells at us from the passenger seat.

"You talking about the movie with Paul Walker?" I ask, still wheezing in laughter.

"Yes, idiot and Steven Zahn."

"Who cares, he's not going to track us down and try to kill us, just laugh and quit being a little bitch."

"You wanna walk the rest of the way?"

I roll my eyes and look at Carter, who's still laughing. At least he's trying to have some fun. Sawyer and Liam need to take a chill pill, or this is going to be the year we all kill each other on this trip.

Five long-ass hours later, including a handful of stops to grab food and switch drivers, we pull up to our Airbnb not a second too soon. Carter throws it in park, and hauls ass up to the front door, fumbling with the keypad to unlock it, I'm assuming to take a leak.

"Fuckin' finally. Being cramped in there with you idiots once a year is enough to drive me mad," Sawyer says as he steps out of the passenger seat and stretches his body.

"You know we still have to drive back, right?" I ask just to piss him off.

"Fuck you, dickhead. Help me get the shit inside."

Liam knocks his shoulder against mine as we open the trunk.

"We need to update his nickname, shithead aint cutting it anymore."

"Crotchety old man seems like it'll fit," I say under my breath.

Liam finally cracks a laugh as we start hauling our duffel bags and gear out of the back to bring inside for the night. Once inside, the yells, grunts, and thumps coming from down the hall get our asses moving to find out what the hell is going on. Liam and I walk in on Sawyer holding Carter to the ground with his arm wrapped around his neck, Carter shifting his body weight to flip Sawyer.

"Tap, little bro. You don't get the master bedroom. I'm the oldest and you're still a little shit. Tap!"

"Ff-u-ck yooou."

Sawyer squeezes a bit more, Carter's face starting to drain of color. I lean back against the door frame and cross my arms, a huge smirk on my face, happy to watch from this side for a change. I'm surprised Liam and Carter break Sawyer and me up so quickly. It's pretty amusing to watch.

"C'mon, Carter, just tap. You were never gettin' this room. We got shit to unpack and stuff to do," Liam says as he walks out and leaves me to my entertainment. Carter tries several more times to get out of Sawyer's hold with no luck before he finally taps out. Sawyer's a natural fighter, boxing is his thing, but he also has dabbled in mixed martial arts. Sawyer releases him and stands, fixing his clothes and reaching for Carter to pull him on his feet.

"We good now? Get your shit out of here and let's get settled." Sawyer runs his hands through his hair, pulls out his phone, and walks away, no doubt to call Ivy and let her know we made it. My fingers itch to call Blaire, but my brothers know I'm never on my phone and would get suspicious. Grabbing my things, I toss them into one of the rooms that isn't Sawyer's special suite and seek out my other two brothers to get a plan together.

Later that night, the four of us are sitting in the living room, drinking beers and talking when I decide to pull out the dice I brought with me for our traditional game of Cee-Lo. I drop them on the coffee table in front of us and sit back with a smug grin. We play this every year, and it gets heated when you've got four heavy-headed competitive fuckers putting money down like it's on fire.

"Oooohhhh! You wanna do this, huh?"

"Pull out your cash you little shits, let's go!" Sawyer yells while rubbing his hands together, moving to the edge of his seat.

I grin ear to ear, ready to get started. Cash is thrown onto the table and we take turns rolling, Sawyer, Carter and I sipping on the whiskey bottle like it's water, the beer no longer cutting it. A few rounds of rolling happen, and money gets passed back and forth before it's my turn to be the banker. I pull out a hundred-dollar bill and drop it in the middle.

"Like fuckin' clockwork. Always the shit-stirrer," Liam jokes, "alright, boys, let's do this."

Everyone matches my hundred, dropping the cash they came prepared with on top of mine.

Shaking the dice in my hand, I drop them on the table, the dice bouncing and spinning before coming to a stop. A four-five-six.

"Motherfucker!" Liam yells as I snatch up the four hundred dollars.

I wake to the blaring god-awful sound of "Never Gonna Give You Up" by Rick Astley and cover my head with my pillow while I groan. It's a bullshit hour and I know I have to get my ass moving but I wait until the smell of bacon travels through the air and I'm sure that Liam has food ready. Dragging my ass from the bed, I pull on my sweats and toss a hoodie over my head to go find coffee and sustenance.

"Plates already on the table, dickhead. How you feelin'?" Liam asks.

"Like ass. How are you so chipper?"

"I didn't drink as much as you did. Didn't want to puke the entire way down the slopes like you're gonna do."

"Well, here's to hoping this grease soaks up all the poison then, yeah? Or I'll be sure to blow chunks all over you."

I search through a bunch of cabinets before finding the mugs and pour some much-needed coffee. After sitting down at the table with my plate of bacon, some sausage links, and scrambled eggs, Sawyer and Carter walk in, grabbing their plates and scarfing down their food in silence, Carter looking similar to how I currently feel. The alcohol is still sloshing around in my stomach and through my veins like sludge.

After breakfast, I pour a second cup of coffee and we go our separate ways, the adrenaline starting to kick in for our day ahead. I get ready, grabbing what I need to, and head outside to find Liam already packing up the car and Sawyer typing away on his phone. I double check that the boards are secured and take a seat in the back of the SUV. Sawyer finally gets off his phone and climbs into the driver's seat, Liam joining us in the passenger.

"Who's going to get him?"

The three of us throw our fists toward the center console while yelling, "Rock, paper, scissors, shoot!"

Losing, I say, "Best of three."

"Fuck you, go get him!" Sawyer yells.

I jump out of the back of the car and jog back up to the house.

"C'mon, Casanova! Move your ass! We got places to be!" I yell from the entryway.

By the time we're pulling in, parking is a nightmare, per usual, but once we find a spot and triple-check that we have everything we need, we get on the shuttle to take us to the lodge. The line to get tickets is longer than I remembered, and I fidget on my feet restlessly, itching to be out on the mountain again. The air is brisk, the sun starting to peek over the mountains, and I know it's going to be a damn good day.

"Shit," Carter moans as we near the ticket counter.

"What now?"

"I forgot my wallet."

"Are you kidding me right now?"

"You were rushing me!"

"We waited for ten minutes!"

"There's nothing we can do about it now, we're almost through this bullshit line. I'm itching to get out there, so shut the hell up and let's just survive this," I tell him.

Once we're finally through all the bullshit, it all fades to the background, because it's me and the trail. We got here at opening so the mountain is still quiet and all seems right in the world. We start on an easy one, getting our footing and finding that muscle memory that hasn't been used in a year. The moment I'm heading out on my board, a rush of adrenaline engulfs me. The crisp, cool air fills my lungs as I look through my goggles at the pure white, flawless powder in front of me.

We start to pump it up after that, branching out. By the third run, we head to the natural halfpipe off the C5 chairlift and it's like coming home. I'm in my element. With every turn and leap, the world melts away behind me. I live for this.

Sitting next to Sawyer on the next lift, I use it as an opportunity to check in with him. Something that both of us have sucked at the last few months. I wish I could come clean to him about Blaire, but I know she's not ready yet and I'll be damned if I betray her trust.

"How are you feeling about becoming a dad?"

"Ready for her to be here, honestly."

"Wait, *her*?"

"Oh shit, yeah. It's a girl. Don't repeat it. Ivy wants it to be a surprise."

"That's amazing, man. I've never seen you happier, I'm happy for you."

"Still doesn't feel real some days. I wasn't living, you know? Just kind of existing because I had to. I don't think I'll ever take for granted waking up next to her after losing her."

"Well, you made damn sure that you won't. Put that baby in her quick."

"First time I had her again," he says with a laugh, "I told her and gave her options, but fuck if I was going waste any time using something like condoms. I love her, swollen with my baby inside her. I'll fuckin' do it again as soon as she's healthy enough to carry another one."

"You're a freak, you know that?"

But even saying the words, I can't help but imagine what it would be like to settle down with Blaire and watch her stomach grow with my child in it. I'm in no way ready for that now, but I wonder if she wants kids and how many. She said all she wished for was a family, and now I feel the desire to know more.

"Remember when Kins was a baby?"

"How could I not? She was so good and sweet. Everything that's right and perfect in the world."

"Now look at her. Feral little gremlin."

"Hey, we made her that way. At least she can hold her own."

We both laugh and I wonder if she's using the time we're away to lose her mind a bit. Even when she was at college, one of us was always checking in on her, never quite giving her the freedom to do whatever she wanted. Overprotective dicks, but we love her too much to let anything happen to her.

After two more runs, we're ready for food and a drink.

"Which lodge for food?" Liam asks on the way out.

"Heather Meadows," I tell him.

"Hell no, we're going to Raven Hut. I'm craving their brisket," Sawyer says.

"Kiss my ass, shithead, I spoke first. Liam, go to Heather Meadows."

My brother's hand connects with the back of my skull with a loud slap. I whip my head in his direction, pushing my palm against the side of his face and knocking his head against the car window, holding it in place.

"What about White Salmon Lodge? Raven Hut's food sucks," Carter chimes in.

"Heather. Meadows."

Sawyer smacks my forearm, knocking his face free of my hold. "Raven. Hut."

"Seriously, let's go to White Salmon, I want to see if that chick is still waitressing. She was a fun time last year."

"NO!" Sawyer and I both yell at Carter.

We end up getting burgers at Raven Hut, everyone except Carter, who orders the same chicken tenders he gets every year.

"They're the best I've ever had, so shut the hell up," he tells us while flagging down our waitress.

"Four tequila shots, please, beautiful."

"Alright, tone it down there, Casanova. Don't need to be bringing your A-game to the lodge. I'm sure she gets hit on enough," Liam tells him.

Two tequila shots later, we drag our asses back out. The next trail is the longest but has a nice S turn to get our post-lunch feet back in motion. I lose myself to the mountain.

Back at our Airbnb, things start to get a little wild. Blame it on the lack of sleep, the delirium of being on the slopes all day, the adrenaline crash, or just being away with no responsibilities, but we tend to lose our minds. Carter stands with his pants pulled down over his ass, bent over the picnic table outside while Sawyer heats up a metal poker in the fire pit we started.

"How 'bout a belt to put between your teeth?" Liam suggests.

Carter just grunts. "How the fuck did I lose this goddamn bet again?"

"You were a shit-eating, cocky-ass motherfucker who thought he could beat us down the slope. Loser gets a branding to his ass. Isn't that what you said? How'd it work out for you, huh, Casanova? The ladies are gonna love to see this one," Sawyer reminds him, and I hunch over in laughter. Liam joins me.

"Hold him down, boys! This one's gonna sting!"

I pull my shirt over my nose, anticipating the rancid smell of burnt flesh as Sawyer holds the poker over Carter's ass cheek, and

Liam and I grab our brother's arms. The sizzle hits my ears before the smell comes and I wince, clenching my ass cheeks together in sympathy.

"MOTHERFUCKER!" Carter wails.

And my brothers and I fall to the ground in a fit of laughter.

blaire

WORK IS BIZARRE WITHOUT THE HAYES BROTHERS running the place. Everything operates smoothly, but I find myself looking for Dallas even though I know I won't find him. After a long day of tours and tastings, I collapse on my futon once I'm home. With Dallas gone, I decide to throw all of my focus into the proposal for changing up the dynamic of the events department of the distillery. I'm positive that the changes could not only benefit the company, but also give Dallas the peace he loves while on the property. Plus, I love creating events that give people their happily ever after much more than I do giving tours.

I work on restructuring what I've already created, putting less focus on the day-to-day tours and more on being a large-scale event venue with a more defined schedule. The research for financial projections is taking a little longer than I had hoped, but the rest of it starts to come together, which gets me excited. Maybe this gesture can bridge the final gap between Dallas and me. Whether I'm personally to blame or not, I know I'm the physical representation of the changes made to the distillery that disturbed his peace. Now that I understand him, I want to give him this. Everyone deserves peace, and I'm starting to accept that he brings me mine.

Losing track of time, I close my laptop after my stomach's protests for hunger get too loud to ignore, when my phone chimes with an incoming text message. Anticipating it being Dallas, I quickly snatch it off my desk to look at the notification. I've only heard from him once, a text last night saying that he hopes I'm sleeping well.

Ivy: Hey Blaire, Kinsey and I are having a girls' night tonight while the guys are away. Want to go out with us? She's dragging me out and to be her DD and I'd love the backup. I hate going out.

Ivy: She wants to let loose while her "overprotective, alpha brothers are fucking off" *laugh emoji*

Me: That sounds great. I'm assuming The Night Owl?

Ivy: Unfortunately. But it should be fun. 7 p.m.

Me: lol! Meet you there!

Excited that I won't be spending another night alone, I start to get ready for a girls' night—something I haven't really had before. Up until I moved to Aspen Ridge, I've stayed reclusive. It's hard for me to put my walls down long enough to get close to people. But I feel at home in AR and want nothing more than to stay here and make it my forever home.

Stripping out of my office clothes, I dig through my little closet to find something cute enough to wear out with Ivy and Kinsey. There's a lingering pressure for them to like me, wanting their approval because I'm sleeping with their family member. Which sounds as crazy as it is. Maybe if Dallas and I decide to come out to everyone, they will be supportive of it because they like me.

I reach for my favorite pair of dark denim jeans that have always made me feel confident. They cling to my shapely bottom half, accentuating every curve that I love so much. I pull on a cream boatneck sweater, my favorite brown booties, big yellow gold hoop earrings, and attempt to tame my hair. The winter air has been kind to me, but once summer arrives it will be a whole different story. Any amount of humidity will wreak havoc on my already wild locks. After I douse it with a hearty spray of dry shampoo and freshen up my makeup, I grab my purse, coat, and lock up, heading down the stairs toward The Night Owl.

"Where do you think you're goin'?" Reid's voice echoes through the small alley I'm walking through between our building and the one next to us on Main Street. A quick burst of fear rushes through me before I register the voice's owner. I look back to find the tattooed beast walking behind me. He's wearing a pair of black jeans, brown boots that lace up the front, a tight white shirt, and a brown jacket. His tattoos peek out over his clothes on every inch of exposed skin, minus his face. His hair is down, slightly wet like he has showered recently, and hanging loosely.

"Out, creeper. Where are you going? It's frowned upon to stalk unsuspecting girls in a dark alley. Don't you know better?" I say jokingly. His steps falter and I cock my head to the side to study him.

"I wouldn't hurt you, B." His voice is laced with hurt and concern.

"Reid, I was just making a joke, of course I know you'd never hurt me. Or anyone for that matter."

He nods in understanding before joining me, and together we walk out of the alley and onto the cobblestone sidewalk of downtown Aspen Ridge. I pull my thick coat closer, the breeze chilling me to my bones.

"I'm heading to girls' night at the bar with Ivy and Kinsey. Want to crash it?"

He gives me a devilish smile and loops his arm in mine, pulling me along with him in the direction of The Night Owl. Reid has to be the most genuine, sweetest man I've ever met in my life, and how he hasn't been snatched up is beyond me. He's going to make someone extremely happy someday.

After a short walk, we arrive at our destination and Reid opens the door for me, the warm heat blasting my face, and I immediately want my coat off of my body. Shrugging out of it, I look around the room until I find the girls sitting in a booth in front of a big window at the back of the bar.

"Look who I found, mind if he joins us?"

"Never! He's an honorary girls' night attendee," Ivy says as Reid takes a seat next to her in the booth. I slide in next to Kinsey, whose face is a little flushed, and who hasn't said a word yet, her eyes darting around nervously.

"Hey, everything okay?" I whisper to her.

"Uhm, yeah, why wouldn't it be? Of course everything is okay."

"Just making sure. You look a little flustered."

"Oh, it's just warm in here. I'm good. Glad you could make it."

"Thanks for inviting me. It's been forever since I had a girls' night."

And by forever, I mean forever. As in, not ever.

"What can I get you lovely ladies to drink?" Reid asks.

"Water for me."

"Midori sour sounds good tonight," Kinsey says, and I agree.

"Same for me. You're the best."

Reid excuses himself to head to the bar and order drinks for everyone while the three of us check in with each other.

"How's pregnancy?" I ask Ivy.

"It was rough at first but now that the all-day sickness has subsided I'm loving it."

"Thank god for that since Sawyer has plans to breed you like a show horse. Which is gross by the way, and he should totally stop announcing it," Kinsey deadpans, and I can't help but toss my head back in a deep laugh.

"You're not wrong though," Ivy says through laughs.

"How's everything with you, Blaire? I haven't really seen you since New Year's Eve."

"Oh, everything has been great," I say, trying not to blush when all the sex I've been having with Dallas flashes through my head, "just been so busy with work. I have several bookings for weddings in the spring that I'm planning for, on top of the day-to-day. I really love it though. Just ready to not do tours in the winter. It's freaking cold, and that's saying something because I'm a winter girl! I definitely didn't expect so many crazies to want to visit in the winter months, so I've been surprised!"

"People are wacky about what they're willing to do. I think the distillery has been so elusive for so long that people are eager to see behind the gates, you know?"

"That's true. Kinsey, you never wanted to work there? All the boys seem so sure that working in some aspect of the business was inevitable for them. How'd you skip out on it?" I ask as Reid sets down a tray of drinks in front of us and takes his seat next to Ivy.

"That was never in the cards for me. It's so hard being the baby, plus the only girl? Forget it. I needed to break away from them and have some autonomy beyond being a Hayes—and Sawyer, Dallas, Liam, or Carter's baby sister. It gives me the ick. I'm not a baby and it would be so nice to be seen as a woman who's independent from her family. Does that make sense?"

"Girl, you are preaching to the choir. I am the poster child of breaking away from parental expectations and building the life that you want. I'm all for you chasing after what makes *you* happy. Just don't waste years like I did," Ivy tells her, and I silently agree because nothing has ever been truer.

"On that note, let's cheers!" Kinsey picks up her pretty

emerald drink and I do the same, clinking it together with Ivy's water, and Reid's soda.

"To living the life you want!" Kinsey yells.

"Cheers!"

I take a sip, the alcohol going down smooth, and quickly find my new favorite drink.

"No alcohol for you, Drogo?"

"Don't drink."

"What? How did I not know this?" Ivy asks him.

"'Cause you've been knocked up since a month after I met you."

"Okay, that's fair."

The four of us spend the next hour talking and laughing like old friends and it fills me with so much happiness. I settle into the comfort of being out with people who genuinely want to be with me, and let myself relax. I have another Midori sour, feeling the alcohol thrum through my bloodstream, and know it's time for some water. Kinsey accompanies me to the bar where she orders four b-52 shots.

"Don't look now, Blaire, but a certain Cole Barnes is here, and he hasn't taken his eyes off you."

Fuck. Cole texted me a few weeks ago asking if he could take me out again but I've been so busy I completely forgot to respond. Feeling somewhat horrible, my mood dampens slightly.

"He is eye fucking the shit out of you. You sure you don't want to hook up with him again? He's hot. So is his friend."

"We never hooked up and I'm for sure good on that front," I tell her.

Kinsey slams back one of her shots just as Cole and his friend join us at the bar. His hand settles on my lower back in a move of confidence, like he's familiar with me in a way that he actually isn't. I turn out of his touch, it feeling all wrong on me. Thankfully, Dallas isn't here because I don't think he would stand idly by and allow it to happen, present company be damned.

"Hey, pretty lady, haven't seen you in a bit, how ya been?"

"Hi, Cole. I'm really well. So busy with the pressure of work but things are great."

"Who's your friend, Coley?"

"Haven't been called that in decades, Kinsey, let's keep it that way, yeah? This is my college buddy, Theo."

"Hi, Theo, I'm Kinsey," she says as she sticks out her hand in his direction.

"Pleasure to meet you, Kinsey. How about a drink?"

"Happily."

Theo moves around Cole and me to stand next to Kinsey at the bar, ordering a drink, and I suddenly feel like a fish out of water. Kinsey slams back another shot that's in front of her, and I snatch the remaining two to keep her from taking all of them. I hand one to Cole, because what else am I supposed to do with it?

"Cheers," I say as I toss back the coffee-flavored shot.

Cole looks at me quizzically for a moment before picking up the shot and drinking it down.

Knowing I can't leave Kinsey alone with this guy, I stand here awkwardly and attempt to make small talk with Cole while Kinsey flirts with his friend.

"So, Coley, huh? How'd you get that nickname?"

"Dallas, actually. Long time ago. Speaking of, I don't see him anywhere," he says as he looks around the bar.

"Why would he be here?"

Cole leans in and whispers in my ear sending a chill down my spine. Not the good kind.

"I think we both know why; you don't need to play games."

"Excuse me?"

He pulls back from me and smiles, licking his lips and letting his eyes trace over my body. I suddenly feel extremely uncomfortable, and as Kinsey takes another shot, Theo gets more and more handsy with her. The hair on my arms stands on end and I start to panic, the situation slowly getting out of control. The alcohol and anxiety mix together, buzzing between my ears as I try to calm myself down.

When I overhear Theo ask Kinsey if she wants to "get out of here" and he takes her hand, I look around frantically to find Reid, his eyes already focused on the situation. Theo pulls Kinsey behind him, stepping away from me, and I move to stand in front of them.

"Hey, you. You seem like you're ready to go home. Want to crash at my place?" I ask her.

She gives me a big, goofy smile as she slurs her next words, "I'm going to go back with Theo." She leans in really close to me, whispering in a not-so-whisper, "It's time I get laid, I want this shit over with."

Before I know what's happening, Reid steps between us, bending down practically to his knees and scooping Kinsey up over his shoulder. She squeals loudly, drawing the attention of everyone in the bar.

"Oh, no you don't. Fuck that, Kins. You think I'm going to let you go home with some out-of-town stranger? Not fucking happening."

"Screw you, Reid! Put me down!"

"Not a chance, sweetheart. You want to get me killed? Your brothers will have my ass six feet under by lunch tomorrow without breaking a sweat. Time to go home, *alone*."

"You're just like my stupid overbearing brothers, you dick! Just let me get it over with!"

I quickly grab her purse and coat and follow them outside to give him her things, catching the tail end of their conversation. Kinsey is back on her feet, Reid's hands on both sides of her face as he crouches down to face her. She looks like a tiny doll in his massive hold. Their size difference is drastic.

"Your virginity is fucking precious, sweetheart. Don't you dare just give that shit away. You're trashed, and that's not when we make huge decisions like this. It's time to go back to Ivy's."

It's hard not to feel like I'm intruding on an intimate moment, but that's just Reid. He has the biggest heart in the world and cares so deeply about everyone. I know he'd do the same for any of us. I don't think he was cut out for this harsh world, being such an empath.

"Hey, here's her coat, she's going to freeze. Ivy was in the bathroom, but I'll go back in and grab her."

"Thanks, B. I'll take them back to Ivy and Sawyer's. Come with us and I'll drop you off after."

"I'm fine, it's just a few blocks. I can hold my own, I promise."

"I don't like that, B."

"I'll text you as soon as I'm inside and the door is locked."

I jog back into The Night Owl and find Ivy putting on her coat.

"Kinsey?"

"Yep. Reid saved the day. He's really a saint."

"We're entirely too lucky to have him in our lives, honestly. I get why he's Sawyer's best friend."

"I couldn't agree more. He's going to bring you two home, I'm going to walk since I'm just up the road a bit."

She looks at me for a moment with confusion and I realize that no one but Reid and Dallas know where I live. Surely it wouldn't be too abnormal to share an apartment downtown with my nonexistent grandparents, right? Luckily, she doesn't press for answers, and we walk outside to Reid's truck, Cole and Theo not saying a word to us. I say my goodbyes and check my surroundings before heading down the sidewalk in the direction of my little apartment.

Once I'm back in my studio, I strip from my clothes and pull on the shirt Dallas left me that smells so much like him, all woodsy and masculine. It's now that my heart starts to pang for him, my mind no longer occupied, left idle to get lost in my thoughts. After being alone for twenty-seven years, it's shocking how quickly I've fallen into a rhythm with him. I should be so used to operating solo that his absence shouldn't be that noticeable. But I miss him.

Last night was okay because we don't spend every night together anyway, but after not seeing him for two days? I wish he was here. A chime rings out from my phone next to me and I nearly jump out of my skin as I reach for it.

Dallas: I miss yur mouth

It's as if I summoned him. I laugh at the typos and quickly type back even though the three little dots bubble at the bottom.

Me: Are you drunk?

Dallas: Want u to suck mee off bsby

Dallas: Very

Dallas: I wwant you on yor knees

He's trashed. I've never seen him this way, and I laugh silently to myself, wishing I could get a glimpse of drunk Dallas in person. I get comfortable under my blankets, holding my phone in front of my face, the glow the only light in the room.

Me: Yeah? What else do you want?

Dallas: I jsu want to hldyou.

Me: You just want to hold me?

Dallas: ya

Dallas: watch u sleep

My heart tumbles in my chest, throbbing painfully against my ribcage. This man has the biggest heart, even when he's drunk at two a.m.

Me: I wish you were here, too

My phone rings with an incoming FaceTime call and I answer it, a smile all over my face.

"Hi."

"Yoursobeautiful."

"You're so drunk."

"I am. Gotta be quiet. Brothers are crashed out hard though. Show me that pussy, baby."

A breath rushes from my lips.

"Dallas . . ."

"Princess, don't make me repeat myself," he slurs. I set the phone down and shimmy out of my panties, pulling the blankets back off me. "Show me what I love."

I spread my legs and move the phone between them so that he can see.

"Spread wide, baby girl."

I do as he says, spreading my legs wider and he moans loudly.

I look down my body, seeing his face that's lit up by the light of his phone. His eyes are glassed over, that look of desire written all over his features.

"Touch yourself. I am. I want to get off watching you touch yourself."

I stay quiet, moving my free hand between my legs and slipping my fingers through my center, finding myself already wet. I dip into my core, gathering up the wetness there and moving up to circle my clit.

"That's it, baby, rub that clit." He's breathing just as hard as I am, his camera shaking, and I know it's because he's jerking himself off, which turns me on further. Thinking about his hand rubbing up and down on that thick, pierced cock like I've seen him do before. I press down harder on that sweet spot between my legs, a moan releasing from my lips.

"Dallas, I want you here."

"I know, my princess. I want to make you come all over my face, wanna lick up all that sweet cum."

"Oh fuck, Dallas." I rub faster, my hips bucking, chasing the impending orgasm.

"That's my good fuckin' girl. Come for me."

I combust, my orgasm swirling through my body, waves of pleasure pulsing through me.

"Baby, I'm coming, fuck." His moans fuel me, pushing me to a new height, flying high, and loving every second of the bliss.

My orgasm ebbs, and I pull my phone back up to my face.

"I wasn't expecting that," I confess. "But I'm not complaining."

He looks at me happily loopy and exhausted, his eyes heavy.

"I'll see you tomorrow. Sleep well, princess. Thank you."

"See you tomorrow."

We hang up and my body aches to be wrapped up in the safety of his big arms. Within a few moments, sleep claims me too.

· · ·

I curl up into a ball, holding my backpack close as I try to stay as small as possible. I huddle closer to the plastic panel on the side of the trailer. Mr. Cain searches everywhere for me.

His footsteps crunch on the gravel driveway. He's been looking for me for a while, and I know the longer I hide, the worse the punishment will be. He expected me home after school today. I hate Wednesdays and being home so much earlier than everyone else. Once he figured out my schedule, his torment shifted from only at night to Wednesday afternoons. If I can just hide long enough the other kids will get home. He never tries to touch me when others are home and awake.

"I know you're out here, you little whore. Come give Daddy what he wants."

Bile turns in my stomach, and I do everything I can to keep it down. I want to take a razor blade to my skin, peel off everywhere he's defiled and touched. I hate him. I hate what he's taken from me. What he's stolen and claimed as his own.

His footsteps crunch closer and I start to panic, caught between fight and flight again, stuck frozen in the in-between, when his hand reaches out and grabs a fistful of my hair. My hands reach up and cover his, trying to break him free as I'm dragged out of my hiding spot and across the rocky gravel.

"Bad girl, Blaire. It's not nice to hide from your daddy when he needs something from you. Time to pay your dues."

He yanks me harder, and I bite my lip to stifle the scream that wants to escape me. I know that if I bring attention to us, it will only make it worse. Even if someone heard me, even if they saw, no one here in this shitty trailer park would do a thing to stop it. I struggle to gain my footing, trying to stand and walk, but his grip is too hard, my hair ripping brutally from my head.

My body thumps hard on each of the crumbling wooden steps as he drags me up them. The door is pushed open and I'm thrown through it. I feel the moment a handful of hair is ripped from my scalp. A scream rips from my throat, and I instantly regret it as his booted foot connects with my stomach.

"You stupid girl. You'll never learn. Don't worry. Daddy's here to teach you a lesson."

He climbs on top of me, pinning me down and shoving the side of my face into the cat-piss-stained carpet. I dry heave, gasping for air and gagging, my stomach trying to purge something that's not there due to the lack of food.

He leans down, his greasy, acne-scarred face rubbing back and forth over my cheek as he smells me, licking up the side of my face. I try to push myself further into the floor, the alternative worse than whatever else has soaked into the threadbare carpet. My eyes squeeze shut, bracing for what's to come and going to the place that keeps me safe. Somewhere far from this hell. Somewhere with someone who loves me and chases all the evil away.

"FUCK!" I jerk from my sleep, sitting up straight, nausea rolling through me. I place my hand over my heart and take a few deep breaths, calming myself down. He can't hurt me anymore, I remind myself. His face in the crowd of people visiting the distillery flashes behind my eyes.

After convincing myself that I've seen Andrew in Aspen Ridge, and now another nightmare, I open up my laptop and do the one thing I've been avoiding out of fear. I pull up the Washington State Department of Corrections website and enter the information for an incarcerated data search, needing to know for sure whether or not he's still locked up. His information loads and my heart plummets into my stomach, my mouth dropping open as nerves hold me hostage.

Released.

He's out.

Grabbing my phone, I call Dallas. I wait while the call is connected, but then it goes straight to voicemail. I end the call without leaving a message. My heart sinks further, stomach acid churning and bile rising. I run to the bathroom and flip up the lid, emptying the contents of my stomach into the toilet.

Laying terrified and exhausted on my tiled bathroom floor, I don't let myself cry this time. I know Dallas would have answered if he hadn't passed out drunk and I can't blame him for that. But part of my heart hurts that I can't hear his voice when it's all I want in this moment.

I pick myself up off the floor and rinse out my mouth before brushing my teeth. Crawling into bed on shaking limbs, I cover myself the way I always do, buried heavily under blankets, cocooning them around me and letting sleep take me, knowing full well what will haunt me once it does.

CHAPTER 28

blaire

THE CHILLY AIR NIPS AT MY CHEEKS AS I WALK OUT into the early winter morning, exhaustion plaguing my entire body. I take a deep breath of it, filling my lungs with the crisp, fresh feeling that is like a balm for my already shot nerves. My drive to the distillery is calm and serene, the sun struggling to break through the thick blankets of clouds, casting a glow over the snow-covered trees. I'm so deeply in love with this town and the people who live here, I can't imagine ever leaving. But if Andrew is out of prison and has found me? If he wants vengeance for getting him locked up? I have to run. I can't prove that the man I saw at the distillery was him, but it's too much of a coincidence not to be.

I pull into the distillery and drive around back to the staff parking lot. As I'm stepping out of my car, Dallas appears in front of me from out of nowhere, causing me to jump back and yelp, my hand flying to my chest.

"What the hell is wrong with you? Will you quit scaring me!"

"Never. Why are you so jumpy?"

"Because you popped up like freaking Michael Myers, you creep. Welcome home. Wait, how are you home so early?"

My body hums to life with him this close to me but I'm

keenly aware of our proximity to everyone else. It takes everything I have not to jump him and lean into his big chest. I'm desperate to feel his arms around me.

"Sawyer couldn't stand to be away from Ivy any longer. Woke us up to get on the road and drove straight through, just got back. Follow me."

He takes a few steps away from me, heading to a large warehouse that I've never been inside, next to the parking lot.

"Where are we going, Dallas? I have work to do and people will be showing up for the first tour at ten," I say as I look down at the watch around my wrist.

"I fucking missed you and if I don't get inside you right now, I'm going to haul you out of here like a caveman."

He grabs my wrist as he slides open a large bay door just enough for us to slip inside. The smell of charred sugar and wood immediately engulfs me. The room is filled floor-to-ceiling with barrels.

"What is this place? This isn't a rickhouse, but it smells like one, and why don't I know of it yet?"

"It's storage for the old barrels waiting to be shipped out. We sell them to make some of the money back on the wood. They're all empty. They typically get turned into wood chips or we sell them to distilleries in Scotland where they don't require new barrels."

"I'll never get used to how much I love the smell of these things. Charred oak and maple, god. I love it."

I turn my focus from the massive lines of barrels to the Hulk in front of me. His eyes are heavy-lidded, his hands curling and uncurling at his sides. I take a hesitant step back from him.

"Dallas. I have a tasting that people will be arriving for. There isn't time for this."

But my god do I want him. My heart starts to beat wildly in my chest as he stalks me backward.

"Then you better come quickly."

He pounces then, like a lion attacking his prey. It's useless to fight, I never stood a chance from the very beginning. His mouth connects with mine as he pushes me against a barrel, pulling my legs up and around his waist. My moans are smothered by his mouth as his hands dig into the flesh of my thighs, gripping me hard, the way I like it. I missed him. Reaching between us, I pull his belt buckle loose, followed by the buttons of his pants. They're pushed down just enough that his massive cock springs free, my hand wrapping around it and tugging.

"Fuck yes, baby girl. Stroke it. Fuck, I missed this. Missed the feel of you."

His kisses are sloppy, rough, and brutal, just as demanding as he is. His talented fingers work their way between us until they meet my center, pulling my panties to the side and finding me already wet.

"Always so ready for my cock."

"Shut up and fuck me, Dallas."

"Shit, I love it when you talk dirty to me."

He grips my hips tightly, lining himself up with my slick entrance and slamming home.

"Aah! Fuuuck!" One of his hands clasps over my mouth, reminding me that we have to be quiet.

"As much as I love hearing you scream for me, I need you to shut the fuck up. Be my good girl, princess. Show me how quiet you can be while I fuck your perfect cunt and fill it with my cum."

The moan that leaves me is primal. His filthy words always spur me on and push me closer to orgasm. His thrusts become brutal, pounding into me with such force, I'm rocking on the whiskey barrel. He buries his face into my neck, sucking on the skin above my shoulder. The feeling of the stubble on his face sends a delicious mix of pain and pleasure through my body.

"Fuck, I love this pussy."

"Oh god I'm close, don't stop, Dallas, please don't stop."

"Milk me, baby girl. You feel so damn good. Make me come."

I lean back from him, balancing on the barrel as he ruthlessly pounds into me. Over and over again.

"I'm coming! Yes! Dallas, I'm coming!"

He pumps into me harder, if possible, my orgasm rolling through me in strong waves, gripping him tightly, my body shaking with the force of it, my arms flying out to grasp anything for purchase.

"That's it, baby girl. Fuck, you're making me come," he groans through clenched teeth. The veins in his neck pop, and his eyes dance around wildly as he watches his cock jerk inside me as he comes.

He slams into me one more time, knocking the barrel back into the others lined next to us. I reach for him at the same time he wraps his arms around me, yanking me off it and shuffling backward. I jerk from his arms at the deafening sound of whiskey barrels crashing to the cement ground around us. My hands cover my ears as Dallas yanks his pants up and pulls me into his chest, his arms wrapping around my head and body. Moments go by as the thundering sound echoes off the walls and rumbles the ground under us, finally coming to a silent stop.

"Holy shit, will you look at that." Liam's voice breaks me out of Dallas' hold, stumbling away from him and righting my dress, quickly running my hands through my hair. My face flames with embarrassment and shock.

Sawyer and Carter rush in next just as Dallas is buckling his belt. Carter's smile could light up a room while Sawyer is shooting daggers at his twin. I can feel his anger from here.

"So, you two fuckers need to pay up. I'll accept cash or Venmo," Carter says, pointing at Sawyer and Liam. My mouth drops open in horror.

"You were betting on this?" Dallas asks his brothers.

"Well, not so much you fucking the barrel house down to the damn ground, but you two fucking? Yep. I won," Carter replies smugly.

I could die right here.

"This isn't what it looks like . . ." I try to explain, even as Dallas' cum leaks from me, sticking to the inside of my thighs.

Everyone looks at me almost identically. Like I'm the village idiot. Because what else could be happening that caused Dallas' pants to be undone and the whiskey barrels to crash around us?

"It's exactly what it looks like. So, you three mind? Why don't you give us a fucking minute to put ourselves back together."

"We need to fucking talk, dickhead. Do what you gotta do and meet me in my office. Now." Sawyer points at his twin. Carter throws his head back in a laugh.

"I love being right. I fucking knew it!" He tries to fist-bump Liam, but he just rolls his eyes and follows Sawyer from the building, Carter right behind him.

My hands come up to cover my face, mortification sinking in. God. This looks terrible. I'm going to lose my damn job. I love my job. I'm just starting to fit in here and I don't want to have to pick up and move again. If I'm going to lose my job over this, maybe I was never meant to be happy here in Aspen Ridge to begin with. Maybe I'm just not meant to be happy at all. Tears escape my eyes before I feel a pair of large hands clasp around my wrists, pulling them gently from my face. He releases me, only to move his hand under my chin, lifting so that I can meet his eyes.

"Hey, no. No tears. I only want your tears when I'm bringing you pleasure. This won't do."

I chuckle through my crying at his statement.

"I look like a hussy, Dallas. I just got caught sleeping with the boss."

"I know that isn't a good look, and I'm so sorry this is how they found out. After I talk to Sawyer, they won't care."

"I do! You're the COO, Dallas. This is *your* family's business! You're the man. I'm a female employee. Not to mention the new girl! Jesus. I'm an idiot. Holy shit, I'm a fucking idiot. This is a bad look. If word gets around, which I'm sure it will, I'll look like a whore. There's no getting around that."

He moves his hands to grasp my head, holding me still and forcing me to look at him.

"Listen to me. No one who works here is going to think that, and if they do, I'll fucking fire them. I'm not going to let anything happen to you, princess. Fuck everything else."

I step out of his hold and he lets me, not wanting to be swayed by the way his body muddles my brain.

"I need to get back to work," I say firmly as I wipe away the tears and straighten my spine, prepared to hold myself together alone like I always do. "I'm sorry about this disaster." I motion to the dozens of whiskey barrels knocked over. He doesn't say anything as I walk from the building, feeling his eyes on me the entire way.

What the hell have I done?

CHAPTER 29

dallas

"WHAT THE FUCK WERE YOU THINKING, DUMBASS?"

"So, dickhead is out then? We're back to Dumbass Dallas now, huh?"

I pull out my phone and open up the group chat.

"What the fuck are you doing, Dallas?"

I hold up my pointer finger in Sawyer's direction. "Hold, please. Just . . . got to . . . there."

Me: FYI dickhead is out dumbass is back in.

"Okay, please, continue," I say as his phone vibrates on the desk in front of him. He picks it up and no doubt reads my message.

"Really?" he chides.

I roll my eyes, spreading my legs in my chair and relaxing backward. Might as well be comfortable for this lecture.

"Dallas, what are you doing?"

I look around the room, slightly confused.

"Uh? Getting comfortable. Figured this was going to take a bit. Anyone ever tell you you can be a bit long-winded?"

"I mean with fucking Blaire, you idiot! How could you do this? I thought you hated her!"

"Oh, I definitely did. Some days I still do." And wasn't that the truth. That woman drives me batshit crazy on her good days. But I know in my heart I'm a goner for her. There won't be anyone else after her.

"I don't want to get into this with you, Sawyer. She didn't want anyone to know. So you all are going to keep your mouths shut until I figure out what's between us." I hope to fuck she wants the same thing I do. I'd move her ass into my house tonight if she'd let me, marry her in the morning and fuck her senseless that evening. But she's about as flighty as a stray fucking cat. I have to tread at her pace. I have to slowly infect her the way she has me, if I haven't already.

"I don't think you understand how fucked-up this is. You're her goddamn boss, Dallas! She could sue us. You were fucking on the grounds! Do I even want to ask how long this has been going on?"

"Since the wedding," I deadpan.

His eyes shoot up at me, widening before squinting into slits.

"*My* fucking wedding? That was almost two months ago!"

"Have we been to any other weddings?" I ask, truly puzzled. His brain has gone to straight mush. I've heard of pregnant women getting "pregnancy brain" but do the fathers get it? His face morphs from irritation to anger, his cheeks reddening and his hands curling into fists around the expensive office chair he loves so much.

"Hey, hey, watch the chair! You don't want to leave marks on her!" I chastise.

"Fuck the chair! Why aren't you taking this seriously, Dallas?" he says as he closes his eyes and tries to keep himself calm. I applaud his effort. "She's our employee. You're fucking a subordinate."

"Hey, now that's not true. We work *with* each other, CEO. You said so yourself, remember? Blaire and I work with each other, not her for me. Remember? That's what you said." My patronizing hits his limit, because the next thing I know, he's launched himself from his seat as his body tackles mine, flipping my chair backward.

"You're so fucking irresponsible! We haven't even been running the company a year!"

I grapple with him, trying to dislodge myself from his arm wrapped around my neck. I toss my leg around his torso, flipping us to the side and spinning out of his hold.

"Is that what you're worried about? How this is going to make *you* look?"

He gets a shot into my ribs and I can't hold back the wince. I try to get his hands locked down to hold him in place, but he's wanting a fight. He bucks me off, flipping us again. I put up my arms, trying to block the blow to the face that I know is coming. He gets one in, his fist connecting with the same cheek that's still got a light bruise from Reid's stinger, the hard punch knocking my head to the side.

"Fuck!" I yell, keeping my forearms up to block the onslaught.

"For fuck's sake, get them off each other," Liam's voice breaks through the current ringing in my ears.

"Why the hell are you two always talking with your fists? Can't we ever just have a normal fucking meeting?" Carter this time, annoyed as usual, and taking a seat in one of the chairs.

Liam pulls Sawyer off me and looks me over.

I stand, righting my clothes and pulling a water from Sawyer's mini fridge before putting the chair back in place and having a seat, catching my breath. I hold the cold water bottle up to my cheek.

"Sawyer, what the fuck man?" Liam asks.

"You saw everything I did!"

"So, you want to beat his ass for having what looked like consensual sex?"

"At the distillery!" Sawyer yells.

"Psh. Like you haven't fucked Ivy ten ways from Sunday in this place," I quip, never having quite learned how to keep my mouth shut when I need to.

Sawyer stands then and moves to come at me again. Liam gets between us, holding his hands extended outward to each of us like he's holding back feral animals.

"Don't you fucking talk about her like that. Next time you do, I'll break your fucking jaw. You got me?" Sawyer hisses in my direction.

"Loud and fucking clear, captain!" I say as I give him a lazy salute.

"He's not wrong though, Sawyer. None of us can be hypocrites about this," Carter adds.

"You fucking employees, too, Carter?"

We all look at him and he just shrugs.

Sawyer throws his head back, exasperated. I take a deep breath and try to settle this.

"Look, we were keeping this to ourselves while we figured things out. You obviously weren't supposed to find out like *that*, and Blaire is mortified. I'd like to wrap this up so I can go check on her."

"And if this goes south? Then what? We lose Blaire?" Sawyer asks, genuinely concerned.

I think about his question for a moment. I can't imagine seeing her and not being able to touch her, take care of her, talk to her. She loves her job more than anything, and even if this ended badly, which I hope to fuck it doesn't, I couldn't take this from her. It means too much to her. She's worked too hard.

"You won't. You have my word. If shit goes south, I won't let that happen. Even if I have to work from home, work nights, do whatever I need to do so that she's comfortable to stay. I will."

All three of my brother's heads snap back in unison.

"You really care about her." Not a question.

Liam's right. I do.

Instead of going straight to Blaire's office to check on her, I decide to give her some space and take a run downtown for some of her favorites first. By the time I return, I hope that she's simmered down enough to have a calm conversation without her running away and shutting me out.

"Knock, knock," I say as I open Blaire's office door and walk in, closing it softly behind me.

"Haven't you done enough damage today?" she asks from behind her desk, her head laying on her crossed arms over her laptop.

"I deserve that, but now I'm here for some damage control. Chocolate croissant?"

She peeks up at me from her position on the desk, eyes squinting, "Bean Haven?"

I scoff, "As if I'd go anywhere else."

Moving to the front of her desk, I set down her black coffee and pastry and take a seat in one of her chairs. Rather than wait for her to sit up and talk, I make the first move.

"I'm sorry. I told you that no one would find out until we were ready, and I failed you. But, I'm not mad about it."

She sits up quickly, her eyes narrowing at me, so I put up my hands defensively.

"I don't want to hide anymore. I don't want to keep you a secret. I know that makes me a selfish bastard. For the first time in my life, I have something that's just for me. You make me happy, Blaire. Being your man makes me proud and I'm sorry if you still aren't ready for us to be open about that with everyone and I'll do whatever you need to make sure you're comfortable, but I can't go back into hiding. I'm sorry how it happened though."

I say my piece and wait. Her eyes haven't left mine and I can't read her expression at all.

"You don't want to keep me hidden?" Her words are slightly vulnerable.

"Fuck no, baby."

"This isn't a good look for me."

"Then let's make it look good. Tell me what you need from me and it's yours."

"You really mean that?"

"I do. I told my brothers that you didn't want anyone to find out and to keep their mouths shut about it. No one knows but the five of us. And probably Ivy because Sawyer can't keep anything from her. I don't want to hide anymore, but if you still need time, I'll give it to you."

"No more fooling around at work. I feel so stupid. We were bound to get caught."

"You aren't stupid. We're just crazed when we're together. I've already imagined taking you sixteen different ways since I've been in your office."

She laughs and I can finally take a deep breath, some of the pressure and worry in my chest lifting.

"You're not what I expected."

"Yeah, well that sure as shit makes two of us, princess."

She stands and walks over to where I'm sitting, and I open my arms for her to sit on my lap. She complies, and I wrap her tightly in a hug, resting my cheek on her head. Her sweet, jasmine scent wafts around me and I inhale deeply.

"It'll be okay, I promise."

"You can't promise those types of things. But I trust you anyway."

Her words hit their mark. If I give her anything in this life, being a safe place she trusts is the most important.

I sit with her while she sips on her hot coffee and picks at her croissant before I have to leave her to start my day, already way behind schedule, and after being gone for three days, I have to play catch-up.

I pass Liam in the hallway on the way to my office and he nods at me, following me into the room and closing the door behind him.

"She alright?"

"Mortified, but she's the strongest woman I've ever met."

"Well shit, that's sayin' something considering the last six months."

"How's Han, everything okay?"

He runs his hand nervously through his hair and paces the length of my office.

"Still trying to process how I'm going to break it to her that her boyfriend slash ex-boyfriend slash baby daddy is a cheating, piece of shit with a live-in girlfriend and another baby on the way. Oh, and he's most definitely not going to marry you so plan on losing your family's business that you love so much."

"Shit. Yeah. So, advice?"

"Please."

"I wouldn't say it like that."

"Well, no shit, Sherlock. Thanks for helping."

"Like I said before, you know Hannah better than anyone in the world, and you literally were the first person to see Charlie when she delivered her on the kitchen floor. No one knows better how to help them through this than you do."

"Shit sucks, man."

"Trust me, I get it. Just be there for her. It's all you can do. Give her a safe shoulder to lean on, something you've been doing for twenty years already."

"Thanks, brother. I got shit to do but I'll see you Sunday."

"Sounds good."

I wonder what Blaire will decide to do and if she'll make a decision before then. I'd love nothing more than to walk into Sunday dinner holding her hand. Being able to enjoy her at my parents' house surrounded by my family would make me so happy. I just wish I knew if she felt remotely the same as I do, or if she still views us as fuck buddies. After the morning we had together before I left for Mount Baker, I thought I felt the shift. I knew I was in love with her, but she was there with me, fully participating, and I know she felt everything I did.

She had to.
Right?

CHAPTER 30

blaire

After the mortification wore off, I was able to think with a clear head. Being thrust into a situation like we were, I was forced to come to terms with everyone knowing that I was sleeping with my boss. I don't know how long I was going to put off telling people, but I know that I definitely didn't want anyone to find out quite like that. But I know the feelings I have for him are real. They're new, but I recognize them for what they are.

I love him.

I park my car in my usual parking spot behind Rogue and walk around to the front to see if Reid is free to talk. Walking into the tattoo shop is always like taking a time machine to a different world. Aspen Ridge is fairly whimsical. Every place has a different vibe, and nothing is ordinary. Bean Haven is very boho chic, while Barrel House screams speakeasy, Book Bound is a woodland fairytale, and The Night Owl is very Manhattan bar scene.

But going into Rogue? It's like walking into an art gallery. Clean black and white lines, and framed artwork covers every inch of wall space in various sized and shaped frames. There's a reception area in front of floor-to-ceiling glass windows and a single door. The floor, which is more like a round fishbowl, has several stations for various artists, both permanent and guest. It's amazing and not at all what I expected from a tattoo shop. Especially one in a small town like ours.

The place is empty when I walk in, so I open the big door to the floor to find Reid.

"Hellooooo?"

Reid pops out of his office, glasses on his face and iPad in his hand, looking happy to see me.

"Hey, B, what's up?"

"Got a second to talk?"

"Always, what's going on?"

"I know you know about me and Dallas, and I'm not mad you told him where I live, so can we skip the weird shit and jump to the present?"

He laughs at me before talking, "Yeah, he's pretty gone for you, I'm glad I'm forgiven. What happened?"

"His brothers walked in on us at work as we were finishing up . . . you know."

His head bobs and he runs his fingers through his long hair, seemingly slightly uncomfortable with the conversation.

"We may have torn down this huge room filled with old barrels. Like, they came crashing down. Then all of his brothers ran in. Everyone was arriving for work and must have heard it. The freaking ground shook under us, I swear."

Reid starts laughing and then starts apologizing for laughing.

"It's not funny, you big jerk!"

"So, what's the issue besides being embarrassed?"

"Well, I wasn't ready for his family to find out we were sleeping together."

"Is that all you're doing?"

I nervously cross and uncross my legs, unsure what to say.

"Look, you need to decide how you're feeling and let him in on it because he's a total goner for you. I've never seen Dallas worked up that bad over anything, and when he knew you were upset and he couldn't get to you? Well, he was dumb enough to try to take his frustration out on me, if that tells you anything."

"I love him," I blurt out.

"Yeah. Kinda thought so. So, what's the reservation?"

"That I won't be enough for him. That he'll tire of me being damaged goods. That he'll leave me and I'll be all alone again."

"Listen up. Dallas or no Dallas, you'll never be alone again because you've got people here who care about you. You've been here six months and you've already buried yourself deep within this community. People love you. I don't want you worrying about that. You don't want to live with regrets and fear. I know that more than anyone. So live, because you can. Not everyone gets that option."

<hr>

The next day, I wait for Dallas to leave his office before I slip inside, closing the door behind me. I'm so ready to tell this man that I love him that it's eating me alive. After my talk with Reid, I went home and spent time by myself, soul-searching and thinking about what I want. Reid was right, I need to live. I may have claimed my body back as my own, after years of therapy, but the lasting effects of the trauma I survived have deeper-reaching consequences outside of the physical ones I sustained. I want to live. And not in fear. And I haven't been doing that.

I slink over to his desk, put the folder down, and shimmy out of my panties, pulling them over my heels and tripping into his desk in the process. I'm so excited to show him my proposal for the events aspect of the distillery, hoping that this will be a huge gesture of my commitment to make him as happy as he makes me.

I take a seat in the chair he loves so much when his computer wakes up from the sleep mode it was on. I recline, kind of loving the feel of it, when I see a file on his computer screen that demands my attention and sends chills down my spine. My palms start to sweat as I study the icon.

Blaire Hollis.

Unable to resist the temptation, I open the file with shaky

hands and my mouth drops open as the preview of each item loads. I click open the first item, my parent's arrest record, making me a ward of the state. The next is a statement from the teacher who noticed the bruises on me. I click to the next, my hands shaking like a leaf, my mouth dry as the Sahara. It's a photo of my face at 17, bruised eye and cheek, cut lip. My eyes are withdrawn, sunken in, with no life behind them. A tear drops from my face onto the top of my hand that hovers over the trackpad. The third file, the police report detailing the sexual and physical abuse, the neglect. The fourth, a hospital report detailing the rape kit results, std and pregnancy screening, and injuries. More photos—the bruises around my wrists and hips. The file is large, extensive, and incredibly thorough. I click through rapidly as the tears cascade down my face. Dallas' door opens then, and when he sees me his face falls.

"Baby, I can explain . . ."

"You aren't even going to try to deny it?"

"I'm a lot of things, princess, but a liar isn't one of them."

He takes two hesitant steps in my direction and I stand.

"Aren't you though?" I yell.

"It's not what it looks like. I never—"

"It's exactly what it looks like! How long, Dallas? How long have you fucking had this?"

"Blaire, give me a chance to explain, dammit." He steps toward me again, his hands extended outward in my direction like he's reaching for me, pleading with his body language.

"You told me to trust you. You told me you'd protect me. You fucking told me you'd make sure no one would hurt me ever again. THIS," I point to his computer, my voice raising, "this fucking hurts me!" I press a hand over my heart and one over my mouth, sobs racking my body. He rushes to me, his arms surrounding me, pulling me into his firm chest. I breathe him in deeply before shoving him off me with all my strength.

"Don't! Don't you dare fucking touch me, Dallas. You just couldn't help yourself, huh? Couldn't stand that I had secrets, you just had to go and dig them up. Because you're a selfish dick. Whatever this is"—I wave between us, his eyes empty and defeated, scared and lost—"this is over. We're done."

"Baby, I promise I never opened it. Sit your ass down and let me explain why I have it in the first place."

"Fuck you, Dallas. Save it."

I move past him to leave his office, tears streaming down my face in an uncontrollable flow. His hand reaches out to grab me, but I jerk away.

"Blaire, sit the hell back down and let me explain."

"I told you not to touch me. You lost that privilege. Remember what you said? I allow it to happen. I don't anymore. I mean it, this is over. I'm done."

I don't look back at him as I race from his office down the hallway to my own, my heart shattered into a million pieces, every inhale like I'm breathing in shards of glass. I grab my purse and jacket and race out of the building to my car. The winter air freezes my wet face and I welcome the sting of pain it brings. I settle into my car, my hands shaking as I try to put the key into the ignition, dropping it several times before I'm able to focus and turn it over. The cold air from the vents blasts my raw face as it works to warm up. My chest aches, the pressure becoming too much. I reverse out of my parking spot and see Dallas jogging my way, I throw it in to drive and step on the gas, spinning on the packed snow, salt, and gravel before straightening and driving away, leaving him standing in the middle of the road behind me.

My eyes fill with more tears, flooding them as I turn out of the long driveway and onto the winding mountain road that will take me away from this place. How could he do this? I opened up to him in my own way, on my own time. Did he already know? This whole time? So many questions rack my brain. He told me he used a private investigator when Ivy was back in town and in trouble, I bet that's exactly what he did for me. But he had no right. That's a complete invasion of my privacy. Fuck. Why? I thought he loved me, too. It felt like he loved me. I swear I fucking felt it!

But now I know the hard truth of it all. He's a fixer and I was just another damaged thing he could try to put back together.

I struggle to catch my breath and focus on the winding road in front of me. All of it was pity. Everything I knew would happen. His behavior was all out of pity. Poor Blaire and her tragic past, all alone with no family, no home, no one but herself to rely on.

"Aaaaahh!" I scream. "I am no one's fucking pity project!"

I slam my hand on my steering wheel as my eyes squint and swell from the onslaught of tears. I wipe vigorously at my face.

I barely notice the blur of a white vehicle coming up fast from my left.

I barely feel the air being pushed from my lungs as my body jerks forward into the exploding airbag when I slam on my brakes.

I barely hear the sounds of my car screeching, the metal crunching.

I barely register the pain in my stomach and chest.

I barely see the snow or smoke.

And then there's nothing at all.

CHAPTER 31

dallas

MY PHONE RINGS FOR THE THIRD TIME AND I PRESS ignore, wanting to sit and wallow in my own created misery. The look on her pretty face is on repeat—the fucking devastation, the shock, the heartbreak. She'll never believe me or understand why I had it. Having no fucking idea how to fix this, I toss back a long pull from the whiskey bottle, not registering the burn. I know how skittish she can get, why the hell I kept that file is beyond me. I should have deleted it the moment it came in.

My phone rings for the fourth time and I jam my fingers onto the ignore button. Sawyer's fucking issues can wait. I just destroyed my fucking life and have to find a solution to put it back together. I can't imagine a world where Blaire isn't in it with me. I know running after her while she's heated like this will be like cornering a wild animal. I'm bound to get my eyes gouged out. I set the bottle on my desk and notice the manila folder that wasn't there earlier. Opening it, my eyes scan over a proposal to change the current dynamic of the events operations. She's suggesting we move the tours to only seasonal in the fall, and focus on hosting major scheduled events on the property like weddings, limiting how many assholes are parading around my space every day, with the financial projections to back it up. It's brilliant. She fucking did this for me. The pressure in my chest tightens further.

My phone vibrates with a text, and I pick it up to throw it across the room when the words flash by my eyes.

Sawyer: Answer your fucking phone NOW

My phone rings again with an incoming call from my twin. This time I pick it up, letting my rage out on him sounds like as good a plan as any right now.

"What? What the fuck do you need so bad that you can't give me five fucking minutes to myself? I'm always there for fucking everyone else. I need a goddamn minute!"

"It's Blaire, motherfucker. I just got a call from the hospital; she was in a car accident. You're sleeping with her, any fucking idea why they called me and not her grandparents? I'm heading there now; they won't give me details over the phone. I don't know how to reach her grandparents, do you?"

I blink twice, registering what he just said, and fear takes over, taking root deep inside me and spreading through my body like a parasite. My heart clenches painfully in my chest as it gnaws at my insides, my body not able to form a sentence or thought.

All that's there is fear.

"Dallas? You there? Do you know how to reach her grand-parents?"

Blaire.

Accident.

Hospital.

She's all alone.

"I'm on my way."

I hang up on my brother and grab the keys to my Audi,

running through the building and peeling out of the distillery parking lot on autopilot. Now I understand what Sawyer felt when Ivy was abducted. Pure, unadulterated fear. This is all my fault, if I hadn't gotten that stupid fucking file on her, she never would have found it, we never would have fought, none of this would be happening. Now she's hurt, all alone in a fucking hospital because of me.

I spin into the Aspen Ridge Medical Center faster than is legal or morally right for being an emergency room parking lot, and run into the building. My brother is already at the nurses' station and turns to face me as I approach.

"She said the doctor will be out shortly to talk to me. She's in surgery."

I fucking crumble. Sawyer grabs my arms to keep my weight from slamming me down to my knees.

"Sawyer, I'm in love with her. I haven't even fucking told her yet. She has to be okay. I can't fucking breathe without her."

I don't register my brother's reaction to the news, just that he hauls me up to my feet and takes my weight, moving us into two waiting room chairs.

"She's going to be fine. It's a good hospital, she's in good hands. We'll get through it. Mom's on her way."

I can't take a full breath. Sawyer pushes me forward, his hand on my back, urging me to put my head between my legs. I work on steadying my breathing, knowing that I need to have my shit together to be strong for my girl. My mom walks in a moment later, taking a seat next to me and rubbing my back.

"Hey, my boy. She's going to be just fine. I feel it. You doing okay?"

"I need her to be okay, Mom."

"She will be. Hang in there. We're here."

I just need to know that she's going to be okay. What feels like hours passes before a doctor walks into the waiting room. The images of her and our last conversation are playing on repeat in my head, the guilt eating me from the inside out.

"Sawyer Hayes?"

My brother and I stand together and walk over to the doctor. He's dressed in surgical scrubs and my heart sinks further. I've never felt so out of control, so scared for anything in my life. My hands shake uncontrollably at my sides.

"That's me, this is my brother, Dallas."

"I'm her boyfriend."

My brother looks at me and nods but doesn't say anything else.

"I'm going to get straight to it, she was in a major accident. It was a hit-and-run. She took damage to the tail end of her car that forced her to spin out of control. Her car flipped three times before it hit a tree."

Nausea rolls through me in heavy waves, my gut churning acid around on a spin cycle, and I'm forced to bend over and brace my hands on my knees.

"Lucky for her, an off-duty police officer was not far behind, saw the smoke, and was able to call in help quickly. She's still in surgery and not out of the woods yet. She has major abdominal damage from her seat belt, but that's what saved her life. There are some things I feel like Blaire should hear first and share with whom she's comfortable with, but I will tell you that because of the complexity of the damage across her lower abdomen, she's going to need support to face what's ahead of her. Otherwise, we're optimistic she'll make a full recovery."

"Thank you, doctor," my brother says.

"Hang tight. Someone will be out to get you as soon as she's out of surgery and stable."

Sawyer grabs my arm and pulls me to stand, but the bile rises with me. I run to the nearest trashcan and flip the lid off, purging the contents of my stomach.

"She's going to be okay, brother. We've got you," Sawyer's voice rushes through the buzzing in my head. My mom joins us, handing me some tissues. I stand slowly, taking them to wipe my mouth when I see Liam, Carter, and Kinsey walking into the waiting room, eyes sweeping the area, looking for us. My mom ushers us over to join them in a section of the room that has enough seating for everyone. I'm met with hugs from each of them, Kinsey holding on to me the longest.

"I need her to be okay. She has to be."

CHAPTER 32

blaire

THE FIRST THING I REGISTER IS INCESSANT BEEPING noises.

The second is how heavy my eyes are.

The third is pain. Everywhere.

I work hard to open my eyes, but they feel glued shut. A dim, blurry light is all I see as I move my head to the side and groan.

"Baby? Thank god. It's Dallas, baby girl. I'm right here."

His warm hand touches my cheek gently as the tears slip free of my eyes. There's shuffling around the room, but my eyes are still only partially open. They feel so heavy. My entire body aches and I'm so tired.

"She just woke up. She hasn't spoken yet." Dallas is talking to someone, but I don't register the other voice. The large, warm hand encompassing mine feels so good, so comforting. I try to open my eyes further, blinking a few times while I adjust to the light.

"Hi, Blaire. I'm Doctor West. You're in the hospital. You were in a car accident. Are you in any pain?"

Car accident. I remember the white car, the noise of my tires skidding across the pavement, the crushing of metal as my car flipped. The tears flow freely now and I try to blink through them, my eyelids heavy.

"Ye-yes," my voice croaks out, followed by a cough. My throat feels like I swallowed crushed glass.

"Can she have water?"

"Of course. Here's the button for her pain meds. She can press it whenever she needs, we want her to be comfortable."

Dallas rubs his hand over my forehead gently and holds a straw to my mouth. I eagerly drink from it, the cold fluid coating my sore throat like a soothing balm.

"Am I okay?"

"You are. We have some things to discuss, but I'd like for you to get some rest," the doctor tells me, and I feel the ominous weight press down on me. I don't like the unknown, I need to know what's wrong now.

"No, thank you. I'd like to know now, please."

The doctor looks from me to Dallas before speaking, "I think it would be best if we spoke privately."

Dallas tenses next to me and a low growl works its way up his throat.

"It's okay, Dallas. Just give us a moment, please?"

He releases a deep breath but stands and kisses my forehead before looking at me, nose to nose.

"I love you. I should have told you sooner. I love you so much, princess, and there is nothing, *nothing*, that will change that. You aren't alone anymore; we'll get through anything. I'm so sorry."

His words coat me in everything I've ever wanted.

Love.

Support.

Safety.

Comfort.

He swipes the tears from my cheeks before kissing me one last time and retreating out of the room.

"He seems like a good man. He hasn't left your side."

"How long have I been here?"

"Three days. You came off the ventilator yesterday but we've kept you heavily sedated so you could heal. You suffered severe damage to your abdomen from your seatbelt. This can happen sometimes in major accidents. We took you into emergency surgery where you received a laparotomy. While rare, you had internal bleeding that was caused by a vessel injury to your uterus. The trauma was quite extensive."

"Okay . . ."

"You received a blood transfusion, but we couldn't fix the lacerations and had to perform a subtotal hysterectomy. Luckily, your colon, liver, and kidneys were spared. Your cervix, ovaries, and both fallopian tubes were left as they were all healthy. But your uterus was surgically removed. You understand what this means?"

I blink back the tears fogging my vision and choke out my next words.

"That I'll never be able to carry children."

"That's correct. I'm so sorry. We have therapists on call that are available to come speak with you when you're ready."

"No. Thank you. That won't be necessary. I have a therapist I'll reach out to."

She goes through the list of my lesser injuries, pats my hand sympathetically, and stands to leave. "You'll be in the hospital for at least a few more days, but your partner is welcome to stay as long as you're comfortable."

I don't bother correcting her. I don't know what Dallas is to me. And like I needed any more pain, the memory of our last talk with each other hits me like a ton of bricks.

The file on his computer. My background. The photos. Every detail of my childhood wrapped up in a little folder for him to view.

I close my eyes and let myself drift off to a place that isn't here. For once, I'll take the chance of my nightmares haunting me rather than be awake any longer in this unfair world.

"Recovery is going to be six to eight weeks. Bed rest for the first two. Do you have anyone at home who can help you?" the nurse asks.

"No. I live alone."

"You're not going home to your apartment. You're coming home with me," Dallas interjects.

"No, Dallas, no. I'm not."

"I'll give you some time to figure things out and come back to go over discharge in the morning," the doctor says before leaving me alone with Dallas and his mom.

"Dallas, can you give me a minute alone with Blaire?" Dallas' mom says. He opens his mouth to talk but she holds up her hand, stopping him. "I'm asking you out of politeness, but as your mother, it's not up for discussion."

Dallas stares-off with his mom before he leans to kiss my forehead. I turn away, but he kisses my head anyway before walking out of the room and closing the door behind him.

Dallas' mom sits at the foot of my bed and thinks for a moment. I sit silently, unsure what to say or where to go from here, bracing myself for a discussion as to how I'm freezing out her son and hurting him.

"My son can be an idiot sometimes. All four of them actually. When they love, they can't see the bigger picture, only doing everything they can in the moment. I'm not making an excuse for anything he has done; I don't have any details. But I do know that he loves you."

Not at all what I was expecting, I meet her eyes.

"It's really much more complicated than that. I don't know how to forgive him for what he's done."

"That's up to you two to figure out. It doesn't change the position you're in now. That, I do have some of the details on. The hospital called Sawyer, because they didn't have anyone else to call. We all know you are here alone. Dallas wouldn't give us much more information than that. So this is what we're going to do. Regardless of your relationship with my son, I want you to know that you're not alone. We have loved getting to know you and you have all of us to lean on. So, when you're discharged in the morning, you'll be coming home with me."

My mouth falls open as tears spring to my eyes, a hard knot in my throat, clogged with emotion. I go to speak but she stops me.

"You heard the doctor. Two weeks of bed rest and a six-to-eight-week recovery total. You need help and I want to help you. We have the space, and I have the time. You aren't alone, sweetie."

I break down, the tears and sobs uncontrollable. All I've ever wanted is to no longer be alone. I've had to claw my way through surviving this world by myself and to have such a beautifully self-less woman want to take me in to care for me is incomprehensible. Dallas and his siblings hit the jackpot with their parents.

"Thank you," I choke out between sobs, "I've never had that before."

"I know, sweetie. But now you don't ever have to go without it again."

She squeezes my hand and grabs the tissue box off the end table, handing one to me and taking one for herself.

"Look at us, a couple of blubbering messes. Get some rest. It was a long day for you. I'll get everything sorted and we'll make you comfortable."

"Thank you, Mrs. Hayes."

"Amy."

I nod and smile at her. Night after night when I was a child, I would lay in bed and wish for a mom who wanted me and cared for me. Dallas' mom encompasses everything I had wished for. With half of my heart firmly gripping onto the feeling of a mother's love, the other half is shielded by heavy guard, unwilling to let them down out of pure fear and a history of nothing but disappointment. But it's so hard not to grasp onto her like a lifeline.

CHAPTER 33

dallas

"SHE'S COMING HOME WITH ME TOMORROW FOR AT least two weeks. She'll stay in your old room on the bottom floor. She'll be comfortable and I'll take good care of her while she heals."

"Like hell she is, Mom. I love you, you're an angel, but she is coming home with me where she belongs. I need to take care of her. I want to take care of her. This is my fault. Mine. I can't be away from her. I have to fix this, and she needs to know that I'm here for her."

"I love you, my boy, but this isn't about you. Sometimes you and your brothers are blinded by what you think is the right thing to do, which you get from your father. But you need to know when to let things fix themselves, rather than force it."

"Mom, I don't know how to do anything else. I love her too much."

"And I told you I will take good care of her. What I didn't do was tell you what *you're* doing." She gives me a wink and a pat on my shoulder before returning to the waiting room.

I walk back into Blaire's hospital room to find her sleeping again. Today was hard on her. They removed her catheter, and she was forced to get up and start walking for the first time since her

301

accident. She bit her lip through every wince I knew was hovering right at the surface. But she pushed through and is healing more and more each day.

Blaire sleeps. And it's torture. Seeing her bruised and battered body causes me a selfish pain that I can't put into words. Guilt. It eats me alive every moment, but I welcome it. This is my fucking fault. I put her here. If I had never asked Wes to pull her background and dig up everything he could on her, we wouldn't be here right now. She wouldn't have to feel pain, she wouldn't have had to fight for her life. She is such a warrior though. Her entire life she's been surviving, and I'm so proud of her. I hate that I promised I would keep her safe from future pain only to be the one who caused so much of it.

I go back and forth between watching her sleep in a heavy slumber and watching her heart rate on the monitor. The bruises on her face have turned from black to a deep purple, but I know her physical pain is nothing compared to the emotional pain she's been through in her life. She's going to heal because she's strong as fuck. I haven't left her once. Haven't showered and have lived off whatever food and coffee my family brings me. There's no way in hell I would be anywhere else. She's all that matters.

I pull the blankets up to her chest and lay a kiss gently on her forehead before taking my spot in the chair next to her. She won't talk to me. The only acknowledgment I get from her is the deep sigh when I touch her. I know I calm her, steady her. I can see it in the way her shoulders relax when I'm near her, the way her eyes flutter closed when I kiss her forehead, the way her breathing settles when I grasp her hand. If she wants to sit in silence for the rest of our lives, and all I do is calm her nervous system, then so fucking be it. I will give this woman anything she needs. Even if it kills me.

There's a knock at the door and I stand back up to pull it open. Reid stands on the outside, looking calm if it weren't for his tell; his hands opening and closing into fists at his side.

"Hey, man, how is she?"

"Sleeping. They finally got her up and moving today and it wore her out. She's such a fighter though."

"That she is."

"Reid?" Blaire asks from behind me, her voice heavy and hoarse from sleep.

I open the door more and step out of the way, welcoming Reid into the room. I don't miss how her face lights up when he comes up next to her, and I try to stomp down the jealous rage that starts to consume me. Reid's a great friend to both of us, and I temper my rash feelings, even if I'd kill for her to look at me like that again. I take a seat in the chair on the far side of the room to give them privacy without actually leaving and pull out my phone to check in with my siblings.

Me: How is everyone?

Kins: That's a stupid question, we're fine. How are you? How is Blaire?

Liam: You guys need anything? We've been keeping Mom stocked with coffee but there were too many of us so they kicked us out and told us to only come one at a time

Me: I'm not in a good place

Sawyer: I'm in the waiting room. Reid's got her. Come take a break.

Sighing, I stand, knowing my brother will come in here and drag me out if I don't go out there willingly. Before leaving, I interrupt Blaire and Reid's talk.

"I'll give you two a few. I'll be right back, baby. I love you," I say loud enough for Reid to hear before kissing her forehead. I leave my woman in her hospital bed, with the large beast of a tattooed man protecting her. Because I know he will with his life. Whether he believes it or not.

I walk through the hospital until I find the exit. Having not left the building, it takes me a minute to navigate my way outside. Thanks to the overcast skies, the light from outside isn't as harsh on my eyes. I pull down the sleeves of my hoodie as the cold air hits me. Sawyer stands leaning against one of the large stone pillars holding up the awning, waiting for me.

"Surprised your wife isn't with you, you're usually not far from her. Can't believe you have time for me."

He turns to face me, the air crackling with tension, his demeanor changing before my eyes. His posture is rigid, and I can see the frustration flashing across his face. He squares his shoulders before talking, his voice thick with irritation.

"You need your ass beat or you want to talk it through? I got all day while Ivy works at Barrel House and I'm happy to do either."

"I'm not leaving Blaire here alone, so you can go fuck yourself if you think I'm going to Dom's."

"I would do anything for you, dumbass, and you fuckin' know it. So, say what you gotta say, hit me if you need something to hit, but don't you dare act like I don't have your back. You may not have seen me, but I've been here every goddamn day in case you needed me. Just like you were there for me when Ivy left."

My shoulders slump inward, realization weighing on my already heavy conscience. I run my hand over my facial hair, which has grown out longer than I like to keep it. Sawyer walks up to me and pulls me into a hug.

"Shit, I know that, I'm just at a loss here," I say, taking a step back. "I don't know what to do anymore. I feel fucking broken."

"Been there, brother. That's why you've got us. So, you love her, huh?"

"More than anything."

"This whole time?"

"From the moment I saw her sitting in your office. I tried to convince myself it was just sexual attraction, that fucking her would get it out of my system, but that just set it in stone. Once I had her . . ."

"She was yours. Whether she felt the same or not."

"Yeah."

"I get it. You know I couldn't move on after Ivy left. She was endgame. Seems like Blaire's yours."

"She is. I just have to fix my fuckups and hope she'll forgive me."

If she doesn't, I don't know how I'll ever recover from that loss.

"Well, speaking of, we gotta talk. You may not remember the details 'cause you weren't holding it together, but I got some info on Blaire's accident."

The hair on the back of my neck stands up as I try to rack my brain for what he could be talking about.

"What do you mean?"

"It wasn't an accident."

"The fuck did you just say?"

"It was a hit-and-run. The police came back to ask some questions, but Officer Hawkins stayed back to talk to me in private. He doesn't think it was an accident but wouldn't give me more details, just asked if I knew of anything that might help him out. But I had Wes pull the police report. The tire marks on the road were only from one vehicle. Blaire's. The other car hit her and didn't even try to pass her or break. They side-swiped her, caused her to fishtail and spin out at a high speed, then bolted."

"Holy fuck."

Nausea churns in my stomach.

"Do you know anyone who would want to hurt her?"

"Fuck!" I yell, pulling the short strands of my hair as I pace, trying to think of anyone who would want to hurt my girl. Only one evil motherfucker comes to mind. The one who still haunts her like a fucking disease she can't shake.

"Look, Blaire isn't who she told us she was when we hired her.

I mean, she's Blaire Hollis, but her background isn't a happy one, and she was trying to protect herself from sharing the details. She's trying to start a new life. This goes to your grave, Sawyer."

"Doesn't need to be said, brother, get to your damn point."

"A few weeks ago, she told me that she thought she saw her abuser at the distillery. He is or maybe was serving a sentence at Washington Pen. I offered to do an inmate search with her to make sure he was still behind bars, but she was insistent she do it on her own. I don't fucking know."

"And you just let it go? What the fuck, Dallas?"

"You don't know Blaire like I do. If I fucking push, she flees. I don't even have his goddamn name."

The fucking file. His name is the goddamn file Wes pulled for me.

"Fucking get it. In the meantime, I'm going to get a plan together."

"We're going to stay at Mom and Dad's. Over my dead body will something happen to her again."

"Get me a goddamn name, Dallas."

How the fuck do I do that without scaring her or breaching her damn privacy again?

blaire

Turns out healing from a hysterectomy while also trying to heal bumps, bruises, and a cracked rib is a total bitch. I have never felt so tired before. It's a bone-deep exhaustion that doesn't get better from sleeping through the night and taking naps. My sleep has been devoid of my usual nightmares, and I don't know if it's tiredness or the fact that Dallas hasn't left my side since before I even woke.

I do my best to listen to the nurse's discharge instructions, but find myself thankful that Dallas and his mom are both paying attention and asking questions. Neither of them knows that my uterus was removed, just that I had internal bleeding that needed surgery to fix. The deep bruises from the seatbelt doing its job are proof enough that healing is going to take a while.

I'm wheeled through the hospital like an invalid by my sweet male nurse, Dallas grumbling that he could do it himself, but the nurse stuck to protocol, which I was happy about. He's been so attentive, and there's a part of me that feels bad that I won't even talk to him, and that I shy away from him even though my body is screaming for his touch. Sawyer pulls up at the roundabout at the front of the hospital and jumps out, opening the door for me.

Together, Dallas and the nurse help me stand and walk slowly to the SUV, assisting me in climbing in.

The moment I'm in the car and Dallas reaches over me to pull the seat belt carefully in place, the panic begins to crawl over my skin like a bad rash. My breathing starts to come in rapid bursts, and my vision goes foggy. I grab for Dallas' wrist, looking at him through my blurry vision. He touches my face, bringing his lips to my forehead and pressing them into me. When he releases his kiss, he looks at me, gently placing his hands on each side of my face.

"You're safe. Do you want me to drive, or do you want me back here with you?"

I hate that he's giving me the option to choose. I don't want to think. I don't want to make decisions. I don't know. All I know is this feeling inside me of fear is incapacitating and making it hard to breathe.

My eyes dart all over his face and I feel the tears slide free, running over my cheeks. I feel so lost, like I'm floating around with nothing to ground me.

"I don't know. I don't— I can't—"

"Okay, baby, shh. I'm going to come sit next to you, and Sawyer's going to drive us home. You're going to just focus on me, okay?"

I nod my head yes. He leaves me for less than a minute after my door is closed, jogging around to the other side and climbing in next to me. Taking both of my hands in his, I rest my head back against the headrest and close my eyes. The vehicle starts to move, and I squeeze Dallas' hand, hard.

"I've got you. You're so damn brave, Blaire. Have I told you that? The bravest person I've ever met. I remember the first time I met you last September, sitting there in Sawyer's office. You were wearing a black pencil skirt with an emerald-colored top. Your hair was down and in wild curls that day. It stunned the shit out of me how breathtakingly beautiful you were. But when you spoke back to me? Damn. I was a goner, princess. No one had ever spoken to me the way you did."

I think back to that moment and remember it clearly. He was wearing black dress pants with a navy blue button-up. He had the top three buttons undone, exposing the thin gold chain that he never takes off. The sleeves were rolled up to his elbows, and I noticed his half-sleeve of tattoos right away. He was so gorgeous. His beard was trimmed to a rough stubble, his hair styled and cropped short on the sides. It took everything in me not to check him out like he had done to me.

"Nice to meet you, Dallas. I'm looking forward to working with you."

"For."

"Excuse me?" I asked, tilting my head to the side in confusion.

"Working for me."

"Ahh. Well, that remains to be seen."

"You were so quick on your toes to talk back to me and call me on my shit." His voice drops low, barely a whisper, "I had to leave his office because I would have hauled you out of there like a caveman ready to claim what's his if I hadn't."

I smile for the first time in days, but my heart aches painfully.

"The night of Sawyer's wedding, I watched you all evening from the bar. Seeing you talk to Cole just kept chipping away at the restraint I had been using to stay away from you. But when you laughed at something he said? I couldn't stay away any longer. If I didn't get to have you, he sure as fuck didn't. He never deserved you."

Dallas uses the back of his knuckles to wipe away a rogue tear that falls over my cheek, and I lean into the touch.

"I didn't plan on taking you that night. I didn't plan on having you at all. But when you followed me to my office and ran that vile little mouth of yours, that restraint snapped. It was the best decision I ever made. And then fate had a hand in making sure we were forced together for three days and there was no coming back from that."

My heart breaks more hearing his confessions. He feels this way now, but he won't once I tell him that I'll no longer be able to have a family of my own someday. He'll abandon me just like everyone else has.

Time flew by and suddenly we are pulling up to the Hayes family home, Dallas talking to me the entire time. Amy walks into the garage and Sawyer and Dallas both climb out, sharing a few words between them that I can't hear. I wait for Dallas to come to my side, opening the door and helping me climb out. I bite the inside of my cheek to hold back the pained gasp that wants to break free.

Dallas stays next to me while I slowly walk through his parents' house, letting him guide me to his childhood bedroom. He drops the paper bags of prescription medications on the dresser and turns to face me.

"I need a shower. I feel so gross."

"It's in here, baby." He motions toward an open door in the room, leading the way for me to follow. I watch him start the water, feeling the temperature with his hand and adjusting it a few times until he's got it right. I start to pull off the scrubs the hospital gave me to go home in, since I didn't have any clothes, and Dallas wouldn't leave the hospital without me. I hiss as my muscles strain and fight against the movement, my battered body aching in every single location.

Warm hands cover mine, pulling them away from the hem of the top as he carefully helps me pull it off. He does the same with the bottoms, letting them fall to the floor in a pile. I stand there naked, my hands moving to cover part of myself, feeling self-conscious as I look down at all the bruises, especially the huge, black ones across my chest and lower stomach where the seat belt cinched.

Dallas reaches behind his head and pulls off his shirt. My eyes dip to his body, roaming over each muscle that he works hard for, the defined V at his pelvis, and my body responds just like it always does to this man. I shake my head, clearing myself of the spell he puts me under. This isn't fair to either of us.

"I can do it myself, Dallas, I don't need you," I snap, even though it's a lie.

Unfortunately, I notice the wince and hurt that flashes across his face and it makes me feel like shit.

"Dammit, Blaire, why do you always have to be so difficult? Let me help you for fuck's sake." His voice cracks on the last word, and his eyes glass over with unshed tears. He blinks them away and takes a deep breath before speaking again. "I'm sorry. I'm being selfish because seeing you in pain is excruciating. Seeing the evidence of your pain on your beautiful body is *killing* me. I would do anything to take it from you, I would bear it ten times over if it meant you didn't have to feel this way. I don't do patient, princess. I'm demanding, I'm possessive, and I take control, because that's how I handle things. I'm trying here."

The expression on his face nearly breaks me. He's so guilt-stricken, so heartbroken, and I want to reach out to him so badly, but I know that I can't. Instead, I nod my head and step into the shower, leaving the glass door open for him to follow. I don't watch him strip from his sweatpants and socks, but I feel the moment he's next to me, my body relaxing as I'm sucked into the orbit he keeps us in. The one place where I can let go and just exist without worry or fear.

We don't speak as we take turns letting the hot spray rain down on us. When he reaches for the shampoo, I don't fight him, leaning back and letting him wash my hair for the first time. His hands massage my scalp, rubbing the soap and pulling away all of the greasy build-up from being at the hospital for days.

He positions me in the spray, running his strong hands through my long strands and rinsing out the shampoo. He repeats the process with the conditioner, and it feels so relaxing, his fingers working to take care of me like no one in my life ever has. My heart aches. It's a pain I've never felt before, because for the first time in my life, I've found a person who makes me feel safe, who makes me feel alive, loved, cherished, and cared for. Someone who's given me experiences to help heal my past, whose only focus has ever been my well-being. Someone who I love for his huge, dedicated heart. The distance between us feels like we're standing on opposite sides of a cliff, a cavernous trench of nothingness keeping us apart.

He picks up the body soap, squirting a small amount on his hand and facing me, silently asking me for permission. I nod, knowing that if I speak, my voice will betray me, giving away all the turmoil I'm trying to keep bottled up. He starts at my shoulder, running his hand over my arm and down to my fingers, massaging between each one. Doing the same thing on the other side, he grabs more soap, this time running both hands across my chest, under my breasts, and sides, gently gliding over my bruised and raw skin, careful not to touch my tiny incisions, before turning me to wash my back.

His hands are strong and smooth, gliding over my soap-covered body like butter. His hand is so much more gentle than a coarse washcloth. I close my eyes and sway slightly, completely relaxed, exhaustion starting to hit me. I face him again as he bends down on his knees, lifting my foot and setting it on his thigh, rubbing between my toes, up my legs, stopping as he gets to the apex between my thighs.

I bite the inside of my cheek, trying to hold back a pleasurable sigh as he washes my other leg. He's attentive, making sure every inch of me is clean and touched. It's a new level of intimacy, and I fall further in love with this man. I wish I had never run out of his office that day. I wish I had stayed and fought. None of that matters anymore. This good, kind, selfless man deserves so much better than me.

Dallas stands and grabs my wrist, pulling my hand out between us so he can drop a bit of soap into my palm, allowing me to finish cleaning my personal areas. The gesture is so considerate, and my heart knocks loudly against my chest, as if it wants to climb out and join its other half that's standing in front of me, looking down at me like I'm the most important thing in the entire world.

We rinse and Dallas turns the water off, stepping out first and grabbing a large, fluffy towel. He wraps it around me before getting one for himself. After we're dry, he grabs a hairbrush from a drawer and pulls me into the bedroom, where I sit between his legs, and he slowly works the brush through my very tangled hair. My eyes start to drift closed as he takes care of me, section by section, pulling out all of the tangles until it's smooth.

I sway back into his large chest, the towel falling as my body starts to demand sleep. Even just the small activity of walking through the house and showering has exhausted me to my core. He carefully helps me move back on the bed, tucking me into the blankets and kissing my forehead.

"Nap, princess. I'll be back with clothes and everything you need. I love you."

A deep sleep claims me, my body desperate for rest in more ways than just one.

CHAPTER 35

dallas

LEAVING BLAIRE IN MY BEDROOM AT MY PARENTS' house doesn't feel right. But I won't be far from her. I gave in to my mom moving Blaire into their house, but that just means I'm moving in too. I'll crash in one of the other rooms if she won't have me in hers. While I know she's safe at my parents' house, I didn't want to take any chances, so Sawyer stuck around and will head back to his place once I'm back.

The drive to my house is lonely as fuck, my brain beating the shit out of my emotions worse than any hit I've taken in the ring. It's hard to believe that just last week we were here, wrapped up in my bed together while she finally slept soundly with my arms around her. It's a heady feeling being able to provide a sense of safety and comfort to another person, and the idea that I may never be able to give her that again makes me feel physically sick.

I don't know what to do with the information Sawyer found out about the wreck not being an accident. The thought alone fuels me with rage and fear, the need to get back to her as soon as possible, strong.

Walking through my house without Blaire here is solemn as fuck. I want her in my space, and I would have given anything to convince her to move in with me as soon as possible. If I hadn't fucked everything up.

Once in my bedroom, I take a deep inhale of the space. Our scents mingle in the air and on the fabric of my pillows and sheets; just as they should. I pack my things into a duffel bag before locking up my house and heading to Blaire's apartment. Pulling my car into a spot in front of the tattoo shop, I decide to take a detour and open the door to Rogue to find Reid. He immediately gets up and walks over to me, pulling me into a hug.

"How is she? Sawyer's been updating me but how is she really?"

I don't know what happens, but everything I've been holding together comes crashing down on me and the floodgates open.

"Hey, man, it'll be alright, let's get off the main floor, my office is right over here."

Reid puts his hand on my back and steers me to his office while I lose my shit, tears falling rapidly down my face. Once inside, I take a seat in one of his chairs and he pulls another one close, sitting in front of me.

"I love her so goddamn much, man. She is everything good, everything so perfect. I promised her that I would keep her safe, that I wouldn't let anyone ever hurt her again. I blame myself for her leaving the distillery that day."

"I know you do. That's why I told you where she lived. I could see it, but the car accident wasn't your fault, man."

"You don't understand. After our days snowed in together at my house, before you told me where she lived, I knew she was hiding something big. When she wouldn't open up to me, I contacted Wes and put a contract out with him on her. He sent me the file after you told me where she was, and she came clean about her past and I never fucking opened the file. I never opened it."

"Fuck, brother. She found it, didn't she?"

I drop my head into the palms of my hands and take a deep breath.

"Yeah. On my computer. I saw it written all over her face. The heartbreak. I'll never be able to forget that look. It'll haunt me forever. She screamed at me and left, and she was so upset. I should have stopped her. I never should have let her drive that upset, but I didn't. And now this."

Reid runs his hands through his long hair, tying it back before rubbing his palms up and down his thighs. Neither of us knows what to say. He can't dispute it. I caused all of this. I wish I could tell him that Sawyer thinks her accident was on purpose, but I can't breach her trust again.

"You'll figure out how to get through it. You and your family always find a way."

"I just don't see a clear path right now. How can she forgive me?"

"Look, it's fucked-up what you did, but I know you had good intentions. She'll see that. You wouldn't do it maliciously. She'll come around because she's crazy about you. You guys weren't as good at hiding it as you think you were."

"Fuck, really?"

He gives me a look that says I'm an idiot, and he's not wrong. I've made a lot of mistakes the last few months and have my work cut out for me on setting them straight. I can't lose my girl.

"Sorry for breaking down, been holding it together as best I can."

"Don't worry about it, brother. I'll swing in to see her again in a few days when she's ready for some visitors."

I nod in agreement, knowing Blaire enjoys his company, and that she needs to see her friends and feel loved.

"Hey, I need to get going so I can grab some things for her from her apartment to bring back to my parents' house, but I'll text you."

He walks over to his desk and grabs a key to Blaire's apartment. I squash the jealous Neanderthal in me that wants to demand he not have access to her space, but I know it's futile and won't get me anywhere. He goes to toss me the key, but I put up my hand showing him that I already have one. I give him my thanks before heading around back to Blaire's studio.

Walking into her space, I'm engulfed in her scent. I move to her bathroom and wash my face, blowing my nose and getting my shit together. Once I've composed myself, I get started on packing things that Blaire will need throughout her stay. I pack all of her toiletries, panties, bras, leggings, and a few pairs of sleep shorts. I purposefully don't pack any T-shirts of her own. She can wear mine.

Leaving her apartment, I step on an envelope that I hadn't noticed when I walked in. There isn't even a mat outside her door, so I'm positive it wasn't here ten minutes ago. Picking it up, I hold it between my fingers, looking at the blank manila envelope with no postage or address on it. I shove it under my arm and jog down to my Audi, looking up and down the street for anyone who could have just been here. Tossing Blaire's things in the back with my own, I climb into the car and lock the doors.

My fingers shake slightly as I open the envelope and pull out a stack of photos with a sticky note attached to the front.

You've been a bad girl.
-Daddy

Bile rises in my throat as I skim through the photos. All of Blaire at various places. Bean Haven, talking with Hannah. Sitting at Rogue with Reid. Walking down Main Street by herself. Talking to a group at the distillery. The last one has my vision blurring and my stomach turning the acid around like a raging storm inside me. Blaire bent over my dining room table with me on my knees behind her.

"FUCK!"

Tossing everything on the seat next to me, I pull out my phone and call Sawyer. He answers on the first ring.

"Blaire near you?"

"No, sleeping right where you left her. What's up?"

"We've got a huge fucking problem."

I peel out of Main Street and gun it back to my parents' house.

"You were right. It wasn't an accident. Someone has been fucking following her and based on the package he left at her front door, my bet is on the motherfucker who tortured her as a teenager."

"Shit. How do you want to deal with this? Want me to call Officer Hopkins?"

"Keep it between us for now. I'm not leaving her side. Keep Ivy close until I figure out how we're going to play this."

"Let me know what you need, brother."

The call disconnects as I fly through Aspen Ridge to get to my girl. I promised her that I would keep her safe. I won't fail again. I'm going to fix everything. I just need to decide how much I should tell her before I do.

"Dallas, there are no T-shirts in here."

"I know, baby." I pull off my Aspen Ridge Distillery tee and walk over to her, bunching it up in my hands and pulling it over her head where she sits on the bed looking through the duffel bag of her things. I don't miss the way she swivels her face to the side into the shirt and inhales deeply. That's my good girl.

"I'm going to need my own T-shirts; I can't live in yours."

"You can and you will. Are you hungry?"

She sighs deeply, her eyes withdrawn, her face battered and pale.

"I don't think so."

"You need to eat. So, what do you feel like having? We have homemade Tuscan vegetable soup with French bread, or I can make you a grilled cheese, French toast, a fruit bowl?"

"I'm really not hungry, Dallas."

"Blaire," I say sternly. "You need food to heal. So, what can I get you?"

"Fine. I'll have whatever you're having."

"That's my good girl. I'll be right back."

I wander off to the kitchen and prepare two bowls of my mom's Tuscan vegetable soup. It's hearty, filled with vegetables, some weird-looking floaty seed thing, beans, and a rich tomato vegetable broth. It's exactly what Blaire needs to start to feel better. I cut off two pieces of the French bread loaf, set everything on a tray, and return to my girl.

"Here you go." I set the tray gently on her lap, grab my bowl off of it, and move to the recliner my brothers brought in here before Blaire was released from the hospital. We eat in comfortable silence, but she eats all of it and I couldn't be happier. She declined seconds, but the fact that she ate something at all is a relief. After I clean up from dinner, I pull out Blaire's lotion from her duffel bag and take a seat on the bed next to her. I hand her the remote so she can put something on the television. Squirting some lotion into my palm, I rub my hands together before picking up one of her feet and massaging it. She moans and my dick perks up in my sweats, the idiot. Not happening, my man, you're confused as fuck. Blaire puts a TV show that she loves on, and I'm not going to lie, Anthony Bridgerton has got some moves, the cheeky bastard. I find myself invested in the show, wondering if he'll continue with the plan to marry Kate's sister, all while rubbing Blaire's feet and legs, massaging her, and showing her the physical affection she deserves.

The show ends, and she turns the TV off.

"It was just getting good!"

"Feel free to finish watching it. I'm falling asleep and need to get some rest."

"How can I help you?" *Please let me help you, it's killing me.*

"I just need to take more ibuprofen and then I'll be okay."

"You haven't touched the narcotics; they'll help you so you can sleep better and feel better."

"My parents were drug addicts, Dallas. I don't want them. I won't touch them, so just dump them down the toilet for all I care. The eight-hundred-milligram ibuprofen has been working fine, I just need to stay on top of it."

Feeling like shit for not putting that together on my own, I pick up the bottle of oxys and set it on the TV stand to dispose of properly later. Her face scrunches up tightly as she bites the side of her cheek through her pain while she tries to get settled in the bed for sleep. I step forward, helping her with the pillows and blankets, tucking her in.

When I look down on her, I can't help but brush the wild red hair from her sweet face, her cheek cool against my fingertips.

"You're so beautiful it hurts."

A tear slips free from her eye and my chest tightens. How did we get here? I lean down to kiss her forehead, my lips pressing down firmly while I take a deep breath of her. She smells like my soap, and I decide I like her covered in my scent most of all.

"Goodnight, princess."

I stand to leave but she stops me, her hand grabbing my wrist. Turning to face her, she's every bit as lost, vulnerable, and confused as I am. Not having any idea how to fix us, I wait for her command, willing to do anything she wants.

"Will you stay with me? Please?" she whispers, and I nearly break right there.

"Yeah, baby, of course I'll stay with you."

I strip down to my boxer briefs and carefully lift the blankets, laying down next to her. Unsure how close she wants me, I settle on resting my hand on her thigh, rubbing my fingertips over her smooth skin in small circles.

Her content sigh is the last thing I hear as she falls fast asleep. With me as her guardian, thankful to be able to watch over her and chase her demons away so she can rest.

CHAPTER 36

blaire

I'M LOST IN MY THOUGHTS, STARING OUT DALLAS' childhood window when there's a knock at the door before it slowly creaks open. Dallas' mom, Amy, and his sister, Kinsey, stand there with a bowl of popcorn and a grocery bag full of things.

"Are you up for some company?" Kinsey chirps, her chocolate brown hair piled high on the top of her head. She's got a head of dark hair like Sawyer and Carter, and the bluest eyes, just like Dallas.

I scoot back on to the bed so that I'm sitting upright against the headboard, the pain in my lower abdomen a mild throb now. Dallas' family has been so incredibly welcoming. They've completely taken me in and treated me like one of their own. Kinsey has stopped by a few times a week to hang out with me and go for walks around the house since it's too cold to walk outside right now. If I hadn't already fallen in love with his family, I would have after this. They've given me something that I've never had before and it comes with appreciation, but also a longing so deep that it mixes with the pain. Dallas won't want me after I finally open up about my hysterectomy, and that breaks my heart most of all. I suppose I should enjoy this time before I lose them, too.

"I'd actually love some company. What did you have in mind?"

"Well, we heard that we share a love of the same movie. How do you feel about a little Mr. Darcy tonight?"

I laugh, always in the mood to watch *Pride and Prejudice*.

"How'd you know that was my favorite?"

"A little birdy told us. It's also Mom's favorite, so I've seen it a million times."

They climb into bed with me, dumping the snacks out in front of us and putting the bowl of popcorn down. Happiness fills me. I reach for the Twizzlers Pull 'n' Peel, opening the package and pulling one out as Amy finds the movie to put on.

"Is everything okay with you and my brother?" Kinsey asks.

"I don't know how to answer that, honestly."

She looks at me with sympathy.

"No one knows better than I do how difficult my brothers can be. Want to talk about it?"

"You're his sister, Kinsey, and I doubt your mom wants to hear all of this."

"I assure you; I don't mind. I know my boys and they take after their father. So if anyone is equipped to listen to what his stubborn ass did and give advice, it's me," Amy says.

Stunned, I blink at them for a few moments. I assumed that they would blindly defend any of their own, but here I stand corrected. Again. Not having anyone else to lean on at the moment and no family of my own, I tell them everything, minus the fact that Dallas is a Dom and all of our sexcapades. I confess my background, my lies to Sawyer in an attempt to make myself not look so pathetic and desperate, trying my best to start a new life. When I tell them that Dallas had hired a PI to dig up my background when I wouldn't initially open up to him, his mom wipes away her tears and finally speaks.

"My stupid, stupid boy. He really is just like his father and brothers. The males in our family are a different breed."

"I know it's not an excuse, Blaire, what my brother did was damn wrong and a huge invasion of privacy, but if he didn't care with every fiber of his being, he wouldn't have done what he did. It does not make it right, he's an idiot. But these Hayes boys see something they want, and they can't see anything else."

"Kinsey's right, unfortunately. Their father was the same way. Brutally protective and possessive. Hell, he still is, the crazy man. But they come from love. In his eyes, he saw an issue you were fighting and wanted to do everything in his power to either fight that battle for you, be educated on the situation enough to help you fight it yourself, or get rid of it completely. He couldn't see past how that may negatively impact you and I hate that his blind, brute stubbornness caused you any amount of pain. You are justified in how you feel."

"He loves you, Blaire. Anyone would be a fool not to see it."

"I know he does. I feel it. I love him, too," I confess. And it feels freeing to say it out loud again, even if it isn't to Dallas. I know that I've already forgiven him for getting all of that information on me. But it's the only thing I can hang onto to keep him at a distance. I continue to keep my infertility a secret, not ready to have anyone try to comfort me regarding it. I've accepted it because what's my alternative? It's a blessing in disguise. The line of Hollis will end with me, so long as they never procreated after I was born.

"Enough of all that! Let's watch Mr. Darcy fall hopelessly in love with Elizabeth and screw it all up in the process."

"So, basically a man in love then?" I add, and we all laugh.

The three of us sit in the big bed together like we've done it all our lives, and I spend more time looking at both of them out of the corner of my eyes than I do watching my favorite movie. We munch on popcorn, skittles, and Twizzlers Pull 'n' Peel, like it's the most comfortable, easy thing in the entire world. And for a moment, I allow myself to imagine they're my mom and sister, helping me through heartbreak, and I'm not so alone in this big world.

When I wake up the next morning, my body is not happy. Everything is tight, sore, and aching. I've healed from physical trauma before, but the mix of internal and external injuries is wreaking havoc on my drained body. I roll over and moan, my full bladder cramping and spasming in protest. Opening my eyes, I look around the empty guestroom and muster the strength to leave the comfort of the warm bed. The bathroom tile is cold on my feet as I walk through the room to do my business. After using the bathroom, something I have to brace myself for since the hysterectomy because it's ridiculously painful, I toss my hair up and leave the bedroom to find some food and stretch my legs.

Not a few steps out of the room, I walk into the living room, stunned to find Dallas sleeping on the couch. I look him over for a brief moment, his large body much too big to lay comfortably where he is. He's in gray sweats and a baggy Aspen Ridge Distillery hoodie, his arm draped over his eyes. I walk slowly into the kitchen, trying to stay quiet, when I find Dallas' dad sitting at the bar drinking a cup of coffee. I haven't spent much time with him outside of Sunday dinners, but he is so loved and respected by his family that I'm at ease in his presence.

He has a full head of salt and pepper hair, a strong jaw that slightly droops on the left side around his mouth, and his eyes are a similar blue to Dallas'. For a fleeting moment, I can picture what he'll look like when he's his father's age.

"Good morning, Mr. Hayes."

"M-morning, Blaire."

"Why is he sleeping on the couch? He didn't go home?"

"He hasn't been to his house since the night of your accident,"

"Wait, he hasn't gone home at all?"

"Nope. Said he's not leaving you."

"Oh. Okay, well why didn't he sleep in one of the other beds?"

"Couch was closest to you."

I cover my mouth with my hand, overwhelmed with emotion. I should have known better. Of course he hasn't left me, he loves me. I feel it in everything he does now, in every look, touch, word, and action. There's no denying that Dallas Hayes is head over heels in love with me. I just don't want that love to be the reason that he gives up on ever becoming a father.

Speaking of the devil himself, he walks into the kitchen where I'm pouring us both a mug of hot black coffee. He walks right up to me and plants a kiss on my temple, my eyes closing the moment his lips touch my skin.

"Good morning, princess. I can do this, want to go sit on the couch?"

"Actually, I need to stretch my legs, are you up for a small walk?"

"Of course I am. Let me throw these into to-go mugs and we can go."

I return to the bedroom and pull on some thick socks and a fleece sweater. When I meet Dallas in the mudroom in the back of the house, he pulls a thick sweatshirt over my head for an added layer and helps me pull on my boots.

"How are your nightmares? Have you had any since your accident?" he asks after a few minutes of walking in silence.

"I haven't. I think my body has been too exhausted to dream."

"Whatever you want to tell yourself, princess."

"What's that supposed to mean?"

"You know I chase every bad dream you have away when I'm close to you. But sure, blame it on being tired."

"That's a pretty pompous assumption, but I expect nothing less from you."

"It's the truth and you damn well know it. Fight it all you want, but you and I both know that pretty little head of yours and that sexy body knows it's safe with me, it's your heart that's fucked-up and not on board right now. But I'm going to fix that."

"Dallas. Please, you need to let this go. There is no us anymore. There barely was an us to begin with."

"Like hell there isn't. Say whatever you want to me, call me every name in the book, hell, fuckin' hit me if you need to, but don't you dare lie to me."

I open my mouth with a retort but close it. I hate that he's mostly right, except my heart is on board. It's pounding loudly in my chest, telling me to go to him, that he's the one man on the planet who's for me, my match in every way.

"I looked up my abuser. He was released from prison. But did you already know that?"

Dallas stops walking and turns to me, his face bearing an unreadable expression that worries me.

"Baby, I never looked at that file. I shouldn't have ever gotten it in the first place. But I need to talk to you about something that I've been putting off."

My feet freeze, and I turn to face Dallas, his gorgeous eyes bouncing back and forth between my own, concern and worry etched into his features.

"Baby girl, we have reason to believe that your crash wasn't an accident." He pauses and studies my face, waiting for a reaction I'm not going to give him. I stand still, standing stronger than I feel, so he continues. "We weren't positive who, even though I had a feeling. But now that you've said he was released . . ."

"It was him."

"Yeah, baby. We think so."

"While we figure out what to do, I can have Wes keep an eye on him. I can make sure he contacts you if you don't want me involved. But if it'll make you feel better, I'll do whatever you need. It's taking all I have to not lead this and hunt him down to make him pay for what he's done to you."

I think about his offer for a moment as we slowly walk up the long driveway, Dallas' warm arm looped through mine to prevent me from falling. I know that the offer is a good one. One that hadn't crossed my mind. At least this time when he hires the PI, he's including me and asking for permission first.

"Yeah, I think I would like to know where he is and that he's staying far away from me. He tried to fucking kill me, Dallas. Shouldn't we take whatever info you have to the police?"

"He won't get close to you again. I'd do anything for you, baby. I'll take care of it and make sure eyes are on him. Maybe if we're lucky he'll just do the world a favor and die."

"We can only hope."

He stops walking again and pulls me gently to a stop before facing me. The features on his face are tight, serious, and I feel an ominous chill slide down my back. I'm suddenly nervous.

"What is it?"

"What if I told you there's a way to make that happen?"

"For him to die?"

"Yeah. What if I could make him go away?"

I search his eyes for any evidence of a lie or being totally full of shit but I see nothing but determination and honesty reflected back in them. I think about my innocence that was taken from me, the pain, trauma, all of the nightmares that haunt me while I sleep, how sick men like him can't be rehabilitated. They're an evil that shouldn't walk the earth.

"Then I'd say thank you."

Dallas' shoulders relax before wrapping his big arms around me, and I lean into him, resting my head on his chest and taking a deep breath. He doesn't say any more. I don't want to ask, and I don't want the details, but imagining a life knowing that my abuser was erased from this earth brings me another level of peace that I didn't think was possible.

Because of Dallas.

CHAPTER 37

reid

I CLOSE UP MY STATION FOR THE NIGHT, WIPING everything down and folding up my chair so I can head home, when Dallas walks into Rogue. I watch him pull open the large glass door to our fishbowl and step inside. The hair on my arms raises as I read his face. He's agitated, nervous, and still looks fucking heartbroken.

"Hey man, you got a minute? Need to talk to you about something."

"Yeah, let's go into my office. Blaire okay?"

Dallas follows me into my office and takes a seat casually across from me.

"She will be. Need you to do something for me. Well, not for me, for Blaire."

"Anything," I answer easily. Blaire's become a good friend of mine since the day she arrived in AR, and like with any of the women in my life, I'm protective.

"Just like that?"

"Yeah, brother. Just like that."

"I wouldn't ask if it wasn't everything to me. I need you to make someone go away."

My eyebrows raise as he sits back in his chair and crosses his legs at his ankles, stretched out in front of him, his arms are next, crossing at his chest. He's serious. I don't know how much Sawyer told his brother, but it was clearly enough to send him my way. I know Sawyer wouldn't have done it if he didn't believe Dallas would take it to his grave.

"Who?"

"Andrew Cain. Released recently from Washington State Penitentiary for serving a little more than a decade sentence for child abuse, neglect, sexual assault of a minor, rape, and a slew of other shit that takes away his right to walk the earth, regardless of what the law says. I want to make sure he doesn't ever hurt Blaire again. Sawyer and I have reason to believe he's the one who caused her accident. We're positive."

I keep my face blank, internally processing while also simultaneously seething with violent anger. I understand what he wants and why he wants it. I can't change my past failures, but I'll be damned if I don't protect those I care about now.

"Okay."

"I owe you."

"You don't. This is my penance. It's not your burden to bear, brother. I'll take care of it."

Dallas nods and walks out. He knows I don't talk about it, and pressing won't get any of them anywhere.

I wait for him to leave the building before I step on the small wood panel of the floorboard under my desk. It pops loose and I kneel down to remove it, making a big enough space for my hand to reach in and pull out the burner phone I keep there.

Flipping it open, I bring up a new text message to the only number in the phone.

Me: Need a hit. Andrew Cain, just released from WSP. Make it happen.

Unknown: You'll owe me

Me: You know how to reach me

Unknown: Consider it done

I erase the text message thread and power down the phone before slipping it back into my stash space. Not feeling anything but peace, I replace the wood and lock up my business for the night.

The world will have one less piece of shit walking on it soon enough, and Blaire will be free.

dallas

Knowing that Blaire and I never got the opportunity to date each other, I decide to take advantage of the forced proximity. This morning, I left a Bean Haven coffee on her bedside table and scrolled out a message for her that I would see her tonight at five. She didn't text me, and while I wish she had, I expected her not to, so I tried not to let it disappoint me. I want to get us to a good place again, and hopefully she'll start to see that I'm not giving up on her.

Creeping into my old bedroom with a large pizza in my hand and a gift bag in the other, I set everything up while Blaire's still in the shower. I queue up *Bridgerton*, lay the pizza out on the bed, dump the candy around it, and set the gift bag on her spot. I haven't ever had a serious relationship before, so buying a gift for a female who isn't my mom or Kinsey was different. But in a good way. I'm glad that she's the only one.

The door to the bathroom opens and steam pours out. It's wild how hot she likes her showers, and I don't know how she can stand the blazing temperature besides being half-demon. She walks into the room in one of my T-shirts—a navy blue Seattle Kraken shirt that makes her eyes pop. Her skin is flushed from the heat of her shower, and her red hair hangs off her shoulders in wet curls. She's so beautiful.

"What's all this?"

"A date."

"Dallas . . ." she says with a little attitude.

"Blaire. Now that everyone knows I am head over heels in love with you, I'm going to date the shit out of you and you're going to like it if you know what's good for you. I can't take you out, so I'm bringing the date to you."

Her eyes widen at my underlying threat. Good. She may be in charge, but I'll be damned if she gets her way one hundred percent of the time. Especially if she's trying to ice me out. Fuck that shit.

"You don't have to go through all of this, Dallas."

"I want to, baby girl. Come open your gift."

Exasperated and a little timid, she pulls the tissue paper from the gift bag and pulls out a beautiful leather-bound sketch pad and charcoal pencils.

"This is gorgeous, Dallas," she says, her voice choking with emotion as she runs her fingers over the soft grain of the cover. I scoot closer to her, watching her face and loving that this makes her happy. "No one has ever . . ."

"I figured, baby. But that's the past. And I'm happy to give you so many firsts."

She reaches her hand out and scratches her fingertips lightly over the scruff of my facial hair, and I melt into her hand. Any touch from her is a gift I won't take for granted.

"Thank you. This is the best gift I've ever been given."

"It's not completely selfish, I have to admit. I'd like you to fill it with sketches, and I'd like to add it to the proposal for the changes to the current structure of the distillery events. You're so talented, baby, and I want to see you reach your dreams."

"How would that even work, Dallas?"

"I don't know yet. It won't be overnight, but I think you're right. If we focus on weddings and large-scale events that are scheduled in advance, it puts us on the map as an elite venue. And you and I will both be happier."

She brushes a tear away from her sweet face. It's so hard not to kiss her right now, but I know she wants space, as much as it's killing me.

"You ready to eat?"

She opens the lid to the pizza and gives me a knowing look.

"Really? You hate pineapple and pepperoni."

"But it's your favorite, so I'll eat it. Next time we can get one loaded with meat."

I hand her the garlic dipping sauce, press play, and we sit together in silence and eat. What was not planned, because I haven't seen it yet, is that this episode is extremely spicy. It's difficult to not get hard watching the scene focus on her pleasure. Blaire shifts next to me, rubbing her thighs together slightly and I know she's just as turned on as I am. Fuck, what I wouldn't give to be able to release her frustration, my own pleasure be dammed. Hell, I could come just from eating her out.

The downside of having such a highly intense sexual relationship is that you notice once it's gone and that connection is severed. On the flip side, it's allowed me to connect with her outside of having sex and only strengthened what I already felt.

As inconspicuously as I can, I rub my palm along my shaft, trying to get the fucker to go down. Her eyes flick down to my hard cock, the outline clear as day through my thin sweatpants.

"You can go to the club, Dallas. No point in holding out."

My mouth involuntarily drops open, and I have to control my immediate reaction to go off the rails. The audacity of this woman knows no bounds and I'd turn her ass bright red if I could.

"Are you fucking serious right now?"

"Even if I was an option, which I'm not, I can't have sex for weeks . . ."

She's so full of shit that she can't even hear how toxic the words she's throwing at me are. How hurtful they could be.

"You're telling me that if I leave you here right now and go fuck someone else you're fine with that? You want me to touch someone else the way I touch you? Sink my cock inside a wet pussy that isn't yours? Make someone else scream my name?"

"If you need to take care of yourself, Dallas, I'm not going to hold it against you."

I'll give it to her. She doesn't falter, and she doesn't let any of her emotions betray her. But I know her better than that and the thought of me being with someone else is ripping her apart. She's only suggesting it because she's trying to piss me off and push me away. Jokes on her.

"You're full of fucking shit, princess."

"Excuse me?"

"Did I stutter? I'm not going to repeat myself."

She opens her mouth to argue but then shuts it without a word. I'd never do that to her. If I have to be celibate for the rest of my life in order to have her, I'll do it in a heartbeat. I've felt how she's pushing me away, but this was the final straw.

"What's really going on, Blaire?"

She pulls her cheek between her teeth, gnawing at it, her eyes darting everywhere but at me.

"Baby, I love you. I'm so sorry about the file. I never should have gotten it."

"I know you are, Dallas. I'm sorry, too."

"Can we move past this? This distance, Blaire? It's killing me. I know you love me. I feel it. I felt it the night before I left for Mount Baker. Tell me you still feel it and don't you dare lie to me."

"Thank you for the date, Dallas. I really just want to go to bed."

I let my head drop in defeat. At least she didn't lie.

blaire

THE NEXT MONTH PASSES IN A BLUR WHILE STAYING AT Dallas' parents' house. I started to slip further and further away into myself in an effort to protect my heart against the loss I was feeling from no longer having the ability to carry a child, and the loss I knew was coming. Dallas continued to sleep on the couch so that he could be close to me, and when I was having an exceptionally weak day, I asked him to sleep next to me. He held me close, and those nights were the nights I slept the best. The first two weeks he showered with me every day, repeating the same process of taking care of me.

"You're precious, let me take care of you. You deserve to be taken care of."

Every morning, he either makes me coffee or has already run out to Bean Haven and woke me up with a coffee and chocolate croissant, still writing a message. He's doting, loving, and everything any woman will be lucky to have from him someday.

I've been meeting once a week with the therapist who worked with me through college and up until I moved to Aspen Ridge. I thought I didn't need it anymore, but I realized that I was wrong, especially now. We've met three times already and while I'm not okay, I'm remembering how to tap into the tools to help me get there again. The fear of Andrew being out there somewhere, that he found me and tried to hurt me again, pushing Dallas away, along with the heartbreak over not being able to have children and wanting to keep it from everyone, has pulled me further and further into a depression that I'm struggling to climb out of on my own.

Dallas' mom, Amy, has been a mother hen and it has simultaneously filled me with more love and joy than I've ever experienced from another woman, and broken my heart. After the first week, when she and Kinsey had watched *Pride and Prejudice* with me, we made it a weekly thing. We all sit together on the couch under a big blanket, and after flipping through a dozen popular TV shows, settle on watching *Schitt's Creek*. We binge a few episodes together before I'm exhausted and ready for sleep again. Ivy joined us last week and has dropped by several times. The baby bump is no longer able to be concealed, and she's the most gorgeous pregnant woman I've ever seen.

Today is the first Sunday dinner they've hosted since my accident, and it's something I've felt extremely guilty about. While I've begged Amy to please get everyone together, and I don't mind skipping, she insisted that her children were wildlings and she wanted to surround me with quiet and peace; things they are not.

I lie on my side at the edge of the bed and look out the window, wondering what it will be like when I move back into my studio apartment above Rogue tomorrow and don't see much of them anymore. There's a knock on my door and I don't bother moving to answer it, knowing that he'll just walk right in anyway like he always does.

"Hey, princess. How are you feeling?" he says as he crouches down on his haunches in front of me.

"I'm fine, Dallas."

He takes a deep breath, no doubt calming himself down to handle me with the kid gloves he now uses. I don't bother looking at him, staring past his head and continuing to watch the heavy clouds slowly move across the dreary sky.

"Baby, will you please talk to me?"

"There's nothing to talk about."

"I'm sorry. I know you're hurting, but this is killing me, too, Blaire. I'm not giving up on you. I'm not giving up on us. I told you that you weren't alone anymore and I'm not going to abandon you the way everyone else in your life has. I see right through you. I know what you need, and until you tell me otherwise, I'm pressing on."

A stray tear falls from my traitorous eyes, so I close them, doing my best to hold the rest at bay. His big hands brush over my cheeks, pushing my wild, tangled hair out of my face.

"Look at me, baby. Tears or no tears, I want your eyes on me. Tell me how to fix this."

I bite the inside of my cheek until I taste the metallic tang of blood before opening my eyes. Tears slowly cascade down his face as he looks at me, eyelids pooled with salty drops ready to rush over. I feel the moment my heart shatters into a million tiny shards, my lungs seizing, my mind swirling in a fuzzy haze of torment. I can survive any physical pain. I've done it before. I know I wouldn't survive Dallas walking away from me. So I have to protect myself. I just can't take that chance after everything that I've been through.

"I just want you to get better."

"Me too," is all I can say before closing my eyes and letting myself drift off to sleep.

Moving back into my tiny apartment is strange after being at the Hayes' for a month. I used to love it here. It's always been small and nothing about it is new and shiny, but it's mine, and it's been home. The adjustment to being alone will hopefully go by quickly, and I'll be able to find my new normal.

After meeting with my therapist virtually yesterday afternoon, we decided that making a plan to focus on the things that make me happy will help propel me into healing. She also encouraged me to talk to Dallas and give him an opportunity to speak for himself and make his own decisions. I plan to, I just don't know when. Being raised with fear as my constant companion, I turned into an adult that prioritizes not being vulnerable, because I don't want to get hurt. It's easier for me to hurt both of us and end it, than to chance Dallas leaving me because I'll never be able to give him a family. Understanding that what I'm doing is wrong is one thing, being able to fix it is a work in progress.

The day goes by quickly, unpacking my things and emailing Sawyer about returning to work as soon as possible. I met with my doctor this morning, who cleared me to return to activity as long as I feel physically well enough to do so. Sawyer insisted that I work from home one more week, and while I'm not thrilled about it, it will be easier than seeing Dallas every day in the office.

I get comfortable on my futon and pick up my phone, scrolling aimlessly through social media, when an article jumps out at me, posted yesterday from *Seattle News Now*.

Ellensburg - The person killed in the trailer fire on Sunday night has now been identified. The Kittitas County Coroner's office has identified the victim as forty-eight-year-old Andrew Cain of Ellensburg. Cain, who was recently released from Washington State Penitentiary on parole, had served a decade-long sentence for child neglect, child abuse, and rape of a minor. The cause of the fire is still under investigation. At the scene, police recovered photographic evidence in a safe that is suspected to be child pornography. The cause of death is still pending. No other injuries were reported.

My phone clatters to the ground as I gasp and cover my face with shaky hands. Scrambling to pick my phone back up, I click on the dozens of comments and scroll through them.

. . .

GOOD RIDDANCE!
ANOTHER PEDO OFF THE STREETS. WON'T BE MISSED
THIS GUY WAS A FOSTER PARENT!
NO ONE'S GONNA MISS HIM
HOPEFULLY HE BURNED REAL SLOW, NICE AND CRISP
SWEET SWEET KARMA
YUCK! WHO CARES!
CLEARLY THESE MONSTERS CAN'T BE FIXED!
ONLY TEN YEARS FOR ALL OF THAT? FUCK OUR JUDI-
CIAL SYSTEM!

I exit out of the app and drop my head back on the futon. He's dead. He'll never be able to hurt me again.

I'm safe.

Because of Dallas.

CHAPTER 40

dallas

THE LAST FEW WEEKS HAVE BEEN THE MOST MISERABLE of my life. I can't remember a time when I've felt this helpless. I need control. Blaire still hasn't flat-out told me that we're done, that she doesn't love or want me, so I haven't given up on her. But it's worn me down and my patience is almost nonexistent now. Nothing is the same without her. My fear over her foster father coming after her again has made sleep and focus near impossible while I wait for Reid to handle this shit as discreetly as possible. Andrew Cain won't get another opportunity to hurt her again.

"Are you listening?" Carter asks from across my desk, where we were supposed to be discussing the feature we're getting in a travel magazine.

"Sorry, man. I'm just not with it."

"Look, I get it, Dal. I do. But we've got to iron out these details."

"I think we should go with your ideas. You know the PR side better than I do. I trust you not to fuck things up for us."

His head snaps back slightly, his facial expression jarred.

"Who are you and what have you done with my brother?"

"I'm serious. You know what you're doing. I'll shut my mouth and follow your lead."

"Well, shit. Okay. By the way, I met with Sawyer and Lorelei, we all agreed with Blaire's proposal and your amendment to it. It's brilliant. But act surprised whenever Sawyer tells you."

Fuck yes. She's going to be so happy.

"And Liam?"

Carter scratches behind his neck nervously.

"He's, uhh, been a little preoccupied."

My phone goes off, and worried that it's Blaire, I snatch it up off my desk. She moved back into her apartment, and it's made me so uneasy, even if I'm finding reasons to show up and make sure she's safe, just needing to lay eyes on her. She hasn't realized it yet, but I've been sleeping in my car outside of Rogue. Sleeping being a relative term, more like watching. I may not be able to hold her through the night anymore, but I'll be damned if I'm not going to watch over my woman.

Reid: She's safe.

I breathe a huge sigh of relief, the weight of the world lifting off my shoulders from those two words. At least we gave her this. She'll never have to worry about him coming after her again. Instead of texting Sawyer, I leave Carter and walk down the hallway to his office, knocking twice before opening the door.

"Get the fuck OUT!" Sawyer roars, before the door is open enough for me to walk through. I pull it closed and laugh, waiting outside for Ivy to leave. The door opens and Sawyer kisses Ivy before she walks away. I face my brother with a smug, shit-eating grin plastered to my face.

"Well, hello pot, meet kettle. I love a day when I get to shove shit in your face. Today, my brother, you are a hypocrite of epic proportions."

He grabs my shirt with his fist and pushes me against the wall. I let him, giving him a toothy smile the entire time.

"You ever walk into my office again without waiting for an invitation, I'll knock your teeth down your throat."

"Shivering in my boots, shithead. Isn't sex supposed to chill us out?"

"Not when it's interrupted by asshole twin brothers. What the hell did you need?"

"Besides giving you an instructional manual on how to lock your door?"

"Get to the point, Dal."

"Everything with Blaire has been taken care of."

He lifts his eyes to me in question.

"Reid?"

I nod.

"Now what are you going to do?"

"Get my girl back."

I juggle our coffees in my hand, along with her chocolate croissant, and rap my knuckles against her door. It's only a few moments that feel like an eternity until she opens it. Her hair is in messy waves that frame her full face that is bare of any makeup. The freckles that dust under her eyes are so prominent when she goes without it, and I wish she'd go barefaced more often. I give her a knowing smirk when I notice that she's wearing one of my Aspen Ridge Distillery T-shirts and nothing else. She wouldn't do that if she didn't miss me.

"What do you want, Dallas?" she snaps, her hand leaning on the door frame, blocking me from entering.

"You, baby."

"That can't happen. So you can stop bringing me coffee and food. Stop being so kind to me. Stop sending me flowers. Just stop."

"If I thought, even for even a moment, that you meant all the bullshit you just spewed, then I would. I would walk out of your life knowing no woman will ever replace you. I'd wish you the best. But your full of fucking shit, princess, and we both know it."

"Dallas . . ." Her eyes flutter closed, her shoulders sagging.

Enough is enough.

"Let me in," I demand. "Now. Or do you finally want to learn what happens when I have to repeat myself?" I use the voice she knows all too well and has always responded to.

Her eyes flash open to meet mine and the emotion reflected in them skyrockets my fucking hope to the moon. She turns and walks into her apartment, leaving the door wide open for me. Walking in, I kick the door shut behind me and follow her to the futon she's currently using as a couch. Handing her the coffee and pastry, I take a seat on the opposite end from her.

"Blaire, I will give you as much time as you need, but I won't stop caring for you. I won't stop showing up for you and being there for you. And there's no fuckin' way I'll stop loving you. I am yours. I want you to be mine."

"You don't understand, Dallas. You don't want me. Why won't you let this go? I'm trying to save you! You thought I was damaged before? That was nothing compared to now!"

"Then tell me what the hell is going on, Blaire. Help me understand!"

"I can't fucking have children! I can't give you a family!" she screams, pushing her hands through her hair and sagging deeper into the couch.

The words confuse me before everything slides in place like a fucked-up missing puzzle piece. The doctor told us that the damage to her abdomen was extensive, but that Blaire would need to share the complications with whom she wanted when she was ready. Holy shit, I didn't even put it together. My heart breaks for my poor girl, and I have to wipe away the tears that fall freely from my eyes. Everything she has been through, and life throws her this to top it off. If that motherfucker wasn't already dead I'd prolong his death for as long as possible to inflict pain on him over and over again before giving him the relief that death would bring. I move closer to her, the front of our bodies facing each other, combing my fingers through her hair and holding her face in my hands.

"I am so fucking sorry, baby. I'm so sorry."

"There's no way you'll want me now. That's why I've been pushing you away. I don't want to be left again, Dallas. No one has ever chosen me until you. And if you left like everyone else has, I wouldn't survive it," she whispers.

My stubborn, traumatized girl. I am not like anyone from her past. I pull her face up, forcing her to look at me. I look into her eyes when I speak so there's no chance of her not hearing my words and the truth behind them.

"I'll gladly repeat this as many times as you need to hear it, princess. You are not damaged, you never have been. I want *you*. I want every version of you. I wanted you the moment I first laid eyes on you. I want you now when we're both young. I want you when we're old and falling apart. There is nothing, *nothing*, Blaire, that will change that."

"You can't mean that, Dallas. Kids are so important to people."

"I mean it with every fiber of my being. All I need is you. Your love, your sass, that fire in your eyes, your body, that vile little mouth. You. Only you. And if you need more than that, if you want kids, baby, we can adopt. Or foster. We can give kids a better childhood and chance at life than the one you had."

Her face finally perks up and looks at me with something other than defeat and heartbreak.

"You mean that? You'd do that with me?"

"Baby, I'd do anything if it means I get you. I should spank your ass for keeping this from me."

Her cheeks bloom with a blush and she bites the inside of her lip.

"I wanted to save you from having to make this choice, Dallas."

"You're such a goddamn pain in the ass. Do you seriously not realize how much I fucking love you?"

She nods her head as the tears fall over her glassy eyes and down her freckled cheeks, I can't hold mine back any longer either. I lean into her, kissing her for the first time in weeks. Connecting with her like this feels like coming home. There's no hesitation from her as she meets me halfway, her mouth opening to accept my tongue as I lick into her mouth, wanting nothing more than to devour her whole. I slow us down, pulling back and pecking a few soft kisses on her plump lips before looking at her again. Her eyes are a stormy mix of emotions, and it makes me wild for her. But first, we need to completely clear the air.

"I'm sorry. I need you to know that I meant what I said, I never opened that file. I started to fall for you when we were snowed in together and when you wouldn't open up to me, I let the fear over what happened to Ivy cloud my judgment. If we hadn't hired the PI, who knows what the outcome would have been for her. I knew you were hiding something big, baby, and I'm so sorry I took that step to breach your privacy. I'm a possessive, protective asshole and I was blinded by wanting to take care of you. And now you never have to worry about someone hurting you again."

"I know, and I'm so sorry, too. I should have stayed and talked and listened to what you had to say, but seeing all of that compiled into a folder of my fucked-up life was a lot to take in. It was a painful reminder of my trust issues. You are the first person who I've felt safe with. You chase all my demons away and allow me to just be, and to see that you had broken that trust was just . . . heartbreaking."

"Baby, I promise I never opened it, and I'm sorry that I got it in the first place, I never should have done that. Please forgive me. I will work every day to make sure you feel safe, loved, and cherished. I want that opportunity. I want us to move forward, I want you to go to sleep every night next to me, I never want you to have a bad dream again. Let me be there for you, let me take care of you, drive me fucking crazy every day like I know you love to do. I will get on my knees and beg if you want me to. I'd be a fucking slave to you, Blaire. Just please, forgive me."

"Then do it."

I freeze for a moment and look at her, reading nothing but a challenge on her face.

"What are you asking, Blaire?"

"Get on your knees, Dallas."

Fucking gladly.

With my eyes on hers, I move to my knees on the floor four feet from her body and wait, hoping like hell she'll let me touch her. I've missed her so damn much. If she had tried this shit months ago I would have punished her. But now? Now I'd get on my knees for her every single fucking day if it meant I could have a piece of her.

"Crawl to me."

Yes ma'am.

I drop to all fours, my heart beating wildly out of my chest, and take a few steps until I'm in front of her, sitting at her feet just the way she's done for me countless times before. My mouth is dry, waiting, and hoping as she looks down at me, her deep blue eyes tracing over all of my features.

This time she's the one to make the first move, shifting her body so that she straddles my legs on the floor, my hands automatically moving to the outside of her thighs, my fingers toying with the hem of the shirt barely covering her ass. She leans down and kisses me, it's languid and passionate, our mouths opening and tongues caressing. Her moan is muffled between our lips as her body softens against mine. I kiss her with everything I have, hoping that she can feel how much she means to me, knowing words alone aren't enough for her. She pulls away, my lips chasing her mouth for more.

"I forgive you, Dallas. What's a queen without her king?"

The growl that leaves me is primal, deep, and possessive. My hand grabs the back of her neck, yanking her mouth into my own, taking back control. I kiss her hard and demanding—exactly how she likes it.

"Fuck, I missed you."

"Then show me how much," she challenges.

I stand, holding her under her ass as I pivot us, laying her down gently on her back and dropping to my knees on the floor in front of her.

"Be my good girl and scream for me."

I push up her shirt, exposing her naked body from the waist down, surprised to see her without panties. I look at the three small scars that are still slightly raised and healing, the faint yellow from the fading bruises. I lean forward, kissing each of them gently before focusing on her pretty, bare pussy. I push her legs further apart, stretching her wide open for me. Her slit is glistening, already wet, and my mouth waters. Just like the first day I got to taste her spread out on my office desk, I waste no time.

I devour her.

Licking up her drenched slit repeatedly, loving her taste as it explodes on my tongue. I use my fingers on either side of her lips to pull her open further, before dipping my tongue into her cunt. I fuck her with it, moving in and out of her tight pussy walls as they clench around me, while my thumb moves over to stroke her little swollen clit. Her body spasms under me, soft moans steadily getting louder. I secretly hope they echo all the way to the studio downstairs. Fuck, I hope the whole fucking town hears her moans so they know she's taken.

"I missed your delicious cunt, my queen." I flick her clit a few times with the pointed tip of my tongue, and she bucks wildly. "I missed the way your thick thighs feel wrapped around my head." I add more pressure, my tongue swirling around exactly how she likes it. "I missed the way you sound when you come."

"Oh, god. Make me come, Dallas, please."

"Like you have to ask, baby."

I suck hard, pulling her throbbing clit into my mouth, and keep a hold of it with pulsing little sucks. She shatters and it's fucking beautiful. Her back arches, her arms stretched out above her head as she digs her nails into the wooden armrest, her screams ricocheting across the walls of the small studio apartment.

"Dallas! Aah! God yes!"

Her body slackens into the futon mattress, and I pull back just enough to move lower. I lick into her pussy, wanting all of her cum, and when she gushes for me, I hum my approval.

"Fuck, you're such a good fucking girl."

"I love you, Dallas," she whispers, and my entire world freezes.

"I love you, princess."

CHAPTER 41

blaire

It took Dallas a week before he moved me into his house. I didn't fight it. Peace. It's a funny thing, really. You crave it. You yearn for it. You work for it. But once it descends on you, you'd do just about anything to keep it. It comes from different things. Mine was found in the least expected of places. My boss. He calms my nervous system, grounds me, loves me, and even while I spent weeks pushing him away as a defense mechanism, he never gave up on me.

We've been living together for a month and found our rhythm. I'm still meeting with my therapist virtually, but have gone down to once a week. Dallas has guided me through leaning on him. We've started to move the BDSM structure into different areas of our life. He likes the control, and I thrive in handing it over to him. I learned that I love being a brat. Pushing his buttons and fighting him brings out one of my favorite versions of him. We haven't gone back to the sex club, but I can't wait until we do.

My nightmares are practically nonexistent. I'm settled and healing. I've had two since my accident and that's a drastic decline in frequency.

Walking into work with Dallas is one of the highlights of my day. Like he said, no one batted an eye. Maybe out of fear of Dallas since he's typically so grumpy, but all of my reservations and fears were squashed, and no one's behavior toward me changed.

"Aren't you going to your office?" I ask him as he walks past his door.

"Nope. I'm walking you to yours."

He slips his hand in mine as we walk the long hallway of offices in our main building. Once at mine, he jerks me forward into him, running his free hand through my hair.

"I love you. You're worthy of the world, princess."

Lost for words, I just smile at him. He opens my office door and pulls me inside, the breath leaving my lungs.

"Oh my god, Dallas," I say in shock. His big palm rubs up my back, grounding me.

"Do you like it?"

"Like it? I love it. I'm blown away. These are mine," I say in awe as I take in the facelift my office received. "When did you do this?"

The room has been completely transformed. The walls are painted a blissful pale blue, and large framed photos of my wedding dress design sketches hang from the walls—the decor is bright and warm and so very me. Sawyer, Liam, and Carter join us a few moments later, each of them smiling.

"Did you guys know about this?" I ask.

"We helped. This dumbass couldn't do this by himself, he's got shit for brains," Carter says, and Dallas reaches out and smacks him on the back of the head.

"Got a minute to talk, Blaire?" Sawyer asks.

We all take a seat around the small lounge area in a corner of my office. It has a new chaise lounge and two wingback chairs.

"We all looked over your proposal. We're in agreement that we'd like to move forward with your changes. Only . . ."

I hold my breath. My heart beating wildly in my chest. This will make Dallas so much happier here.

"Dallas added an addendum to it, and we think it's important to adopt that change as well."

My eyes shoot to Dallas, suddenly nervous. I created this proposal for him, to benefit him and fix everything that was negatively impacting him day-to-day here at the distillery. Did he not like it?

"We'd like you to also focus on creating a one-stop shop for weddings. Create a master vendor list, companies that are local and source local, and . . ."

I hold my breath as Sawyer looks to Dallas.

"Baby, we'd like you to give some thought to designing wedding dresses. You're extremely talented."

"Dallas, that's just a hobby."

"But it's your dream. It won't be overnight, but it's something we want to leave open to you if someday you want to do something with your designs."

"It's a good idea. I like keeping us as exclusive as possible. Especially if you only offer it to brides who book their wedding here. Think about it," Carter says, surprising me.

"Thank you. All of you. I don't know what to say."

"You're part of the family now, Blaire. Our dad gave us all a role here, and now you've got yours."

The tears freely flow now, and Dallas gets up to wrap his arms around me.

"Thank you so much. You've all given me more than I could ever ask for."

"I love you, princess. You're not alone anymore."

The guys leave Dallas and me alone and shut the door behind them. I continue to look around the space and I can't believe it's really mine.

"I can't wait to fuck you in here."

"No fooling around at work. I don't ever want a repeat of the empty barrel house."

"Don't push me, my cock's already hard for you. I'll bend you over this couch right now, baby girl."

I jump up from my seat and move behind my desk quickly. He stands slowly, eyes trained on me, and prowls, each step sure and purposeful.

"Dallas . . . No. Not here."

"Oh, baby, I like it when you say no. Especially because your body is always screaming yes. I know that pussy is already weeping for me."

My heart flips over in my chest, beating erratically, and I know he can see how he affects me. I feel the heat rising in my cheeks, my breasts rising and falling rapidly with each ragged breath.

"We can't."

"Get on your knees, Blaire. Be my good girl."

He takes two steps in my direction on the furthest side of my desk away from the door. I use that as my chance to bolt. I barely rip the door open and make a pace into the hallway when he's wrapping his large, strong arms around me. I bite the inside of my cheek so as not to squeal loudly.

"You're going to pay for that little stunt later, princess."

He releases me and kisses my forehead before walking away, leaving me wondering and excited about how he'll punish me for it.

"Fuck, baby. I love you tied up like this."

"Please, Dallas. Please let me come," I whine and plead.

"Dammit, I love it when you beg, princess. But you were a bad girl today. And bad girls don't get orgasms."

My arousal leaks between my legs and I feel crazy as he leans his head back down, licking slowly from my clit to my tight little hole. My ass is in the air, my wrists and ankles cuffed tightly to our bedposts, spreading me out for him to do whatever he wants. He's been edging me for almost an hour, alternating between his mouth, his fingers, and that glorious, pierced cock. Tears stream down my face as I whine and cry out, my body hovering on the edge where pain meets pleasure.

"I can't take it anymore! Fuck, Dallas, I'm begging you. Please, I'll be good. Let me come."

He moves up my body, straddling my thighs and grabbing a handful of my ass, gripping and kneading the flesh there tightly.

"Fuck, I love this ass."

His hand connects hard with my right cheek, and I cry out loudly at the sting. He spreads me wide before spitting onto my hole. I feel his fingers next, rimming that tight area just like he loves to do.

"Going to fill you, princess. You want to come?"

"Yes! Please!"

He breaches my ass with his finger as his dick thrusts inside my pussy. He fucks me hard, filling both of my holes and gripping the flesh of my ass with his free hand.

"Baby girl. You're so filthy. Did you learn a lesson?"

"Yes! I'll be good! Oh, oh, god! Yesss!"

He pounds into me, adding a second finger and scissoring inside me.

"Good. Come for me. Let me hear you scream."

I feel him everywhere. In one more thrust, everything snaps inside me. The orgasm is ten times more powerful than anything I've ever experienced before. I scream, my voice drowned out by the ringing between my ears, my body shaking uncontrollably as the pleasure pummels me.

"That's it. That's my good fucking girl. You take my dick so well, baby. Gonna come. Ohhh, fuck."

I feel his cock jerking inside me, his piercings making him feel so thick and rigid in the best way possible. He collapses on top of me, removing his fingers but keeping his dick buried inside my pussy.

"Fuck, I love you."

"I love you too. But now I need you to untie me, and hurry up. We're going to be late!"

"It's Sunday dinner, it's not like we're missing anything. It's the same every week."

"I look forward to it every week! Move your ass, Dallas or I'll leave without you."

"You little liar. You didn't learn shit. You need me to punish you again? I'll keep you tied up and make you miss dinner altogether."

"You wouldn't," I challenge.

We arrive at his parents' house late, but luckily with plenty of time to spare before dinner starts. The sun is peeking through the clouds today and I don't hate how it feels on my face, although I'm going to miss winter once it's gone. The house is filled with everyone, and the rowdiness can be heard from outside. His mom meets us at the door and Dallas leans in to hug and kiss her. She scoots to the left, dodging his advance, and wraps me in a huge hug.

"Hi, sweetie. Glad you two are home," she says to me.

"Need help with anything?"

"Not today. I made it easy on all of us. We're having chili and it's been slow cooking all day, toppings are already in bowls. Ivy made crème brûlée for everyone for dessert so that will be a refreshing treat after."

"That sounds delicious."

She cups my cheek in her hand and gives me a smile that melts my heart before walking away. I watch her go before looking up at Dallas to find his eyes already on me, a satisfied smile on his face.

"What?"

"She loves you."

"I love her. She's everything I wished for in a mother."

"Well, now you've got her."

"Dinner, heathens!"

The rest of the family stampedes into the kitchen as loudly as a pack of elephants. Dallas leans into my ear and whispers, "And the rest of the family. It's too late to run, by the way. You're stuck."

"I wouldn't dare."

epilogue

FIVE YEARS LATER

HOLDING MY WIFE'S HAND TIGHTLY IN MINE WHILE I drive, nerves and excitement pulse through me.

"Are we really doing this?"

"We're really doing it, princess. Are you excited?"

"I am, but my god, I'm nervous. What if she doesn't like us?"

"She will, baby."

I pull into a large government building and put my car in park. Turning to face Blaire, I grab her face in my palms.

"Listen to me, we're ready for this. We've gone through all the training, and you've been through this, you're ready. And you've gotten me ready. Is it going to be perfect? No. But it's going to be ours and we're going to make a difference no matter the outcome. You understand?"

"I love you."

"I love you, princess."

We walk into the building and meet the case worker. After going through all of our paperwork and a briefing, we're led to a room where a nine-year-old girl sits alone at a table, writing on a pad of paper. We walk in, Blaire leading the way, when she perks up in her seat and looks at us.

She has the lightest blue eyes, strawberry-blonde hair, and is very thin. I'm already thinking about all the food items I want to stock in the house to make sure she has access to everything she needs. I know the neglect was bad.

"Hi," Blaire says hesitantly, "I'm Blaire. This is my husband, Dallas."

"Hi. I'm Nadia Hope. Which is silly because Nadia means hope."

We both chuckle at her and I relax further. We take our seats across from her and she returns to her notebook.

"So, I'm going home with you, huh? Since my parents died?"

"That's right. You're going to come home with us. We have a room all set up for you that's all yours. And lots of people who are excited to meet you when you're ready."

"I've never had a room before. Are there other kids?"

"There are five kids with another one on the way. We have a really big family."

"That sounds nice. I'd like to meet them."

Nadia's parents were drug addicts like Blaire's. They lived in and out of shelters and couch surfing at who knows whose houses. They both overdosed on the side of the road with Nadia in the backseat. She fished the phone out of her mother's purse and called 9-1-1. She's so mature for her age and it's so unfair.

"Do you like writing?" Blaire asks her.

"Oh, I love it. I want to be an author when I grow up."

"That's a really incredible dream, kiddo. What do you like to write about?"

"Fairy tales. I love making up worlds. Nothing bad happens in them and everyone is safe."

"I used to dream like that, too, when I was a little girl. But I dreamed of having a big family that kept me safe and loved me more than anything."

"Did you get it?"

"I did, sweetie."

On the trip home, I drive with both hands on the wheel, constantly checking on the little girl in the back of my SUV through the rearview mirror. Blaire and Nadia both seem to be handling this well, while my insides feel like they've been torn out and lit on fire in front of me. I can't stop thinking about my beautiful girl at Nadia's age, alone and scared, and then the evil that descended on her later in life. I know at this moment that I'll die before anyone tries to hurt either one of them. Nadia has been given a shit start at life, but Blaire and I are determined to make sure not a day goes by that she doesn't feel love and support.

I hang back and give the two of them some space while Blaire shows Nadia to her new room. When we found out that she would be coming home with us, our entire family worked through the weekend to transform the room into one a little girl would dream of.

"This is all for me?"

"It is. And if you don't like something, we can change it. We want it to be your space and you should love to be in here."

"It's perfect! These are my favorite colors! And look at all of those books!"

Her face lights up and it makes me feel proud that we could provide her a safe place to call home. Once upon a time, I was able to chase all of Blaire's demons away, I hope that together we can do the same for this little girl.

My phone buzzes in my pocket and I excuse myself to let them talk while I check it.

Sawyer: How's it going?

Kins: Yeah, kinda dying over here wanting to know

Me: We're home. She's so sweet. Needs patience, love, and food.

Liam: You guys are the best people

Me: Have you met yourself?

Sawyer: Everyone is eager to meet her when you all are ready

Me: I will. One of her first questions was if there were any other kids. I think she's gonna want the friends and family

Carter: Well we've got that in spades

Me: I'll be in touch soon

Kins: We love you

Me: Love you all

I go into our kitchen and put the lasagna that Ivy had made for us into the oven to heat up and quickly put together a salad. When the timer beeps, I plate everything and get the girls for dinner. We eat in silence, Nadia scarfing down her food way faster than she should.

"So, Nadia, what are some of your favorite foods? Anything you haven't had that you'd like to try?"

She thinks for a moment before answering. She's so methodical, and I prepare myself to take mental notes because I feel a list coming, which I appreciate.

"I read an American Girl book once about a Korean family and their food sounded so good, so I've always wanted to try that. I really like learning about other countries."

"I think I'd like to try that too. Blaire's favorite food is Mediterranean, specifically Turkish. Would you like to try that, too?"

"That sounds so good!"

And just like that, my new little family became foodies.

After dinner, we let Nadia pick a movie for all of us to watch. She chose *The Nightmare Before Christmas* and I couldn't contain my smile at the memory of my blizzard lock-in with Blaire over Christmas when we had a movie marathon.

We both bring Nadia to her room and tuck her in, making sure she knows where to find us if she needs anything, and we walk to the doorway to leave.

"Blaire?" her little voice says softly.

"Yes, sweetie?"

"Will you stay with me?"

I watch my beautiful wife as she wipes a tear from her face, walks back into Nadia's new room, and takes a seat in the bright pink papasan chair next to her bed.

"I'll stay here for as long as you need. Get some sleep. You're safe."

And just like that, I fall in love with my wife all over again.

thank you for reading!

LOVED DALLAS & BLAIRE'S STORY?

Please consider leaving a review! As an indie author, reviews are so important! Thank you so much for your support.

Liam's story, book three in the Aspen Ridge series, is next! Find out how our master distiller finds love with his best friend in Love Me.

also by jenn plummer

Aspen Ridge Series

Unravel Me

Love Me

Wreck Me

Complete Me

Aspen Ridge Holiday Novellas

Ready or Not

Sweet Girl

Daddy Issues

acknowledgments

Thank you all for coming along on this journey with me. I hope you enjoyed reading Dallas and Blaire's story as much as I did writing it. Blaire had a lot of trauma to unpack. Her decisions, while sometimes not fair to others, always come from a place of self-preservation. While I usually dislike the miscommunication trope and never thought I would write one, Blaire's response to her trauma and the news of her infertility are accurate for her character as she worked through her trauma and abandonment issues, and I love the end result. Dallas refused to give up on her, and that's what she needed most. Thank you all for trusting me and for reading.

Michael,

Thank you for your support while I juggled writing two books while our kids were on summer break. I don't know what I was thinking, but you got me through it. Not a day has gone by that I haven't felt like I was the center of your world, and your love and support is what keeps me going. Thank you for everything you do for me and for always pushing me to continue to write. I love you more than I'll ever be able to put into words.

My friend and editor, Katie,

I hope you enjoyed all the little gifts I left you throughout my first draft and that we don't miss replacing any during our final pass through. Thank you for constantly making me laugh and pushing me to grow as a writer. I couldn't do this without you and I'm so proud of the work that we do. I love you!

My PA, Meighan,

Girl, how did I ever survive without you? Thank you for jumping in and taking so much off my plate, for having my back, cheering me on, and pushing me forward. I'm so glad I have you by my side and that I get to work with you every day. I love you!

Lemmy,

I am forever grateful to be a Luna Literary Management author and that I get to work with you. I am so thankful for everything you do for me. Your constant encouragement, hype, love, and support fuels me to keep going when I start to question myself. I know my brand of crazy pushes you hard, but I know you're a glutton for it. I love you!

Najla and the entire Qamber team,

Thank you for bringing Dallas & Blaire to life. Creating this cover was a dream come true and I am forever thankful to the work you did to make this happen.

My alpha readers, Lauren and Laura,

I couldn't (and wouldn't) do this without you two in-document with me. You constantly adapt to my insane writing process, you keep me on track, grounded, focused, and push me to grow as a writer. I'm so thankful for your love of Aspen Ridge and seeing each of these characters' stories told. Per usual, it's a race to the end, and one I couldn't do without your encouragement. Thank you for pushing me and having faith in me that I sometimes lose in myself. But most of all, thank you for loving me. I love you both an insane amount.

My alpha reader, Dylan,

Thanks for sending the guys to Mount Baker. It was a needed trip for them all and really gave the opportunity to bring some of their personalities to life outside of their relationships. I hope you're proud of the work we did! Thank you for your support and for giving me your time and all of your crazy-ass stories to share with the world!

Dani,

Thank you for the endless pep talks and vent sessions to keep me in check and focused. It was exactly what I needed!

My personal ARC team,

Thank you for believing in me enough after the release of Unravel Me to support me through my permanent ARC team. I am so grateful to every single one of you. You're all my favorite humans and I'll be forever thankful for each of you.

To every bookstagrammer, reviewer, and blogger,

Thank you for reading. Every post, review, and tag means the world to me. Thank you for your support!

To every reader,

You are making my dreams come true. Thank you for reading!

about the author

Author, wife, mother, lover of reading, overcast skies, chilly weather, and hockey.

A romantic at heart, Jenn has always been a lover of books and is constantly dreaming up heart-wrenching stories that will have you reaching for tissues and make you blush.

When Jenn's not writing, she can be found reading a spicy romance novel, watching scary movies, and enjoying her quiet life in New England, living out her real-life romance story.

Follow along for updates on new releases and book news.

www.jennplummer.com
Instagram @authorjennplummer
Goodreads @jennplummer
Amazon @jennplummer
Threads @authorjennplummer